Sexiful

Rose II
Back with A Vengeance

Sexiful

Rose II
Back with A Vengeance

CLARA WILLIAMS

ISBN: 978-1-64826-548-8   (Paperback Edition)
ISBN: 978-1-64826-549-5   (Hardcover Edition)
ISBN: 978-1-64826-547-1   (E-book Edition)

This is a work of fiction. Names, characters, places and incidents either are the product of the author's imagination or are used fictitiously, and any resemblance to any actual persons, living or dead, events, or locales is entirely coincidental.

Book Ordering Information

Phone Number: 347-901-4929 or 347-901-4920
Email: info@globalsummithouse.com
Global Summit House
www.globalsummithouse.com

Printed in the United States of America

This book is dedicated to my family—most of all,
to my mother, Sarah; my sister, Sylvia; Jahi; Al;
my daughter, Lacretia; "Tia" Taylor;
and my grandson, Rodney Shakiel Taylor.

Thank you for your support.

PROLOGUE

La'Roc and her best friends have an organization to promote cancer and HIV/AIDS awareness. To head the organization, La'Roc called in the best—her sister, L'Oreal, and her brother-in-law, Casey. L'Oreal and her husband have their own organization: Hope, Love, & Survival Instinct.

Just to give you a little background on L'Oreal and Casey: L'Oreal and Casey's organization has been very successful and is well-known all over the world. The organization has served and helped many people in and out of the community as well as all over the United States.

L'Oreal is five foot three, with a beauty mark right below her left eye. She keeps her beautiful brown hair cut in short layers to accommodate her gorgeous face. She is always driving around in her BMW SUV, with her music blasting, just like her sister, La'Roc. L'Oreal is the youngest of four siblings.

L'Oreal is a kindhearted person and is well loved and respected in her community. She and her husband birthed one child who died of crib death at three months old. Since the death of their only child, she and Casey have continued to try to become pregnant, with no luck.

However, at the time of Courtney's birth, L'Oreal and Casey made a pact with La'Roc to always have a parental presence in Courtney's life. And, of course, the same held true when Courtney birthed Devon. To be honest, if you didn't know better, you would think L'Oreal and Casey were their biological parents. They have spoiled them rotten. La'Roc smiled with pride.

Casey and his wife retired and own their own business. This couple should open up a marriage counseling agency because they are so good at keeping their marriage together. They have been married for seventeen wonderful years and they act as though they just met. Yes, they are so much in love with each other, which is a wonderful way to be, according to L'Oreal. La'Roc smiled to herself.

La'Roc looked at her sister. "L'Oreal, it is a pleasure having Casey as a brother-in-law."

She said, "Thumbs up, L'Oreal." La'Roc pointed her two thumbs toward the sky with approval.

La'Roc has had a hectic schedule helping her daughter Courtney cope with her boyfriend's—Justin's—paralysis and his other medical conditions.

The good news is La'Roc's grandson, Devon, is a law student at Howard University.

He is a very smart young man and graduated at the top of his class. Devon graduated from high school at an early age, and from high school, he went straight into college. He was the youngest student in his class. Devon started taking college courses during his junior year in high school. He entered college at the age of sixteen.

The family is so proud of him, especially his mother. La'Roc is very close to her daughter and her grandson.

Courtney and Devon have a very close relationship. They played around more like sister and brother than mother and son. La'Roc enjoyed watching the two of them play like kids.

La'Roc loves Courtney and Devon's relationship. She likes the way Devon plays around with his mother yet has the utmost respect for her. He never forgets that Courtney is his mother.

Devon is doing very well at Howard University Law School. He is taking his internship at his grandmother's firm. The family is extremely proud of him. Courtney is a wonderful mother and has been doing a great job raising Devon as a single parent.

You will also continue to enjoy reading about La'Roc's two best friends, Chantal and Denise.

Paris and Biscuit are still in La'Roc's life as her babies.

You will learn more about La'Roc's family: her mother, sister, brother-in-law, and employees.

Shawn is still in Upland State Prison waiting for his pretrial to get out on bail.

As you all read in the first book, *Sexiful Rose,* La'Roc had semiretired. She is back in court as a consultant, fully ready to fight to bring her sexy man back home, where he belongs. La'Roc soon will be back in Shawn's arms one more time, holding him close to her heart. She will be in the courtroom with her three best friends and her partner, Alex, by her side, fighting for her man's freedom. Alex has been appointed by La'Roc to be head attorney in charge of Shawn's trial.

La'Roc will act as a consultant—a conflict of interest.

SEXIFUL ROSE IS BACK WITH A VENGEANCE ... TO FREE HER MAN

Well, well. Sexiful is back, and this time with a vengeance, as she promised. On the day of Shawn's trial, La'Roc will walk into court facing the biggest challenge of her life.

The day of the trial, La'Roc could not get her bearings together as she was waiting for the judge to announce Shawn's sentence. She turned and looked away from her friends with tears in her eyes.

The judge looked over to Shawn's table, and the bailiff said to Shawn's lawyers, "Please rise." Then the judge made his announcement: "There will not be a bail set for Mr. Parker. Mr. Parker will be returning to Upland Correctional Facility immediately." La'Roc looked at her friends and reality hit. *Oh my God!* It was true. Shawn was not going home with her that evening. However, she knew in her heart that he would not be in prison for long because she knew he was innocent, and nothing could stop her from proving his innocence. La'Roc would fight until the end for her man.

Chantal and Denise noticed that La'Roc was walking very aggressively from the courtroom, trying to control the tears that were running down her face; without hesitation, Chantal and Denise ran after their hysterical friend to comfort her.

La'Roc knew as she ran out of the courtroom that Shawn's case was going to be her most challenging case yet. Shawn was her soul mate and the love of her life. She continued to repeat, "I have to save Shawn. I have to save him." Her friends held her in a group hug, and they all cried together.

La'Roc just knew in her heart that Shawn's case would be going to trial because of Kelly Brown's condition. Kelly remained in the hospital in a coma and was unable to breathe without oxygen tubes. At this point, La'Roc was a little worried about the outcome of this trial.

La'Roc had only one possible witness, and she wasn't too sure about his credibility. Her only witness had been Mr. Johnston, the buyer that was at Shawn's complex the day of the incident. La'Roc had a gut feeling that he had lied on the statement that he had provided to La'Roc's partner, Alex Power. The statement was taken the day that Ms. Kelly Carlotta Brown fell three floors down in one of Shawn's building complexes.

There was just something about Mr. Johnston's statement that just did not make any sense. His story was too conflicted. He had changed his story several times on the day in question. La'Roc had an excellent reputation as a lawyer, and she had a suspicion that he was being dishonest, which really pissed her off. La'Roc hated being lied to, especially when it came to her profession. La'Roc just didn't trust Mr. Johnston. He showed little or no concern for Shawn's life or Shawn's imprisonment. That again pissed her off.

Mr. Johnston's focus seemed to have been on Ms. Brown being able to speak after she had fallen three floors down at Shawn's complex. Ms. Brown had allegedly been pushed down three floors by Shawn. (Remember the word *allegedly*.)

La'Roc recalled Mr. Johnston saying, "Ms. Rose, will Ms. Brown be able to testify about what actually happened at the complex the day the incident occurred? Will she remember any of what happened that day or the day before?" Those were his questions. He seemed to be worrying more about her speaking about what happened before the fall and not her ability to wake up from the coma that she had been in since falling on that dreadful day.

La'Roc had something on her mind that was bothering her. She could not figure out how Kelly Brown knew that Shawn would be showing that particular townhouse on the day in question. Shawn had other complexes he could have shown to Mr. Johnston on the day of that horrible accident, which occurred in April of 2010.

La'Roc Rose swore she would win this case because Shawn was innocent. She also felt that Kelly Carlotta Brown would make a full recovery. She knew that she would have to put up a damn good defense to free her soul mate.

According to Shawn, Ms. Brown's last words to the police officers before leaving for Gateway Hospital were that he was responsible for her falling down three floors. Shawn supposedly pushed her.

When La'Roc was informed by her partner that Ms. Brown pointed her finger at Shawn, this petrified her; it was like a dying person using her last words to say, "He did it." The DA was going to have a field day with those three words.

Those words frightened La'Roc and it terrified her to even think that Shawn would be away from her for a long period of time if Ms. Brown passed away. La'Roc's team needed a strong witness to help back Shawn's testimony.

La'Roc had all the confidence in the world that she would free her soul mate from that horrible place called Upland Prison. It was now time to put on the gloves and get Shawn released on bail. The only hope La'Roc had to get Shawn released on bail as soon as possible. However, as long as Ms. Brown stayed in critical condition in intensive care, Shawn would remain in prison. La'Roc closed her eyes and started daydreaming; in her dream, Kelly Brown was making some positive progress and had been moved from intensive care into a private room. However, it was only a dream. Ms. Brown remained in a coma. If Kelly was discharged from intensive care, it would be in La'Roc's favor and a strong element in Shawn's case. Her only hope of getting Shawn's bail posted was if Ms. Brown's came out of her coma and her condition improved. Then Shawn would have a better chance of coming home.

La'Roc just knew that Shawn would be walking out of court with her on the day of his bail hearing. She had a good feeling about that particular day in July that Shawn would be leaving the courtroom with a big smile on his face; and she would be giggling like a schoolgirl on her first date, with pure happiness all the way home.

She knew everything was going to work out just fine because she would have her baby back in her arms again. Most of all, she would be able to listen to his lame jokes and his singing in the shower once again. Shawn had been incarcerated for three weeks, and La'Roc missed him something awful. She missed his strong arms around her toned body, feeling his hot breath against her face as he made sweaty love to her entire body all night long, licking her from her head to each one of her toes. He'd whisper sweet, sexual, provocative words into her ear, telling her how much he loved her and would never leave her for another. La'Roc decided to take a nap. It really didn't matter what she did; Shawn was always on her mind.

Thinking about Shawn's trial, La'Roc had a beautiful dream that she and Shawn had gotten married in a small ceremony in the presence of her family and friends.

Everything seemed so real: the exchanging of the vows and rings, the DJ playing their favorite songs. Most important, all of La'Roc's family was there to witness her and Shawn's love for each other. Her two best friends, Chantal and Denise, participated in the wedding as her bridesmaids. Her sister and daughter were the maids of honor. Of course, Devon was Shawn's best man. It was a disturbing dream because Shawn was still in prison for a crime he allegedly committed, yet it was a wonderful dream because it felt like Shawn was there in her arms, sleeping like a baby, with her head on his chest, just like old times. However, when she woke up completely, she was alone. It was only a dream, but it had seemed so real. She cried out loud, "Oh, Shawn, please help me. I cannot do this alone. I need you."

La'Roc decided to leave the guest room and go lie down in her master bedroom where she and Shawn had spent so many nights together in each other's arms. Before going back to sleep, she thought about Paris and Biscuit. *Oh, my babies will be home tomorrow. Ms. Holiday will be bringing Paris and Biscuit back from Manhattan late tomorrow evening.*

La'Roc drifted off to sleep.

It had been very hard for her to really sleep since Shawn had been incarcerated. She thought to herself, *Wow! There is a lot of work to be done.* She kept tossing and turning, thinking about the hearing for Shawn's bail, until she finally got back out of bed to call Alex. La'Roc invited Alex over to start working on Shawn's case early the next morning. "Alex, please come over early so we can get started on your presentation."

"I will be there as early as possible," Alex had said.

La'Roc could not keep her mind off Mr. Johnston. She believed that Ms. Brown and Mr. Johnston had set Shawn up. She felt that neither one of them believed Ms. Brown would get hurt pulling off their little scheme. But there was no proof of them working together at that time.

If Ms. Brown and Mr. Johnston were working together, La'Roc and her team would get to the bottom of their little deception. How did Ms. Brown know where Shawn was working on the day the accident occurred? La'Roc started to cry. She cried out loud, "Oh, God, please help me get through this."

La'Roc could not stop crying. Everything in her townhouse smelled of Shawn's Calvin Klein cologne, and in her head, she could hear him singing in the shower like he had done in the past before getting dressed to go to work or just going to hang out with his friends.

The day of the accident, before Shawn left that morning for work, he was singing one of his favorite songs in the shower, "Send for me."

But tonight, La'Roc was only imagining that Shawn was in the shower singing. *Oh, please make this pain go away.* She missed Shawn so much; her heart was racing like it was going to burst. She said out loud, "I'm hurting so bad, my body is in pain. I have an awful pain in my chest. Please make the ache go away." She tried to fall asleep, but it was impossible. So she cried until there were no more tears left. La'Roc's eyes were swollen and red from all the crying she did that night. Her tears continued to roll down her cheeks. She cried until she finally fell asleep. Tossing and turning, she fell asleep; thinking about the day Shawn had told her about his childhood.

According to Shawn, he grew up in a very abusive and dysfunctional home. He was raised by his mother, without his father's presence. His mother had seven children, and Shawn was the fifth child. His father walked out on the family when Shawn was four years old. He stated that his father was physically, mentally, and verbally abusive to his mother.

"Sexiful, my father was also abusive to all of his children, including me. After my father left, my mother became addicted to alcohol and heroin. Then she became physically and mentally abusive toward me, my brothers, and my sisters. One day, she hit me so hard; I fell against a table and busted my head wide open. My aunt said I was unconscious about five seconds, lying in a pool of blood. No doctor was called. The next day I ran away from home. I was eight years old at that time. I ran five blocks to my friend's house. I lived in my friend house for about two weeks before my mother realized that I was missing. When she found out that I was at my friend's house, she came to pick me up and beat me for five blocks. I mean all the way home. She beat me so bad; I couldn't walk for a few days, Sexiful. When I was able to walk, I ran away again and never looked back. I never returned to my mother's house again. But, baby, that is not me; I am not an abusive person.

"I will never treat my wife or any other women like my father treated my mother. I couldn't never hurt my son's mother. I am not a violent person. La'Roc, I didn't have a real family when I was a child. I grew up with someone else's family. I adopted my friend's family. But I have my own family now. I have you, baby, and I have your family. Baby, every time I see a man yell at or hit a woman, I get pissed off because it brings back memories of my father hitting my mother, my siblings, or me. Sexiful, that's my childhood story.

"I was a troublesome child, but you know what? I am glad I ran away from home. I think I turned out pretty good. I have my own business, I own my own home, and now I have you. What else could a man ask for?"

"Shawn, sweetheart, I think you turned out very well," La'Roc responded. La'Roc thought to herself, *For Shawn to have come from an abusive and dysfunctional home, he has a big heart. I cannot believe that he could be so loving, caring, respectful, and thoughtful of others. I've never met a man like Shawn before. Coming from that type of home, he did well for himself. He accomplished a lot. He had to raise himself in the streets because he had no family to turn too.*

"Sexiful, I was confronted each and every day with different types of drugs, and I turned it all down because I didn't want to be like my mother or my father. My sister April started using cocaine and other drugs when she was in high school when she was hanging out with Kelly."

As a man who spoke about not being abusive toward women or using drugs, how could Shawn hurt anyone? Especially his son's mother; Shawn was not a killer or an abusive person. He was a sweet, kind, and loving man. He wouldn't hurt a fly, La'Roc thought to herself.

Shawn said, "I never saw either one of my parents again." According to Shawn, they both died. His mother died of kidney failure, and his father was shot and killed by his common-law wife, the same woman he left his family for.

"Sexiful, my mother and father died three months apart. Isn't that a kick in the ass?" he had said with an expression of sadness on his face.

At 11:45 p.m., the phone ringing startled her. La'Roc jumped from her bed, frightened as hell.

Before answering the phone, she wondered who the hell was calling her at this time of night. "Hello, who is this? And it better be good!"

"Hi, baby girl. This is Jordan. I'm on my way to New York. I'm going to be working on Shawn's case with you and Alex. Baby girl, you know that Shawn will walk the next time he goes to court, right? I will be right by your side, just like when we were in law school. Shawn will walk! He will have the three best lawyers in the country fighting for his life. He will also have justice on his side. We will not lose this case. Shawn is innocent, and we'll prove his innocence in court."

"Oh, Jordan, you are a gift of love. Thank you so much for coming to help me fight for my baby. I had better warn you, this case is going to be a tough one, even for the three of us, because of Kelly's last words before going into the hospital; now she is in a coma. If Kelly Brown dies and we have no witness, Shawn doesn't stand a chance. We have one weak witness, and I myself don't trust him." La'Roc continued, "His name is Mr. Johnston. He is one of Shawn's so-called buyers.

I don't think he is telling the truth. Hurry and get your handsome ass on that plane. Love you."

"Baby girl, I am almost there. I will use my key to get in. See you soon." "I will wait up for you. Hurry; I am so excited. Courtney and Devon will be so enchanted and surprised to see you. I will call Chantal and Denise tomorrow morning. Alex will be here early. I want you all to myself tonight. How do you feel, babe?"

"La'Roc, we'll talk when I arrive, okay? See you soon, baby girl." They both hung up.

La'Roc started crying just thinking about Jordan and that terrible virus that had claimed his body and was sucking the life right out of him. She thought to herself, *We will beat this just as we have won all our cases in court, hands down.* HIV had her worried about her friend. She had just told Courtney and Devon about Jordan's mother passing away and now this virus. *Jordan and I will tell them together,* she thought to herself. *However, if money can save him then he will be saved without any problems or hesitation.*

Several hours later, La'Roc heard the front door open. She knew it was Jordan. She ran downstairs to greet him.

La'Roc was crying, and Jordan was smiling. She noticed that he had lost a lot of weight. He looked very thin, and his face seemed darker than she was accustomed to, but he was just as handsome as ever. They ran into each other's arms with tears running down their faces; they held each other for a short period of time just crying.

Jordan looked at La'Roc with a smile. "Come on, baby girl, let's talk before the other part of the team arrives tomorrow morning. Baby girl, you look damn good under the circumstances."

"Thanks, Jordan. Would you like something to drink or something to eat?" "La'Roc, I know where everything is. If I wanted something to eat or drink, I know how to get it. I don't drink anymore. I'm good; just don't fuss over me. Don't treat me any different than you would Alex or any of your other friends."

"Jordan, I want you to know and understand that I am not judging you.

I just want to know, Mr. Diaz, when were you diagnosed? And how did you contract this hideous virus? Was it through blood transfusion or a one-night stand?" She paused. "It really doesn't matter. I will always love you, Mr. Diaz." Jordan's explanation to La'Roc on how he might have contracted the virus was: He was at one of his law firm's holiday parties. He got drunk, and he didn't know if it was a man or a woman he slept with that night. He said, "You know I had to be drunk to have had unprotected sex. She/he was dressed like a woman and looked good, I may add."

It had been several years prior, and the person he had slept with that night was a transsexual. La'Roc sat very quietly, listening to her friend give a narrative of what happened that night. Jordan said, "I am still in shock."

Then he continued with his story. "Since then, I found out that Jess was her name, or that is what she called herself. She had the full operation, and now her balls are bigger than my balls." They both laughed. "That is why I said a man or a woman. Jordan finished telling his story, they decided to go upstairs take a shower and get ready for bed."

La'Roc said, "Jordan, sweetie, we are going to beat that damn virus shit before it turns into AIDS. We'll focus, and we will *win*. Thanks for telling me your story Jordan." La'Roc winked at her best friend. She was glad Jordan couldn't see inside of her heart because she was terrified for Jordan's life and what that crazy-ass virus would do to her BFF.

"Baby girl, if I didn't tell you, who was I going to tell?" Jordan answered with a wink and a smile.

La'Roc and her team had a long several months ahead of them to prepare for Shawn's bail hearing.

La'Roc was not going to be working directly on Shawn's case due to a conflict of interest. However, she would be in court each and every day as a consultant to Alex and Jordan.

Before La'Roc retired to bed, she called Chantal and Denise and left messages for the both of them. She gave them instructions on what to do when they arrived the following morning. She informed them she would be visiting Shawn, and she had a surprise for the both of them.

La'Roc then placed a call to Manhattan to notify Ms. Holiday and Ms. Cotton to check on Paris and Biscuit. She knew that Ms. Holiday always stayed up late at night, watching *The Late Show*. La'Roc left a message with Ms. Holiday to inform Courtney and Devon that she would be stopping by later that evening because she had a surprise for them. "As a matter of fact, Ms. Holiday, the surprise is for all of you." She then asked Ms. Holiday to wait at the condo until she arrived the following evening.

After Jordan got into bed, La'Roc decided to make herself a nightcap. She was hoping that the drink would help her to get a decent night's sleep. She was wrong. She was up all night, pacing back and forth, and thinking about all the men in her life. Thinking back, La'Roc realized that they all had problems in one way or another.

That night seemed to be the longest night in history for La'Roc. She paced the floor, crying and thinking about ways to keep Jordan alive and get Shawn back into her arms again.

She cried out, "I need Shawn's strength to keep me moving forward. I know as long as we're together, we can do almost anything. We need to help Jordan. Oh, Shawn, I cannot do this without you and God," La'Roc pleaded. She believed that she and Shawn could master anything together, but Shawn was locked away in prison. La'Roc felt so helpless and all alone without her young lover by her side. She was lost in transition and could not find her way out of the maze that she had created for herself.

However, La'Roc begin to look at the positive side: Shawn's imprisonment would not be forever, and that's one thing she knew for sure.

She cursed out loud, "That damn Kelly Carlotta Brown and that lying ass Mr. Johnston!" She punched her fist into the sofa cushion.

She knew in her heart when Shawn got released, together they would help Jordan find the help he needed so badly.

Finally, La'Roc crawled into her king-size bed, covered her head with her gold silk sheets, and went to dreamland.

The next morning, Jordan let La'Roc sleep in late. He decided to wake her with breakfast in bed after Alex arrived. She had explained to Jordan she hadn't been able to sleep well since Shawn had been incarcerated. He felt that his friend needed the rest.

Alex arrived bright and early at 7:30 a.m. The two lawyers greeted each other with hellos and bumping of the shoulders. They sat at the table, drinking juice and coffee.

Alex brought Jordan up to date on Shawn's case. Jordan went over some of his strategy with Alex while La'Roc continued to get some much-needed sleep.

The guys didn't think about themselves; the focus was mostly on Shawn's bail hearing. Alex and Jordan continued to discuss Shawn's case through breakfast.

At 10:30 a.m., La'Roc crept down the stairs very slowly, rubbing her eyes, still half-asleep.

Alex and Jordan said, spontaneously, "Good morning, sleepyhead. How are you feeling this morning?"

"I feel better. Thanks for letting me sleep in. Jordan, you made breakfast too? Thanks, babe." She grabbed a cup of coffee and a glass of juice.

"Partner, what time is your appointment set up to visit with Shawn today?"

"Around 1:30 p.m.," Alex responded.

La'Roc excused herself and ran upstairs to take a hot shower. She felt better than she had since Shawn had been arrested, thanks to her best friend, Jordan.

Jordan and Alex put the breakfast dishes in the dishwasher and cleaned the kitchen while they waited for La'Roc to finish her shower and get dressed, so they could get started on their journey to visit Shawn.

La'Roc decided to wear a yellow pantsuit and a purple top with a pair of yellow Louis Vuitton four-and-a-half-inch heels and matching Louis Vuitton bag. She liked to look tall when she was standing next to Shawn. She walked downstairs, looking and feeling as confident as ever.

"Baby girl, you look just like Courtney walking down those stairs," Jordan said. The three of them walked out the door, laughing, after listening to one of Jordan's lame jokes.

La'Roc hadn't laughed in months. Today was a good day for her.

It was a good day because she was with her partner and one of her dearest best friends, one on each arm. Plus she was on her way to visit her soul mate, Mr. Shawn Parker.

La'Roc yelled, "Wow! I cannot wait to see Shawn's face when I tell him that Jordan is working with you, Alex; he's going to be ecstatic."

Jordan wanted to drive the Hummer. La'Roc was happy to see Jordan in a good mood and up to driving. This was his first time driving her Hummer. La'Roc looked with teary eyes at her friend driving; she turned away so neither Jordan nor Alex would notice her watery eyes. She put her shades on to cover up the sadness.

"Alex, how are you and Jordan going to approach the hearing? What are your strategies?"

Alex began to elaborate on what he and Jordan had discussed at breakfast. The three lawyers drove into the parking lot at the Upland Prison at 12:45 p.m. La'Roc felt like butterflies were having a party inside of her stomach. She was excited to see Shawn, although she visited him every week. She still felt nervous every time she saw him. Jordan parked the Hummer in the prison parking lot.

They walked across the street to a restaurant to get something to drink and to go over the case before meeting with Shawn. They ordered bottled water and apple juice. They then sat down and went over Shawn's case.

After a while, Jordan excused himself and walked outside. La'Roc followed him.

"Jordan, are you all right?"

"Yes, baby girl. I'm fine. Please don't worry about me."

A few minutes later, Alex joined La'Roc and Jordan outside the restaurant. "Everything all right, partner?" Alex asked.

"Yes, everything's fine," La'Roc answered with a smile.

The three attorneys walked back across the street for their scheduled appointment with Shawn.

La'Roc stopped. "Partner, you okay?" Alex inquired quietly.

"Yes, I just need a La'Roc moment alone before I see Shawn. Keep walking. I will catch up with you guys. Don't worry about me. I am doing terrific." She added, "I am really excited today because today is the day I get to see Shawn again and introduce him to his new lawyer."

La'Roc and her team walked into the prison with more confidence than ever. They showed their identification to the officer at the front desk. And then Mr. Power requested to see #000523, Mr. Shawn Parker.

While they waited for Shawn to enter the conference room, they continued to discuss his case.

Five minutes into the wait, Shawn walked into the conference room escorted by an officer. La'Roc started to tear up as Shawn walked toward her with his open arms. She fell right into his arms with tears streaming down her cheeks.

Shawn's eyes were watery as he tried to hold back his tears from rolling down his handsome face. They held each other close crying like infants.

"Sexiful, I missed you so much. Baby, when can I leave this place and come home with you?"

"Sweetheart, trust me, I missed you too; you will be going home soon, I promise you. Just be patient, sweetheart."

"Baby, I am patient," Shawn responded. La'Roc looked at him and smiled at his response.

"Remember, Shawn, I informed you that you'll have the best lawyer in the state working on your case, and look who you have here: Jordan, Alex, and yours truly."

Shawn smiled and gave Jordan a high five and a bump on the shoulder. Alex and Shawn repeated the high five and the shoulder-bumping thing. Looking at her baby, La'Roc noticed he had lost a little weight since her last visit a week ago.

"Baby, we have something we want to run by you. We have worked out a plan for your case, and we need you to listen very carefully."

She told him about the plan to investigate Kelly's relationship and background with Mr. Johnston. "We will start the investigation back from when Kelly and Mr. Johnston were in kindergarten, middle school, and high school, etc.

"I think they have known each other for a while," La'Roc added.

"Listen, Shawn, the day we walk into the courtroom with you on July 14, 2010, my plan will be to walk out with you on my arm. On the day of your bail hearing, I will take you home, where you belong. I promise you that." La'Roc looked into Shawn's eyes and said, "Trust me."

La'Roc looked over at Jordan and Alex. "Okay, partners, let's get busy so we can get Shawn home."

La'Roc watched Shawn's face as tears rolled down his cheeks. "Baby, what's wrong?" La'Roc asked with concern.

"Baby, I am just happy to see you. These tears are happy tears." Shawn responded to her with a smile. "Sexiful, always remember that I love you, and my heart will always belong to you."

After going over the plans for the bail hearing, she kissed Shawn goodbye and walked out with her partners.

Alex said, "We think everything is going to be all right, La'Roc."

Jordan added confidently, "I know that everything is going to be all right because Shawn is innocent. This case is finished. We have won this case already. We just need some concrete evidence, and we know how to get the evidence that we need to free Shawn."

Heading back home, the three were talking about the bail hearing. "Jordan, we're going to the condo remember?"

"Right, baby girl, I didn't forget. I cannot wait to see Courtney and Devon. How is Justin doing?"

"He's making great progress today, but tomorrow he could have a horrible day on oxygen etc. … Justin's health has been touch and go. We just take it one day at a time. We just pray for him and Courtney each and every day. He will be going back to rehab soon, according to

Courtney. He had a relapse and was readmitted back into the hospital. He has his good days as well as his bad days.

He still has a long way to go, in terms of healing. As you know, he will never be able to walk again or have children."

Jordan asked, "Has Justin heard from his father?"

"No, but we will find him. Right now, I just want to focus on Shawn's trial and Justin getting better. I will get to Justin's father when he least expects it. Jordan, I still feel that Justin's father is responsible for him getting shot."

As they approached the condominium, Jordan parked the Hummer, got out, and walked around to the back of the vehicle. La'Roc got out of the vehicle and ran behind Jordan and asked if he was all right.

"Yes, baby girl, I just needed to get out of the car for a moment to stretch my legs and give thanks for all of my wonderful friends that I am surrounded by. La'Roc you are the best."

"Thanks, bro."

Alex decided to join La'Roc and Jordan.

La'Roc was the only person who really knew about Jordan's medical condition. However, the rest of the team would soon know that he had been diagnosed with HIV. That would include Chantal, Denise, Alex, Courtney, and Devon. The rest of La'Roc's family would be informed later.

La'Roc decided to tell Ms. Holiday and Ms. Cotton later on during the week, after returning to Westchester.

Ms. Holiday and Ms. Cotton needed to know about Jordan's medical condition because they would be working closely with him while he was in New York.

As they reached the condominium, La'Roc called and alerted Ms. Holiday to have some mixed drinks for her and Alex. "Please, Ms. Holiday, make a nonalcoholic drink for a friend of mine."

"Ms. Rose, Courtney and Devon are upstairs waiting for their surprise." "Thanks, Ms. Holiday. Tell them that I am outside. Ask

Devon and Courtney to bring my babies down. The surprise is also for you and Ms. Cotton." As La'Roc came around the Hummer, her cell phone rang.

The voice on the other end of the phone said, "Hello, girlfriend!"

"Hi Chantal. Where are you?"

"I am at work in my office. Why?"

"I need you and Denise to drive down to the condo after work. I have a surprise for you guys."

"La'Roc, how did your visit go with Shawn today?"

"The visit went very well. I left Shawn with a big smile on his face. After hearing our presentation, he seemed excited about his bail hearing."

"La'Roc, we will see you within the hour. Denise is at work. I'll call her and tell her to meet me there. Denise and I were in Westchester today for lunch to set up things for tonight. We are still working on Shawn's case tonight, right?" Denise and Chantal were very helpful in terms of keeping things in perspective. They kept all of the files on Shawn's case in order and placed phone calls for the team.

"Yes, we are working on the case tonight." "All right, girlfriend. Love you."

Courtney ran outside with La'Roc's beautiful babies. She gave La'Roc Paris in one hand and Biscuit in the other.

She walked over to the driveway and spotted Jordan. "Oh my God, Mommy, it is Uncle Jordan! Why didn't you tell me he was here?"

She started to cry and ran into Jordan's arms. "Uncle Jordan, I am so happy you're here. I missed you so much."

Jordan picked her up and held her real close to his chest. "Baby girl, let me look at you. Baby, you look just like your mother. Courtney, you are so beautiful. Just look at you. Where is my man Devon?"

Courtney responded, "He is upstairs on the phone talking to one of his friends. He is going to be really surprised to see you."

La'Roc was playing with her babies and not thinking about Jordan and Courtney's conversation. She was happy running around the grounds with her babies. In her four and half inch heels.

Jordan said, "Let's go upstairs and surprise Devon."

While waiting for Chantal and Denise, La'Roc said, "Alex you look like you're worried about something. What's up, partner?"

"I am fine. What did you think about our presentation today?"

"Don't worry, partner. We've got this one. You trust me, right?" La'Roc asked Alex.

"Yes, I trust you, partner. I trust you with my life."

"The three of us are going to walk into that courtroom and walk out with Shawn. I am working on something. I will discuss it with you and Jordan later on tonight. So please don't worry, okay, babe?" La'Roc said.

"Come on; let's go inside. Denise and Chantal are on their way over."

Devon finally came outside ...

Devon was so excited to see Jordan; he ran into Jordan's arms, and then they did the shoulder bump.

Devon looked over his shoulder and spotted his grandmother. "Hi, Grams." He ran over to her, kissed her, and then ran back to Jordan to continue their conversation.

Devon and Courtney were very close to Jordan. During their stay in California, Jordan was their guardian angel. He took care of them as if they were his children. He loved Courtney and Devon dearly. It's going to be really hard for Jordan to tell them about his being diagnosed with the HIV virus. La'Roc felt so helpless.

There was nothing she could do to help Jordan get though the heartbreaking story he was about to convey to Devon, Courtney, Chantal, and Denise. La'Roc said, "Chantal and Denise should be arriving soon."

La'Roc's mind drifted back to high school, when she first met her two best friends. They all were deprived of money; they were some sad-looking little creatures. The girls were smart; however, their financial status was zero. Being financially disabled brought the three friends closer together. Chantal, Denise, and La'Roc became as one. Meeting Jordan in college was like meeting a banker. He was the cute little rich boy. (Howard University was on one side of the street, and on the other side was Morris Medical University and Business School.) Jordan and La'Roc attended Howard University together. They were like two peas in a pod. All three girls were granted financial aid and student loans to get through their first three years of college. The rest is history.

A little background on Chantal: Chantal was born to a single parent. Her father left the home when her mother was seven months pregnant with her, according to what Chantal said her mother told her. Her mother turned to drugs and alcohol after she gave birth to Chantal. Her mother kept a job as long as she could because of her outstanding drug habit and her alcohol dependency. Ms. Miller gave up on raising her daughter after her drug problem would not allow her to hold down a job. According to Chantal, at the age of five, her mother drove her to Anna Adoption Agency, not to put her up for adoption but to place her in foster care until she could provide for her daughter.

At five years old, Chantal Miller became a ward of the state. When she was six years old, she was placed in a foster home with a family: Mr. and Mrs. Bob Murphy.

Chantal said she was removed from the Murphy's' home at the age of eight by her social worker. She reported being raped and molested by Mr. and Ms. Murphy from the age of six, and it continued until the age of eight. She ran away from the Murphy and went back to Anna Agency. The agency was the only place she knew. At the age of nine, she was adopted into a nice family: the Freemans. This family gave her love and everything that she needed to grow up to love herself as well as build up her self-esteem and self-confidence. The Freemans were not a rich family but were rich in love. They had to struggle to keep food on the table just like La'Roc's family. But they had a lot of love for Chantal.

The only thing difference was La'Roc was raised by her biological parents. Chantal wasn't. However, the Freemans became Chantal's loving family.

Chantal started college before La'Roc and Denise because of La'Roc and Denise's financial difficulty.

Chantal's adopted family was all about education. Chantal didn't have money to buy lunch, but she was able to buy some of her needed books.

Chantal never saw her biological parents again. They both died of drug overdoses. However, Chantal was very close to La'Roc's family. La'Roc's family was Chantal's second family. Chantal went on to be one of the greatest heart surgeons in the country. She was also semiretired now.

However, she still worked as a cardiology consultant all over the world. She was hardly ever in her office. Chantal was always flying across the country to consult with other doctors about new ways of saving heart patients' lives. She was often called out of the country to do motivational speaking.

Snap out of it, La'Roc. It's time to refocus on the problem at hand, which is Jordan.

La'Roc wanted Jordan to tell everybody at the same time about his contracting the HIV virus. She did not want him to have to keep repeating this horrible story.

Jordan insisted on telling Courtney and Devon in private. La'Roc responded by nodded in agreement. "Jordan, whatever makes you happy."

Ms. Cotton and Ms. Holiday ran downstairs with big smiles on their faces.

"Oh, Mr. Diaz, is that you? How nice to see you. We all missed you."

Jordan said, "Come over and give me a hug, both of you." They both ran into Jordan's arms.

La'Roc said, "You see Jordan, we all love you, and we'll never stop loving you. You will always have us as your extended family, and you will always have a home here in New York with us."

"Thanks, baby girl." La'Roc hugged Jordan. They kissed each other, and tears started running down her cheeks.

Courtney walked back into the entertainment room from the kitchen. "Mommy, what's wrong? Why are you crying?"

"Sweetie, Mommy's all right. I am just happy because Jordan will be working on Shawn's case with me and Alex."

"Oh, that's really cool. You guys will be working together again."

Jordan walked into the gray room. "Courtney, where is your deadbeat son?"

"He's upstairs getting dressed for dinner. I'll go get him."

"No, baby, let's go upstairs together. I need to talk to both of you."

"Jordan, what's wrong? I don't like where this is going. Something is up. Spill it, Uncle Jordan."

"Courtney, you are just like your mother. You can't wait. Everything has to be rush, rush, rush. Calm down. I want to tell you and Devon together."

La'Roc and Alex waited downstairs for Chantal and Denise.

Paris and Biscuit ran inside, following Ms. Holiday and Ms. Cotton from their walk.

La'Roc grabbed Paris and Biscuit in her arms; she held her babies close to her chest with tears forming in her eyes. She started to cry, thinking about the sadness that her daughter and grandson were getting ready to face.

I don't know how much more Courtney can take after going through so much with Justin and now Jordan. Justin is not making progress. He's back in the hospital, unable to breathe on his own.

He's on life support most of the time to help him to breathe, La Roc thought. *As Courtney's mother, I will always be there for her.*

"No, no. Tell me that's not true." Courtney ran downstairs, crying. Alex jumped from his seat and held her in his arms. Devon ran after his mother with tears running down his face.

La'Roc knew at that second she had to tell the rest of Jordan's friend's about his illness.

At that moment, Chantal and Denise walked into the living room. Denise cried out, "What the hell is going on?"

Chantal spoke. "Tell me what the fuck happened! Ms. Holiday, will you please tell me what's going on here?"

La'Roc said, "I will tell you. Please sit down. I need to check on Jordan." Denise and Chantal asked simultaneously, "Jordan is here?"

"Yes, he is upstairs," La'Roc responded.

La'Roc ran upstairs to check on Jordan; to her surprise she found him sitting on Devon's bed, crying. La'Roc put her arms around him and assured him that everything was going to be all right.

La'Roc approached her friend with tears in her eyes. "Jordan, we have our friends downstairs. We need to tell them why Devon and Courtney are crying their eyes out."

He stopped crying long enough to give La'Roc a hug. "I am ready to go downstairs and tell my friends what going on with my health," Jordan responded in a soft tone. He looked at La'Roc with sadness in his eyes.

"Yes, all of your friends are here to support you. You are not alone. Just remember, we all love you, baby. Let's go downstairs and tell the group. How do you feel about telling Alex?"

"La'Roc, Alex needs to know. We're working together on Shawn's case, remember? I will not keep something like this from him. Yes, he needs to know about my diagnosis." La'Roc entered into the great room.

"What is going on?" Chantal asked La'Roc. "My godchildren are crying like somebody died, and you are walking around as if you lost your best friend. What the hell is going on?" Devon and Courtney went back upstairs with their heads down, holding hands.

Denise asked, "This is about Shawn, right? Is Shawn all right?"

La'Roc responded, "Yes, Shawn is fine. Jordan would like to talk to all of you in the sitting room. He has something very important to tell you, and you will understand why my children were upset."

Courtney and Devon were upstairs, grieving. La'Roc felt that they needed some alone time together before she went upstairs to grieve with them. Courtney and Devon had received some shocking news about their godfather and needed some space. They both loved Jordan like a father and understood what the virus could do to their godfather.

Jordan came downstairs; he looked totally drained. He tried to put on a happy smile for his friends. Chantal, Denise, and Alex were sitting in the den, waiting for La'Roc to tell them what the commotion was all about.

Alex, Chantal, and Denise followed La'Roc into the sitting room as if they were La'Roc's children.

Jordan walked into the room with drinks for everybody.

Before Jordan got started, La'Roc decided to send Ms. Cotton and Ms. Holiday out into the backyard with Paris and Biscuit.

Chantal and Denise noticed that Jordan looked darker and slimmer. Denise yelled, "Jordan, good to see you again." Denise walked over to Jordan and gave him a kiss.

Chantal said, "Hi, friend; what's wrong with your black ass? You look sick as hell, babe." Jordan walked over to Chantal and gave her a hug.

"Same old Chantal. I love you too, baby," Jordan responded.

After Jordan finished talking to his friends and Alex about his health, he went upstairs to bed. Before he left the room, he made it clear to all of his friends, "Please do not treat me any different than you do your other friends." Jordan then turned around, left the room, and walked back upstairs to Devon's bedroom.

The girls and Alex sat downstairs with a stiff drink. Chantal and Denise were devastated after hearing that Jordan had been diagnosed positive with the HIV virus.

Denise asked, "La'Roc, how long has you known about Jordan testing positive for the virus?"

"He told me last night after he arrived," responded La'Roc.

She lied to her friends. Jordan told her weeks prior to his visit to New York. He asked her to keep his secret ... she did because she wanted him to be the one to tell his friends. She felt it wasn't her story to tell.

The three girls hugged each other and just cried. Alex tried to console them. That was useless. "La'Roc, I really feel bad about what I said about Jordan when he came downstairs," Chantal responded with an embarrassed look on her face. "He looked so skinny and dark, and now I know why."

La'Roc said, "Don't worry about it; he knows that you love him and that you will always have his back."

"Thanks, La'Roc, I needed to hear that."

La'Roc excused herself and ran upstairs to check on Courtney and Devon. When she opened the door, she found Courtney and Devon lying in Jordan's arms. All three of them were sleeping.

La'Roc tiptoed back downstairs to be with her friends.

"Hey, guys, snap out of it! We have work to do. Jordan will not like this sulking around. Remember what he said, okay? We have to get to work—not only on Shawn's case, but we have to think about Jordan and his needs as well."

La'Roc said, "Justin is back in the hospital, and he's not responding to the treatment he is receiving. It just seems like everything is falling apart."

Chantal, Denise, Alex, and La'Roc made a promise to each other that every day they would work together to help find Jordan the best doctors in the country.

"Money is no object," Denise responded.

"Denise, you are right about that. Money is no object," Chantal said. "I will contact all of my connections, and I have quite a few. I'll get on it right away." La'Roc said, looking out the window, "We all have money, but will money be enough to save our friend Jordan?"

Ms. Holiday and Ms. Cotton came into the sitting room with Paris and Biscuit. Both pets ran into La'Roc's arms. She picked them both up with a playful kiss and a hug. How she missed Paris and Biscuit. La'Roc had been so busy during the past few months, she had no time to play with her babies or take them out for their morning walks.

La'Roc's family was Jordan's family. That was one of the reasons she wanted Jordan to live there in New York—to be close to her and her family.

La'Roc yelled out to Paris and Biscuit, "Let's go upstairs for a long, hot bath and wash Mommy's problems away."

La'Roc would never turn her back on Jordan. He took care of Chantal and Denise, and he also took care of her all through college. That was why she would always be there for him. She loved him so much, and she was not ready to let go of him or let him be eaten up by that horrible virus. She would fight to the end to keep him alive. Even if helping Jordan took her last dime, it would be worth it. Because if you cannot spend your money helping your best friends, what's the purpose of having money?

La'Roc decided to relax in a hot bubble bath while Paris and Biscuit looked on. "What a beautiful Kodak moment."

La'Roc undressed and stepped into her bath, with Paris and Biscuit by her side. She closed her eyes and thought about how much she loved her mother. *I am so blessed to have a loving family, unlike Jordan. He has no family left.* His father died when Jordan was in his third year of law school. Jordan's mother had passed away several months prior to him finding out about his health crisis.

Jordan's father was a very rich man. He made his money in real estate and was a well-known movie producer-director who made good investments. Jordan and his mother never had to worry about money. They had always been blessed with the good life.

In college, Jordan had the money, and the three ladies had Jordan.

Jordan was an only child. He had one aunt left, whose whereabouts were unknown. She was like the black sheep of the family, or at least, that was what Jordan told La'Roc.

La'Roc and her friends believed that Jordan's Aunt Ruth had passed on. La'Roc and her team had searched high and low without ever finding Jordan's aunt.

Jordan had never discussed his aunt in great length to any of his friends. Jordan looked at his friend. "La'Roc, please stop searching for Aunt Ruth. I really don't know her that well. I met her twice in my life. So just leave it alone, okay, babe?" He added, "You guys are my family now. Drop the search party, okay, baby girl?"

That day, La'Roc heard anguish in Jordan's voice, and his facial expressions showed unhappiness.

She said, "We need to talk about Aunt Ruth. I feel the pain, baby, that you're feeling." La'Roc looked him straight in his eyes. "Talk to me, Jordan." She realized that day that Jordan had a deep secret that he was with holding within his heart. A secret he had shielded for many years.

La'Roc thought about everything that she and Jordan had discussed about his aunt that day. The sadness in his face during the conversation was unbelievable. "La'Roc, I will tell you everything about Aunt Ruth later. Talking about Aunt Ruth brings back some painful memories. It has something to do with my mother, and I just don't feel like talking about it right now. La'Roc, I need for you to respect my feelings on that. Are we good?" Looking at him, La'Roc knew that she would never disrespect her best friend's feelings under any circumstances.

"Oh, Jordan, you know that I respect you, and I will have no problem with respecting your feelings. I love you, Jordan, and you just remember, your pain is my pain."

"I know that you will always have my back, La'Roc," Jordan said.

La'Roc jumped up from her bath pillow and realized she had fallen asleep in her bubble bath while her companions, Paris and Biscuit, were lying in their doggie bed by her bathtub, asleep.

Oh my goodness, I look like a dried-up prune. She smiled to herself. *What would Shawn say if he saw this old prune standing in front of him? He would say, "Hey, babe, let's make love." He would be smiling, and I would return the smile.* She laughed out loud.

There was a knock on her bathroom door. "Yes," she answered. "Mommy, may I come in?"

"Of course, baby, come in and talk to your old, dried-up mother." They both laughed.

"Courtney, how are you and what are your feelings about the news Jordan just relayed to you and Devon?"

"Mommy, I really don't know what I feel. I am angry, sad, and confused." La'Roc pulled a robe from her bathroom closet and ran into her master bedroom. Courtney followed her into the bedroom. They jumped on La'Roc's round, king-sized bed.

"Talk to me, sweetheart. Mommy is here. Let me call Devon down so we all can talk about the bad news that you guys just received from Jordan," La'Roc said.

Courtney responded, "Okay, I will call Devon."

She dialed Devon's number from her cell. "Mom, he is on his way down. "Mommy, I want to sleep with you tonight. Will that be all right with you?" Courtney changed the subject, not wanting to express her feeling about Jordan's health.

"Sweetheart, you can sleep with me any time you like. When you're ready to talk about Uncle Jordan, please don't hesitate," La'Roc said.

"Mommy, what happened to the rest of the team?"

"Oh, baby, they left to begin working on Shawn's case. Jordan and I will be leaving later on this evening. Courtney, I would like for you and Devon to come with me to Westchester to hang out with Jordan for a few days. Jordan needs all of us right now. However, we cannot pity him; remember that. Since Justin is back in the hospital, you will have some time to spend with Uncle Jordan. First of all, Courtney, let's talk about your feelings about what Jordan just told you.

"Remember, his mother just passed away, and you and Devon never expressed your feeling about her demise. I will be here to discuss her passing as well as Jordan's illness as soon as you guys are ready. I will be here for you always."

"Okay, Mother dear," Courtney said with a tearful smile.

Courtney responded to her mother, "How could this happen to Uncle Jordan ... how did he contract HIV?"

"Sweetheart, you know Uncle Jordan. He will tell you when he is ready. Just be patient with him. Okay, baby?" La'Roc responded.

Devon walked into La'Roc's bedroom and laid his head on her lap. His eyes were swollen from crying. Courtney and Devon were well educated on the HIV virus. They both knew that it could mean death.

La'Roc explained to Devon how important it was for him to share his feelings.

She looked at Devon with sadness in her eyes. "Devon, you don't have to share your feelings this evening; but you must talk about it soon."

"I will, Gram. I promise you will be the first person I talk to."

La'Roc put her arms around both of her little darlings, and they all cried together. Courtney and Devon fell asleep in La'Roc's bed.

While they slept, La'Roc went downstairs to inform Ms. Cotton and Ms. Holiday of Jordan's serious health problem. She felt they needed to know. Neither Ms. Holiday nor Ms. Cotton could verbalize their feelings when they were told; they were only able to express themselves by the tears running down their faces.

They also loved Jordan. They were aware of the HIV virus.

Ms. Cotton and Ms. Holiday had known Jordan for years and, of course, they were sad because they too were a part of the family. They both treated him as a son.

La'Roc looked down on the floor where Paris and Biscuit were sitting on their pillows, looking at her, licking their lips; they seemed to be crying about Jordan's health as well ... they loved Jordan too. La'Roc smiled at them. *We will never know if they are actually crying or not. Remember, puppies have feelings too,* she thought.

She walked back upstairs to Devon's room to check on Jordan, and to her surprise, he was still sleeping. He had had a long day. She kissed him gently on the forehead and then walked quietly out of the room with sadness in her eyes. As she walked away, her thoughts wandered. *Where will I stay tonight? Will I stay here at the condo or shall I go to Westchester tonight?* She snapped her fingers and then said out loud, "I'll just stay here tonight. But first, I will call my partner."

She went into her office to call and check on the team. She talked to Alex for a while about Shawn's case. After collaborating with Alex, she instructed him and the others to get some sleep. Before saying her goodnights, she asked about Chantal and Denise.

Alex responded, "They're sleeping."

"Good." And she disconnected her call and then realized she had a few more calls to make ...

La'Roc called her mother; they talked for a while and then made a date for lunch and hung up. She then called her sister, talked for a few minutes, made a date for lunch as well, hung up, and sighed deeply. She needed to tell her family about Jordan but not right now. When Jordan was ready, he would tell them everything.

La'Roc took her babies upstairs and put them into their bed. Then she proceeded to go back into her bedroom to join her daughter and grandson in bed for hopefully a good night sleep. They were all exhausted, trying to put Jordan's heart-breaking news in perspective because they all loved him, including La'Roc's Mother.

Before she fell off to sleep, she heard the vacuum cleaner running. Thinking out loud, she said, "What the fuck? Oh well, Ms. Holiday and Ms. Cotton cleaning downstairs."

Ms. Holiday and Ms. Cotton were indeed downstairs cleaning the first floor's sitting area and the kitchen before going to bed. They both were very sad after hearing about Jordan's condition.

For the second time in months, La'Roc finally got a good night's sleep. The next morning, La'Roc was awakened by the ringing of her phone. "Hello, who is this?"

"Good morning, partner. Sorry to wake you so early, but Shawn just called me and woke me up, so I decided to take it upon myself and wake you up." Alex explained to La'Roc how Shawn was allowed to make the phone call. "One of the officer's I knew gave Shawn permission to call me as a lawyer-client phone call."

"What's wrong, Alex?" La'Roc asked.

"Nothing is wrong," he responded. "Oh, by the way, a message from Shawn ... he said he loves you and can't wait to see you on the next visit."

"Thanks, for the message; you can wake me anytime with a message from Shawn," La'Roc responded, smiling.

"When is your next visit with Shawn, Alex?" La'Roc asked.

"As soon as you and Jordan get here, I need to go over some notes with you both. I wonder if Jordan feels up to taking the ride with me to visit Shawn today." He continued, "I made a few call last night and, La'Roc, you are not going to believe what I found out about Mr. Johnston and Ms. Brown. I can come to Manhattan if you'd like?"

"No, Alex, we're coming to Westchester as soon as we get ourselves together. It's now 8:30 a.m. We should be there around noon. I think you should wait until tomorrow to make that visit to see Shawn. I need Jordan to go with you. I would like for him to be well rested and prepared to present the case to Shawn. We all have to be on the same page during this trial; this is my man, my soul mate, you are defending. Please calm down, Alex; you are going to be fine. Alex, you are a damn good lawyer, and don't you ever forget that."

After talking to Alex, La'Roc went into one of the guest bedroom showers because she didn't want to wake her daughter or her grandson. La'Roc had a good night's sleep. She felt that she slept so well because she was sleeping with her two loving children, Courtney and Devon.

She looked at her daughter and grandson sleeping and thought how blessed she was to have them both in her bed, by her side. Tears of happiness ran down her face to have her beautiful children lying in her bed, sleeping soundly.

La'Roc finished her long, hot shower. She then called over the intercom and instructed Ms. Cotton and Ms. Holiday to get breakfast ready and start packing for the trip to Westchester. La'Roc said that she would take Paris and Biscuit out for their morning walk in the meantime.

Ms. Holiday responded, "Yes, Ms. Rose, we will get breakfast started and start packing for the trip. Mr. Diaz is already up dressed, has had his breakfast, and said he was going for a long walk before leaving for Westchester."

"Thank you, Ms. Holiday. Courtney and Devon will be going back to Westchester with us for a while, so don't forget to pack for the both of them, okay?"

La'Roc heard Jordan's voice downstairs. She finished dressing, ran downstairs, and greeted him with a kiss.

"Good morning, baby girl. How did you sleep last night?"

"I slept wonderfully. How was your night? Did you get a good night's sleep, Mr. Diaz?"

"Baby girl, I slept like a baby. It seemed like I was sleeping for hours. I just could not wake up. What time did Chantal, Denise, and Alex leave?" Jordan asked.

"They left real early yesterday to beat the traffic to Westchester," La'Roc responded. "They went to the townhouse to go through the files for Shawn's case. By the way, Alex is waiting to share some information with you and me concerning the case. "Alex is going to visit Shawn tomorrow, and I want you to ride with him. I need for you to get to know Shawn as well as Alex does. That is, if you are feeling up to it. I know you think you know Shawn because of his ties to me. Jordan, you need to know Shawn for who he really is. He is everything I told you he was. Baby, you need to build a relationship with him as his lawyer and not as his friend. Shawn has enough friends right now. What he needs now are three damn good lawyers to get him home. Jordan, are you following me?"

"Baby girl, I am with you all the way. You're the boss." He put both hands on her face and pulled her gently into his arms and kissed her on the forehead. "La'Roc, stop worrying; we have it under control, baby girl. I will never let you down, and you know that. Are you taking the ride with Alex and me tomorrow?"

"No, I don't think so. If I make the trip, I will be a distraction. I want you and Alex to get to know Shawn. Work on his case and consult with me. I have faith in the both of you. I know that you can do it."

Ms. Holiday called on the intercom and announced breakfast was ready. Courtney and Devon ran downstairs into Jordan's arms.

"Good morning, my precious godchildren."

They laughed. "Good morning, Godfather. We love you."

"Courtney, are you going to the hospital to see Justin before you leave?" La'Roc asked her daughter. "If you are, Jordan would like to ride with you for your visit."

"Oh, Uncle Jordan, that would be great. Justin would love to see you. Thank you for coming with me," Courtney responded.

"You, Jordan, and Devon can take the Lexus. I'll drive Ms. Holiday, Ms. Cotton, and my babies in the hummer," La'Roc said.

"Okay, Mom that will be great. Uncle Jordan, you are down with me driving, aren't you?" Courtney asked.

"Of course, little La'Roc; you know that I trust you. I trust you and your mother with my life," Jordan answered.

Devon appeared from the dining room with a glass of juice in one hand and a sandwich in the other hand.

"Mom, what time are we going to visit Justin?" He then turned to La'Roc. "Grams, did you know I am leaving for California next week to have my SUV and my mother's car shipped back to New York?"

"How long will you be gone?"

"I will be gone for several days. My partner is flying out with me," Devon answered.

"You know, Devon, your mother needs you here with her. It is very important that you remember that she needs you and why she needs you," La'Roc responded.

"I know, Grams. You know me. I will always be where my mother can reach me."

"We will talk before you leave for California. Okay, little man?" La'Roc said.

"I got you, Grams. I know my mother is going through a lot with Uncle Jordan's health situation, and Justin's health is not improving. Believe me, Grams. I got it under control."

"I know, little man; you are the best son a mother could have," La'Roc whispered with a smile.

"Mom, let's get out of here. We need to get to the hospital and get on the highway before the traffic gets too heavy."

"I'm coming, Devon. I'm waiting for Uncle Jordan, and you know how slow he is," Courtney responded jokingly to her son.

La'Roc yelled out, "We're leaving! Later, kids."

La'Roc called out so Pairs and Biscuit could come downstairs. She also informed Ms. Holiday and Ms. Cotton to meet her outside because it was time to leave.

Ms. Cotton and Ms. Holiday got into the vehicle with Paris and Biscuit in their arms. Devon pulled out and sped off. They said their goodbyes with the blowing of a kiss. They both went their separate ways. La'Roc headed toward Westchester while Courtney, Devon, and Jordan left for the hospital to visit Justin, with Devon behind the wheel.

With a change of heart, Courtney decided to let Devon drive. He drove like a speeding bullet, just like his mother and grandmother. Speeding was just a part of the Rose family.

La'Roc got into the Hummer and headed north on I-95. She popped in a CD, and music started blasting out of the speakers: R. Kelly *When a woman loves, she loves for real.* She began to speed with tears in her eyes, thinking of how many times she and Shawn had traveled this highway together. Now she was alone, fighting back tears and fighting for his freedom.

La'Roc knew in her heart that Shawn would be free, but she needed him now. She needed his strong arms around her and him breathing down her neck. She needed his tongue between her thighs making love to that hairy thing that people call a vagina. Oh, how she missed her boy toy. When he made love to her, she knew that she had been loved. Shawn was so good in bed that even when he was not around, she felt him inside of her as well as his lips on her lips.

As La'Roc drove up I-95, her cell phone started to ring. She answered with her headset, "Hello, who's speaking?"

The voice on the other end responded, "Hello, Sexiful. What do you mean?

'Who's speaking?'" Shawn said jokingly. "How're you, babe?"

"Shawn, I am good. What's going on, and how did you manage to make this call? Are you breaking the rules, young man?" La'Roc said with a loud giggle.

"Baby, is everything all right?"

"Yes, everything is good. I just spoke to Alex, and he made arrangements with the officer. The officer allowed me to call and speak to you for five beautiful minutes."

"Oh, I must thank Alex for this wonderful surprise when I get to Westchester. Sweetheart, how are you really?"

"I was a little down until I called Alex. I am feeling better now talking to you."

"Baby, I will see you next week. However, Alex and Jordan will visit you tomorrow," La'Roc said.

"Sexiful, you are not coming with Alex?"

"No, I want you to get comfortable with your lawyers. I will always be there by your side, but not as your lawyer. Remember, I am Alex and Jordan's consultant. I need them to meet with you tomorrow alone, and you let me know if you want them to represent you as your lawyers," La'Roc responded.

"Baby, you guys are the best. Why wouldn't I want the best?" Shawn responded to La'Roc's question.

"Baby, I want you to be happy and pleased with your lawyers. When you are happy, Sexiful is happy." She chuckled. "Shawn, when I get to Westchester, I will have Alex reconnect with you again with permission from one of the officers. Okay, baby? Shawn, don't worry. Alex will get through, and he will touch base with you around 3:30. And at that time, you will be able to speak to Courtney, Devon, and Jordan. Okay, sweetheart? Talk to you soon, sweetie." She disconnected her cell headset.

La'Roc pressed her foot down on the gas, with her music blasting loud just the way she liked it when driving on the highway. The loud music woke Paris and Biscuit from their nap. Paris and Biscuit looked at La'Roc as if to say, *Please, let the both of us sleep. We were up all last night crying about Shawn, and now we have to cry about Jordan. Don't you realize that we need our beauty sleep?*

35

La'Roc looked into her rearview mirror. *We'll be home soon, my little ones.*

"Ms. Cotton, are you and Ms. Holiday all right sitting back there?" "Yes, Ms. Rose, we're fine."

"We are almost there, family." Minutes later, after the conversation with her employees,

La'Roc pulled into the garage. She noticed Chantal and Alex's car. Denise ran outside to greet La'Roc.

"Hi, sis. Where's Jordan?"

"Hi, Denise. He's riding with Devon and Courtney. They stopped by the hospital to visit with Justin. I just hope Courtney is all right," La'Roc said.

"I'm glad she'll be with you for a while. Chantal and I will be around whenever you or she needs us," Denise said.

Chantal walked out to help unpack. "Well, hello, sister," Chantal yelled out. "Where's the other part of our family?"

"Courtney wanted to stop by the hospital to see Justin before coming. She, Jordan, and Devon will be driving up to the townhouse in a few hours."

"La'Roc, we should talk about what we're going to do to help Jordan," Denise said.

Chantal spoke up. "Yes, we need to get working on finding the best doctor who specializes in HIV. We have got to save our friend."

La'Roc said, "If Jordan can be saved, we'll save him. We have the money to get the best doctors in the country."

"Okay, girls, let's not lose focus. We've got to get Shawn home because Jordan is ready to fight to prove his innocence and bring him back to La'Roc, where he belongs."

"Don't worry, girls. We'll help Jordan, just like we're helping Shawn. He'll have the best of care."

La'Roc pointed at herself smiling.

As they all walked into the townhouse, Alex dashed from La'Roc's office. "Hi, partner. Are you ready to get to work? I have something that I know you want to hear." La'Roc gave Alex a quizzical look. "Kelly Brown and Mr. Johnston knew each other back in high school. She was his prom date; can you believe that?"

La'Roc said out loud, "Thank you, Alex. When I chose you for my partner, I knew it was the right decision for my firm. That's the type of investigating I'm talking about. When you investigate, you always find what you are looking for.

"Alex you've done a wonderful job. My hunches are never wrong. I knew they had a history, but I couldn't prove it until now. Shawn will be so happy when he finds out that we have evidence of a connection between Brown and Johnston. This case needs everything we can find to help prove that Shawn was set up."

La'Roc knew she couldn't say anything to Shawn about her hunch. She knew if she told him about her feeling and it turned out to be false, Shawn would be devastated.

La'Roc was overwhelmed with happiness. She thought to herself, *Maybe we can get Shawn off without going to trial.* She asked herself, *would that be great or what?*

"Alex, after Jordan arrives, I need you and him to pay a visit to Shawn's sister, April, because I think she can free her brother with the information I believe she has about Mr. Johnston and Ms. Brown." La'Roc had a gut feeling that April had a hand in setting Shawn up because of her friendship with Kelly Brown.

"Good idea, partner. Maybe we can shake her up a little," Alex responded.

"Alex, she needs to know if she lies, she will go to jail." "Hello, everybody," Jordan yelled out.

"Come downstairs and join the team in my office," La'Roc called back.

When Jordan joined them, La'Roc said, "Alex, you and Jordan do your shoulder-bumping thing, and Chantal and Denise, do all your kissing. Get it over because we've got work to do. Jordan, where are my children?"

"They are outside, playing with Paris and Biscuit."

"Jordan, how was Justin?" La'Roc inquired, a worried look traveling across her beautiful face.

"Justin responded to seeing Courtney, but the doctor said he is still not responding to his treatment."

"How is Courtney handling it?"

"She seemed okay. She is just like you. She hides her feeling very well." "Baby girl, I think Courtney has come to accept Justin's condition and is ready to move forward. I am really proud of her, La'Roc. I am proud of her mother too," Jordan said.

"Thanks, baby, for your support," La'Roc responded. "Alex, give Jordan an update on what you found out on the Brown case. As your consultant, I need to know how you got this important information and from where."

Alex responded, "I met Ms. Brown's sister, Sandra Brown, at the hospital one night, and after introducing myself, we got into a conversation about Ms. Brown's condition. She was about to give me her phone number without hesitation, and to be honest, I was quite surprised. Before I accepted the number, I showed her my identification and informed her that I was Shawn's lawyer. Today I decided to call her, and with good results, I may add. I reintroduced myself stated my reason for calling, and she started talking," Alex continued excitedly.

"She gave me some useful information about Mr. Johnston and her sister. She said her family never did like Mr. Johnston, even when Kelly Brown and Mr. Johnston were dating.

"She also said Kelly told her the baby she was carrying was not Shawn's baby, but Shawn was going to take care of both of her children. Sandra Brown stated that Kelly's two-year-old son's father was Mr. Johnston. He is not Shawn's child. She said, 'My sister has always been a troublemaker. I can't figure out how a man like Shawn ever looked twice at her. Kelly is a very nasty person; she has stolen from our mother and other family members as well as Shawn.' Sandra continued her story by saying, 'One day, Kelly slapped my mother so hard, she fell to the kitchen floor. That's the day my father kicked her ass out the house. Mr. Power, if you need me to testify, please call me. You have all of my information. Shawn's sister April is no angel. She's bad blood too.'

"At that point, I stopped the conversation and explained to her, as Shawn's lawyer, that we may need her to testify on Shawn's behalf," Alex reported.

"Oh wow! My baby is coming home soon. Alex, Jordan, things are looking up for the team. I love you, guys." La'Roc ran over and hugged Alex. "Baby, I love you. Keep up the good work."

"La'Roc, may I get in on the hug?" Jordan asked.

"Alex, will Ms. Brown's sister go to trial to testify, and did you do a background check on her?" Jordan asked.

"Jordan, weren't you listening?" La'Roc noticed that Jordan was trying to rain on Alex's report; she wasn't going to have it. They would work together or Jordan could just sit this one out. *I don't play that shit, and Jordan knows it.* Jordan thought his little smart statement went over La'Roc's head.

That little smart remark would come back to bite him up his ass.

"Yes, I didn't leave any stones unturned. Sandra is a second-grade teacher at a local school in her community, and she's also very active in her church. Sandra Lee is married to a well-to-do restaurant owner in Long Island City and has two teenage children. I had one of my sources check out the information on her and her husband. Everything checked out just as Ms. S. Brown Lee had said.

"The people in the community spoke very highly of the Lee family. She said testifying will not be a problem," Alex responded to Jordan with a hard stare. Alex gazed back at La'Roc for approval.

La'Roc smiled and said, "Good job, Alex."

Jordan rolled his eyes with a smirk on his face. La'Roc also caught that little childish attitude and called him on his smirk. "What's that smirk about, Jordan?" La'Roc questioned, annoyance slipping into her voice.

"I'm all right, baby girl," Jordan responded, looking embarrassed because he knew La'Roc peeped his whole card.

"Jordan, I need to speak to you and Alex later regarding a personal business matter, and, Jordan, I think you know what it's about."

Alex asked, "You need us now, partner?"

"No, not now," La'Roc responded. "I'll meet with you both later."

Alex continued with his report. "Although Sandra Brown is saying all of this stuff about the babies who may or may not be Shawn's, we are still waiting for the DNA results for the two-year-old son. We got the DNA back from the fetus. We do know that was not Shawn's child. I am sure that Shawn is not the father of Kelly's two-year-old son, and that's going to kill him.

"Knowing that information, which we received from Ms. Sandra Brown Lee ... Please do not let Shawn know what we discovered today because we need hardcore evidence, and we don't have that. Before Shawn is informed of this hopefully wonderful news, we need proof. I don't need him becoming overwhelmed with thoughts about the son that he may have never fathered," La'Roc stated.

"Alex, I need you to go and interview April today. Let her know that we know about Ms. Johnston and Kelly dating," La'Roc said.

"I just don't understand how a sister does this to a brother. April seemed to have all of this anger penned up inside of her for her brother. Ms. Brown had stated in one of her conversations that April was very angry with her brother because he made it out of the streets and she didn't. Shawn has a business, his own home, and three of the damn best lawyers in New York State," stated Alex as he shook his head.

Jordan got up from his seat and pointed toward Alex. "Come on, man. We've got work to do. Let's go get Shawn out of prison."

Chantal, Denise, Courtney, and Devon walked into the room. "Oh, Mommy, Shawn's coming home?"

Denise yelled out, "Come on, La'Roc. Tell the girl. Is Shawn coming home or not?"

"Yes, if everything works out with the interview that Jordan and Alex will be having with Shawn's sister today; he may be home sooner than you think and back in my arms, where he should be. If all goes well, Shawn will be home this month."

Alex stuck his head back into the door and called for Devon.

"Devon, come on, man. Take a ride with Jordan and me. Come on, dude, and get your hands dirty."

"I love the sound of that. Let's ride, man. Grams, I am going to drive the Hummer," Devon yelled to La'Roc. "Okay, baby; drive careful."

La'Roc dashed to the door. "Jordan, you and Alex take care of my baby, all right?

"Alex, before you leave, see if you can reach Shawn. I told him that I would call him around 3:30 p.m. And when you see Shawn tomorrow, I repeat, you are not to utter a word to Shawn about what we found out today regarding Kelly and Mr. Johnston."

"I'm on it, partner," Alex responded.

"La'Roc, Shawn is on the phone," Alex yelled over his shoulder as he was walking out the door.

Courtney picked up the phone. "Hello, Shawn, this is Courtney. How are you?"

"I'm good as can be; looking forward to my visit tomorrow with my lawyers. The part I'm not happy about is I'll not be able to see your mother tomorrow."

41

"Why is that, Shawn?"

"Courtney, this is the way it goes. Your mother is not my lawyer on record. She is behind the scenes. She is Alex and Jordan's consultant. She advises them on what to do and how to present my case. Being a consultant, she has to come on regular visiting days. You got that, little La'Roc?"

Courtney said, pretending surprise, "Oh, I get it, because of conflict of interest, right?"

"You got it, Courtney," Shawn responded.

Courtney then said her goodbyes to Shawn and yelled to her mother to pick up the phone.

"Mom, Shawn's on the phone." "Thank you baby I'll take it upstairs."

La'Roc picked up the phone. "Hi, handsome. I am overly excited to hear from you. Baby, I miss you so much it hurts. Handsome, when you come home, we'll hang a 'Do Not Disturb' sign on the door for three days. Are you feeling me, baby?"

"Sexiful, I love you so much, sweetheart. I miss holding you in my arms at night. I'm always full and unable to eat or drink. I go to bed each and every night hungry for your love. I can't stand it anymore.

"Sexiful, I don't want to live without you … I want to always be in your life.

"Sexiful, when I get released from this place, I'll never leave you again. I will always be by your side. Baby, you know that I'm innocent, right? Just get me out of here and I'll prove my love to you each and every day. Kelly was not carrying my child. Sweetheart, I need you to believe me.

"Sweetheart, my time is almost up, but before you go, tell Courtney it was nice talking to her today, and ask Devon to take a ride with Alex and Jordan tomorrow. I'd love to see him too."

"I have a surprise for you Devon will be coming with them. He is a part of the team. I forgot! You didn't you know that? I didn't tell Devon yet, but he will be in the courtroom sitting with Alex, Jordan, and myself at your hearing. He will be overjoyed when I tell him tonight."

"Devon will be working on my case? Yes as an intern. That is awesome," Shawn said with pride in his voice. Shawn really liked Devon and Courtney. He always said how proud he was of the both of them.

"I am going to let you go but first remember the day at the airport when Courtney and Devon gave me the boxes. I think I will open them tonight after dinner while we are all here together."

"Oh, Sexiful, that will be great. I wish I could be there with you when you open your gifts. Give Chantal and Denise my regards. See you tomorrow, Sexiful. I love you. See you in a couple days. Remember, Sexiful, I am always inside of you. You feel me, baby?" Shawn responded.

"Baby, you know what we are doing right now? Close your eyes. We are lying in bed together, snuggling close and reflecting on the lovemaking that we shared so many nights in this bed. I feel your hands against my thighs, and you are deep inside of me. Can you feel my hot body, Shawn, rubbing against your hot, sweaty body, baby? Keep your eyes closed and feel me. Good night, handsome. Pleasant dreams. I love you. See you soon." La'Roc said her goodbyes and hung up the phone.

La'Roc summoned Ms. Holiday and Ms. Cotton on the intercom. She told Ms. Holiday to bring her babies downstairs. She wanted to take them for a walk around the grounds of the townhouse.

Ms. Holiday responded, "Yes, Ms. Rose. I'm on my way downstairs now." "Ms. Cotton, ask Courtney to come down if she's not busy."

"Ms. Rose, she left with Ms. Chantal and Ms. Denise a while ago."

"No problem. I'll call her on her cell. Thank you. Please bring my babies downstairs."

Biscuit and Paris ran downstairs to La'Roc's open arms. At the end of the stairs, her babies jumped up into her arms. La'Roc fell to the floor with laughter.

"Oh boy, you are happy to see me, huh?"

"Come, guys, let's go jogging." As you know, puppies don't jog. Her babies were in their little carriage, being pushed by the runner.

La'Roc yelled, "We will be out running. If I get a phone call, send it to my cell, ladies. Thank you."

La'Roc and her babies ran out the door for their afternoon run.

They finished their run as she fell on the ground with them on top of her.

She heard Ms. Holiday calling her name. "Ms. Rose, Mr. Diaz is on the phone."

"Thanks, Ms. Holiday. Ask him to call me on my cell." "Okay, I will give him the message."

Sexiful's phone rang soon after.

"Hello, Mr. Diaz. What can I do for you?"

"Well, La'Roc, we got here just a little late. We were informed by one of the tenants that Ms. April Parker moved out three days ago and left no forwarding address."

"Don't worry, Jordan, we will find her. That is why I pay my private investigators so handsomely so they can find the bad guys." They both laughed.

"La'Roc, you don't miss a thing."

"Thanks, Jordan. That is one of the reasons I am the best lawyer in New York State. May I speak to my intern?" La'Roc asked, walking into her house with her babies' right behind her.

"Hello, Grandmother." La'Roc smiled when she heard Devon's voice. "Hi, sweetheart. How was your first day as an intern?"

"Grams, it was real cool, but there was no action. We were informed that Shawn's sister had left town. We'll give you a report when we get back to the townhouse."

"Devon, I have a job for you tomorrow."

"Now you got my attention. I'm ready for whatever. What's the job?"

"I want you to take a ride to Upland Prison with Alex and Jordan to visit Shawn tomorrow."

"Grams that is a great idea. I'd like to see old Shawn."

"That's great, baby. I'll inform Alex and Jordan that you will be going with them."

"This will be your first paying job: a jail interview. How cool is that? Devon, you must be very professional at all times tomorrow. Alex and Jordan will be there to do the actual interview. You are only there to learn how to conduct a professional interview in lockup. You are there to be educated for when you become a certified lawyer."

"Grams, I am excited about this trip. Please let me tell my mother about my first paying job. She's going to be extremely happy and excited for me. So please, Grams, don't tell her."

"Devon, you have my word. This will be our secret." "Thanks, Grams. See you soon."

After hanging up the phone, she turned on the surround sound and snapped her fingers to the music.

La'Roc looked out the great room window and saw Courtney, Chantal, Denise, and, to her surprise, her mother and sister driving into the driveway.

La'Roc ran to the front door to greet everyone. It had been a while since she had spent time with her family.

She gave her mother a hug and a big fat kiss on her cheek. She stretched out her arms to her sister and gave her a tight hug and a kiss.

"I love you, guys. Thanks, Courtney, for bringing Mom and L'Oreal to visit." Everyone walked inside, laughing and talking, while Chantal danced to the music.

Then said, "La'Roc, come into the office. I need to talk to you and Denise. I'm ready to work on getting Jordan well. We need to talk in private since Mom and sis don't know what's going on with Jordan.

"I have contacted some of my colleagues about working on an organization in Jordan's name. The organization would open doors for kids as well as adults who suffer from HIV, and it would help the kids, mainly teenagers and their families, be aware of the dangers of having unprotected sex," Chantal explained.

Denise responded to Chantal. "Good idea, girlfriend. My contacts will donate a five-million-dollar scholarship to the organization to help underprivileged families with the virus send their children to college, etc."

La'Roc said, "*Wow!* You guys have been working. We'll run all of this good news by Jordan when he returns from Brooklyn. Right about now, I need to spend some time with my mother and sister.

"Good work, girls," La'Roc responded with a smile.

"Chantal, Denise, please come onto the terrace with me for a second. I'm going to ask L'Oreal and Casey to run the organization. They have all the experience we need to run a big organization like this one. If they say yes, then I'll be able to sleep at night because I trust them."

Chantal said, "That is a wonderful idea." Denise also agreed with La'Roc's decision.

La'Roc said, "I'll speak to L'Oreal tonight after dinner. I know she'll have to inform her husband of this request. As I said, we'll update Jordan later on this evening."

La'Roc yelled, "Courtney come up with a menu for dinner and give it to Ms. Holiday and Ms. Cotton. Ask Chantal and Denise to help." "Okay, Mother, we're working on it."

"Set up the big dining room because we're having ten guests for dinner," La'Roc responded. Whenever La'Roc had her friends over for dinner, it was always set up as if it were a *dinner party*.

"Okay, Mother."

"Courtney, you guys don't have to cook. Cooking is Ms. Holiday and Ms. Cotton's job."

"Yes, Mother dear," Courtney responded.

La'Roc, her mother, and her sister entered the guest living room.

"So, Mom, what's been going on? We haven't talked in a while. Tell me about your love life." They all laughed.

L'Oreal looked at her mother. *"Love life what* love life?"

La'Roc said, "Oh, sis, you're late. Mom has a man in her life." They looked at each other and had a big laugh.

The three of them each had a glass of red wine; they laughed like schoolgirls and talked for hours.

"Courtney, come and rescue your grandmother from your mother and your aunt."

"I am coming Grandmother. I am on my way to rescue you from your nosy daughters."

Chantal and Denise poked their heads in the door. "May we come in?" "We would like to talk to Mom and L'Oreal too. You always hog up Mom and L'Oreal when they visit. Why is that?"

"Denise, you really want me to answer that stupid question?" La'Roc answered with her hands on her hips.

Chantal said, "Yes, Sexiful. Explain. Why is that?"

La'Roc responded, "Okay, assholes, maybe you forget. This is my mother and my sister. I don't have to hog up my mother or my sister's time from you guys. However, I'll share them with you if you're nice to me. Would you like to share my mother and sister?"

Denise responded with her hands on her hips. "Oh, please, let Chantal and me share your family," she said jokingly.

Everybody burst into tears from laughter.

Alex, Jordan, and Devon returned from their investigation out in Brooklyn with no statement from April Parker.

La'Roc was not worried since things were looking good for Shawn. Devon ran into the house and saw his great-grandmother and gave her a hug and a kiss.

He looked at his mother, walked over to her, and gave her a high five and then kissed his grandmother.

Jordan entered the house. "Hi, family, what's for dinner?" He looked into the den and spotted La'Roc's mother.

"Hello, Mother dear. Are you ready to go on that date you promised me five years ago?"

Geneva responded with a smile. "Get over here, boy. Give me a kiss. And where is my hug?" Geneva noticed that Jordan was walking very slowly to greet her with that hug she had requested. She said, "Baby, what's wrong? You and these three girls are up to something. What is it?" Geneva said, laughing.

Jordan walked over and gave Geneva a big hug but avoided the kiss.

He explained to La'Roc he wanted Geneva to have the choice of kissing him or not because Geneva was uneducated on the transmission of AIDS. She was from the old school, and she believed that a person could contract the AIDS virus from a kiss. He didn't want to offend her.

La'Roc's mother was very smart in so many other ways, but not when it came to the HIV virus. La'Roc's mother was no different from any of her peers.

HIV was something Geneva didn't really understand. AIDS was never discussed in Geneva's home.

La'Roc agreed with Jordan.

Jordan decided to tell his story to L'Oreal and La'Roc's mom after dinner, in private.

"Good idea, Jordan," La'Roc said with approval.

Courtney ran from the dining room with Devon following her.

Chantal stopped in her tracks. "I don't know what's going on with my godchildren. Tell Auntie all of your problems."

Devon said, "There's no problem. We need to talk to Grams."

La'Roc said, "Chantal, will you please leave my children alone? You're just a nosy-ass person. Go help Denise with my four-legged babies, okay, sweetie?" Seeing Devon running around, playing with his mother, her mind drifted back to Devon's father and how proud he would've been of his little man. With all the noise, La'Roc decided to go on the terrace to read her newspaper. "Grams, where are you?"

"I am sitting on the terrace, trying to read my newspaper."

Shyly, Devon approached La'Roc and asked her about his father. She said, "What would you like to know?"

"Just tell me what was he like and did you like him?"

"Oh, Devon, I wished you had met your father. Your father was a wonderful man. He made your mother very happy. They were planning on getting married five months before his death. He was killed when he was thrown from his motorcycle. Courtney took it very hard when your father passed away. Your mother was a young mother—still in high school, as a matter of fact—when she gave birth to you. Your father never left her side. In spite of being a single mother, baby, she has done a wonderful job raising you."

"Thanks, Grams, for that information," Devon said.

Devon sat quietly looking at his grandmother, before saying, "My mother is always talking about my father and how much I look like him. Do I really look like him, Grams?"

"Yes, baby, you look as if he spit you out. That is how much you look like your father," La'Roc answered.

"Grams, you know what? I wish my father were here too," Devon responded. "My mom said that she misses her dad too. I see her sometimes looking at old pictures of her father, and she becomes very sad. At those times, I just put my arms around her and hold her real tight to reassure her that she is not alone. Grams don't worry. We have each other to lean on."

Courtney's father, Omar, had been killed in Vietnam. La'Roc was very young when she had Courtney. Courtney and Omar had been the loves of her life. Courtney knew her father for a very short time. She was five years old when he was killed. She still remembered her father.

Devon kissed his grandmother and left the terrace. La'Roc's daydream was later interrupted.

"Courtney and Devon, what's going on? You guys are too loud. Uncle Jordan is trying to rest ..."

"Oh, Momma, we are so sorry."

"Momma, Devon said his first paying job begins tomorrow and he'll get his first check on Friday ... I'm so proud of him! He won't tell me the client's name. Who is the client?"

While they were playing with each other, La'Roc thought about opening the boxes. La'Roc thought out loud that this would be the perfect time to open the two boxes that Devon and Courtney gave her after she gave Devon his Jeep and Courtney her car. She never had a chance to open them because as soon as she and Shawn returned from California, Justin was shot and the shit with Kelly happened.

This would be the perfect time to open the gifts. Shawn would not be home when she opened them. He would understand. Shawn was understood when it came to La'Roc's happiness. However, she did tell him earlier that she was going to open the present. La'Roc snapped back to Courtney and Devon.

"Devon, give your mother the client's name," La'Roc said with a smile. Looking at Courtney and Devon playing with each other, La'Roc thought about earlier when she had talked to Devon about his father. Devon's father would be so proud of him and his mother.

"Okay, Grams, I will tell her just for you. My client's name is Shawn Parker." Devon looked at his mother and said, "Are you satisfied?"

Courtney ran over and hugged her son. "Baby, I am so proud of you. Look at my little lawyer." Tears ran down her face. "Oh, Mommy, I am so happy for Devon and so sad for Jordan. I know he will get the help he needs because he has you as his best friend, and I know he'll get the best medical care in the world." Courtney looked over at Devon. "My little man has a paying job. I am so proud of you."

La'Roc hugged her daughter, and her grandson got in on the hug. They all cried sad tears for Jordan and happy tears for Devon.

Ms. Cotton called out over the intercom that dinner would be served in five minutes.

La'Roc went outside to get Chantal, Paris, and Biscuit for dinner. She thought to herself, *Hell, my babies have to eat too.*

Mr. Holiday then announced on the intercom that dinner was being served in the dining room.

They all sat down to a wonderful dinner. Jordan blessed the table, and they all dug into the food. After dinner, La'Roc decided to open the boxes that were given to her several months ago by Courtney and Devon the day she and Shawn left California. They had each given La'Roc a box with their name on it.

This was the first opportunity La'Roc had to open them. What with Justin getting shot and Shawn with his baby momma drama, there had been no time to open the boxes. She figured this was the perfect time, because her mother, sister, and friends were there to witness the surprise.

Everyone was there except Shawn.

La'Roc said first, "I would like to thank Ms. Holiday, Ms. Cotton, and my friend Denise for a wonderful dinner."

La'Roc suggested they all go into the living room to have dessert and open up the surprise boxes.

Jordan asked L'Oreal and La'Roc's mother to come to the guest room with him.

Jordan called out, "La'Roc, we'll join you guys in a few minutes. I need to talk to Mom and my little sister."

La'Roc acknowledged Jordan with a nod.

Fifteen minutes later, the three of them walked out of the guest room. Mrs. Rose and L'Oreal walked out of the room holding Jordan's hand with tears in their eyes. La'Roc knew at that time he had told them the sad news.

Jordan said, "La'Roc, you can continue with your surprise boxes. Right Mom, L'Oreal? We're okay, right?" L'Oreal said, "Yes, we're good."

La'Roc looked across the room at her mother. "Mom, are you all right?" "Baby, I will be okay. Just take care of Jordan. I'm good."

"Oh, Mother. Jordan will be all right, I promise you. He's going to be just fine. Okay, let's get this party started." La'Roc called Courtney and Devon, "Come with me, guys. I want to show you something." She asked if they remembered the boxes they had given her several months ago at the airport.

Courtney and Devon responded, "Yes."

Courtney said, "You really haven't opened them yet?"

"Grams, you are good. I would've opened that box as soon as I sat down on the plane," Devon said with a smile.

La'Roc held the boxes and motioned for Courtney and Devon to come and sit by her.

Everyone gathered around, and La'Roc opened Devon's box first.

It was a pure gold key to his SUV. The key had La'Roc's name engraved in the inside of the key ring.

And now it was time for La'Roc to open Courtney's box. Inside the box was a bronze key to her car that La'Roc had given her, with La'Roc's initials engraved in the inside of the key ring as well.

Courtney and Devon hugged La'Roc and thanked her for the car, the SUV, and all the things she had done for them. Courtney and Devon showed her their appreciation by giving La'Roc a part of things they loved.

Courtney said, "Devon and I decided to give you something that you will keep forever. The keys are keepsakes. So you will always remember that we love you."

"I love you, Grams," said Devon.

"I love you, Mommy," Courtney said La'Roc said, with tears in her eyes, "I love both of you with all my heart, and I love giving you beautiful things. With that, I would like to give Courtney and Devon something else."

La'Roc gave Devon and Courtney a piece of paper. "Please open it and tell me what it says."

"Grams, this is awesome. Is this for real?"

"Yes, I'm thinking about buying the condo next door and having it renovated for Devon so he can have his own space. I think he deserves to have his own condo. Do you agree, team?"

"We all agree."

"Yes, my loves, the condo in Manhattan is all yours."

Chantal and Denise gave Courtney and Devon a check to relocate from California to New York. The check was for fifty thousand dollars. Courtney could not stop crying; they were so happy.

La'Roc's sister, L'Oreal, and her mother were very excited that Courtney and Devon would be moving back to New York.

Jordan, Devon, and Courtney hugged each other, with tears rolling down their faces. Looking at Jordan, she felt really bad for him because of his serious health issues, and Courtney and Devon would be moving into their new condo. She knew he was falling apart, and there was nothing she could do to help him.

Alex congratulated Courtney and Devon on their decision to move back to New York to be with their family.

Courtney said, "This is wonderful! I can see Justin every day, and I can drive the Hummer every other day." She looked at her mother, smiling "Thanks, Mom, for everything," Courtney said.

"Love you, Grams. Thanks, for all you have given me," Devon thanked his grandmother with a hug.

"Okay, guys, we have work to do. Please come into my office, Alex, Jordan, Chantal, Denise, and Devon." She added, "Mom, you and L'Oreal hang out with Courtney. She will entertain you guys. L'Oreal, I need to talk to you later on this evening or tomorrow."

"Okay, sis."

"Ms. Holiday and Ms. Cotton, please give the babies their bath. Thank you," La'Roc yelled from her office.

La'Roc closed her office door. "Okay, let's get down to business. Let's start with Shawn's case.

"When you visit with Shawn tomorrow, do not relay any information that Kelly's sister provided to Alex because they need to do a little more investigation on that story. I really think we're onto something, but I need Mr. Johnston to admit that he knew Ms. Brown before the accident occurred." La'Roc paused and looked around at her team. They all nodded, so she continued.

"Devon will be going with you to Upland Prison to visit with Shawn tomorrow. How do you feel about him making the trip with you guys?"

"I like the idea. I think it will be great since he's already on payroll," Alex said with a little grin.

Jordan responded, "You know how I feel about Devon. I'd like to see Devon by my side tomorrow during the visit and by my side in the courtroom the day of the bail hearing."

"Remember, after the trip, Devon will be going back to California to close up the house and put it on the market.

"Jordan, we will fly out to California to take care of your home and all of your other property as soon as Shawn comes home.

"Shawn will be home soon, I promise you. He'll be home within a month; trust me on that," La'Roc said. Oh, by the way, Chantal and Denise have some good news to share with the team." Chantal was called into the office to share her good news.

Chantal then told the team about the AIDS foundation she had started, and Denise also enlightened the team about the donation that was offered for the organization.

La'Roc looked at Jordan. "Jordan, we would like to name the foundation after you. Is that okay?"

Jordan had tears rolling down his cheeks as he hugged all three girls. "Thank you. I love all of you." He looked over at Alex "I love you too, man." Alex walked over, took Jordan's hand, pulled him into his chest, and cried as Jordan cried.

The whole team was hugging Jordan and crying. Devon left the room with his head down after the meeting was over, trying to hide the tears from his mother. He didn't want to upset Courtney or make her think about Jordan's health.

La'Roc was crying because she didn't know how long she would have her best friend around. He seemed to be getting weaker by the day.

She would never allow him to go back to California. He would continue to live with her and Shawn. A few months ago, La'Roc purchased the adjoining condo to the one she had given to Courtney and Devon some weeks back, and Jordan would have his pick of where he wanted to live. He and Devon could share the condo. La'Roc knew Jordan would never go back to California. La'Roc liked investing her money in real estate.

Jordan had been looking a little sad, and at times, he seemed so distant. Chantal stated that she had noticed a change in Jordan's behavior.

After the meeting, Chantal asked La'Roc if Jordan was okay. "I'm asking you because he seems to be a little on edge."

"He is okay. He had been worried about telling my mother and sister about his health problem. However, he told them tonight after dinner. And after the conversation, Mother came out of the room in tears, and L'Oreal appeared as if she had just seen a ghost. Chantal, did I answer your question?"

"Yes, I guess I have to be more understanding about Jordan's health," Chantal responded. La'Roc nodded in agreement.

"Chantal, where's Alex and why is he hanging around Denise so much lately?" La'Roc asked, changing the subject.

Chantal responded, "I really don't know. I think something is going on with that slut and Mr. Cool."

"Chantal, you know what they say: What happens in the dark will come out to light. If something is going on between Alex and Denise, we will find out. Trust me.

"Anyway who would like to join me for a drink?" La'Roc asked with a smile as she entered the great room.

La'Roc walked over to the bar to mix her mother and sister a nightcap, Chantal and Denise poured themselves a glass of red wine. Alex got himself a beer and some chips.

Jordan, Courtney, and Devon took Paris and Biscuit out for their evening walk.

"L'Oreal," La'Roc yelled over her shoulder. "Come with me. I need to talk to you about the foundation that we are starting in Jordan's name."

"I'm all yours, sis."

"Come into my office and have a seat. Chantal, Denise, and I would like for you and Casey to run the Jordan Foundation. Run it the way you see fit. You both will serve as CEO and will hire as many people as you need to and fire as many as you have to. However, the team will need a monthly report. I will inform the team if you agree with the terms and the management of the Jordan Foundation. Please feel free to speak to Denise about the large donation that she has pending." L'Oreal happily agreed to be the head of the foundation.

La'Roc said, "Thanks, L'Oreal, and thank Casey for the team as well. I'll thank him after he returns from visiting his family in North Carolina."

"Oh, sis, we'll be honored to do it," L'Oreal said.

"We'll discuss this more when Casey returns from his trip."

"Thanks, sis," L'Oreal said as she walked back into the great room with everyone else.

La'Roc spoke to Denise and Chantal about the meeting she had with L'Oreal. They were both happy about L'Oreal and Casey being the CEOs of the organization.

La'Roc said her good nights to her mother and sister as they went upstairs to their bedrooms.

Alex, Jordan, and Devon would be going to visit Shawn the following day. Oh, how she wished Shawn were there with her that night and every night.

She loved him unconditionally. Chantal and Denise stopped by La'Roc's room to say good night before they returned to Manhattan.

La'Roc thanked them for everything that they had done for her and Shawn. The three of them kissed each other and left. La'Roc stood in her bedroom door holding a glass of wine, blowing kisses at her friends.

Alex yelled from downstairs. "Hey, partner, it's time for me to get out of here. I'll see you tomorrow before I make that trip."

"Alex, I need to talk to you. I am on my way downstairs. Give me a minute, okay?"

When she got downstairs, La'Roc asked, "Alex are you coming back tomorrow or do you want Jordan and Devon to meet you at the office?"

"I will be here first thing in the morning," Alex answered.

La'Roc replied, "Good. Also, I need for you and Jordan to follow all of the instructions we discussed today at the meeting. No more and no less. You understand what I am saying to you, right?" Alex nodded.

"Alex, please don't give Shawn any information that we don't have proof of. Don't even mention that you spoke to Kelly's sister or that his sister has left town." La'Roc couldn't stress enough to Alex about giving Shawn inaccurate information. "Alex, it is very important to keep a level head. Remember, my grandson will be there to learn; you and Jordan are there to teach him. So make me proud.

"You understand everything, Alex?"

Alex responded, "We're good. Everything will be just fine."
"Good night, Alex."

"Good night, La'Roc."

La'Roc knew that Alex was an excellent lawyer, and she knew he could win this case hands down. However, Alex was a little nervous because the client he'd be defending was his boss's fiancé, and he didn't want to make any mistakes. La'Roc had to remind Alex daily how good of a lawyer he had become.

La'Roc called down to Ms. Holiday and Ms. Cotton, "When the babies come in from their walk, give them a bath. Thank you." Ms. Cotton responded, "Yes, Ms. Rose."

"Thank you, Ms. Cotton. I am going to get into the whirlpool for a while to relax. My mother and sister are in the guest rooms. Please see if they have everything to facilitate their needs for tonight. Thank you, Ms. Cotton."

La'Roc mixed herself another drink and went into her bathroom and stepped into her whirlpool for some much-needed La'Roc time to think about Shawn.

But her relaxing didn't last very long as her mind raced to Upland Correctional Facility. She thought about her handsome, tall, young man and her desire to hold him close to her body. She wanted to feel Shawn inside of her as they made love all night and woke up holding each other oh so tightly.

After forty-five minutes in the whirlpool, she got out, went to her bedroom, and dressed for bed. She slipped on a pair of yellow silk boxers from Victoria's Secret and a matching yellow t-shirt. Yellow was one of Shawn's favorite colors.

La'Roc slipped under the gold comforter Shawn purchased the week before he was arrested.

La'Roc fell into a deep sleep with nothing on her mind but Shawn. Her thoughts were all about Shawn coming home and how he was going to make love to her, from her head to the bottom of her feet.

In her dream, Shawn was there making love to her entire body. Whenever he touched her, she felt as if her body were going to explode ... his lovemaking was oh so exhilarating.

She couldn't get enough of this man. In her dream, she could feel Shawn rotating his penis in and out of her vagina. The loud sounds of moaning and groaning she made once again awakened her to an empty bed; there was no Shawn in sight. As usual, she cried herself back to sleep.

After a few hours of tossing and turning, it seems there was no sleep in store for her.

La'Roc climbed out of bed, ran into the bathroom, and stepped into the shower to calm down. She yelled out during her shower, "Please help me! I need Shawn here with me. He needs to come home *now*!"

She finished her shower and went back to bed, hoping to get some much-needed sleep, which she knew was going to be impossible. She knew she'd never get a good night's sleep until Shawn returned to her bed once again.

La'Roc finally dozed off to sleep again, and her reoccurring dream continued ... Shawn was there in bed with her, kissing her shoulders and making love to her, with his tongue licking her all over her body. During her dream, he made love to her as sweat dripped from his chest into her face as he went deep inside of her. She begged for more of his sweet, devoted lovemaking as he continued to go deeper and deeper inside of her walls.

La'Roc dreamed Shawn was saying, "Sexiful is what you are asking for? You can have all of me."

She screamed out, "Yes, don't stop loving me."

This dream was so real, she could hear Shawn whispering in her ear, "Sexiful, I promise you I will never stop loving you, not ever."

His lovemaking was always amazing. Every time she and Shawn made love, it seemed as though it got better and more incredible, as if that were possible.

Oh the way he made her feel, the way he made love to her, she wanted to call every talk show, newspaper, and television station to inform the world that she had the best lover in the whole wide world and he was La'Roc's creation.

The dream La'Roc was having seemed so realistic. Again she was so exhausted when she awoke. However, her dream, as always, was just wishful thinking.

La'Roc had one thing going for her—that is, she knew that Shawn would be home soon.

La'Roc sat on the edge of her bed, grabbed her silk robe, and then walked into her babies' room to find they were still sleeping like little angels. Biscuit and Paris looked so beautiful lying in their beds. Their cute faces made her smile. Before tiptoeing out of their room, La'Roc turned and whispered to them, "Daddy will be home soon." La'Roc then walked out and closed the door.

Since she was up, she decided to check on her mother and sister, who were sleeping soundly in the upstairs bedroom.

La'Roc also poked her head into Jordan's bedroom. He seemed to be resting peacefully.

Then on to Devon's room and he too was fast asleep.

As she walked toward Courtney's room, she prayed that Courtney was resting comfortably. Earlier, La'Roc had learned from Devon that Courtney wasn't sleeping well at night, and she had hoped this wasn't one of those sleepless nights. Since Justin had been readmitted back into the hospital and Jordan had been diagnosed with HIV, Courtney had a lot to think about. Tonight Courtney seemed to have no problem sleeping—*Thank God,* La'Roc thought.

As she was walking out of Courtney's room, she heard her call out, "Mommy, I want to sleep with you. I had a bad dream about Uncle Jordan and Justin." La'Roc stopped in the hall to wait for her daughter to follow her to her bedroom.

La'Roc responded, "Yes, baby, of course; you can sleep with me. I'd love for you to sleep with me so I can hold you in my arms all night like when you were a little girl" They walked down the hallway to La'Roc's bedroom. "Sweetheart, how would you like to go visit Justin tomorrow?"

"Mother, I'd love to go to Manhattan to visit Justin. You and I, right?" Courtney asked while climbing into her mother's bed.

"Yes, you and me, baby."

Courtney turned toward her mother and snuggled up into her arms. "Good night, Mother."

"Good night, my only child," La'Roc responded.

They fell asleep with Courtney wrapped in her mother's arms like a little baby. La'Roc loved it when Courtney and Devon slept in her bed and told bad jokes. If only she could keep them as babies and never allow them to grow up, she would be happy. However, deep down inside, La'Roc had to remember that her daughter and grandson were full-grown adults. She understood that sooner or later, she would have to let go.

La'Roc and Courtney slept throughout the night without any interruptions. The next morning, La'Roc was awakened by Ms. Holiday's loud voice on the intercom. "Mr. Alex and Ms. Denise are downstairs having breakfast. Ms. Rose, would you like for me to wake Mr. Jordan and Devon? Mr. Alex said he is here to pick them up for their trip to visit Mr. Parker." La'Roc had asked Ms. Holiday to inform her room only over the intercom when Alex arrived I *had no idea it was going to be so early.*

I just fell asleep, she thought.

La'Roc responded, "Yes. Please wake them both up." A few seconds later, Ms. Holiday went upstairs to talk to La'Roc. She knocked on the bedroom door.

"Ms. Rose, they're not in their room. Maybe Jordan and Devon went for a walk this morning."

La'Roc replied, "Yes, perhaps. Well ... Please inform Alex that I'm on my way downstairs. Thank you, Ms. Holiday."

Sometime later, Ms. Cotton informed La'Roc, "Ms. Rose, your babies are out with Mr. Jordan and Devon. As I was taking them for their morning walk, Mr. Jordan and Devon were jogging and asked if they could take Paris and Biscuit for a walk. Ms. Rose, I gave them permission to do so. I hope you don't mind."

La'Roc responded, "No, Ms. Cotton, there's no problem with you leaving Paris and Biscuit with Jordan and Devon. Paris and Biscuit will be well taken care of."

La'Roc went into the bathroom to take a shower before going downstairs. She took a long, hot, steamy shower and then went into her large, custom, walk-in closet to get a pair of indigo-blue sweats and a tight, white T-shirt that clung to her tiny body.

While walking down the hall to wake her mother and sister, she met Courtney going into the adjoining bathroom of her bedroom. "Hi, baby. You feel better this morning?"

"Momma, I slept better last night than I've slept in months.

The sleep came so easy after we had our little talk. Thanks, Mom." "Courtney, I'm always here for you, and anytime you want to sleep with me, you're more than welcome. Sweetheart, I love you and Devon. You guys are the most important people in my life. I'm going to wake your aunt and grandmother up for breakfast, and I'll meet you downstairs."

"Sorry, Mom, but you're too late. Grams and Aunt L'Oreal went downstairs earlier. I could hear them laughing and talking on the terrace from my bedroom."

La'Roc strolled downstairs although her mind was in the moment as she was still thinking of the beautiful dream she had about Shawn that had her so exhausted the night before. Even in her dream, Shawn could make her cry with his lovemaking. He was so damn good with the rotation of his body, she could feel him inside of her twenty-four seven.

La'Roc said out loud, "Oh my God!" as she thought about how she yearned each and every day for Shawn's skillful hands to slide slowly and lovingly over her body, pumping all of his natural juice inside of her.

La'Roc walked onto the terrace and greeted her family and friends good morning. She kissed her mother on her soft cheek and then kissed her sister on the forehead. She looked at her watch to check the time because she didn't want Alex to be late for his visit with Shawn.

La'Roc turned her attention toward Denise. She said playfully, "Denise, did we have an appointment that I forgot about?"

Denise responded, "No, madam. I just wanted to see my godson before he left for his first paying job. Do you mind, Ms. Rose?" Denise stated with a flip of her hand.

"Denise, is that what this is about? My grandson going on his first job today? Denise is that so hard to believe." La'Roc laughed out loud. And then whispered to her, "I really think something is going on between you and Alex."

Then she continued to tease, "Denise, I really don't give a damn who you fuck as long as Alex is on point with his clients and my law firm."

Denise replied, "Let's talk later when Chantal arrives, okay?"

"No problem. However, you'll have to wait until I get back from Manhattan. Courtney and I are going to visit Justin. We'll talk when I return; is that all right?"

"I have a presentation to give this morning, but I can also work on the donation for the Jordan Foundation as well. As soon as I connect with my contacts, I'll call you with a report."

"That will be great, Denise. Thanks.

"Oh, by the way, I need a favor, can take my mother and sister out to lunch today? And remember, I'll be with Courtney all afternoon, so please keep them busy until I return."

Denise responded, "No problem, sis. I will call Chantal and ask her to meet us for lunch."

La'Roc's mother and L'Oreal came back onto the terrace. L'Oreal asked some questions about Jordan, wanting to know if he had any family in New York.

La'Roc answered, "No, we're his family. He has an aunt, but he won't talk about her for some reason. He said when he was ready to talk about her, he would, and he asked me not to pressure him." L'Oreal and Denise both shook their heads sadly.

Then L'Oreal said, "Well, La'Roc, Denise, and Chantal are taking Momma and me out to lunch. We'll see you guys later. Give Justin our love."

"Okay, I'll give Justin your love and blessing," La'Roc replied.

La'Roc wanted to play with her babies. Before leaving, she asked Ms. Holiday to bring them downstairs to the gym.

Jordan, Alex, and Devon walked on to the terrace to speak with La'Roc before she left to see Shawn. Devon kissed her on the cheek. Alex winked at her and leaned against the railing.

"Okay, guys. You have a student with you today, so make La'Roc proud. Jordan, how do you feel? Are you okay?"

Jordan responded, "I'm good, baby girl. I've asked you not to worry about me. So stop it and give me a wet one right here on the left side of my face." He continued, "La'Roc, we have some unfinished business to take care of when we return from our visit with Shawn."

"Jordan, I've been putting off the job you asked me to do for you, but I promise you, I'll make time for you after you finish the investigation on Shawn's case. Just you and I, working together like old times."

"No problem, baby girl," Jordan answered.

La'Roc walked over to Devon and gave him a big hug and a kiss on his cheek. "Love you, baby. You're my little man, right?"

"I'm going to make you proud, Grams."

Jordan spoke to La'Roc's mother for a short period. After their conversation, the two lawyers and law student left with their briefcases in hand.

La'Roc smiled with teary eyes. She was excited that Devon was working as an intern defense lawyer in her firm. She was so proud of her grandson.

She knew that when Shawn saw Devon working with Alex and Jordan, he would be delighted. *He is going to love Devon being a part of his freedom.* La'Roc wished that she could be there to capture Shawn's expression.

"Courtney, what time are we leaving?" La'Roc asked her daughter. Courtney responded, "We'll be leaving in about an hour and a half. Is that okay with you?"

"Good. That'll give me some time to get a quick workout," La'Roc responded.

"Momma, where are Ms. Holiday and Ms. Cotton?"

"Oh, they wanted to go shopping to buy Devon a present for his first day of work. They are crazy about the both of you. Courtney, you know that Ms. Cotton will still be working for you at the condo, right? You can also have Ms. Holiday to help out whenever you like. Okay, baby?"

"Momma, I know you love me and my son, but I cannot believe you gave us your condo. You are the best mom in the whole world, and I love you very much! Are you buying another condo in Manhattan?"

"I already did. You know the condo next to yours? I am going to connect the two together. However, that was supposed be a surprise for Devon.

"Momma, you can stay with me when you're in Manhattan."

"Thanks, sweetie. I love your offer, but right now, please join me and my babies for a quick workout before we leave for our visit into Manhattan to see Justin."

La'Roc and Courtney walked into her gym while Paris and Biscuit followed her onto the mat.

La'Roc and Courtney exercised for an hour. When their workout was complete, Courtney headed for the shower. La'Roc poured herself a glass of Nuevo on the rocks, and as she began to relax for a moment, she could vaguely hear Ms. Holiday and Ms. Cotton enter the house.

Paris and Biscuit were too tired to bark; they just laid on their mats with their legs up in the air.

La'Roc finished her drink and got into the shower.

After showering and putting on a golden silk dress, she and Courtney left to visit Justin.

As they drove into Manhattan, La'Roc asked Courtney about her feelings toward Justin. "Since he's been paralyzed, have your feelings changed at all? Baby, you've been devoting all your time to taking care of Justin. Courtney, sweetheart, you have to remember you have a life of your own to live. You can't live Justin's life for him. I suggest you start thinking about what you want out of your life without Justin. I am not telling you to walk out on Justin, but he'll understand if you continue living your life without him. I'll always be there for you. Whatever decision you make I'm there."

Courtney turned to look at her Mother and replied. "Mother, I'm not in love with Justin anymore. However, I can't walk away from him in his condition or turn my back on him. Mom, I understand what you're saying, and I know you want the best for me. That's why I love you so much—because you take care of my son and me so well.

"Have I told you today that I love you?" Courtney said, changing the subject. La'Roc looked at her daughter. "Yes, you did, but tell me again. I love hearing you say it. Courtney, I understand you clearly, baby. I want you to be happy in whatever you do,"

"I'm happy when I am with you and Devon," Courtney replied. La'Roc smiled.

"Oh, Momma, I have something to show you when we get to the condo. I have a surprise for you. I think you'll be very pleased with your surprise." Courtney and La'Roc arrived at North General Hospital. Justin had been living there since being released by Dr. Mitchell, his primary doctor in California, several months ago.

Courtney and La'Roc took the elevator to the third floor and then proceeded walking to Justin's room, 33- 08. His nurse was inserting an IV into his arm. Courtney looked anxiously at the nurse and asked, "Ms. Walker, how's he doing, and what is the name of the medication you are giving him?"

The nurse responded in a soft, low voice, "I was just giving him his pain medication because his body has been rejecting most of the medications the doctor has prescribed. He's not doing well, and his health is deteriorating fast." "Ms. Walker, I'm sorry for not introducing you to my mother. This is my Mother, Ms. La'Roc Rose. Mom, this is Justin's nurse, Ms. Walker."

"Ms. Rose pleases to meet you, Ms. Rose. I've heard a lot about you. I should have known you when you first walked into Justin's room because your daughter looks just like you. Your daughter is a beautiful girl," Ms. Walker continued with a smile. "Another reason I should know your name is because you sign my check each month."

La'Roc smiled.

La'Roc and Courtney walked over to Justin's bedside. Justin stared at both of them as if they were strangers. Courtney had been away for only two days. She was shocked to see how he had deteriorated so quickly. *I will not allow my child to go through this guilt trip over Justin.* La'Roc and the Rose team would always be there for financial support, etc. She made a promise to herself she wouldn't let Courtney wallow in guilt over Justin. Yes, La'Roc liked Justin, but she loved Courtney!

Courtney was her daughter, and La'Roc would die for her family, especially her only child. She would do everything in her power to get Courtney away from Justin and save her from self-destruction.

Courtney turned to her Mother. "Mom, talk to Justin."

"Hello, Justin, is the staff and doctors treating you all right?" La'Roc knew Justin was unable to respond to her question, but she would do anything to please her daughter.

To see Justin lying there in bed, not moving, was very devastating. Justin's bed was surrounded by various monitors and other pieces of equipment, all designed to monitor his life force. A breathing tube was secured down his throat. From his right arm ran an IV tube for feeding and medication.

Justin looked so pale lying in bed so still, totally unable to turn his small, frail body. He would remain in whatever position the doctor or nurse left him in—that was where he stayed. To see him in that condition was demoralizing.

La'Roc looked on, she thought, *we need to find Justin's father as soon as possible.* La'Roc knew finding Justin's father would be beneficial to Justin. Finding his father could be helpful for Courtney, and maybe she would be able to sleep at night. *We need his father!* And then hopefully she would be able to release the guilt that she held so deeply within her heart.

The night of the shooting, Courtney, and Justin had a dinner date, but Courtney had a few other matters to attend to. She told Justin they would meet up later for a late dinner that evening. She blamed herself for postponing their date: "Mother, if only I kept our date that evening, Justin would not be in the hospital, paralyzed." Courtney kept blaming herself for Justin being paralyzed. She told Courtney each and every day she's not responsible for Justin unfortunate condition—she wasn't the one who pulled the trigger.

Before the accident occurred, Justin was alert, vibrant, and so full of life. And now the only way he was able to communicate was by blinking his eyes for "yes" and keeping his eyes closed to the answer "no," and that was on a good day. Justin had shown no improvement in the past week. He'd been in critical condition since being rushed back into the hospital. "Poor Justin," said La'Roc as she stared deeply at her daughter. Justin was dying slowly right before their eyes. La'Roc turned away so Courtney couldn't witness the tears that were forming in her eyes.

La'Roc knew Courtney was not allowed to sign any medical papers for Justin's treatments because she was not his wife. Only his father could; that was the law.

Not even La'Roc could do anything about that. Bottom line, they needed Justin's father, and La'Roc wanted the doctor to explain that to Courtney. At that point, Justin's doctor walked into the room. "Good afternoon. How are you today, Ms. Rose?" he said, referring to Courtney.

"I'm hanging in there, doc. I want you to meet my mother ...

"Mom, this is Justin's doctor, Dr. Moore. Dr. Moore, this is La'Roc Rose, my mother."

"What a pleasure meeting you, Ms. Rose," Dr. Moore said as he extended his hand to La'Roc.

The doctor began to explain Justin's condition. "Justin's body has rejected all treatment and medication; however, there are several other medications we could try on him, though authorization is needed to do so."

"Ms. Rose, would you and your mother stop by my office today around four o'clock this afternoon. I would like to discuss this new medication with you so we can get started as soon as possible. I will be working with a specialist, Dr. Berry. This new treatment will not make him walk again; however, he will become more responsive and alert, and after a few treatments, he should be able to recognize familiar faces and his surroundings. I'm not going to give you any promises or false hopes. This medication doesn't work for all patients. We will talk more in my office this afternoon," Dr. Moore continued,

"Dr. Moore, when you say authorization, would you elaborate a little more about that and who will be responsible for giving this authorization?" Courtney asked.

"Of course, Ms. Courtney. Let me explain. The authorization forms are for his parent, guardian, or his spouse if he's married. They would have to sign for the treatment that Justin so badly needs."

Courtney held her head down in disappointment and said, "Don't get me wrong, I do understand authorizations and the terms, but I just needed more clarification as to who that person will be for Justin ... this is going to be hard.

"Thank you, Dr. Moore, for that information."

"Ms. Courtney, you are more than welcome. Hopefully, I will see you and your mother this afternoon. Bye now." Dr. Moore walked down the corridor, checking his notes.

"Mom, will you be free this afternoon?" Courtney asked La'Roc.

"Yes," La'Roc responded. "Baby, you have me for the whole day. *We* will go to the condo, have something to eat, and you can give me my surprise; you do remember my big surprise?" La'Roc asked. "Oh, by the way, I have a surprise for you too, baby." La'Roc teared up as she thought of all she and Courtney had to cope with over the last year—Jordan's mother passing, Justin, and now Jordan being diagnosed with HIV.

La'Roc walked over to her daughter and hugged her real tight. "I love you, Courtney."

"I love you too, Mom."

"Are you okay?" asked La'Roc. "Baby, we need to talk about Justin. I really don't want you to feel guilty about Justin's condition. You didn't put Justin in that hospital bed; his father did. So stop feeling guilty about something you couldn't control. This would have happened to Justin even if you and he weren't involved."

"I know you just want the best for me, but, Mom, he is my special friend. We have a history together," Courtney responded.

"Baby, please come out of guilt mode and bring me back my beautiful daughter," La'Roc said with concern.

"I understand that you and Justin have a history, but, baby, I just don't want you to feel that you owe Justin anything. I know he's your friend, and he'll always have a special place in your heart," La'Roc concluded.

"Thanks, Mom."

"Mom, you know who I would love to talk to?" "No, baby, who would you like to talk to?"

"I would like to speak to Dr. Kim. Mom, do you think she would fly to New York?" Courtney asked.

"It's funny you asked that question because she called last week to get an update on you and Justin. I'm sorry I forgot to tell you. I'll call her as soon as we get home. I know she'd be pleased that you reached out for her assistance. I'd even pay her expenses to visit with Justin if you would like; would you like that, Courtney?"

"That would be awesome mom." I can't wait to see her again."

"Okay, as soon as we get home, I will make the call to Dr. Kim," La'Roc responded. La'Roc thought about Courtney's reaction to Justin's condition. During the visit, Courtney showed no emotional reaction to Dr. Moore's report on Justin's condition. La'Roc was terrified that Courtney was slipping into a deep depression or a hell of a case of denial. La'Roc tried not to panic, thinking about Courtney's lack of emotional response. She knew she'd ask Dr. Kim how best to handle Courtney's lack of response.

La'Roc and Courtney left Justin's room and then headed to the elevator. They rode down in silence. La'Roc's cell phone started to ring, and without looking, she pulled her phone from her purse as she and Courtney continued walking through the hospital parking lot to her car. Before La'Roc could answer, the strong voice on the other end said, "Hello, Ms. Rose." La'Roc smiled.

"Hello, my young lawyer. What can I do for you?"

"My client would like to speak to you. Alex got him about five minutes of talk time."

If La'Roc had been seated, her heart would have fallen into her lap. She took a deep breath and then said, "Thank you, sweetheart. Now please put my man on the phone."

"Hi, baby. It's beautiful music to my ears when I hear your voice."

"I miss you, Shawn. I'm bringing you home soon; I promise."

"Sexiful, I miss you and can't wait to hold you in my arms again." He began to whisper these words over the phone. "Baby, I love you with all my heart. Just remember those three words. I love you, and I promise you, Sexiful, I'll never let you out of my sight again. Oh, by the way, thank you for my surprise visit today. I think Devon is going to make a damn good lawyer one day, just like his grandmother. I mean, off the record, of course, he asked some excellent questions. I hear a lot of noise; where are you, anyway?"

"Courtney and I are in Manhattan, visiting Justin. Today, we were informed that Justin's body has been rejecting all of the prescribed medications, and Dr. Moore will be bringing in a specialist to work on his case. Courtney and I have an appointment to meet with the specialist this afternoon to hear about alternative medication."

"Baby, I am sorry to hear that about Justin. I only have a few minutes; so tell me, what's on your mind?"

"What's on my mind? Good question. Shawn the same thing that's has been on my mind since you were taken away from me. I wanted be in your strong arms, laying my head on your chest, and staying there throughout the night."

"Sexiful, I am making love to you right now. Do you feel me inside of you, baby?" That's all she could think about. As Shawn's voice swept over her, she could feel her silk bikini panties getting wet.

La'Roc walked away from Courtney and then answered, "Yes, I can feel you inside of me. My daughter needs me right now. You and I will be fine; however, Courtney is heading for a bad place, and I need to catch her before she hit the darkness she about to enter."

Before he disconnected he said, "Sexiful, I understand, and remember, I love you. Please say hello to all the family, especially your mother. Give Denise and Chantal my regards. Love you, Sexiful."

"Love you too. See you soon, and think only good thoughts, okay, baby? Oh ... and tell your lawyers I will see them at home with a full report."

"Baby, the session went well today. I have full confidence in my lawyers. They give me hope, and having Devon on the Rose team blew my fucking mind. Give Courtney my love. Bye, sweetheart. See you soon." They disconnected.

La'Roc and Courtney's ride home was quiet. They drove into the garage, and La'Roc watched as Courtney removed herself from the car and began to cry.

"Come, baby, let's go inside, and I'll give you something to calm you down. Sweetheart, it's going to be all right. I promise you, baby."

As soon as they walked inside the house, La'Roc took Courtney into one of the rooms downstairs and gave her some of her prescribed medication to relax her. As she gave the medication to Courtney, she thought to herself, *My Poor baby has had a long day, and I know when she awakes, she'll probably be hungry, and so I will make soup for the both of us.*

Once she got Courtney down for a nap, La'Roc placed a call to Dr. Kim and explained the situation with Courtney and Justin. "Dr. Kim, Courtney specifically asked for you."

"I'll be on the next flight out to New York later this evening. I'll refer all of my clients to my associates, and I'll see you and Courtney soon."

La'Roc was ecstatic that Dr. Kim's schedule allowed her to come to New York so quickly. Before hanging up, La'Roc informed Dr. Kim that her black car service would be waiting at the airport to drive her to the appropriate house. La'Roc gave Dr. Kim all the information that she would need for the car services and thanked her, with a promise to see her soon.

La'Roc decided she'd lie down with Courtney and take a nap as well. Before taking a nap or making soup, La'Roc decided to check on the workers who were doing the renovating at the condo. At a glance, everything seemed to be on point. *It is definitely time for a drink,* she thought to herself. Once La'Roc placed all the ingredients in the pot to make the perfect soup, she checked on the time. *Um, it's three o'clock.* She then remembered Courtney had that four-thirty appointment with Dr. Moore to discuss Justin's treatment plan, so she decided against taking her nap.

La'Roc felt Courtney was ready to give up being committed to Justin but was willing to keep the friendship intact. It was hard for her to break her ties from Justin on her own. She needed Dr. Kim's expertise.

La'Roc went to Courtney's room to wake her for their meeting with Dr. Moore.

"Hi, baby, you feel better?" La'Roc asked her daughter.

"Yes Mom. I feel a lot better. Oh, I see you made some lunch." Courtney smiled at the thought of her mom preparing anything in the kitchen that wasn't a sandwich.

"I made a little something for you, Courtney, and by the way, Dr. Kim will be arriving this evening. We'll meet her at the townhouse. Isn't that nice, sweetheart?"

"Mom, maybe we can change the appointment with Dr. Moore today and reschedule for tomorrow when Dr. Kim is present; that's if Dr. Moore has an opening tomorrow. What do you think?"

"That's a wonderful idea. Perhaps Devon could sit in on this meeting as well." While sipping on her soup, Courtney walked down the hall to place a call to Dr. Moore's office to reschedule their appointment for a later date. Before entering the office, she poked her head out and said, "Mother this is the best soup *ever*—thanks, Mom!"

Courtney came back into the playroom where La'Roc was lying on a floor mat, relaxing.

"He said tomorrow will be fine, Mother. He has an opening at five thirty tomorrow afternoon.

"I explained to him I was bringing Dr. Kim and my son with me for support," Courtney stated.

"Sounds good, sweetheart," replied La'Roc.

"Now let's head back to Westchester before we get stuck in traffic," she added. *Courtney, you know your mother hates getting stuck in traffic …*

"Okay, Mommy, but first I want to give you your present. Close your eyes." La'Roc closed her eyes and announced that she was ready for her surprise.

"Now you can open your eyes," Courtney said with a big smile on her face. La'Roc was presented with a large yellow envelope.

"Open the envelope, Mommy! Hurry. I am getting nervous!" Courtney said with excitement.

La'Roc accepted the yellow envelope from her daughter, and what a huge surprise! Courtney had been accepted to one of the most prestigious law schools in the country. "I'm so excited and elated!" exclaimed La'Roc. "Now both my children are in law school: you at Princeton, and Devon at Howard," La'Roc continued wiping the tears from her eyes.

La'Roc could not believe her eyes or what she was hearing. She had no idea that Courtney was interested in becoming a lawyer. What a shock!

Courtney finally had her own practice as a leading surgeon; now she wanted to become a lawyer.

La'Roc was overwhelmed with happiness as she held her daughter and cried. She had always wanted her daughter to become a lawyer, but never pushed her or Devon.

When Courtney graduated from medical school, La'Roc was ecstatic. But the news La'Roc received from her daughter this afternoon was exhilarating.

"Baby, you have made me the happiest mother in the world. Courtney, why didn't you tell me?" La'Roc asked.

"Mom, it wouldn't have been a surprise if I had told you, right?" Courtney smiled.

Mother and daughter held each other for what seemed like hours. La'Roc cried as Courtney consoled her.

"Courtney, I will be all right. I just need to absorb this wonderful news that I just received. Give me a La'Roc moment, sweetie."

"Mom, how are we going to celebrate my accomplishment?" "Let's have a dinner party and have the guys cook. We'll buy the food, and they'll cook," La'Roc answered.

"Good idea," Courtney laughed.

"That'll be a good time to tell Devon about the other part of the condo," Courtney agreed.

Courtney's cell phone rang, breaking into their conversation. "Hello, Devon. Where are you?"

"Hi Mom. The question is; where are you and Grams?"

"We're in Manhattan, getting ready to drive to Westchester. I can't wait to hear about your first day at work. Devon, I have some good news to share with you when you get home—can't wait to see your face when I tell you." She added, "Oh, by the way, you guys are cooking tonight. Let Alex and Uncle Jordan know they will be cooking dinner tonight. I love you, Devon," Courtney said.

"I love you too, Mom. Give Grams my love; can't wait to see you guys."

"See you soon, babe," Courtney responded.

As La'Roc and Courtney were walking to the car to head home, Courtney said, "Mom, you said you had a surprise to show me. Give it up."

La'Roc looked at her daughter and smiled. "I will show you the surprise when we get back home. You think you can wait that long?"

Courtney responded, "Oh, I think I can wait until we get home. We will be there shortly because I am driving." Courtney made a playful face.

"Courtney, I can see the funny face, you know." They both smiled.

La'Roc was extremely happy regarding Courtney, Devon, and Jordan living in New York again. She was especially jubilant that Devon and Courtney had decided to follow in her footsteps and become defense attorneys.

As Courtney and La'Roc coasted down the highway, La'Roc popped in one of Shawn's favorite CDs, *If I Could I Would,* by Tia T.

La'Roc adjusted her seatbelt and lay back in her seat. "Take me home, Courtney." Courtney stepped on the gas and continued speeding up I-95.

Courtney always drove fast, just like her mother.

La'Roc lay back and thought about how much she admired her daughter and grandson. The surprise she had for Courtney was a gift from Jordan. Jordan's gift was a house La'Roc had been admiring for some time.

La'Roc was shocked when Jordan had asked her to take a ride with him three nights prior. She responded reluctantly and accepted the drive, not knowing the beautiful outcome. He wanted it to be a surprise for Devon and Courtney.

Before she left to go to the city, she had asked Chantal, Denise, L'Oreal, and her mother to go to the big house to help Ms. Holiday and Ms. Cotton set up for the party. The party was to celebrate her new house. Everyone was shocked and amazed when La'Roc told them about the new house.

She thought to herself that it would be a great idea to have a big party to celebrate getting the new house, Courtney being accepted to a prestigious law school, and Devon's first paying job as an intern. La'Roc was elated. With her left hand under her chin and a happy smile on her face, she thought, *Hmmmm I forgot Devon's condo in the celebration. Oh well, another time and another place.*

She thought about Shawn not being there to partake in the festivities with the family. With tears in her eyes, she turned away so Courtney couldn't see the sadness and pain in her facial expression.

In the months since Shawn had been arrested, La'Roc had lost noticeable weight due to her lack of appetite and excessive exercise.

La'Roc's doctor warned her she was burning more calories than she was consuming. He demanded, "Eat more, and exercise less." La'Roc ignored his concerned advice.

"Wake up, Mom. We're home. Where's everybody?" Courtney asked.

"Oh, sweetie, I forgot to tell you, Jordan took everyone out for dinner tonight to celebrate Devon's first day at work and to celebrate you and Devon becoming the proud owners of the condo.

"Courtney, remember, I have a surprise for you and Devon. We have a lot to be thankful for, and believe me; we have a lot to celebrate. Jordan, Denise, and Chantal will be overjoyed when you tell them about your acceptance. I want to see Mom's, L'Oreal, Denise, and Chantal's faces when they find out about you becoming a lawyer.

"What about your practice?"

"I will never give up my practice—I worked too hard for my medical license. I will be a good lawyer. Just like my momma."

"Thank you, Courtney, for that wonderful compliment."

Courtney looked out the window, "I cannot wait to get to the restaurant. I am so hungry; I just want to take a big bite out of Biscuit." They both started to laugh.

La'Roc acknowledged her with a smile.

"Courtney, we have about five more minutes before we get to the restaurant. Stop the car and let me drive."

"Good idea, Mom. I've never been to this place before." Courtney removed herself from the driver's seat and gave La'Roc the car keys.

"Oh, Mom, why did I take the keys out of the ignition?"

La'Roc responded, "Baby, maybe you're anxious to tell Devon the good news.

"Sweetheart, you're going to be flabbergasted when you see how the restaurant is decorated. Jordan and the team decorated it yesterday just for you and Devon. Your grandmother, L'Oreal, Ms. Cotton, and Ms. Holiday are in on the surprise as well.

"Guess who else is going to be at the restaurant?" La'Roc teased. "Paris and Biscuit will be there to greet you at the door."

What a joke. Courtney thought she was going to a high-class restaurant. However, La'Roc was going to show her daughter her beautiful new home. La'Roc looked over at Courtney; her eyes were closed.

"Open your eyes, Courtney," La'Roc said.

"Oh Mother what a beautiful house; who in the world lives here?

Mom don't tell me. I think I know—one of your big-time lawyer friends, right?"

"Baby, you are right; one of the best lawyers in the world lives here. That is why I want you and Devon to meet the three of them tonight. Since you and Devon are going to be lawyers, you are going to need a good lawyer with good connections on your side.

"Courtney, will you be in court for Shawn's trial next month?"

"Of course Mom I'll be there to watch Uncle Jordan and Alex in action," Courtney responded. "And don't forget my son."

"Come on, Courtney. Let's go into the house so you can meet your new friends and the owner of this beautiful house." La'Roc looked over at Courtney. "Go and ring the doorbell. I'm right behind you, honey."

Courtney rang the doorbell, and her grandmother opened the door. As they both stepped inside the house they heard voices yell, "Congratulations on your condo!"

Everyone turned to Devon. "This young lawyer worked on his first case today. Shawn Parker is his first client." They all clapped.

"Courtney also has something she would like to share once we get seated in the great room. Wow!" La'Roc said.

Courtney reached into her Lobo bag and pulled out a yellow envelope and opened it. She pulled out the letter and gave it to Devon.

Devon said, "Oh, sweet. Guess what, family?

"My mother is going to become a lawyer—she has been accepted to Princeton. Congratulations, Mom!"

Everyone said, "Congratulations, Courtney!"

Chantal yelled out, "Courtney you're going to make a damn good lawyer." Denise walked over to where Courtney was sitting and kissed her.

"Congratulations, Courtney. You are going to be a great lawyer."

L'Oreal said, "Courtney, come over here and give your aunt a hug." Courtney walked over to her aunt and kissed her. "Congratulations, baby. I am so proud of you and Devon, walking in your mother's footsteps."

"Grandmother, are you all right?" Courtney asked.

"Yes baby, I am fine—just very happy for all of my children and wishing your grandfather was here to see your accomplishments," Geneva responded.

Jordan said, "There is one more surprise." Jordan walked over to La'Roc. "Baby girl, this is for you." He gave her a set of keys and a yellow envelope. Jordan said with a smile, "I hope you like your gift."

La'Roc told Denise, L'Oreal, Chantal, Alex, and her mother to sit down next to her. "Before I open this envelope, I wanted all my friends to be near me. I need Ms. Holiday and Ms. Cotton and my babies."

When La'Roc opened the envelope, there was a deed inside for the beautiful home. La'Roc had to pretend that she was surprised. "Oh, Jordan, you didn't buy me this house! I told you that I wanted the house, not for you buy it."

"Baby girl, I wanted to buy you something nice. You are my lawyer, so you will pay for this house by working for me. La'Roc, I knew you weren't going to charge me for my legal work, so I gave you a gift you would like."

"I love this house. My goodness, how many rooms does it have?" La'Roc asked.

Jordan responded, "Enough for you and your family … more important, enough for you and Shawn to hide from Denise and Chantal."

Jordan looked over his shoulder, searching for Denise and Chantal. They were nowhere to be found. They had slipped out of the great room and gone upstairs, checking out their bedrooms.

Courtney said, "Uncle Jordan, this is unbelievable! I cannot believe you bought my mother this gorgeous house. Mother, you said, this house belongs to one of the best lawyers in New York State, and you were right. I should have known that this was your house when you said 'the best lawyer in New York State.'"

"I didn't know at the time that this house was mine, baby. I was just as surprised as you were," La'Roc responded with her fingers crossed behind her back as she told a little white lie.

Alex said, "This is a dream. Please wake me because I am dreaming. I've never been around friends that give money and homes to each other before. I am totally in shock. This is amazing. Congratulations, partner. *Wow!*"

Not only did Jordan buy the house, he furnished all twenty-five rooms. Besides the numerous bedrooms, the house contained a gym, Jacuzzis, laundry room, game rooms, and a special place for Paris and Biscuit.

Geneva said, "Baby, you have some great friends. You are so well blessed, La'Roc."

Ms. Cotton called over the intercom for dinner.

"Oh, Ms. Cotton, you have the table set up so beautifully," L'Oreal said. "I love the centerpiece. I love everything about this house. This dream house is perfect for your wedding."

"L'Oreal, will you be my wedding planner? Money is no object. I just want it to be the best wedding ever," La'Roc asked.

L'Oreal answered, "I wouldn't have it any other way, sis. I'll be delighted to plan your wedding."

"Yes L'Oreal that's a great idea. I'll speak to Shawn about it when I see him on Friday. I really want the house to be a surprise."

"La'Roc, why didn't you tell us this was your house when we left you this morning?" L'Oreal asked.

"Because, L'Oreal, Jordan asked me not to tell anyone, not even my mother," La'Roc responded.

Ms. Cotton called out again for dinner. "Please, everyone, come into the dining room for dinner."

"Thank you, Ms. Cotton," Jordan responded.

"After dinner, we need to discuss your visit with Shawn today. I'd like for Devon to give his report first." Devon described what he observed during the visit and, of course, it was off the record questions he asked Shawn.

After dinner, Devon stated, "I had a great experience talking with Shawn today as an attorney and not as his *little man*." Before Devon could continue, he was interrupted by his grandmother handing him a set of keys. "These are your keys to your new condo. I brought you a condo next to your mother's."

La'Roc continued, "They are renovating it as we speak. That's your gift from me. The two condos will be connected; so we all will have space when we visit." They all laughed. Devon and the others were clapping and yelling so loud that the rest of the group ran back into the dining room.

L'Oreal said, "What's going on?" With tears in his eyes, and hugging his grandmother, Devon explained, "My grandmother just gave me my own condo next door to my mother. Gran, I love you so much."

"I love you too, baby ..." Courtney walked over to her son and kissed him. They all had to face the fact that Devon was becoming a man. "Okay, guys, let's get back to the meeting."

Jordan and Alex both said simultaneously, "We have nothing to worry about."

With dinner over, everyone was relaxed and exclaimed about the fantastic dinner they had just eaten.

"Come on, guys; it's time to get to work. It is time to get Shawn out of lockup and get him home," La'Roc announced.

"Why don't you all take a tour of the house while we discuss what we're going to do about Shawn," suggested La'Roc.

"Chantal and I have something to talk to you about later, Ms. Thing." Chantal and La'Roc smiled at each other.

"Denise, where are Ms. Holiday and Ms. Cotton?" La'Roc asked. "They are cleaning the kitchen," Denise responded.

"Thanks friend." She winked at her friend and walked toward her office, smiling.

Jordan, Alex, and Devon followed La'Roc into her new office. They all took their seats in the gold leather chairs and looked around the beautifully designed room. For a few moments, La'Roc was overwhelmed by the beauty of the room and the generosity of her friend.

"All right, let's get started," La'Roc announced.

"Devon, are you ready to give your report?" La'Roc asked.

Devon stood up and gave his report. His report was well written and very professional.

Once he was done, the team applauded and congratulated him on a wonderful job. La'Roc was smiling from ear to ear.

"Baby, I am so proud of you," La'Roc exclaimed as she nodded to her grandson. Devon proudly left the office immediately after he gave his report. Jordan and Alex were equally as proud of Devon and his handling of his assignment.

Jordan and Alex gave their report, and everything appeared to work in Shawn's favor.

Alex reported that he had gone to Kelly's parents, sister, and other people in the community. He reported some very important and positive information.

La'Roc waved her hands to get Jordan's attention. "Jordan, you are very quiet. What's wrong? Are you all right?"

"Yes, baby girl, I'm good. My feeling about Shawn's case is that he's a free man. When we go to his bail hearing, he'll be coming home with you. Tomorrow I'm taking a ride to see Mr. Johnston and, baby girl, he will talk. La'Roc, you know I mean that. He will tell the truth. I promise you, he will talk. I have my own little ways of getting information," Jordan quipped. Devon walked back into the study. "Devon, I want you to ride with me tomorrow. We need to pay Mr. Johnston a visit. I want you to see me in action."

"It's part of your lesson, Devon. I'm talking about teaching you how to cross-examine a witness. Just watch me in action, little man."

Jordan looked over in Alex's direction. "Alex, you're still going to check on Kelly tomorrow, right?"

Alex responded, "Yes, I have an appointment with her doctor at three. I'll bring a report back on her condition."

La'Roc looked across her desk and thought to herself, *What a magnificent group of lawyers, including my grandson.*

La'Roc said, "It's getting late. We're all staying here tonight. So let's go out and say good night to everyone."

As they walked out of the office, La'Roc spotted Dr. Kim. "Hi, doctor. How was your flight?"

"It was fine. It is so nice to see you and your family. I met your mother and sister. Ms. Rose, you have a lovely family."

Devon and Courtney came out of the dining room, laughing with each other.

Courtney ran over and hugged Dr. Kim. Devon gave her a hug as well as a handshake.

"Dr. Kim, you know the rest of my extended family. You met Alex and Denise out in California. However, you didn't meet Jordan. Dr. Kim, this is my very dear friend Jordan. You already know Chantal. If it weren't for Chantal, I would never have met you."

Dr. Kim walked over to Chantal. "Hello, Chantal. Nice to see you again."

Jordan extended his hand to Dr. Kim. "It is a pleasure meeting you, Dr. Kim. I've heard great things about you. Welcome to our home."

La'Roc said, "Ms. Holiday, will one of you please show Dr. Kim to one of the guest bedrooms. Please use the elevator."

"All right, Ms. Rose," Ms. Holiday responded.

Alex grabbed Dr. Kim's bags and followed Ms. Holiday to the elevator. "Ms. Rose, you have a beautiful home," Dr. Kim said.

"Please, Dr. Kim, call me La'Roc."

"La'Roc. And you can call me Debbie. I believe we're going to be friends." She added, "La'Roc this house is breathtaking. I am speechless—I cannot get over this house."

"Debbie, this house was a gift from Jordan. This is my first night sleeping in my beautiful home."

"La'Roc, find me a friend like Jordan," laughed Debbie. "Sorry, he's the only one, and he is mine." La'Roc smiled.

Courtney and Devon got on the elevator with Dr. Kim and followed her and Alex to her room.

Courtney gave Devon and Dr. Kim an update on Justin's condition and told him about the meeting they were going to have with Justin's doctor the following day. However, Devon would be able to attend because he would be working with Jordan on Shawn's case. Dr. Kim would update Devon on Justin's progress after the meeting with Dr. Moore.

La'Roc explained everything to the team and updated them on Justin's condition.

Everyone went to their rooms, except Jordan and La'Roc. They sat downstairs and talked about the good old days.

"La'Roc, I don't want you to worry about me. I'm going to be all right. I am very happy being here with you and my godchildren. It will be nice being around Chantal and Denise again too. I love talking to your mother, your sister, and her husband. By the way, where is Casey?"

"He went to North Carolina to visit his family. As soon as he returns, we're going to ask him to head the Jordan Foundation. I have spoken to L'Oreal already; she will speak to Casey when he returns. They are a great team, and I'll be able to sleep at night as long as I know they're in charge. Do you agree?" La'Roc asked.

Jordan agreed. "That is a great idea. I love it."

"Jordan, let's go to the gym and play with my babies before Ms. Holiday and Ms. Cotton put them down for tonight." Jordan said, "That sounds like fun."

Jordan hugged La'Roc as they walked into Paris and Biscuit's room, laughing like they were still in college. Jordan grabbed Paris, La'Roc grabbed Biscuit, and they ran down the long hallway to the gym.

La'Roc looked at Jordan with admiration in her eyes. Oh, how she wanted to keep him from the pain that he would be facing as his illness progressed.

"Thank you Jordan, for my beautiful home. I love you and my new house. You have given me everything, and I know you will give me Shawn the next time we go back to court. Then I'll have everything. What else could a woman ask for?"

Jordan responded, "La'Roc, you deserve everything you have. You've earned all of this and more. I'll do anything for you because I know you would do the same for me."

"Jordan, I'll always be there for you—without a doubt. You are my best friend, and you will always be my friend. I love you so much."

"I love you too, baby girl."

As La'Roc held Jordan in her arms, she wondered how long she would be able to hold him without crying out loud.

The two best friends played with the puppies for a while and then walked them back to their room.

"La'Roc, come with me. I need to show you something."

"Okay," La'Roc replied without question. She followed him up the stairs to the second floor, whispering, "What is it? Shall I close my eyes?"

"Now wait. You have to be patient, La'Roc," Jordan responded. "And yes, baby girl, close your eyes. I'll lead you up the stairs." Following his instructions, the two of them walked to the second floor. She heard him unlock a door. "You can open your eyes now."

La'Roc screamed out loud, "Oh wow! This is fantastic! Jordan, what is this beautiful room?"

"Baby girl, this is your big office, and down the hall is Shawn's office! Courtney and Devon also have an office on this floor. I hope this makes you happy. The office on the first floor is your small office for when you are having a small meeting like the one we had tonight. Go down the hall next door to Devon's office. We'll call this the office floor ... I forget to tell you, La'Roc, my office is across the hall from Courtney's office."

Jordan smiled.

"Jordan, I don't know what to say. I am at a loss for words."

"I forgot to tell you that your office is soundproof. You and Shawn can make whoopee in your office and no one will hear. How cool is that, baby girl?"

"Oh, my God, you didn't really say *whoopee*, did you?" La'Roc's heart was filled with so much love and so much Joy. Her heart raced as she went down the hall to see Shawn's office, which Jordan had laid out so beautifully.

"I cannot wait to tell Courtney and Devon. I'd like for you to show them yourself. Surprise them both in the morning."

Jordan said, "That sounds like a plan. I'll show them before we go out for our assignments tomorrow."

"Courtney and Devon are going to be so overjoyed," La'Roc said.

La'Roc hugged and kissed Jordan. "It's bedtime, Mr. Diaz. You have work to do tomorrow, and I have a shopping spree to go on with

Courtney. After the shopping trip, Courtney, Dr. Kim, and I have an appointment with Justin's doctor in Manhattan."

"Good night, La'Roc. I'll see you when Devon and I return from questioning the witness tomorrow. Alex is going to the hospital tomorrow to get some information on Kelly's medical condition and to see if she'll be able to appear in court."

"Sounds like a plan," La'Roc answered.

La'Roc and Jordan retired for the night.

Going into her bedroom, La'Roc decided to check on Paris and Biscuit. They both were asleep. She left Paris and Biscuit's door open so they could walk out to her room when they woke up. *Oh shit,* she thought, *I'll just take them into my room now.*

She grabbed both of her babies and went to her bedroom with puppies in her hands.

La'Roc mixed herself a nice strong drink and headed for her whirlpool to relax.

Once in the whirlpool, she closed her eyes, and the memories about Shawn started to form in her head.

Shawn had been locked away for almost one month. However, to La'Roc, it seemed more like years. If everything went according to plan, her baby would be walking out of the courtroom on the same day of his bail hearing, hopefully a free man. Shawn would be free from prison, and most of all, he would be free of Kelly C. Brown.

La'Roc's team of lawyers felt that there would be no trial after the bail hearing because they all knew that Shawn was innocent.

"Shawn is not responsible for Kelly's fall. Shawn is a lover, not a fighter. If Shawn fought like he made love, then he'd be a damn good fighter," La'Roc sighed, licking her lips. Provocative thoughts rushed through her mind as she thought of her man coming home.

She pulled herself from the whirlpool while wrapping a plush bath sheet around her beautiful body. She entered her luxurious bedroom and fell across the king-sized bed, draped in a sea-foam green, raw-silk quilt.

After a moment of lying on the bed and stroking the sensual silk cover, La'Roc moved to the large walk-in closet. Thank goodness for Ms. Holiday's foresight; she had packed La'Roc an overnight bag.

La'Roc dressed for bed in a pair of light blue silk boxers and a matching top. She crawled into bed and hugged the pillow next to her. *Shawn's pillow*, she thought. All of La'Roc's nights had been long and lonely, waiting for her man to come home. La'Roc knew that she would have Shawn's name embroidered on the pillow within a couple of days. She needed the physical comfort to help her fall asleep until he got home.

Oh well, La'Roc thought to herself. *I have his pillow and my wet dreams to send me to dreamland.*

As La'Roc dozed off to sleep, she heard a soft tap on her bedroom door. "Mother its Courtney. May I come in?"

"Of course; come in. What's wrong?" La'Roc asked. Courtney entered the room and noticed Paris and Biscuit sleeping on the floor. Courtney indicated that she would move the dogs. Her mother waved her hand in a gesture to leave the sleeping pets.

La'Roc patted the bed, and Courtney sat nervously on the edge, rubbing her hands along the quilt.

"I just need to talk to you before we meet with Dr. Moore tomorrow. I just left Dr. Kim's room—we had a long talk about Justin."

La'Roc looked at her daughter. "Courtney, I will be there to support you, but you are the only one who can answer the questions Dr. Moore will ask tomorrow." La'Roc continued, "Follow your heart and think about what you want to do for the rest of your life. Ask yourself, 'Do I want a career or do I want to take care of Justin the rest of my life without a life of my own?' Courtney, whatever the doctor says, it will be your decision to make. That is not mother's decision or Dr. Kim's decision to make. At the end of the day, the decision is yours, but I will be right there by your side and will support whatever decision you make, okay, baby? I know you will make the right decision, sweetheart.

"Courtney, you are intelligent, and you will make the right decision. Go to sleep and get some rest. Don't worry about the meeting tomorrow. Everything will work out just fine."

Courtney looked over at her mother. "Mom, let's talk about Shawn's party that we are going to give him when he comes home."

"Oh, sweetheart, that is a good idea. That is why you are my daughter, because you think like your mother." They both laughed.

They talked for what seemed like for hours about Shawn's welcome home party and the appropriate people to invite to the enormous blowout.

La'Roc and Courtney talked about everything imaginable before Courtney fell asleep with her arms around her mother. La'Roc knew her daughter was afraid of the outcome of tomorrow's meeting. All she could do was just be there for her; that was pretty much it.

La'Roc managed to release her body from Courtney's arms.

She looked around in her new bedroom and realized, as she had many times before, how truly blessed she was to have family and friends who loved her so dearly.

Thinking about the gift Jordan had just given to her, she found herself crying softly. She didn't want to wake Courtney.

La'Roc finally dozed off to a long-awaited sleep. That was the first night she did not dream about Shawn. She felt that Courtney was her lucky charm.

The next morning, La'Roc was awakened by Ms. Cotton's voice over the intercom calling everyone to come down for breakfast.

Jordan ran into La'Roc's room and leaped on the bed to wake Courtney. Then he asked, "Courtney, why didn't you invite me to your mother's room last night? It would have been nice if I had been invited to the party."

"Jordan, my daughter is a little worried about the meeting she scheduled today with Justin's doctor."

"I understand. Courtney, you will be all right. You will have your mother and Dr. Kim with you. I'm sorry I won't be able to join you. Devon and I will be working on Shawn's release."

"Uncle Jordan, I'll be all right. I'll have Dr. Kim and Mother with me. I'm good. It's time for me to take my life back. I'm ready to push forward, Uncle Jordan."

"Courtney I have a beautiful surprise for you and Devon. I'll show you your surprise now if you'd like. It could make you feel better." Jordan and Courtney left La'Roc's bedroom and took the elevator to the second floor. La'Roc sat on her bed, smiling.

Courtney returned to her mother's bedroom with tears in her eyes. "Oh, Mom, my office is beautiful. I can't wait for Devon to see his office. Thank you, Uncle Jordan," she said as she ran into his arms.

"Jordan, I want you and Alex to update Devon about his role during the interview," La'Roc announced. She continued, "Remember, he's not a lawyer until he passes the bar."

"Jordan thanks again for my beautiful present. Sweetheart, can you go wake Devon; have breakfast and go bring me back a reliable witness." They both laughed.

"Okay, La'Roc. I'm going to wake Devon, have some breakfast, and we're out of here. You guys have a wonderful day. Remember, guys, I love you both." Jordan kissed La'Roc and Courtney goodbye and then left the room.

Courtney hugged her mother with a kiss. "I'm going to take a long, hot shower. Thanks, Mom, for letting me sleep with you last night. It was fun, and the conversation we had made me feel better about seeing Dr. Moore this afternoon."

Before walking out of La'Roc's bedroom, Courtney looked back and said, "Mom, I have to get started on the welcome home party for Shawn. This party is going to be off the hook." She smiled and ran down the hall to her room. La'Roc smiled to herself as Courtney bounced down the hall, yelling about the party they were planning for Shawn. "We are having a party! Not just any party, a welcome home party for Shawn Parker!" Courtney yelled at the top of her voice.

"Shawn is going to be really excited about coming home to a wonderful family that loves him and an outstanding welcome home party. Thanks for the gesture, baby," La'Roc yelled down the hall to Courtney.

Courtney went to her room, and La'Roc returned to her bathroom to take a shower.

La'Roc showered and then joined her guests downstairs for breakfast. Dr. Kim was already downstairs, waiting for La'Roc to join them.

La'Roc's mother, sister, Chantal, Alex, Denise, Jordan, Devon, and Courtney were all seated, having breakfast. La'Roc joined her friends as Jordan pulled out a chair at the head of the table.

"Breakfast is served," Mr. Holiday announced.

"Thank you, Ms. Holiday," La'Roc said.

They were served coffee, juice, hot tea, bacon, toast, eggs sausages, pancakes, and fruit salad.

"Thank you, Ms. Cotton," Courtney said.

"Denise, what do you and Chantal have on your agenda today?" La'Roc asked.

Chantal responded, "We're going to hang out with Mommy and L'Oreal. I'm taking them out to lunch, and we're going to a play."

"Sounds like a fun day. Will you be in Manhattan?" La'Roc asked.

"Yes, the play is off-Broadway. We're going to see Tyler Perry's latest play, Have you seen the play Colored Girl yet?" Denise asked.

"No, but I'm looking forward to seeing it with Shawn," La'Roc said with excitement. "That'll be great. We can all meet up at the condo later on in the evening. Denise, remember the little talk we are supposed to have concerning you and Alex?" La'Roc smiled as she ran upstairs. La'Roc yelled over her shoulder, "See you later at the condo. Courtney, Dr. Kim, and I myself are having a meeting in Manhattan with Dr. Moore."

Devon walked in on the conversation and asked, "Who is Dr. Moore?" "Dr. Moore is Justin's doctor. I wanted you to come with us to meet with him, but you have to go to work today. You'll meet him at the next scheduled meeting. I've concerns about Justin's treatment. I need to get some answers and reasons why his body is rejecting the medication. That is why I wanted you to be in on this meeting," Courtney responded to Devon's question.

Everyone left to go on their assignments. Courtney and La'Roc decided to go shopping before they headed into Manhattan. Dr. Kim informed La'Roc that she had a couple of conference calls to make before going into Manhattan. That would give Courtney and La'Roc about four hours to shop.

They could easily spend ten thousand to fifty thousand dollars or more in four hours. La'Roc smiled to herself.

The shopping trip was a blast.

La'Roc and Courtney purchased dresses by Stella McCartney and other well-known designers. La'Roc knew Jason Woo had a new line out and was anxious to see what she would like. After leaving Neiman Marcus, the two women ventured to several boutiques. Shopping was such a stress reliever. Their next stop was to an exclusive jewelry boutique. La'Roc treated Courtney to a rose-colored diamond necklace with rose diamond and ruby earrings. For herself, she purchased the emerald and diamond ring she had been admiring for some time. She thought about getting something for Shawn but decided she'd wait until he was released. However, La'Roc went shopping a week later and purchased a beautiful diamond ring for Shawn's welcome home gift.

La'Roc continued with her generous spending by purchasing gifts for her other family members and legal staff.

La'Roc spent over one hundred thousand dollars with no regret, and she enjoyed every minute spending money on her family. La'Roc also purchased gifts for Dr. Kim, Ms. Cotton, and Ms. Holiday. After shopping, it was lunchtime; mother and daughter decided to have lunch at Seafood Wallace's place. He had the best seafood in Westchester County.

After having lunch, they gathered up their packages and left for La'Roc's beautiful new home.

La'Roc and Courtney picked up Dr. Kim and then drove to Manhattan for their scheduled appointment with Dr. Moore.

As La'Roc drove into the garage, Dr. Kim commented with surprise, "Wow! What a beautiful home."

La'Roc said, "Thanks, Debbie. Come in. Make yourself at home. Feel free to go in and look around. I'll have Ms. Sanchez make you something to eat."

"Good afternoon, Ms. Sanchez. This is Dr. Debbie Kim, and you know Courtney," La'Roc said, introducing Dr. Kim to Ms. Sanchez.

"Good afternoon, Dr. Kim. Pleased to meet you. Hi, Courtney, how're you this afternoon?"

Dr. Kim greeted the housekeeper, "Good afternoon, Ms. Sanchez, nice to meet you."

"Ms. Sanchez, please take Dr. Kim into the dining room and make her a salad or whatever she likes. I'm going to take a shower. Thank you, Ms. Sanchez," La'Roc responded.

"You're welcome, Ms. Rose," Ms. Sanchez answered.

"Make yourself at home, Debbie. I'm going to grab a quick shower." "I am fine, La'Roc," Debbie answered.

"Courtney, are you all right?"

"Yes, Momma, I am good. I'm going to take a quick shower as well. All that shopping has left me a little sticky," laughed Courtney.

After their quick, refreshing shower and a sandwich, Courtney and La'Roc, along with Dr. Kim, left for their scheduled appointment with Dr. Moore.

Driving toward I-95, La'Roc popped in the CD *I Fly Above*, which was one of her favorites. From the backseat, Courtney continued discussing Justin's progress with Dr. Kim.

La'Roc hoped that the music would help to soothe Courtney so that she wouldn't be so tense during the conference with Dr. Moore.

"We are here, ladies. Let's go inside. We don't want to keep Dr. Moore waiting. Courtney, are you okay?" La'Roc asked.

"Mom, I am great. I have you and Dr. Kim with me."

The three women arrived at the Doctor's office. Courtney held Dr. Kim's hand. La'Roc could see from the pinched expression on her daughter's face that she was very nervous about this meeting.

The three women entered Dr. Moore's office. The plants and cream-colored walls decorated with photographs offered a sense of comfort. The heavy upholstered chair continued to convey the sense of comfort and security.

Ms. Harris, Dr. Moore's secretary, offered the three women coffee and juice.

Within a matter of minutes, Dr. Moore entered the office along with another doctor, Dr. Woo.

Dr. Moore introduced Dr. Woo and explained that he asked him to consult on Justin's case due to his concerns about him not responding to his current treatment.

"What is the treatment that he is on now, and what is the new treatment that you would like to try? Also what would be the possible side effects we have to look for, Dr. Woo?" Dr. Kim inquired.

Dr. Woo explained the new medications they wanted to try on Justin. "For the new treatment, we will need authorization from his father in order to proceed with the treatment."

The doctors explained and discussed the possible side effects. Courtney and Dr. Kim walked out of the room to discuss the options in terms of the new treatment.

Courtney would still be unable to authorize the documents for Justin's treatment because she wasn't married to him.

"Who signed for his surgery in California?" Dr. Kim asked.

Dr. Moore checked Justin's chart. "I have it right here—it was his father." "His father, that's who took Justin to the hospital the night he was shot. Mr. Justin Holloway Sr. called Courtney that night and then left the hospital,"

La'Roc said from her chair in the corner of the office.

"Dr. Moore, without the new treatment, what will happen to Justin?" Courtney asked.

She needed Dr. Moore expertise to help her to cope and understand Justin's current condition.

"Well, Courtney, I will not give you false hope. As you know, the treatment that he's receiving now is not working. His body is rejecting the treatment. I hate to say it, but I don't see him getting better. Without the new treatment, he will die," Dr. Moore responded. Dr. Moore repeated without hesitation, "He'll die."

"Ms. Rose, do you think we can locate Justin's father?" Dr. Kim asked La'Roc.

"Dr. Kim, I'll put one of my private investigators on this right away," La'Roc responded. "Courtney, baby, do you have any idea where Justin's father could be? When was the last time you spoke to him?" La'Roc asked.

"The last time I actually spoke to Mr. Holloway was the night Justin was shot," Courtney answered sadly.

With the meeting over, Courtney and Dr. Kim left Dr. Moore's office and headed to the hospital to visit with Justin.

La'Roc stayed to assure the doctors that she would find Justin's father. She thanked the doctors and left.

As La'Roc approached the parking lot, she observed Dr. Kim holding Courtney in her arms, comforting her.

With tearful eyes, Courtney saw her mother and ran into her arms, crying. "Courtney, we will find Justin's father. I promise you. Calm down and let's go visit Justin." La'Roc soothed her as she stroked Courtney's bent head.

Upon arriving at Justin's room, they saw that Justin was sleeping. Courtney tried to wake him, with no luck. Dr. Kim went over to check on him to confirm if he was sleeping and not in a coma. Lapsing in and out of coma was his body's way of rejecting the treatment he was being given.

Justin's nurse walked into the room and checked on his medication, which was pumping though the tubes running down his arms. The only sounds that could be heard were the constant beeping of the monitoring machines keeping track of Justin's vital signs.

La'Roc looked down at Justin, this once-handsome young man who had a damn good future ahead of him. Now he was unable to speak his name. *How sad,* she thought to herself with tears in her eyes.

La'Roc, Dr. Kim, and Courtney stood around Justin's bed, holding each other's hands, praying.

After they prayed, La'Roc noticed Dr. Moore and Dr. Woo standing in the doorway of Justin's room.

Dr. Woo said, "We are sorry to interrupt your prayer, Ms. Rose." "No problem," La'Roc answered with teary eyes.

"Dr. Moore and I would like to evaluate Justin. We also must inform him that the treatment he is receiving now is not allowing him to make progress. He needs to know that his body has been rejecting the medication that he is now on. He also needs to know that we need to try a different treatment and hope his body responds to the new medication.

"Dr. Moore and I will not ask Justin to sign any documents because he is not responsive enough to be responsible for his treatment." The doctors said, explaining the treatment to Justin was healthy. Although Justin was incoherent, the doctors stated that talking to Justin about the new treatment could be helpful; they were also hoping that he would come out of his coma for a moment. Even though Justin would show some signs of awareness, it wasn't enough to authorize his new treatment.

Quietly and with a stern look, Dr. Moore informed Courtney that it was imperative that Justin's father be found right away.

La'Roc, Courtney, and Dr. Kim said their goodbyes and left Justin's room. Before leaving, Courtney reassured Dr. Moore that they would find Justin's father. Silently, Courtney vowed that she would find Mr. Holloway. She wasn't sure where she stood in regard to Justin, but she was going to fight damn hard to save his life.

Dr. Moore reassured Courtney that Justin would be fine and he would give him the message.

The ride back to the condo was silent. Dr. Kim and Courtney were sitting in the back seat. Dr. Kim was holding Courtney in her arms, rocking her back and forth.

Courtney wasn't crying because she loved Justin; she was crying because she had to give up being Justin's caregiver. She determined months ago that she had stopped loving him; however, she also realized that she felt obligated to him as his friend. Courtney was now facing reality, the reality that she was no longer capable of giving Justin the help he so badly needed.

La'Roc's cell phone brought her thoughts back to the present. Answering, she heard Alex's exciting news about Shawn. La'Roc advised him to contact Jordan and Devon in order for them to all meet at the condo.

"I'll call them now, and I'll see you later. How did your meeting with Justin's doctor go?" Alex asked.

"Alex, I'll fill you in later tonight," La'Roc responded and ended the call.

La'Roc's phone screen quickly flashed Jordan's image. Answering, Jordan acknowledged that he got Alex's message and would meet her at the condo along with Devon. Jordan teased her with the possibility that Shawn's release was quickly coming into view.

La'Roc's nerves were twisting as she tried to slow everything down. What she didn't want to do was get her hopes up too high only to be disappointed. She hoped the possible information the team acquired would be sufficient enough to free Shawn.

By the time La'Roc drove into the garage, Courtney had calmed herself down.

After conferring with the kitchen staff concerning the dinner menu, La'Roc gathered up Paris and Biscuit for their walk.

After her shower, she walked into the great room, where Dr. Kim was having a drink.

"I hope you don't mind that I fixed myself a glass of red wine."

"No, make yourself at home. I'm making myself a drink, but something a bit stronger than yours," laughed La'Roc as she mixed a vodka and cranberry juice cocktail.

La'Roc stopped by Courtney's room only to discover that she was curled up under her comforter, asleep. She looked at her with a mother's concern and knew that she needed the rest after her visit with Justin.

Setting her drink aside, La'Roc turned on the shower in her large bathroom. She set the shower for heavy steam and turned on the music setting to her smooth jazz. Once the shower filled with her favorite scented steam, she stepped in.

Spreading the scented gel over her body, La'Roc thought about how Shawn's large hands felt caressing her breasts and then moving down over her still-flat stomach. They finally came to rest between her legs, tangling in her soft curls. She could feel his fingers working their magic, stroking the inside folds of her core, slowly bringing her to a fantastic, mind-blowing orgasm. La'Roc hear herself gasp and realized that, in her daydream, she had had brought herself to a climax.

After stumbling out of the shower and to her bed, La'Roc drifted off to sleep, her last thoughts of Shawn. "I love you," she whispered.

La'Roc was awakened when Chantal and Denise ran into her bedroom and jumped on her bed.

La'Roc said, "What is going on with you bitches?"

"Oh, bitch, we missed you. Mom and L'Oreal are downstairs asking about you. We haven't seen you all day," Denise said.

La'Roc responded, "You see me now, right? I'm all right, just a little tired. Since I've taken a nap, I feel better.

La'Roc, Chantal, Denise, and Courtney entered the great room; La'Roc found her mother and sister out on the terrace, laughing, talking, and telling jokes to each other.

"Hi, sleepyhead," Geneva said, hugging La'Roc. "I had a lovely time with my two beautiful adopted daughters today. We had lunch at a fantastic restaurant called Sarah's place, and then we went to see an unforgettable play on Broadway."

Everyone talked over how their day went. L'Oreal mentioned that Casey would be returning home shortly. "I think I know now how you feel when you talk about missing Shawn. How is Shawn's case going?"

"Thanks for asking, L'Oreal. If everything works out the way the team plans, Shawn will be home soon," La'Roc responded.

"That's great, sis. I can't wait to see him," L'Oreal replied.

"I asked Casey to meet me here. I hope that it's all right with you,"

"What do you mean, if I don't mind? Casey is always welcome in my home, and you know that."

"Just being respectful, sis," L'Oreal smiled.

"I know. That's the way we were raised. Mom always said, 'Give each other respect at all times.'" They both laughed and hugged each other.

Through the laughter, La'Roc heard the doorbell and knew the guys had arrived. Soon the suspense would be over, and she would know what they had found. *Slow down*, she cautioned herself. It wouldn't pay to get her hopes up to high only to see them crash to the floor. She could hear Alex and Devon, along with Jordan, greeting the housekeeper.

"Good evening, Ms. Cotton," greeted Jordan as he entered the house, sniffing the air. "Something smells good. What did you beautiful ladies whip up today?" he continued as he headed straight for the kitchen. Ms. Holiday popped her head out of the kitchen door, a happy smile to lighting up her face.

Ms. Cotton said, "Oh, Mr. Jordan, you're too much."

Alex asked, "Where's La'Roc and the rest of the group?"

Ms. Holiday answered, "They're all sitting on the terrace, enjoying the sunshine. Courtney is upstairs, sleeping. She had a long day with Justin." She couldn't keep the concern out of her voice.

"She'll be all right, Ms. Holiday. I promise you. Don't worry about her. She's going to be okay," Jordan responded.

The three lawyers walked onto the terrace, smiling.

Alex, Jordan, and Devon walked over and kissed all the ladies; Alex stated, "We have good news!"

Devon continued, "We went to the co-op to compare notes, and guess what? Once you see all the information we collected today, you'll be surprised. Shawn could be coming home next week. I'm so excited, Grams. Just wait until you hear the information we have for you."

La'Roc stood up from her seat. Tears rolled down her face as she walked over to Devon and hugged him. "Come on, guys. Let's get this over with. Let's bring Shawn home. I cannot wait to hear the breaking news that you have for me."

They excused themselves from the rest of the family and walked to La'Roc's office.

La'Roc took her seat at the small oak conference table. The rest of the team took their seats around the table. Devon was taking the lead in conducting the conference.

There were all kinds of evidence that showed Shawn was innocent. There were statements from Mr. Johnston, Ms. Brown, Kelly's sister, and her brother-in-law, and both DNA tests. La'Roc said, "*Wow*, I love you, guys. However, tomorrow we need to speak to the judge and set up a court date for a bail hearing.

"I am so proud of all of you. Alex, I told you … you didn't have anything to worry about. All it takes is a little confidence and Jordan on your side." They all laughed.

La'Roc looked over to her right to where Devon was sitting and said to her newest lawyer, "Devon, I am *so* proud of you, sweetheart. You did a wonderful job. Thank you."

Jordan, Alex, and La'Roc gave Devon high fives and a toast for the incredible work he had accomplished on the Parker case.

La'Roc spoke directly to Alex. "Alex, you need to get in touch with Judge Oliver. If he is busy, try Judge Cohen or whomever you can get to put Shawn on the calendar for next week. Jordan and Alex, you need to connect with these judges right away. I believe, personally, it is time to bring my baby home," La'Roc avowed with a serious face.

Alex said, "Yes, it's time to bring Mr. Parker home, and we're in the driver's seat. We have this case in the bag."

"Shawn is already a free man. We have everything we need, signed, sealed, and ready to be presented in court. So let's roll, Alex, and get one of these judges to put Shawn's case on the calendar," Jordan replied.

La'Roc walked back into the great room, where her friends and family were having a ball, laughing and talking about something funny that Devon had said since he was such a practical joker.

He always made his mother and his great-grandmother laugh.

"Hi, guys, you seem to be happy about something. Tell me the joke. I love to laugh too, Mr. Lawyer." La'Roc looked over at Devon smiling.

"I will tell you the joke later, Grams," Devon responded.

"So, what was all the laughter about?" inquired Chantal.

"Lawyer stuff," Devon chuckled. "You know we can't discuss the case with you guys," he stated as he winked at his grandmother. La'Roc acknowledged her grandson's quick thinking with a slight nod of her head.

After dinner, La'Roc allowed herself a moment to think over the news she had received from her team.

La'Roc and her team would be defending the man she loved in several days and there could not—would not—be any mistakes. On the day of the bail hearing, they all would have to be on point and on the same page.

That also included Devon. Earlier, La'Roc looked around the room at Devon after the meeting; she thought to herself that Devon was going to make a damn good lawyer someday. Just like her colleagues, Alex and Jordan. She laughed out loud.

"Ms. Holiday, where are Courtney and Dr. Kim?"

"Ms. Rose, Dr. Kim and Courtney went for a walk," Ms. Holiday answered. "Thank you, Ms. Holiday. Where is Ms. Cotton? Is she all right? She seemed a little quiet at dinner."

La'Roc had noticed that Ms. Cotton had been a little distant from the family.

When asked what was bothering her, she would always say, "I'm fine; don't worry about me, Ms. Rose."

"I think she is okay, Ms. Rose," Ms. Holiday answered.

"Thanks, Ms. Holiday. Please ask Ms. Cotton to come downstairs for a second. I need you both to meet me in my old office for a short meeting. I want to discuss arrangement involving the five houses. Thank you, Ms. Holiday," La'Roc said.

"I will give her the message, Ms. Rose."

A few minutes later, Ms. Holiday and Ms. Cotton entered La'Roc's office. "Hello. Please come in and have a seat. First of all, I would like to say thanks to both of you for taking good care of me and my family over the past two or three decades." La'Roc gave Ms. Holiday and Ms. Cotton each a white envelope with a check inside. "Well, this meeting is well overdue. I want you both to know how much I appreciate you and your dedication; and most of all, I value your loyalty. Ms. Cotton, you have been employed with the Rose agency for twelve years. Ms. Holiday, you have been with me for how long?"

"Ms. Rose, I have been with you for twenty-eight years. I started working for you before Devon was born; Courtney was a little girl with two long braids down her back and at that time, you had a two-bedroom apartment. Remember, Ms. Rose? I raised Paris, and I also help raised Biscuit," Ms. Holiday said with a smile. La'Roc returned her smile.

"Ms. Cotton, Courtney would like for you to continue to work for her in her and Devon's condominium. At some point, you will be summoned to work at the townhouse as well as the big house in Westchester. Ms. Holiday will inform you of parties, events, etc. However, you will be in charge of things here. I will send Ms. Sanchez down to work in the co-op from time to time until you hire more help. We have five homes and need more help right?"

"I love working for you and Ms. Courtney. Thank you, Ms. Rose," Ms. Cotton responded.

"Ms. Holiday, what am I going to do with you?" La'Roc asked with a grin. "Ms. Holiday you will be at the town house and you will also be in charge of the house in Westchester. I'll be meeting with the Sanchez's tomorrow to inform them that you'll be in charge, and they will have to inform you of any decision have to be made. The Sanchez's are working at the house in Westchester as we speak. I'll e-mail them tonight with my decision and the changes I've made. Mr. Sanchez will be in charge of transportation and the landscaping. Ms. Holiday, you are in charge, and if any decision has to be made, it will have to go though you. Of course, the CEO will approve whatever needs to be approved. Ms. Holiday, you cannot designate any decision on your own. Do you understand?"

"Yes, Ms. Rose. I understand."

La'Roc decided to call her secretary. She informed her to send out an e-mail to the housekeeping department and transportation department about all the changes that were facilitated by the CEO during the morning meeting. "Thank you all for your cooperation during these changes.

"Ms. Holiday will be in charge and the supervisor of the housekeeping department. Ms. Holiday, I have appointed Mr. Sanchez to be in charge of maintenance," La'Roc said. "Remember, Ms. Cotton, if there is to be a dinner party, Ms. Holiday will summon all staff to participate in getting it together. During dinner parties, events, big birthday parties etc., we will then hire more staff.

"Ms. Holiday you are the number-one person in charge, and Ms. Cotton, you are the second person in charge," La'Roc announced.

"Thank you for your patience, your time, and for putting up with me as your boss all these years. You can go now and open up your envelopes." La'Roc smiled.

Ms. Holiday and Ms. Cotton hugged La'Roc and started to leave the office. They Stopped, turned around, and said, "Thank you, Ms. Rose."

"Please get my babies ready for their walk," La'Roc said. "Hurry, ladies.

I need to see my babies," La'Roc teased.

Once alone, La'Roc walked over to the window and looked at the beautiful view. Tears began to flow down her face. She yelled out to whoever would listen, "Oh, somebody please send Shawn home to me." La'Roc was so tired of being alone. She needed Shawn to be there for her; she wanted to hold him close to her and never let him go. She loved him more than words could ever express, and soon her man would be back in her arms. *I love you, baby,* she thought to herself as she gazed at the picture that she kept in the locket that hung around her neck ... the irony was that Shawn had given her the locket the night before he was arrested. He said it was a token of his love. *My love for you is forever, Sexiful,* was engraved inside the necklace.

While La'Roc continued to gaze out the window, the two housekeepers knocked and entered the quiet office. Both wanted to express their appreciation for the generous gifts La'Roc had presented.

As the evening wound down, Chantal, Denise La'Roc's mother, and her sister said their goodbyes as they were getting ready to leave. Alex and Jordan agreed that they would work together to prepare their opening statement for when Shawn's trial began.

La'Roc decided that she would make a trip tomorrow to see Shawn. She just had to see him and hear his voice.

The workout was great. She needed that workout to take her mind off Shawn's case.

Jordan and Alex noticed La'Roc sitting on the terrace. They walked over to join her.

Jordan and Alex outlined their statements. La'Roc nodded her head as she listened to the two men; she was very happy with their statement.

La'Roc kissed them both. "Thank you, guys, for all the hard work you've done. I love you both. I am going to visit Shawn tomorrow. You're welcome to come with me," commented La'Roc as she gazed out over the terrace. "If you all do, remember; don't tell him about the DNA outcome."

"La'Roc, you know we have your back, no matter what," Jordan stated, with Alex nodding in agreement.

Jordan looked over at La'Roc and smiled. "I told you some weeks ago that Shawn would be free."

La'Roc volunteered her car and asked Jordan to drive. Usually, she was a calm, cool person; however, when it came to Shawn and his imprisonment, she was rattled.

While talking to La'Roc, Jordan realized that Alex was no longer on the terrace. When questioned, La'Roc stated that Alex left with Denise and Chantal.

Looking closely, Jordan noticed that La'Roc's shoulders were shaking, and he could hear soft sobbing sounds. Moving quickly, he gathered her in his arms and just held her without speaking.

"Jordan, I am hurting. Please help me to stay strong and focused. I need your support and, as always, your friendship," La'Roc sobbed.

The two of them dozed off in the lover's lounger as the tiny fairy lights twinkled in the bushes.

Later that evening, Devon informed his grandmother that he had to return to California to tie up a few loose ends. Devon's phone rang, and he left the room.

Walking around her mother's room, Courtney stopped in front of La'Roc. "Momma, are you and Uncle Jordan okay?"

"Yes, sweetie, why do you ask?" La'Roc responded.

"Oh, because you guys were sleeping when we came in."

"Nothing is wrong. I was having a Shawn moment. I am going to visit him tomorrow. Devon walked back into the bedroom, eating a sandwich and drinking a soda.

"Grams, I think Shawn will be coming home once we bring him in for his bail hearing. I really don't think there will be a trial. We have nothing but solid evidence. Don't worry, Grams. Shawn is coming home. I am positive," Devon declared.

"Thank you, Devon, for your confidence and for believing in Shawn's innocence."

"Grams, I never told you this before—however, I am telling you now. Shawn is a good man for you. Mom adores him, and I like him. What more do you want?" At that point, a slight grin split his face. "Shawn makes you laugh all the time with his funny jokes, and when Shawn makes you laugh, that's what makes me happy—seeing you laugh. Are we having a welcome home party for Shawn?"

La'Roc answered, "Ask your mother. Thank you, Devon. Shawn is a good man, and yes, I love him with all my heart."

"Oh! I overheard you and Mom's conversation about the townhouse in California. I think it's a great idea. Personally, I like having two homes: one home in California, and one home here in New York, right? And I will be able to see you every day," Devon said with that little handsome smirk on his face.

"Devon, you will be riding with Jordan and me to visit Shawn tomorrow, all right, baby?"

"I'd love to. I really want to see Shawn's face when we give him the good news about his early trial," Devon responded.

"Shawn is going to be very excited," La'Roc stated as she walked away. Once upstairs, she buzzed for Jordan. Jordan answered the intercom. "Yes, my love, what can I do for you?" Jordan responded.

"Did you get one of the agency detectives to find Justin's father?" La'Roc inquired.

"Yes, we have detective Ross on the case." "Okay. Good work, Jordan."

La'Roc further instructed Jordan to make sure Alex knew to try to get the earliest date possible on the court calendar for Shawn.

"That's fine if my name will get Shawn on the calendar. By all means, use La'Roc. Thanks, Jordan. You are the man."

La'Roc mixed a drink and headed for her whirlpool to relax before Biscuit and Paris woke up.

La'Roc looked at her Michael Kors watch to check the time. At 6:35 p.m. tomorrow, Shawn would be holding his Sexiful in his strong arms, the arms that she missed so dearly. Tomorrow, Shawn and La'Roc both would be expressing their love for each other through tears of joy.

La'Roc fell asleep in the whirlpool with her music playing: Michael Jackson's "This is it." To La'Roc, it felt like an appropriate song to play since Shawn would be coming home soon. *Please get me through tonight.* La'Roc knew she would be delighted when she saw her husband-to-be that following day. "This is going to be a long and dreamless night," La'Roc said as she laughed out loud at the sexual thoughts she had running around in her head about her and Shawn making rough love all throughout the night like two untamed animals.

La'Roc stepped out of the whirlpool, ran into the bedroom, and jumped on her king-size bed. She was so exhausted from all the running around with her friends and family, getting things ready for what would hopefully be Shawn's homecoming.

She decided to get ready for bed. She slipped on a tight green T-shirt and boxers to match. Before she retired to bed, she pressed the power button on the TV. She clicked the remote control to channel forty-five. La'Roc had positioned herself in her bed when she heard a knock at her door. "Yes, come in."

"La'Roc its Debbie are you sleeping?"

"No, Debbie. Come in. I am having a drink. Feel free to join me."

"Yes, I think I will have that drink." Debbie walked over to the bar and mixed herself a drink.

"Well, Debbie, what's on your mind and how is my daughter?"

"Your daughter is fine. Dr. Moore gave me a report on Justin's progress; the progress report wasn't too hopeful. He is worried about Justin going into a coma if he doesn't get the appropriate documents signed for the treatment that he discussed with Courtney at our last meeting. Dr. Moore is afraid Justin won't make it another month. Justin's father is the only person who can save him," Debbie replied.

"Debbie, let me update you on the finding of Justin's father. I have an investigator on the case as we speak. We should know something by tomorrow. When you speak with Dr. Moore, please inform him that Courtney will contact him as soon as she hears from Justin's father." For a moment La'Roc looked away from Debbie. It was just too hard to imagine a parent dropping out of contact with their child. She also agonized over that fact that neither she nor Courtney could authorize Justin's treatment.

"Damn him!" whispered La'Roc as she continued to pace around the room. Debbie turned to her in surprise at the venomous sound coming from her new friend.

"What happen to Justin?" Debbie inquired gently.

"It was a drive-by shooting. I was told the shooting was a message to Justin's father. His father was involved with a lot of illegal business, drugs, money laundering, etc. Justin's mother was reported to have been run off the highway by one of his father's business partners." Debbie quietly listened as La'Roc continued to explain her suspicions of Justin's father's shady business deals. She also explained that as far as Justin knew, his mother was just in a car accident, and nothing had ever been mentioned about his father's possible involvement.

"So, you're saying that, at this point, Justin has no real family, and the closest thing he does have to family is Courtney and the rest of you guys," stated Debbie with a worried frown. La'Roc acknowledged that she was correct.

The two women continued to lounge in La'Roc's spacious bedroom. Each one was turning over the day's events and wondering how soon the investigators would locate Justin's father. La'Roc informed Debbie that she planned on seeing Shawn the next day. She also informed her that she was considering having a contest to name her new home. La'Roc laughed, saying that she couldn't keep calling the place "the big house." It sounded like something from the days of slavery or a prison. Debbie had to giggle in agreement.

After wishing Debbie a good night, La'Roc made her rounds, walking quietly through the house before returning to her bedroom. Settling deep in her bed, she was quickly claimed by sleep.

La'Roc could hear the chiming of her cell phone. Reaching out a hand, searching for the noisy thing, she cursed at having her sleep interrupted. Checking the screen, she didn't recognize the number. Who the hell would be calling her at this ungodly hour?

"Hello," La'Roc answered.

"Ms. Rose, this is April, Shawn's sister."

La'Roc was instantly awake and shot up to a sitting position.

"I got your number from one of Shawn's notebooks that he left at my apartment some time ago." April continued in a rush, "I need to talk to you about Shawn's case."

"What the hell!" shouted La'Roc?

"I have made some terrible mistakes concerning my brother and Kelly. I've lied, and I'm sorry," continued April tearfully.

"April, it's too late to talk about Shawn's case, and it's really too late to be talking to me. I'll tell you what: if you want to talk, I'll see you in court okay. Goodnight, and don't call me again," stated La'Roc, wishing that she had a vintage phone that could be slammed down for a dramatic effect.

Flopping back down on her many pillows, La'Roc made a mental note to call Jordan in the morning to tell him about the surprise call from April. She laid there for several minutes thinking that April was a *crazy bitch* and couldn't be trusted. She was also convinced that April was aware of Kelly's scheme to get money from Shawn.

La'Roc thought she had everything she needed in Shawn. With Shawn, she believed that she could take on the world and not have any worries about anything because she knew Shawn would always have her back. She knew that Shawn would never leave her.

La'Roc had never met anyone like Shawn: he was kind, loving, giving, thoughtful, and a respectful human being. "Shawn loves me, and he treats my family as if they were his own family." She knew in her heart he would make a good husband.

In the beginning of their relationship, La'Roc was terrified of the age difference. However, Shawn convinced her to give him a chance and take a chance on loving him. He said, "Sexiful, you take chances every day in the courtroom Please take a chance on our love." He continued to pursue her, and she gave in to his charms. That was the best thing that could have ever happened to her—giving in to Shawn.

La'Roc said when she first met Shawn, she really didn't like him because of the age thing. However, she wanted his body; she wanted him to pick her up in his strong arms and rip her clothing off and make passionate love to her on her living room floor. Yeah, it was like that.

When she thought of Shawn making love to her, it made her shiver with satisfaction. He was so damn good in bed.

La'Roc fell asleep with thoughts of Shawn. At six in the morning, she was awakened by Paris and Biscuit playing around in her bedroom, tugging at the comforter on her bed. She said in a loud, playful, deep voice, *"Leave this room now! I am speaking to Biscuit and Paris!"*

Paris and Biscuit ran closer to the bed. They both were terrified. Their little tails were wagging and ears dropped and became very quiet.

La'Roc continued to play her game with her babies. They continued to squirm and wriggle, their little tails trying to get La'Roc's attention.

La'Roc quickly went through her morning routine before going through her exercise routine. She was looking forward to her visit with Shawn.

La'Roc went into her walk-in closet and grabbed a black sweat suit for her morning run before her visit with Shawn.

Entering the kitchen, La'Roc saw Ms. Holiday pouring her a cup of coffee. "Ms. Holiday, could you ask Jordan to join me for breakfast."

"Mr. Diaz, Courtney, and Devon went for a run. They are not back yet," Ms. Holiday responded.

La'Roc laughed and decided that she was totally not speaking to the three of them because they did not include her in their little run.

All three crooks—Jordan, Courtney, and Devon—ran into the kitchen where La'Roc was sipping her cup of espresso.

Courtney ran over to her and kissed her. Jordan and Devon followed. La'Roc pretended that she was angry. She didn't even crack a smile. She grabbed her coffee and left the kitchen, smiling to herself. She ran upstairs to the gym to work out before her visit with Shawn.

Jordan, Devon, and Courtney ran up the stairs and jumped on the mat where La'Roc was doing her sit-ups, which was a part of her daily regimen.

Jordan said, "Courtney, your mother—and my best friend—seems to have an attitude because she wasn't invited on our little venture this morning. Right baby girl?"

La'Roc continued to count, "Ninety-eight, ninety-nine, and one hundred." La'Roc stopped counting and looked at her family, shaking her head. "My family and friend, are you proud of yourselves?" She said, "Get out of my gym and go take your showers. Mr. Diaz and Devon, you remember, we have an appointment to see Shawn. Devon, you have the pleasure of giving him the good news."

"You are telling me that I can give Shawn the good news?" She said, "Yes, my little lawyer. It is all yours."

"Thanks, Grams."

As Courtney was doing her last set of sit-ups, she looked at her mother. "Hello, mother dear. I heard you said a few minutes ago to get out of your gym. Remember, this is our gym now."

They all started to laugh, and La'Roc joined in on the funny joke that Courtney had made.

"That is right, Courtney. Keep her grounded because I cannot do a thing with her," Jordan said, still laughing.

La'Roc's cell rang. "Hello, Mr. Power. What's on your agenda today?" "Good morning, partner I have some good news. We have a calendar date for the hearing. It's Thursday, the twenty-third of this month. We're all set as far as time is concerned.

"While in the courthouse, I recognized one of the judges. I saw Judge Perkins walking out of the courthouse. I asked for a minute of his time. I gave him your name. I explained to him everything about Shawn's case and the reason we needed a calendar date. He smiled. 'Walk with me. I'll check to see if I can get you on the docket right away.' We walked back to his chamber; he checked his calendar and gave me a date for next Thursday. He said to give you his regards. I think you have a secret admirer," Alex teased.

"Judge Perkins was on the Boston case, right?"

Alex answered, "Yes, he is the same judge. Shawn better watch it. I think the judge is on your case." La'Roc heard Alex chuckle.

"Thank you. I love you, and Shawn loves you too. I will give him your regards on my visit today."

"La'Roc, do you need me to come with you guys?" Alex asked.

"Alex, do you have all of the witnesses lined up?"

"Partner, I have my entire opening statement prepared and ready for your approval," Alex answered, his voice edged with excitement.

"Great job Alex. I'm going to visit Shawn today, and he'll be glad to hear the good news."

For some time, La'Roc had been noticing a little tension between Alex and Jordan. At first, she tried to dismiss it as just competition between friends, but recently, it had taken on a sharp edge that had the possibility of wrecking the team. She figured she'd follow her gut and call the boys on this matter; after all, her man's life was at stake here. "Alex, would you please stop by the condo later. There's something I need to discuss with you?" La'Roc assured Alex that their future discussion had nothing to do with the impending case; it was personal.

When Alex arrived and was seated in her office, La'Roc came straight to the point. "Alex, recently I've noticed that there has been some tension between you and Jordan, and I'm not talking about simple kidding around. I'm noticing some serious sniping going on. You want to explain this to me?" inquired La'Roc as she leaned back in her leather chair. Alex studied the serious look on his best friend and partner's face.

"Well, La'Roc, sometimes he's a little cross with me. I really don't let it get to me because of what he's going through," Alex replied.

"You know I've had enough of this, so I'll just have Jordan join us now and get to the bottom of this mess. Right now there's nothing more important than getting Shawn free. Do you feel me?" stated La'Roc with a steely edge in her voice.

Coming downstairs and hearing voices coming from La'Roc's office, Jordan headed in that direction. Stopping by the door, Jordan knocked and was waved in by La'Roc.

Upon entering the room, Jordan pulled up a chair and joined Alex and his best friend at the conference table.

La'Roc looked back and forth between Jordan and Alex with concern. "I just want you both to know that I have noticed some negative vibes between you two, and I will not tolerate this juvenile behavior. I care about Jordan. The love I have for you is inexpressible. I cannot verbalize words to express how much I love you. I want you and Alex to listen to me." La'Roc continued, "I don't know what is going on between the two of you, but I want it to stop now. If you have a problem with one another, fix it! I have two of the best attorneys in the country, and I need you to work together. I don't need you to love each other. I need you to work for Shawn. Cut the shit, and make it happen."

The two men apologized, shook hands, and then left the office, promising not to repeat their childish behavior.

As the two men left the office, Jordan turned to Alex, "Alex, any word from the PI you hired to find Justin's father?" Jordan asked. "He's supposed to call me today," Alex responded.

"Thanks, Alex," Jordan said. Following the guys out of the office, La'Roc called after Alex.

"Alex, whatever you do, don't forget Roger's murder case. Whoever killed Roger will not get away with murdering my friend," La'Roc affirmed.

"I have Detective Juan Nunez on Roger's case. I'll check in with him today. I'll give you a report as soon as I finish my call with Mr. Nunez."

As La'Roc turned to go upstairs, her cell phone rang. It was Chantal. She grabbed the phone excitedly.

"Hi, honey," La'Roc answered.

Chantal said, "Hello, slut, what's up? First of all, I got your message about April calling. I know you cursed her ass out, right?"

"I said some things to her and referred her to Shawn's lawyers. I'm so suspicious of that woman. I will never trust her when it comes to Shawn's safety," La'Roc responded.

Chantal said, "You got that right. That bitch can't be trusted. If you'll help set up your brother, you'll do anything. Oh, by the way, Dr. Mitchell called me last night; he's flying into New York tomorrow night to a conference and asked me if I was free to escort him to the affair. I agreed to be his date."

La'Roc said, "Is that name supposed to mean something to me? Who is Dr. Mitchell?"

Chantal responded, "O.M.G. From California! Justin's doctor. Don't you remember, fool?"

"Oh right, I remember. The nice doctor you threw yourself at like a bonfire slut. I'm only playing with you, girl; that is some wonderful news, girlfriend. I'm so happy for you. Now it's time for us to find Denise a man so she can be happy just like we are. You sound really excited," La'Roc responded.

"I'm really excited. We have been keeping in touch with each other ever since we left California. We call each other once or twice every month," Chantal responded.

"I'm thrilled for you, sis," La'Roc said with approval in her voice as she headed toward her room.

"Have you talked to Denise since she left yesterday?" Chantal asked.

"No, I was going to call you and her tonight before I went to bed to check on you bitches," La'Roc said out of concern.

"Well, La'Roc, the bitch is okay," Chantal laughed.

"Just to let you know, Chantal, I'm going to visit Shawn, and from there, I am going to the townhouse.

"Sis, are you bringing Shawn home or what's up with that?"

"We have a bail hearing next week. Sweetheart, we have all the evidence we need to bring my baby home. However, he may still have to go to trial because we have to prove he's innocent. We have a calendar date for next week for his bail hearing. As a matter of fact, it's next Thursday. We would love it if you guys were there for moral support."

"Of course we'll be there," Chantal answered.

"Thanks friend. I miss you," La'Roc said. "I have been so busy with Shawn's case and dealing with Justin. I'm a little worried about Courtney and her reaction to Justin's condition. However, if my detective doesn't find Justin's father, Justin will not make it," La'Roc said. "Courtney will be fine. She is just like her mother: tough and strong."

"How is Devon?" Chantal asked.

"Devon is doing great," La'Roc said proudly.

Chantal said with pride in her voice, "That's my man."

Concluding their conversation, La'Roc walked into the walk-in closet and tried to select an outfit to wear to visit Shawn.

Standing there, she finally chose a yellow raw-silk suit. She smiled, acknowledging that this was Shawn's favorite color. Checking the racks again, La'Roc settled on a mint green blouse with matching four-inch heels and a Calvin Klein bag.

La'Roc went to Dr. Kim's room to thank her for her services and gave her a check.

"Dr. Kim, I will be leaving early in the morning to visit Shawn, so I will say my goodbyes tonight. My driver will take you to the airport tomorrow morning. I gave him your flight information. Thank you for all of the help you have provided for my daughter. Thanks again."

"As soon as they find Mr. Holloway, I will be back. I love working with your daughter. As a matter of fact, I love your whole family. Consequently, I will be back if you will have me," Dr. Kim responded.

"You are welcome anytime, Dr. Kim. You don't need an invitation," La'Roc replied.

While working in her office, La'Roc's phone rang. Glancing at the screen, she realized it was an unfamiliar number.

"Hello, who is this?" she asked.

"Hello, Ms. Rose. This is Detective Don Ross. I was hired by Mr. Alex Power to locate a Mr. Justin Holloway Sr. I have him here in a hospital in California." La'Roc's heart began to rapidly beat in her chest.

"Mr. Power advised me to contact you as soon as I had some information concerning Mr. Holloway."

"You stated that Mr. Holloway was in a hospital in California. I hope it's nothing serious," she said. Even as she said this, La'Roc knew that Slick Holloway had somehow run afoul of someone who wanted him out of the way.

"I was told that he had been shot several times. There's no other information at this time." Mr. Ross continued, "From the information that I received, he could be relocated to New York. However, his doctor is going to want proof as to why the move is necessary."

La'Roc explained, "I understand, Mr. Ross. I'll have Mr. Power send Mr. Holloway's doctor all the information that is needed to get Mr. Holloway to New York. This is a matter of life or death."

"Thank you for your help. You've done a monumental job," La'Roc said. "Mr. Power will contact you soon. Thanks again." La'Roc hung up the phone and hit the express dial for Alex's number.

On the second ring, Alex picked up. "Hello, partner. What's up?"

Trying hard to slow down her breathing, La'Roc replied, "I just received a call from Mr. Ross, the detective you hired to find Holloway.

"Mr. Ross confirmed that he found Justin's father in a hospital in California. You need to get the name of the hospital, the city that the hospital is located in, and all of the documentation that Dr. Moore will need for Justin's father to sign to get started on his new treatment.

We need that information like yesterday," La'Roc stated anxiously as she paced the floor.

Alex said with surprise, "What is he doing in a hospital?"

"The report Ross gave to me was that Justin's father was shot several times. He didn't give any other information. Do your job and get him to New York, and get those papers signed. I really don't care about Mr. Holloway being shot or who shot him. My concern is Justin!

"This is the phone number where he can be reached." La'Roc repeated the number Ross gave her. "Call him right away, Alex."

"I'm on it, partner. Talk to you later."

"Good job, Alex. We need him here, like, now."

Before she hung up the phone, she gave Alex some instructions.

She asked Alex to call her right away with the information that was needed to get the new treatment for Justin. "California time is three hours behind our time, so that gives you enough time to get the information to Dr. Moore tonight."

La'Roc called Dr. Moore as soon as she hung up the phone. Alex called back an hour later.

"Hello partner. I have some good news for you and Justin." He explained everything to La'Roc.

"Thanks, Alex. That is wonderful news. Courtney will be overly delighted when I give her this news."

La'Roc left her bedroom, walked down the hall to Courtney's room and Dr. Kim's room to share the wonderful news she received regarding Justin's father and Alex's report.

After hearing the good news, Courtney became teary-eyed, and Dr. Kim had tears running down her face. The tears they shed together were happy and joyful tears.

Dr. Kim stated she was going to postpone her trip back to California. "I would like to stay and be with Courtney when Dr. Moore tries the new treatment on Justin. Ms. Rose, I hope you don't mind," Dr. Kim said with concern.

"Debbie, are you sure? I would love for you to stay. I didn't give you the best part of the good news. I listened very closely to Alex's report," La'Roc said with a big smile. "Alex said he was instructed by Mr. Holloway's lawyer that Justin's doctor needs to contact Justin's father's doctor in California and work out the details. Mr. Holloway is able to sign the documents that are needed. Once he signs the documents, the doctor can overnight the paperwork to Dr. Moore. Once Dr. Moore receives the signed documents, he can start Justin's new treatment immediately." La'Roc explained all the details to Dr. Kim and Courtney.

"Thank you, Mother dear. The sooner Dr. Moore starts the new treatment, the better it will be for all of us," cried Courtney as she held her mother in a tight hug.

La'Roc excused herself after saying good night. She left her daughter's room and walked down the hall to her bedroom as Paris and Biscuit followed.

La'Roc was so excited about seeing Shawn the following day. She knew in her heart that she wouldn't be able to sleep. Oh, she thought that mixing herself a strong drink would guide her into the beautiful world of dreamland. Paris and Biscuit ran into La'Roc's room; she played with her babies until she got tired. La'Roc looked over at Paris and Biscuit; she smiled thinking of what tomorrow could bring.

"I swear you guys are human. I think sometimes you guys are thinking about ways to kick my ass. Paris, you and Biscuit can erase that thought from your dog minds because that will never happen. Get off my bed and go to your room," she said. "Oh, I have a better idea. I will walk you to your room to make sure you go into your room and not Courtney's room."

She walked Biscuit and Paris to their room and ran back to her bedroom. La'Roc jumped into her big, round, king-size bed as she pulled the beautiful, floral sheet and comforter over her gorgeous body. Her dreams took her to a world of beauty. That beauty was being wrapped into Shawn's arms. Again, when she awakened from her dream, there was no Shawn.

But that was okay, she was going to get a good night's sleep—that was one night in a million. She needed that one night of sleep before facing her future husband the following morning.

The day dawned sunny and bright, and La'Roc was excited on two fronts. Justin's father had been found, and she was going to see Shawn today. Strolling through the walk in closet, she double-checked the outfit she had picked out the day before.

After checking her original outfit, she decided that the yellow suit didn't fit her mood, so La'Roc selected the mint green suit instead. After all, it was a woman's prerogative to change her mind.

She wanted to look her best when she greeted Shawn. This visit would be different because she had some excellent news for him— news he had been waiting to hear for the past several months. Shawn was going to be extremely excited.

La'Roc thought out loud, "My baby will be home in the next few days." And she would be waiting for her handsome fiancé, Mr. Parker, to hold her in his big, strong arms.

Her heart was pounding with excitement like an adolescent. Imagine your first date or the first time you had sex or if you could imagine something that was exceptionally exciting; then you'll know how La'Roc felt. Since Shawn had been locked away, she realized that Shawn was the most important person in her life besides her family.

La'Roc thought to herself, *Shawn is my lover, my confidant, my man, and, most of all, he is my best friend.*

Tears started to form in her eyes; however, these tears were positive tears as she sat in the backseat, thinking about the day her baby would be released. She looked on as Jordan continued talking to Devon about Shawn's court cases.

Devon seemed to be excited about the upcoming trial. He was sitting in the passenger seat, and he looked back at his grandmother.

"Grams, one of these days, I'll be an excellent lawyer just like you and Uncle Jordan. I've also been thinking that I might even become a judge," Devon pondered. "I'm not sure whether I want to be a local judge or move up in the system. I've got time," he laughed.

La'Roc said, "Yes, Devon, you'll make a great attorney one day, and we are all very proud of you. Isn't that right, Jordan?" La'Roc added, "Devon, furthering your education in law is a wonderful idea. Sweetheart, you are just full of surprises, aren't you? Your Honor Devon Rose Simmons." (Devon used his father's last name, Simmons). "That has a good ring to it, right, Jordan?" La'Roc said, teasing with Devon.

Devon looked at his grandmother and smiled. "I love you, Grandma." "Devon already knows how I feel about him and his mother. I am very proud of my godchildren," Jordan responded.

The ride seemed to take longer than she expected. La'Roc repositioned herself in the back seat.

La'Roc hated being chauffeured around. She preferred driving herself and using her chauffeur for special occasions when she felt like being spoiled.

"Attention, guys! I forgot to mention that the detective Alex hired to find Justin's father found him in California, in a hospital. And by this time tomorrow, if everything works as planned, Justin should be on his new medication, and his new treatment will start. Courtney is hoping he'll be on his way to recovery. Dr. Kim and Courtney will be there for his first treatment, which supposedly starts today."

Jordan said, "That is great news."

"Grams, are you for real? I'm happy for my mother. I'm going to call her before we go in to see Shawn."

La'Roc acknowledged Devon's statement with a smile.

"Give her my love, Devon," Jordan said. "Baby girl, we are almost there. Just be patient a little while longer. In a few minutes, you'll be in Mr. Parker's arms, and next week, he'll be home with you in your bed, planning your wedding," Jordan replied with a smirk.

As Jordan drove into the facility, La'Roc declared that she felt anxious and a little edgy, but she didn't understand why, because she had made this trip so many times before. *What happened? Oh well ...* she thought to herself. *It could be the good news that his lawyer will present to Shawn today. Come on, La'Roc, and pull up your big panties and walk into the facility with pride.*

"Okay, Grams we're here. Let's go give Shawn his Get-out-of-Jail-Free card," Devon said, winking at Jordan.

Devon called his mother before going into the facility.

La'Roc smiled. "Let's go give Shawn the good news," La'Roc said. "How do I look?"

Jordan said, "Like the beautiful woman that you are. In that outfit, you are going to knock Shawn out. Baby, you look like a million dollars." Jordan laughed.

"Grandmother, you look great. Shawn will love your outfit."

They all laughed at Devon's remark and walked toward the facility.

As they enter the facility, they walked up to the front desk and showed their identification badges. Devon said to the officer, "We're here to visit 000523, Mr. Shawn Parker." After being searched, the officer motioned for the team to follow him though the open doors, into the conference room, to wait for Shawn.

La'Roc paced back and forth while Devon and Jordan were engaged in a deep conversation about something that La'Roc wasn't interested in. Her mind was on Shawn.

La'Roc was so deep in thought, she didn't hear the officer bring Shawn into the room. "Hi, baby."

La'Roc turned around, and there he was, standing behind her with that beautiful smile. She ran into his open arms, weeping like a child who had just fallen off her bike. He looked so damn handsome in his blue prison uniform. That man could look good in anything he put on that body of his.

Shawn said, "Sexiful, you look so damn good, baby. Look at you: you are wearing some of my favorite colors."

He pulled La'Roc into his big, strong arms. He kissed her and held her as tight as he possibly could.

La'Roc was so turned on by Shawn's touch. She whispered softly as she looked up into his eyes, "Please hold me and never let go."

"Baby, when I leave this place, I will never leave you again, I promise you. Sexiful, the first thing I want to do when I am a free man is to marry you." Shawn looked down into her eyes. "Sexiful, I love you."

"I know, baby. Our feelings are mutual, and I love you too." La'Roc turned in Shawn's arms.

She called Jordan and Devon, and then in walked Alex. In the course of Shawn and La'Roc greeting each other, Alex had shown up. La'Roc had no idea that Alex had made it to the facility; she was delighted that he showed up for the duration of the conference. La'Roc wanted the team and Devon to be together when they informed Shawn of the good news. Well, it was time for La'Roc to step back and let her lawyers and intern do their job.

She looked over her left shoulder and spoke. "Do a good job and prove to me that you're worthy of your paychecks. Remember, you are working with precious cargo."

La'Roc smiled as she turned her back, waving her hand, and walked out of the conference area.

She decided to go over some notes for Shawn's bail hearing just in case her team needed her expertise.

Just thinking about Shawn's release made her feel damp between her legs, as though he was making love to her right there in Upland Prison.

She thought to herself, *Oh my darling Shawn. You don't know how much I missed you making love to me night after night and day after day. My body cries out for your body every minute of the day.*

As La'Roc sat in the waiting room, tears started running down her face, thinking about Shawn's lovemaking and knowing that she had to leave him there at Upland.

La'Roc was in her own little world when she heard someone call out her name. "La'Roc."

She jumped up from her seat. "What is it? Has something happened to Devon?"

"Devon is fine. It's Shawn asking for you. Shawn is so excited with the news, he is dancing and pacing the floor, waiting for you to come back into the conference/interrogation room," Alex said, laughing.

"I'll be right there." She wanted to pull herself together before she returned to Shawn's lovely arms again.

When La'Roc walked back into the area where her team was sitting, Shawn was the only one standing. As she walked toward Shawn, all eyes were on her. Shawn ran over and took her into his arms "Thank you, baby. I am going home." He just kept repeating, "I'm going home," with tears running down his face as he held her. He picked her up into his arms and kissed her firmly on her lips.

"Oh, baby, we made it. I'm going home next week with you, right?" Shawn asked.

La'Roc and Shawn walked over to the table and sat down across from each other. She held his hand and looked into his eyes. "Shawn, we are hoping for an early release. But first, we have to get you out on bail. The bail hearing will be held next week. Thursday, as a matter of fact. Shawn, you will hear testimony in court that you may not be aware of, and you will not be happy with some of the testimonies that will be presented. All these testimonies will come out at the trial, not the bail hearing next week.

"My lawyers are always ready; they just have to prepare you for the questions that you will have to endure on the stand if you are called to testify on your behalf. I personally don't think it will go that far. However, your lawyers will update you before going into court."

"Oh, Sexiful, I am so excited about going home. I will be with my baby once again. And, Sexiful, I promise you, I will always be there for you." Shawn smiled as he held La'Roc's hands.

They both looked at each other with teary eyes; the way they were looking at each other ... nothing could ever separate the two of them again. La'Roc and Shawn were so in love with each other.

Jordan, Alex, and Devon walked over to the table and sat down with Shawn and La'Roc. Devon sat next to his grandmother with a big smile on his face.

"What are you smiling about?" she asked, smiling back at her grandson. Devon looked at Shawn. "Man I'm going to get you out of here. Are you ready to leave this place?"

Shawn looked over at Devon. "Yes, man. To answer your question, I've been ready to leave this prison since the first day I arrived here. I am ready to go home like yesterday."

Jordan said, "Don't worry, my friend. You'll be getting out of here soon, but we still have more work to do."

Alex said, "We're not out of the woods yet, Mr. Parker. However, next week, everything will be in place."

La'Roc reached for Shawn's hand and walked around the table to sit next to her future husband. The lawyers left the room to give Shawn and La'Roc some privacy.

"Baby, what's wrong? Are you okay?" Shawn asked her.

"Sweetheart, I'm fine. I just want this week to end so we can go to court and get this shit over with," whispered La'Roc as she made small circular motions on Shawn's hand. La'Roc turned to face Shawn. "Baby, I need you home with me. I miss your body next to mine. I miss laying my head on your chest and feeling you kissing my neck until I go to sleep. I really love you, Shawn, and there is no one I would rather be with." Finally, La'Roc said, "Shawn, it's time to go. I will see you next week in court. Alex will bring you your clothing for the hearing." Shawn was reluctant to release La'Roc from his arms.

La'Roc turned and spoke to her team. "Come on. Move it toward the door. It's time to leave this place. Or I can make arrangements for you guys to stay here in Shawn's place, and I will take him home tonight," She teased Jordan, Alex, and Devon yelled, "We're coming."

Devon said, "No hard feelings about me staying in your little house, but I like my big house better." Everyone laughed, including Shawn.

La'Roc kissed Shawn goodbye and walked out of the facility.

Jordan put his arms around her body and kissed her tears away. "Baby girl, it's going to be all right. I promise you with all my heart. Shawn will be home next week; just mark my words, baby girl."

Jordan called Alex as he was getting into his car. "Alex, we'll meet in Westchester at the townhouse because the contractors are working at the big house. I'm going to put La'Roc to bed. She's had a long day."

"Okay. On my way, Jordan," Alex responded.

"Grandmother, are you all right? Missing Shawn? He'll be home before you know it. So don't worry your pretty little head, okay, Gram?"

"Devon, I'm good, baby. Just take me home, my little lawyer," La'Roc teased her grandson.

Devon jumped into the driver's seat, and Jordan climbed into the backseat with his friend La'Roc.

On the drive back to the city, La'Roc laid her head on Jordan's shoulder and was about to go to sleep when she heard Devon and Jordan talking about Shawn's trial.

Five minutes into Devon and Jordan's conversation, she finally cried herself to sleep on Jordan's shoulder.

The ride home was very dark for La'Roc. Even on the ride to Westchester, she was only thinking of Shawn, dreaming that he would be home, waiting for her in bed with two drinks in his big hands, like always.

La'Roc's cell phone awakened her. She answered, "Hello. Yes, who is this?"

"This is Justin's doctor, Dr. Moore," the caller on the other end of the phone said.

La'Roc answered, "Yes, doctor, how can I help you?"

"We have all the paperwork and we're ready to get started with the treatment. Where is Courtney? I tried to reach her at the number we have on file, but it has been disconnected."

"Oh, doctor, I'm sorry. She just picked up a new phone yesterday. I'll have her to call you right away. She and Dr. Kim were supposed to be coming to the hospital today because she was informed last night about the documents, and she wanted to be there for the first treatment. She should be there soon. I'll try her on her cell." She continued, "That is great news, Dr. Moore. Justin can now get the treatment he so badly needs."

"Ms. Rose, he should be very thankful to you, Courtney, and your team of lawyers. I will always keep your business card in my possession. I would like to talk to you about your firm representing me if I ever have need a good lawyer," chuckled Dr. Moore.

"Thank you for all of your help, Dr. Moore." Before hanging up, she said, "Take care of Justin."

La'Roc turned to Jordan and Devon. "That was Dr. Moore." She told the two of them what she had discussed with Dr. Moore concerning Justin's treatment. As they journeyed home, La'Roc gazed out at the star-filled night. Even though she lived in the suburbs, she forgot how awe-inspiring the night sky could be. Remembering something from childhood, she gazed at the stars and made her wish that all would go well for Shawn's release.

Devon looked in the rearview mirror at his grandmother and asked if everything was going to be all right.

"I think so, baby," La'Roc answered.

"Baby girl, are you all right?" Jordan asked with concern.

"I feel much better. It was just so overwhelming leaving Shawn in that place again," La'Roc responded.

Devon said, "Shawn, will be home soon; I promise." Leaning back into the plush leather seat La'Roc dialed Courtney's cell.

Courtney picked up on the first ring. La'Roc briefly explained about the call from Mr. Ross and what had happened to Justin's father. She further explained how Alex was able to make arrangements for Holloway Sr. to give permission for Justin's treatment. Courtney was overwhelmed with the news. La'Roc continued by informing her that Dr. Moore now had her new cell number and should be in contact soon.

"Mom, you're the best. Thank you so much for your help."

"I couldn't do less, Courtney. You're my child, my heart," spoke La'Roc gently. Courtney then suggested that maybe she and Dr. Kim might make an appointment to see Dr. Moore.

"Okay, Mom. I love you." "Love you too, Courtney."

They both hung up their cell phones.

La'Roc decided to call Denise to share the good news with her and Chantal at the same time; however, Chantal was out of town for a seminar, and that left Denise to get the good news first.

Remembering that she was still in the car with Jordan and Devon, she decided she would hold off on the call until she got home. After all, the guys didn't need to be in on this girl-to-girl conversation. Knowing her friend as she did, La'Roc could just imagine the conversation.

"Hi girl. I just want to give you heads-up on the visit with Shawn today. The conference went well. Shawn was thrilled with the information his lawyers presented to him about his upcoming bail hearing next week. He is all ready to come home so he can get into my Victoria's Secret panties." They both would laugh.

"La'Roc, that is wonderful! I know you cannot wait to get that hunk into your arms and, most of all, into your bed," Denise would tease her best friend.

La'Roc chuckled to herself; they could get so raunchy sometimes.

As the ride continued, La'Roc closed her eyes and thought about Courtney and her meeting with Dr. Moore. She was confident that Courtney would be all right.

La'Roc dozed off to sleep. She was awakened by Jordan and Devon.

She heard them joking around with each other. Devon said to Jordan, "Go get Paris and Biscuit; that will wake her up."

La'Roc pretended she was still sleeping when Jordan and Devon returned with her two babies. They eased open the door and sat Paris on one side of her and Biscuit on the other side. Both puppies licked her hands and started to jump around in the Hummer to wake her up.

La'Roc pretended to wake up. "Oh wow! My Babies. Devon, are we home already, and why didn't you guys wake me?"

"Grams, you seemed to be resting, so I did the next best thing—I felt you would love it if your babies woke you," Devon said, smiling.

"Yes, that was a great idea, Mr. Lawyer. Come walk with me; tell me what you learned today during the conference with Shawn." The two of them walked into the house and out onto the terrace, talking about their visit with Shawn.

"Well, Grams, I learned one thing for sure: I really want to be a defense lawyer, just like you, but a better one." He looked at his grandmother with a sly smile.

"That's great, Devon, but what did you learn in the interview that was presented to Shawn about his bail hearing?"

"I enjoyed the way Alex and Jordan put Shawn on a make-believe stand, getting him prepared for the trial. They were really good, and Shawn answered the questions without breaking a sweat. Grams, I'm not a lawyer. However, I do know that Shawn is innocent. I cannot wait to pass my bar exam so my mom and I can work together as partners. Grams," Devon said with excitement, "you are going to be proud of me and my mother. To answer your question, I learned a lot today as a law student—everything I learned today, I'll apply to my work, and I'll always remember this day."

"Sweetheart, I'm already proud of you and your mother. I want you to be happy and proud of yourself.

"Devon, will you please ask Alex and Jordan to come out on the terrace." "No problem, Grams," Devon said and ran upstairs to Jordan's room.

Alex was sitting in the kitchen talking to Ms. Holiday.

"Alex, Grams wants you on the terrace," Devon yelled as he was running upstairs to give Jordan the message.

Jordan walked out on the terrace.

"La'Roc, what's going on?" Jordan asked. "Where are Alex and Devon?"

"We're here," Alex responded, walking onto the terrace.

While everyone was settling on the terrace, La'Roc asked Ms. Holiday to fix drinks for them.

Ms. Holiday left the terrace to mix the drinks. She returned a few minutes later with the drinks, dip, and chips.

"Here are your drinks, Ms. Rose."

"Thanks, Ms. Holiday. Hold all of my calls unless it is an emergency and my family are always an emergency.

"Oh, and please close the terrace door on your way out. Thanks again," La'Roc said. She turned to Alex, Jordan, and Devon.

"I will just jump right into it: We've got a bail hearing this week, on Thursday. I will pay his bail on Thursday, and Wednesday night will be his last day incarcerated. I will confer with Judge Perkins about the court date for next Thursday. Remember, next week we will continue with the trial because Shawn will already be out on bail. This should be easy—we have all the evidence and witnesses to prove he was set up. Shawn is innocent, and he needs to come home. I know you guys can bring him home to his family."

"Grams if the judge said yes, we will have the bail hearing, and then we will have Shawn home by Friday."

"Thanks, all of you, for helping out with this decision to bring Shawn home. I know that you're his lawyers and this is your case, but I needed to butt in, in order to get Shawn home on Friday. I hope you understand. Please forgive me. Please, guys, let's keep this among ourselves," La'Roc said.

La'Roc looked at her team of lawyers with pride flowing throughout her body. The pride she felt most of all was for her grandson, Devon.

"Grandmother, have you heard from my mother and Dr. Kim? What is taking them so long? I am going to call her cell right now," Devon said as he walked into the entertainment room from the terrace.

Devon had been extra worried about his mother since Justin was shot. "Devon, she will be all right. I spoke to her when we were on our way home from seeing Shawn. I relayed news about finding Justin's father. Things should turn around for Justin very soon," La'Roc responded.

"Okay, Grams," he said, looking out at the garden.

La'Roc left the terrace and went upstairs to soak in the Jacuzzi and dream about Shawn making love to her each and every night for the rest of her life.

La'Roc's waiting was about to come to an end. Her baby would be coming home before long, and they would be together forever.

While soaking in her Jacuzzi, she thought about how hurt Shawn would be when he found out that Kelly's son was not his child. He needed to know, and she had to be the one to tell him before his trial. He would also learn about Jordan's illness because it was important for him to know. La'Roc's quiet thoughts were interrupted by a gentle knock on the bathroom door.

"Momma, may I come in?"

"Courtney, yes, come in. What's wrong? Are you okay?"

"I just want to tell you the outcome from the meeting we had with Dr. Moore."

"Courtney, you okay?" "Mother, I am fine."

"Okay, baby, I am all yours."

"Dr. Moore said if Justin's body accepts the medication, he will be fine. However, for the next three to four days, he will be going through some horrible side effects. Dr. Moore also informed Dr. Kim and me that his body may still reject the treatment. After four days, we will know if his body accepted the new medication, and he will be on the road for recovery." Courtney explained the doctor's report to her mother. "Mother, Justin will never walk again; that part of his life will never change."

"I know, baby. It was explained to all of us that Justin will never walk; however, Justin is a lucky man because he has you as a friend. Oh, baby, that is wonderful. I hope the treatment will be what Justin needs. Courtney, it is now time for you to sit back, relax, and wait for the outcome," La'Roc continued, "Courtney, we seem to have good news all around us. I want you to go and rest before dinner. I will tell you all about my visit with Shawn later. Chantal is back in town, so she will be here. Denise, Alex, your grandmother, Casey, and L'Oreal will be joining us. We have a lot to talk about. See you at dinner." Courtney left her mother feeling the best she had felt in a long time. Justin might not have the use of his legs anymore, but he was alive and given a fighting chance to have a good life.

La'Roc walked down the foyer to her office to place a call to Judge Perkins. She dialed the judge's number. The phone rang, and the judge answered on the second ring.

"Hello, Judge Perkins. This is La'Roc Rose. How are you?"

"Hello, Ms. Rose," he said excitedly. "It is a pleasure hearing from you. What can I do for you? I see you have a court date on the twenty-third of this month, which will be next Friday."

"Yes, that is correct. Next Friday it is. Judge Perkins, I would like to bring Shawn home on Thursday. Today is Tuesday, and I was just wondering if we could have the bail hearing this week and the trial next week, as planned. Shawn is innocent."

"Ms. Rose, hold on for a second. I need to check on something. My datebook is open just for you this Thursday."

"Oh! Judge Perkins, you have made my day. I really appreciate this. Please, if there's anything I can do for you, please don't hesitate to ask."

"Ms. Rose, you have helped me so many times. You don't owe me anything, but get your lawyers in here and win your case. That will be my reward," Judge Perkins replied.

"Thank you, Judge. Before you hang up, there is something I need to say to you ..."

"Ms. Rose, there's a lot of things about you. However, what I like most of all is that you put your clients first."

"Yes, my client is always my primary concern. I thank you for your observation. I will forward a copy of Mr. Parker's transcript over to your office this afternoon."

"That will be just fine, Ms. Rose," Judge Perkins replied. They said their goodbyes and hung up.

Judge Perkins was one of the judges who mentored La'Roc when she was interning in the courthouse. She formed a close relationship with him right away because of his kindness and caring for the law and what justice represented.

It was never revealed to her friends or her associates that he mentored her, and it would always remain between the two of them.

La'Roc and Judge Perkins would always have a close relationship. He respected her work as well as her professional methodology.

She would never forget what Judge Perkins had once said: "La'Roc, I've always been proud of you; I like the way you put all of your energy into your cases with such a professional attitude, which is one of the reasons you're a winner." Judge Perkins smiled and winked.

La'Roc thought to herself, *Thank you, God! My baby will be home on Thursday if things go as planned.* At this point, she didn't foresee any problems. She yelled out, *"Shawn, Shawn! You will be coming home to me— Sexiful Rose."*

La'Roc decided to enlighten everyone at dinner with the good news about Shawn being released on Thursday.

She was deep in thought about Shawn's release when the office phone started to ring. She ran to the office from the great room to answer her phone.

On the third ring, she answered, "Hello, this is La'Roc speaking." It was Mr. Alex on the phone. "What a pleasure to hear from you, Mr. Power. I am in a very good mood today, so don't blow it if you want to keep your J-O-B," she said with a smirk.

"What's up, my dear?" La'Roc laughed.

"Oh! Partner, I have some good news for you. Number one, I have a statement from April—signed, sealed, and delivered to my office. A messenger just delivered it," Alex was overjoyed, excitement dancing in his voice.

"Alex, don't shit me. Are you really serious? That is wonderful, Alex! And number two?" La'Roc said, trying to contain her joy. "Good work partner."

"The detective that I assigned to Roger Harris's case, he called me this morning and said he found one of the guys who were involved in Roger's murder."

"Oh my God, this is amazing!" La'Roc exclaimed. She continued, "I also have good news. I have the date for Shawn's bail hearing. The hearing is on Thursday, and next Friday will be the trial, if there is one. Good job, Alex. I will be looking forward to seeing you in Westchester this evening for dinner, and we can share our good news with the rest of the team and family. Alex, please bring all of April's statements with you. We need to get them to Judge Perkins's office this afternoon. So please come over as soon as possible."

Alex lets back to Roger. "Alex was the perpetrator arrested for this alleged crime or was he arrested for just participating in the beating of Roger?" La'Roc asked.

"Yes, he's on lockdown as we speak. I went to the PCT to make sure he was behind bars."

"Thanks, Alex. See you soon," La'Roc replied as she disconnected the call. La'Roc placed calls to all of her friends and family to remind them of the dinner party for that night. Her phone calls ended with, *"Please don't be late!"* La'Roc wandered around the room and then headed for the kitchen office to inform Ms. Holiday that there would be several guest for dinner that evening.

She explained that it was a special event and wanted the meal to reflect it.

La'Roc further informed Ms. Holiday that there would also be a large gathering the following Friday to celebrate Shawn's release. She told the housekeeper to spare no expense for the celebration. "Ms. Holiday, please make sure you include some of Shawn's favorite foods. I'll leave the menu up to you. Just run it by me for a final check, okay?" stated La'Roc as she exited the office.

"I understand, Ms. Rose. I will get on it right away. Everything will be just fine. Don't you worry about anything—you have other things to worry about," Ms. Holiday responded.

La'Roc walked to the terrace window with tears running down her face. *I have waited for so long for this day—wow, the wait is almost over.*

While in her home office, La'Roc contacted her law office and left word for her secretary, Kayla, to contact her. Within a few minutes, she heard her phone ring.

La'Roc picked up the phone from her desk. "Hello, Ms. Kayla. Just to let you know, I need you in court on Thursday with all of the reports from Shawn's case. Alex will be dropping off some documents that we will need you to type and have ready for Thursday. I need you in court at 8:00 a.m. No later than 8:30 a.m. Listen, Kayla, don't leave out anything. When you finish the work, please get it to me by messenger. You keep the originals and messenger me the copies.

Bring the originals with you to court on Thursday morning. This is very important. Thank you, Kayla. If you need help, don't hesitate to ask." Kayla acknowledged the information she had been given and reviewed it for understanding. Then she assured her boss that she understood everything.

La'Roc had been waiting for Shawn for months, and now her wait was coming to an end. On Thursday, Shawn would be facing Judge Galloway for his second bail hearing.

Things looked better for Shawn being awarded bail because the alleged victim, Kelly C. Brown, came out of the coma and was now in a rehabilitation center, recovering from her fall.

Shawn's bail was set for one hundred thousand dollars—not a problem for La'Roc. The check was already made out.

Her cell phone rang, which brought her back to reality. The caller ID let her know it was Alex.

"Hello, Mr. Power. How much money do I owe you for this call?" Alex chuckled.

"I just spoke to one of our detectives: the one I have on Roger's murder case. I found out that the district attorney's office is thinking about closing Roger's case."

La'Roc said, "That will never happen. Who is the district attorney on the case?"

"Just a minute, partner." Alex checked his notes. "I got it. Mr. Gateway." "Thanks, Alex. Have I told you lately how much I appreciate you?"

"Yes, in every paycheck," Alex responded with a hard laugh. "Partner, I almost forgot to inform you about Roger's sexual activities—he was into men as well as women. That was the report I got from the witness on the day he was arrested. The witness said he was never a friend of Roger's. Roger was his brother's lover.

"Alex, what happened to the perpetrator that was arrested for Roger's case?" La'Roc asked.

Alex responded, "The DA informed me that this witness had an air-tight alibi on that night of the incident."

"Alex, we will handle it. Don't worry about it. I will see you tonight for dinner, and I will be deducting your dinner from your paycheck," La'Roc said, joking with Alex. They both laughed. "See you tonight." They both said their goodbyes and hung up their phones.

La'Roc placed a call to Jordan's room to remind him of the dinner party that was planned for that night.

Jordan answered with a sleepy voice. "Hello, baby girl. Are you all right?"

"Hi brother dear, I was the happiest person in the world until I spoke to Alex. Jordan sat up alert, all thoughts of sleep instantly gone. He listened as La'Roc continued. "Jordan, I called you to remind you about dinner tonight. However, Alex just called and told me that the judge was going to release the asshole who was involved in Roger's death today because he has an airtight alibi on the night in question."

"Oh wow! That is not good. Don't worry, baby girl. Everything is going to be just fine. Are you all right?" Jordan asked.

"I am fine," La'Roc lied to her friend.

"Baby girl, I didn't forget. I just needed a little rest. Where are you?"

"I am in my office. Jordan, are you okay?"

"La'Roc, I am on my way downstairs," Jordan said, wheezing as he spoke to her.

"No! Stay upstairs. I am on my way up to you." La'Roc didn't like the way he seemed to be struggling to breathe.

La'Roc closed her cell as she made her way up to see Jordan. On her way, she couldn't help but shout out loud. "That damn! Roger, still fucking with me even in his grave. He just cannot stand to see me and Shawn happy." First thing's first: She needed to take care of Jordan and call her two BFFs. *Oh! What if I have AIDS? That cannot happen. Shawn is coming home soon and I need some validation on my health.* Although, it had been three years since Roger and La'Roc had sex. There was no way she could have contracted the virus. She never had to worry about this type of betrayal.

Don't panic, La'Roc told herself. *Everything is going to be all right once Chantal and Denise get involved.* She would keep her fear of contracting the virus from Jordan. He really didn't need to hear this; he had enough problems of his own. *What am I going to do?*

La'Roc ran upstairs to her friend. She remembered that Jordan had a doctor's appointment earlier today. However, she was so caught up in her own personal thing with Shawn's case. She really had forgotten all about his appointment.

She tapped on Jordan's bedroom door and entered. She heard a voice that didn't sound like her friend. The voice sounded very weak, unlike her smart-mouthed friend.

"Jordan! Baby, talk to me." Jordan was soaked in his own sweat and vomit. He appeared to be nervous, and his facial expression showed fear of what was happening to his body. La'Roc grabbed a pair of gloves from Jordan's nightstand and put on an apron and took charge in helping her friend. La'Roc was terrified of the unknown.

La'Roc reached out to her friend and held him as tight as she could as sweat ran down his face profusely.

Jordan was crying uncontrollably as La'Roc cried with her best friend. Jordan and La'Roc seemed to cry for hours.

She thought, *Oh my God! Is this what I have to look forward to? Oh please, don't let me have the virus. Oh, Shawn. I am so sorry, Shawn; please try and understand, baby. I love you with all my heart. I need you to hold me in your strong arms and tell me you love me more than life itself.* Jordan's voice brought her back to reality.

"Baby girl, this will pass. I should have told you about these episodes. This is the first time this has happened since I've been here. One of the medications I take makes my body feel like it is on fire; that was the pill I just took. Sometimes I become very weak—I gag and throw up all over the place. It is not easy, and for me, this is my life from this day forward. La'Roc, this disease is not to be played with; this is some serious shit," Jordan said weakly as he lay back on his pillow.

"Jordan, we'll deal with this virus. You do believe me, don't you?" La'Roc asked.

"La'Roc, you have my life in your hands. That is how much I trust you and believe in you. You may be Shawn's, La'Roc, but, baby, you are my rock."

She turned to face Jordan and smiled.

"I am sorry you had to see me like that. Sorry for not telling you about the outburst you witnessed earlier. Baby girl, please forgive me," Jordan said as gave her a tight hug. "Baby girl, I am okay now.

"We smell horribly," Jordan teased her as he smiled. La'Roc continued to care for her friend, cleaning him up personally.

La'Roc said, "Jordan, you are forgiven, but don't you ever, as long as you are my best friend, scare me like that again. That was very scary. I was terrified; I didn't have a clue of what to do with you at that moment. The only thing I could do was to hold you in my arms and not let go. I think it would be a good idea for you to type out what I am supposed to look forward to in terms of the reactions from your medications. Baby, I need that typed up like yesterday. I am not going to lose you, Jordan, I promise you that."

Tears ran down her beautiful face. She was shaking as she held her friend in her arms.

Jordan continued to protest La'Roc's help, but the friend would hear nothing from him as she completed her task of cleaning away the remains of sickness. La'Roc turned, questioning Jordan about his strength.

"La'Roc, I am okay. I wouldn't miss this dinner party for the world," Jordan said, smiling.

"Yes, baby girl, I will take a shower and nap before dinner," Jordan assured La'Roc as he made his way to the on-suite bathroom.

La'Roc returned to her room, stripping as soon as she closed the door. Heading toward the shower, she made a mental note to contact her two BFFs. \She has not receiving any answer from either friend, she left both of them a 911 message.

Please call me back right away. It is very important! I need you guys like yesterday!

The echo of Alex's words continued to haunt her. "According to my source on the street, Roger was a male prostitute, and he had contracted AIDS."

La'Roc had asked if his source had any idea of when Roger started selling his assets. Alex answered, "Yes, some years ago."

La'Roc said, "Oh no! This cannot be happening!" She covered her mouth with both hands. "Oh my God what have I done?" She'd been so busy working on Shawn's trial, she forgot about her own health. She hadn't even considered the fact that her health and possibly her life could be in danger.

La'Roc paced back and forth with her hands over her ears as if she could hear Roger saying, "I have my revenge, La'Roc. Now I can rest." No, this couldn't be happening.

During the time she and Roger were together, she never, ever thought Roger was having unprotected sex with other people, especially with men. *Oh my God. What am I going to do? Shawn will be coming home in a couple of days.*

She walked into her room and looked on her bedroom wall. There was a picture of the four of them: Chantal, Denise, Jordan, and herself. She couldn't help crying, seeing Jordan getting weaker right before her eyes. Now, she had to deal with the possibility of being infected with the HIV virus herself thanks to Roger.

Oh well. In a few days, Shawn would be home, and he would be able to help her take care of Jordan. She needed help now with her possible health crisis.

The phone rang. La'Roc answered, "Hello. Hi, Chantal. I see you got my message. I need you to come over right away and bring Denise with you. Please come over as soon as possible."

"I am on my way, sis. What's up?" Chantal asked.

"I will explain when you get here," La'Roc answered.

She decided to call her sister and ask her to come to dinner early. She needed to tell her what was going on.

La'Roc decided not to tell Courtney or Devon.

Hours later, the doorbell distracted her; she heard Denise and Chantal entering the townhouse.

Chantal yelled out, "The cavalry is here." Denise yelled out, "Where are you?"

La'Roc answered, "I am upstairs. Come on up." She thought to herself *that was fast.*

The three gave their group hugs.

"Hi girl what's going on, and what is the emergency?" Denise asked. La'Roc mixed drinks and gave each of them a glass. She sat across from her friends and thought how grateful she was to have them in her life. Quietly, L'Oreal entered the room.

"Hello, people. What the emergency? Shawn is okay, right?" "Shawn is fine. This is about me," La'Roc said.

Chantal looked at Denise and L'Oreal. "What do you mean, about you? What's wrong, La'Roc?" For a moment, La'Roc looked down at her hands. Then she raised her head and looked her close friends and sister in the eye.

La'Roc said, "I just found out that Roger was a male prostitute."

The women looked at her in stunned silence; then Chantal broke the silence. "What can we do?"

Denise couldn't contain her anger. "Dig Roger's ass up and kill him again."

La'Roc leaned her head back on the chaise longue and closed her eyes for a moment. A million and one thoughts raced through her mind at once. Speaking in a soft, controlled voice, she said, "Chantal, use your contacts and reach out to one of your doctor friends. I need to be tested, and I need it done discreetly."

"I'm on it, sis," Chantal answered. "I'll call my friend Dr. Cunningham."

He'll know what to do," Chantal said as she left the room to place the call.

L'Oreal asked, "What can I do, big sis?"

La'Roc rose from the chaise and reached out to her sister and best friend. "You and Denise can give me a hug 'cause I need one right now."

The three of them embraced, giving each other comfort. Chantal returned and confirmed that the doctor could and would conduct the required HIV test for La'Roc at her home.

After the women left, La'Roc went in search for Paris and Biscuit; at this point, she needed a cuddle, and they just fit the bill.

As she cuddled with the dogs, she decided that she would share the information about Jordan and his recent episode.

Sometime later, Chantal told La'Roc to meet her in the conference room next to her office downstairs. As La'Roc entered the room she immediately noticed a strikingly handsome man standing alongside her sister. She noticed his beautiful brown skin and then the thin mustache that rose above his generously shaped lips. His hair was fashioned in short, layered locks. His clothes hung well on his tall, muscular frame. *Beautiful eyes*, La'Roc thought. Even though her heart belonged to Shawn, she could still appreciate a good-looking man.

Chantal smiled, recognizing the look in her friend's eye. "La'Roc, I'd like to introduce you to my friend, Dr. Kevin Cunningham."

Extending his hand, Dr. Cunningham greeted La'Roc. "I've heard a lot of good things about you, Ms. Rose. Chantal speaks very highly of you."

"Yes, she is one of my dearest friends." La'Roc continued, "This is Denise, my other close friend, and my sister, L'Oreal."

"It is a pleasure to meet all of you." He smiled Denise and L'Oreal returned the smile.

After the introductions, La'Roc led the doctor to her private office, where he could conduct his test. Dr. Cunningham questioned her about her sexual activities, and La'Roc went on to explain her concern about the recent news she received about Roger. The doctor made notes and pulled out all the necessary tools he would need to conduct the test. La'Roc informed him that she wasn't fond of being stuck. He assured her that the stick would be as painless as he could make it. He further explained that it would take a few hours before he could get the results of the test. Dr. Cunningham further explained that he was using his private lab to have the test processed; this would also secure her privacy.

A million thoughts were running through La'Roc's mind as the doctor continued drawing blood into the test tubes. She watched her blood flow through the thin plastic tubing. She thought about how her life could change if the test proved to be positive. La'Roc told her inner self to be strong and that things were going to turn out okay; they just had to. She and Shawn had plans, and they were going to fulfill them. They had gone through so much to not have a happy life. Having AIDS was just not in her plans. After the doctor concluded his test, he told La'Roc that he was taking the samples directly to his lab and had to decline her invitation for dinner. As Chantal escorted Dr. Cunningham to the front door, La'Roc observed them and wondered if they could become a couple. She liked the good doctor.

This should have been the happiest time of her life, but after Jordan's episode, she was very sad. She began to realize that she had been neglecting her friends, family, even her babies, because of Shawn's trial. But tonight, La'Roc felt that this dinner party would bring the family and friend back to where they were before Shawn was arrested.

She walked upstairs to her bedroom. She fell across her bed.

La'Roc hadn't told Shawn about Jordan's health issues. She felt that it would be better to wait and tell him when he got home. Shawn had enough to deal with right now.

She said out loud, "Shawn will understand because he loves me, and he likes Jordan." La'Roc cried until her eyes were swollen and red.

She went into her bathroom, washed her face, changed her outfit, and ran down to play with Paris and Biscuit. Playing with them always made her feel extremely great.

La'Roc checked with Ms. Holiday about dinner again and made a few reminder calls concerning the dinner party for that evening.

Courtney came into La'Roc's office. "Mother, are you all right? Your eyes are swollen. What's wrong?"

"Baby, I am okay, crying happy tears. I am happy because I have my family and friends, and soon Shawn will be home with all of us."

"Okay. You sure you're okay?" Courtney asked with a sideways glance at her mother.

"Yes, baby. I'm fine," responded La'Roc.

Courtney looked at her mother. "Mother dear, did Devon tell you that he was bringing a friend home for dinner tonight?"

La'Roc paused as she was arranging a vase of flowers on the hallway table. "No, this is all news to me. Is there something you want to tell me about this friend?" she asked with a slow chuckle.

"Oh, it's nothing really. Just a girl he met at school. Not sure if she's a girlfriend, but who knows," Courtney responded with a wink.

La'Roc continued to ponder the idea of her grandson having a girlfriend. She had to remind herself that after all the boy, was grown. Imagine that. Courtney informed her mother that she and Dr. Kim would be visiting Justin the following day. La'Roc then enlightened Courtney about Jordan's current health issue.

Mother and daughter continued to chat as they sat in the great room. La'Roc eventually got around to the thing that had been playing in her mind "So, what did you think of Dr. Cunningham, sweetheart?"

La'Roc asked. Courtney gave her mother a sidelong glance, knowing that this question wasn't just out of the blue. "He seems to have his head on straight." Taking a deep breath, she continued, "He asked me out on a date."

"Is that something you want to do right now?" inquired La'Roc. "Yes, I think so. I want to run it by Devon first," replied Courtney.

They both busted out in a loud laugh. "Good luck with that one," La'Roc said.

Before going upstairs, La'Roc went into the entertainment room to mix herself a drink.

La'Roc was so excited about the dinner that night; she couldn't wait to give the group the wonderful news about Shawn's homecoming and to tell them his trial would be coming up the following week. She thought to herself, *I won't let anything happen to sabotage my plans to get Shawn home. Today is Tuesday, and Thursday I'll be in my future husband's arms, making love throughout the day. Just about forty-eight more hours and Shawn will be walking through my door. He's going to love the big house.* She said out loud, "I'll give Shawn the privilege of taking a part in the naming of the house in Westchester. Shawn will love that; naming the house will make him feel like he's a part of Jordan's gift."

After a brief nap, La'Roc assessed her plans for the dinner party. This was going to be a pre-celebration of Shawn's release.

She asked them to meet her in the great room.

La'Roc explained to them what she had witnessed when she went into Jordan's room.

L'Oreal said, "That must have been terrifying for you."

"Yes, I was really afraid for Jordan. I thought he was dying," La'Roc responded. "I thought I wanted to talk about Jordan and what I witnessed, but I just cannot speak about it in full detail right now; it was very painful. So, L'Oreal, let's talk about the foundation," La'Roc stated.

Jordan walked toward the great room, looking well and rested. He looked like he had when he was in college. He was still a handsome man.

Jordan tapped on the door; La'Roc said, "Come in, the love of my life."

He walked in. Denise, Chantal, and L'Oreal greeted him as he entered the great room, giving him a heartfelt hug. His facial expression showed he was happy to see his friends.

He joined in on the conversation about the Jordan Foundation. He was amazed at the amount of progress that had been made in such a short period of time.

"Okay, we've finished talking about the foundation. Let's get ready for this big dinner party."

Courtney yelled out to the group, "Devon went to pick up his girlfriend. I told him to call when he is on his way back."

L'Oreal said, "What! Devon has a girlfriend?"

La'Roc said, "This is something new, honey. I just found out today. We'll meet her tonight, together, sis. She is a lucky female to be dating my grandson." She flashed a brilliant smile.

Behind that smile, La'Roc could still hear Alex's voice echoing in her brain, "Roger died of AIDS." *That bastard,* she thought. How could he be so cruel to do this to her? So much for Roger's love. Yeah right! This had to be the most horrible news a person could receive. La'Roc knew she had to keep her face neutral because her family and friends would read her and gather something was wrong. She knew she could trust Alex, Denise, L'Oreal, and Chantal with her secret.

I need a stiff drink, La'Roc thought to herself to calm her nerves.

Enough of Roger's disgrace and humiliation; it was time for her to go on with her life.

La'Roc went into the kitchen to check on the progress of the meal. She knew she could trust Ms. Cotton and Ms. Holiday to pull out all the stops.

Ms. Holiday and Ms. Cotton had hired additional staff to help with the serving tonight.

"Ms. Cotton and Ms. Holiday, you have outdone yourselves with all of this food. Who are we inviting, the army?" La'Roc laughed out loud.

Ms. Holiday responded, "Yes, we want everything to be nice for you and your guests. I like cooking for you, Ms. Rose."

"I feel the same as Ms. Holiday," Ms. Cotton responded.

"Oh! Ms. Holiday, I forgot to tell you, Dr. Cunningham will be dining with the team tonight as Courtney's guest. Sorry I didn't tell you about Dr. Cunningham earlier. Thank you. Also, I would like for you and Ms. Holiday to join us for dinner."

"We would love to join you and your family for dinner," Ms. Holiday responded.

Ms. Cotton said, "Thank you, Ms. Rose."

By six o'clock, all the guests had arrived. They all were served hors d'oeuvres and drinks. La'Roc loved having large dinner parties. She loved entertaining and did it quite often.

As the guests gathered downstairs, La'Roc entered the great room, escorted by Jordan. This evening, La'Roc chose to wear her barley there long-sleeve blouse with flowing navy-blue silk skirt. The overhead light bounced off the large diamond engagement ring that graced her left hand.

Alex escorted La'Roc's mother to the great room as well.

The dining room was especially beautiful. Large bowls of flowers filled the room with a heady perfume that reminded one of being in a garden during a spring rain. The food was plentiful and fantastic. All of the guests applauded the cooks for a wonderful meal.

The guests retired to the entertainment room for coffee and desserts.

La'Roc realized that the events of the past several days had finally caught up with her, and she felt exhausted. She said her goodbyes to her guests and reminded Mr. Sanchez to deliver the leftover food to the local soup kitchen at the Brown Street Baptist church.

Now, she thought, it was time for her to give the good news to the team. La'Roc's cell phone began to ring. She answered, "Hello. Judge Perkins. How're you feeling these days?"

"I am doing just great. It is lovely to hear your voice, Ms. Rose. I miss you coming in and out of court every day. But what I called you about—first, I would like to apologize for not attending your dinner party tonight. Please forgive me."

"You're forgiven, Judge Perkins," La'Roc responded.

"Just to let you know, Ms. Rose, I read your report, and I cannot anticipate any problems with Mr. Parker going home with his family on the day in question," Judge Perkins said.

"Oh, Judge Perkins, you have made my day. I don't know how to thank you."

"I am just doing my job, Ms. Rose."

La'Roc could hear Judge Perkins laughing over the phone.

La'Roc was overjoyed with the phone conversation that she just received from Judge Perkins.

Oh, Shawn, you're on your way home, baby. In a few more nights, you will be in my arms. When La'Roc finished her call with Judge Perkins, she joined the team in the dayroom.

La'Roc's team was sitting in the dayroom, talking to Devon's girlfriend. "First of all, Grams, I want to apologize for being late for dinner. The traffic was crazy out there.

"Grams, I had a good time. I enjoyed meeting Judge Peterson. It was exciting meeting a State Supreme Court justice. He told me that I might consider clerking for him."

"That is wonderful, Devon."

La'Roc responded, "Devon, why don't you set August up with a movie while we're in the office."

"No problem, Gram. Come, August, let me show you this cool set up." Devon smiled as he led his girlfriend to the home theater.

The team members followed La'Roc as she entered the conference room. When Devon joined them a short time later, La'Roc made her announcement.

"Well, folks, we got our date for Shawn's hearing. Judge Perkins called and stated that everything looked in order for our defense," she proudly announced.

Courtney asked, "Mom does that mean Shawn will be home tomorrow?" La'Roc yelled out, "Yes, that is what that means!"

The whole team ran over to hug La'Roc. Everybody in the room was crying happy tears for her.

La'Roc's mother and August ran into the office to check out the noise. "What is going on?" La'Roc's mother demanded to know as August looked on in fear.

"Devon, take August out and assure her that everything is all right and explain to her your family is not crazy. Tell her we just received some good news, and we all are happy about it," La'Roc instructed.

L'Oreal was hugging her mother. "Mom, everything is all right. Shawn is coming home tomorrow."

La'Roc's mother walked over and hugged her daughter. "Baby, I am so happy for you."

Devon entered the room. "Wow! Shawn is coming home. What time should we pick him up?"

"Little man, Shawn won't be allowed to ride with you; an officer will transport him to the city," La'Roc responded.

"We'll all be there at 10:00 a.m. The hearing is at 10:30. Alex, you need to take Shawn his gray suit and gray shoes, and Devon will pick out a shirt and a tie for him to wear."

Devon yelled to Alex, "I'll ride with you tomorrow to take Shawn his clothes. I want to see his face when we break the good news to him."

"That will be fantastic," Alex said. "I need your input, little lawyer."

Devon smiled. "Wow! you want my input?"

Courtney said, "What are we going to do about the welcome home party for Shawn?"

Denise said, "We will get started on the party right away."

"I have an appointment first thing in the morning. I will be free around noon. I will meet you here at the townhouse," Chantal responded.

"You guys are aware that the party will be at Mother's new house, right?" Courtney asked, sitting on her Mother's desk with her hands beneath her chin.

Denise spoke up. "I'll get the DJ, and we'll get together and draw up a plan on how we will set up and figure out what part of the house we'll be using, etc." "Sounds like a plan, Denise. However, Wednesday and Thursday we can do all the decorations. This party is going to be the best ever," Courtney said with that silly little laugh she always had when she was happy.

La'Roc said, "The party is next Friday, not this Friday, fools. Shawn and I will be staying in the Bronx until Sunday. Next Thursday is Shawn's pretrial date. After the trial, we will go to the townhouse and stay there for the night. You guys have a week to get the party in order.

"Denise, please ask Ms. Holiday to come into my office," asked La'Roc. When the housekeeper found La'Roc, she was advised to make sure the house in the Bronx was prepared for a special event. La'Roc also told Ms. Holiday to have Mr. Sanchez secure a driver for Courtney and Dr. Kim.

Courtney stopped by her mother's office and observed her sitting with her hands over her eyes. She thought her mother looked tired. She was always amazed how La'Roc was able to keep going in spite of the heavy burdens she carried with regard to her family and friends. Courtney often wondered if she would ever be able to match her mother. Then she shook her head and decided her mother was something else.

"Mother, are you all right?" Courtney asked as her mother leaned forward.

"Yes, dear, I'm fine. I was wondering what happened to Dr. Kim. She missed dinner tonight."

"Oh snap, I forgot to tell you she had to fly out to L.A," Courtney replied, looking a little guilty. "She stated she was going to take the red eye back tomorrow," continued Courtney.

"Will you be working on the party list tonight?" asked La'Roc. "Don't forget to invite Dr. Cunningham and Dr. Moore."

"Of course, I invited Dr. Cunningham." Courtney smiled as she was walking toward the door. Before leaving, she turned and looked back at her mother. "They are already on the list." She opened the door and walked out into the foyer, smiling from ear to ear.

Geneva walked into La'Roc's office. "Baby, I love you, and remember what I said to you the day Shawn was arrested. I said you would work it out and you would get him out if he were innocent. Baby, you believed in yourself, and you believed in Shawn. La'Roc, Shawn is not a killer—if he was, you wouldn't be with him. Remember, you're a damn good person and a fantastic lawyer." Tears began to form in La'Roc's eyes. "If only your father were here, he would be so proud of you."

"Yes Mom. I know he would be proud of my success. And yes, Mother, I do remember that conversation very well. I am so happy tonight, Mother. Shawn will be home tomorrow. *Oh Mother, what a feeling! I am so happy!*" La'Roc said to her mother. She had tears of joy trailing down her face as she kissed her mother good night.

"Good night, Mother dear," La'Roc said. "Good night, baby," Geneva responded.

La'Roc closed her office door, walked over to the window, and looked out at the view. *Tomorrow, Shawn and I will be looking out at the view together.*

It had been a long four months since Shawn held her in his big, strong arms. She needed to hear him say, "Sexiful, please come into my arms and lay your head on my chest."

Oh, dear God, thank you for giving me the strength and the power to keep my sanity for the past several months; it seemed like years. I also thank you for the negative HIV test. I am free of the virus, and that gives me the freedom to love Shawn in any way, at any time I want to, without worrying about giving him the virus.

Not for the first time, she prayed that the HIV test turned up negative. La'Roc was pretty sure the test would be negative. She hadn't shown any sign of the symptoms; however, she wanted to be absolutely sure, hence the test. Dr. Cunningham promised he'd have the results in a couple of days.

La'Roc promised herself that she would tell Shawn about the test and why she had to take it. This was going to be a private matter between her and Shawn.

She thought Shawn would understand about her scare after finding out that Roger had been a male prostitute.

Oh well, tomorrow isn't coming fast enough; well, Vibrator, back in your box.

La'Roc though out loud, "I don't need you anymore Mr. Vibrator, my little Rabbit. I have a human vibrator coming into town tomorrow. He will take care of all of my sexual needs."

She closed her eyes with a big sigh!

La'Roc quickly filled her deep soaking tub with her favorite scent and stepped into the swirling bubbles. She leaned her head back as the soft, smooth jazz saxophone of Marion Meadows filled the room. She thought about her loving family and loyal friends, but most of all, she thought about her man, Shawn.

Shortly after finishing her bath, La'Roc heard the two puppies outside her bedroom door. When she opened it, not only were Biscuit and Paris there, but Jordan as well. The two of them played with the dogs for a while and then returned them to their own room.

La'Roc reminded Jordan that she wanted the list of the medications he was taking.

"La'Roc, what time are we due in court?" Jordan inquired.

"We're due at 10:00 a.m. The procedure starts at 10:30," La'Roc responded as she headed back toward her room.

"This will be a surprise for Shawn as well. He doesn't know that he is coming home tomorrow. He just thinks he is going to court to get his bail lowered."

"That will be some surprise," chuckled Jordan. "Jordan, where is Devon?"

"He drove August home. I think she'll be good for him. We had a long talk tonight. He seems to like her very much. He was concerned if you and Courtney would like her. I think she's nice. I spoke to her too; she gave the appropriate answer when she was being interrogated by Mr. Diaz." Jordan smiled.

"Jordan, I hope you didn't run the poor girl away," laughed La'Roc.

"Devon seems to be serious about this one," La'Roc responded.

"La'Roc, don't give him a hard time about this," Jordan said.

"I will never give Devon a hard time. I love him too much to give him a hard time. I just need Devon to stay focused on his education," La'Roc answered.

As Jordan and La'Roc continued their discussion of Devon's love life, the person in question called his grandmother to alert her about the fact that he was home. Devon also wanted to confirm their departure time for tomorrow.

After concluding their conversation, La'Roc said her goodnights to Jordan as well.

Just as La'Roc was settling into her bed, she heard a knock on the bedroom door. The door cracked open, and Courtney poked her head in, looking around the room for her mother. La'Roc signaled her to join her on the large king-size bed. They talked about Shawn's anticipated arrival and the surprise homecoming party. Finally, the subject of Devon's girlfriend, August, arose.

"So, Momma, what do you think about August?" asked Courtney.

"Don't worry about what I think. What do you think about her?" In true lawyer fashion, La'Roc had turned the question to her daughter.

"I like her. I think they'll be okay," replied Courtney.

"Mother, I just wanted you to know we're not going to visit Justin tomorrow. I am going to court to support Shawn. I talked to Dr. Kim, and she thinks it's a good idea to wait until after Shawn's hearing tomorrow. We'll visit Justin another day. Maybe I will go on Sunday."

"Oh, is that something you want to do?" La'Roc asked.

"Yes. I just want to see Shawn's face when he becomes a free man. It has been four months since I looked into Shawn's face. That reunion is going to be off the hook. Oh, Mom. He has to be surprised. He has no idea he is coming home tomorrow. He is going to be blown away," Courtney said excitedly.

"Mom, aren't you excited about Shawn's homecoming?"

"Yes, baby. I am very excited." Mother and daughter talked awhile longer about Justine, Devon, and Shawn's release and party. Finally, Courtney kissed her mother goodnight and returned to her room.

La'Roc shut off the lights and dozed off to sleep.

She was amazed when she did not fall asleep right away. She thought maybe she was overly anxious because of Shawn's release.

She finally dozed off to sleep and was awakened by Devon kissing her. "Good morning, Gram. I am on my way to meet up with Alex, and we'll be on our way to take Shawn his clothing. We'll see you at the courthouse at ten fifteen. Alex has all the paperwork for Shawn's release."

"No, baby, he has to be escorted by the officers from the prison to the courthouse for his hearing. Your mother decided to ride with me and Jordan to the hearing. We'll see you there. Please, Devon, do not tell Shawn that he will be coming home after the process of the hearing. He will know he is going home in time."

"Okay Grams, I am out of here; I will see you in court," Devon said as he was walking out the door with his black briefcase. "Tell my mother I love her. I really don't want to wake her."

"I will deliver the message, little man. I promise. By the way, little man, you look too handsome to be a student lawyer," La'Roc responded proudly.

La'Roc made her way to the bathroom for her morning routine. When finished, she walked downstairs to the spacious kitchen. Opening the refrigerator, she poured herself a glass of orange juice. Sitting at the kitchen island, she went over the schedule with Ms. Holiday.

After their conversation, La'Roc spent thirty minutes in the gym, exercising and burning off excited energy.

When leaving the gym, she encountered Jordan in the hall.

Observing La'Roc walking toward him, Jordan spoke. "Shawn is a lucky man."

She picked up her babies and kissed them both. "Daddy is coming home."

"La'Roc you have that little glow about you that says, 'I'm in love.'" "I'm happy, Jordan."

Jordan hesitated before asking her about Shawn's supposed son. "La'Roc, when are you telling Shawn about his so-called son?"

"Well, that is one of the reasons we'll be staying in the Bronx at the co-op for the next few days. I want to tell him in private. I have to tell him before the trial next week. I want him to be prepared for what he's going to hear."

"Okay, baby, no time for chatting. We have to get ready to leave. Devon has left already. He woke me up very early this morning. It is now eight thirty. We need to be there at ten. I'll be sitting in the back of the courtroom until almost the end of the hearing," stated La'Roc as she continued to her room to shower and change.

La'Roc placed her light-gray two-piece suit and yellow blouse with gray stripes on her bed, and placed her gray five-inch heels on her shoe stand. Her accessories matched her gray shoes and her gray Chanel bag.

La'Roc's cell phone started to ring. She looked at her caller ID and saw it was Alex.

"Hello, partner. I have someone here in a gray suit and looking good, I must add."

"Alex, if you don't put my baby on the phone, I will have to discharge you." They both laughed. Shawn's smooth, sexy voice soon caressed her ear.

"Hi, Sexiful I will see you in court, right?"

"I know what the judge is going to say already. I just want to hold you in my arms and never let you go," Shawn said.

"Baby, I want that too and don't be so negative. I'll be in your arms before you know it, I promise," La'Roc said.

La'Roc pulled the phone away from her ear with tears of joy rolling down her face.

"Hello, hello? Baby, are you there?"

"Yes, baby. I'm here."

"I love you, baby. I'll see you in court. The officers are ready to drive me to Manhattan. Baby, they told me to bring all of my belongings. What's that about?"

"Don't worry, baby. I asked Alex to bring your things today so I can take them home with me."

Well, she had to tell him something when he asked about his belongings. "Okay, I'll see you soon," Shawn said.

"See you in court."

A secret smile drifted across La'Roc's face as she thought of her plan to drive Shawn back to Upland Correction Facility to pick up some of his forgotten belongings. Oh, there was still going to be a surprise party for Shawn; however, she wanted her man first. So she decided to be Shawn's chauffeur and not drive to Upland but to drive him to a romantic spot in the woods to have a rumble in the back seat with her man.

La'Roc, Courtney, and Jordan left for court. The traffic was flowing, and La'Roc stepped on the gas, moving with the swift traffic. She reached over and turned on the sound of Shawn's favorite song, "Send for Me," by Atlantic Starr.

Entering the courtroom, La'Roc saw that the team was gathered around the defense table. She knew Shawn was in the holding cell, so she flashed her ID so that the officer would let her see him.

La'Roc looked at Shawn, and he looked handsome as ever. He was wearing his gray suit, a yellow shirt with gray stripes, gray shoes, and a gray necktie to match.

She couldn't wait for Shawn to be released. She was so damn horny for his lovemaking.

When Shawn walked out of that holding cell, she looked at him as if it were her first time meeting him. She noticed that he had gained a little weight; he was toned as a motherfucker.

She couldn't see the weight gain during her visit in the holding cell; but looking at him now, the only thing she could say was, "Wow! What a hunk, and he's all mine." As La'Roc approached the cell, Shawn rose and looked at the love of his life. As far as he was concerned, there was no finer woman than his Sexiful Rose. They talked quietly for a few minutes in the language that lovers understood.

Shortly, they were told that it was time to go into the courtroom. The hearing had begun.

The judge walked from his chambers, and the bailiff said, "Please rise. The Honorable Judge Perkins presiding."

After the judge was seated, the bailiff said, "Please be seated."

"Judge, we have docket number 554432, Mr. Shawn Parker. Here in court today to represent Mr. Parker is—his lawyers, Mr. Alex Power and Mr. Jordan Diaz."

Jordan rose from his seat and began his opening statement. Then he turned the case over to Alex. Alex continued and asked for Shawn to be released on bail.

DA Hernandez argued that Shawn was a flight risk and he should remain in Upland State Prison until his trial. The DA and Alex argued back and forth about all of Shawn's assets, property, homes, land, and bank accounts.

DA Hernandez continued to argue that Shawn was a fight risk because he had the assets to leave town and live wherever he wanted to live.

The judge denied the DA's request and posted bail for fifty thousand dollars. During the hearing, La'Roc sat in the back of the courtroom, watching the team work the DA just like she taught them to do.

Courtney came in and whispered in her ear that everything was ready. "Mr. Sanchez will be waiting at the secluded area that we talked about." Mr. Sanchez left the limousine at the courthouse for La'Roc, and another driver drove him to the secluded drop-off to wait for the lovers.

Shawn's bail was reduced from a hundred thousand to fifty thousand dollars. Alex left the courtroom to do the paperwork and to post bail.

La'Roc watched as Jordan and Devon gathered their notes and spoke quietly to Shawn. She was so proud of her team, especially Devon; one day he would be arguing his first case, and she was sure he would be terrific.

La'Roc looked over at her daughter and smiled.

Her daughter was crying; Denise and Chantal's eyes were teary. They all cried because Devon had become a man right in front of their eyes.

La'Roc walked up to the front of the courtroom and congratulated the team on the fantastic job they had just completed.

She then turned to Shawn and gave him a gentle kiss. Even though it was the first time in four months that they were free to express themselves, they kept it PG-13.

"Oh my dear Shawn, I will see you at Upland," she said. "Mr. Sanchez will drive me to Upland. I will be right behind you and the officer." La'Roc's phone started to rang.

"Hello, Ms. Rose, is everything okay?"

"Yes, Judge Perkins. We're fine. Thank you," La'Roc responded. That call was another part of the plan.

"Shawn that was Judge Perkins, he said you could ride in the limo; the flipside is, I cannot ride with you. I have to meet you at the prison." She kissed Shawn and walked away to get dressed for his surprise.

La'Roc smiled and walked out of the courtroom with tears of joy running down her face.

La'Roc decided to have Shawn driven away from the courthouse in her white limo with a red rose drawn on the back door on the passenger side.

There would also be a red rose placed on the backseat of the limo. As Shawn opened the car door, his favorite music would start to play.

Part of La'Roc's plan was to disguise herself as the chauffeur. She planned to have the privacy panel so that Shawn wouldn't clearly see who she was. She fought hard to control her giggle because she knew beneath her uniform she was wearing a lacy black thong and matching black lace bra.

La'Roc met the girls at the door of the courtroom and grabbed her uniform and ran out the door to her limo.

Shawn asked, "Devon, where is your grandmother?"

Devon responded, "She left; she will be at Upland when you get there. Shawn, you know how my grandmother drives."

Shawn opened the door; he saw the red rose. "Devon, I see a gift from your grandmother. She has been in the limo; I can smell her. Oh, man. Hurry and get me out of here so I can see my baby. Guys, I'll see you at the facility." Shawn and his lawyer's bumped shoulders; then Shawn stepped into the limo and stretched his long legs across the seat. One of their favorite songs started to play: "I Will Love You Forever" by Johnny Gateway.

A recording came over the microphone. "Ms. Rose wanted me to remind you that you are free to mix yourself a drink; the bar is stocked with your favorites." That should have been a clue that he was not going back to prison.

The microphone turned off. "Thank you," Shawn responded.

La'Roc could not wait to feel Shawn's arms around her body.

La'Roc was almost at her destination. She pulled off the highway into a deserted area where Mr. Sanchez would take over in the next hour.

This was where the party started.

La'Roc exited the driver's seat and opened the back door on the driver side. Her uniform was still intact. After opening the limo door, she pushed the button for the microphone to automatically come on and speak in Mr. Sanchez's voice. It was a tape recorder with Mr. Sanchez's voice recorded. "Mr. Parker, you may get out and stretch your legs if you like."

"Thanks," Shawn responded.

La'Roc was standing in front of the limo with her back turned, opposite from Shawn. Her chauffeur hat and fitted jacket were still in place.

Before she turned to Shawn, she hit the recorder button that was in her pocket. Mr. Sanchez's voice. "Mr. Parker, are you ready to leave? I have to get you back to the facility on time. If not, Ms. Rose will have my head. We really don't want that to happen, do we?"

Shawn entered the backseat of the limo; La'Roc followed with a red rose in her right hand.

Shawn was getting in the limo headfirst. That was just what she wanted. That gave her a chance to be standing by the open door when he turned around to sit down in his seat. La'Roc was standing with a red rose in her right hand and a glass of champagne in her left hand.

Shawn looked as if he was having a heart attack.

She gave him the red rose and the glass of champagne. She put her hands up so he could hold her in his arms to kiss her. Shawn placed his glass of champagne on the bar and pulled her into his arms and kissed her very aggressively.

"Oh no Sexiful, Oh, my baby is here," Shawn said with tears in his eyes. "Sexiful, I love you so much. I just wanted hold you and never let you go," Shawn said through his tears of excitement "Shawn, sweetheart, you don't have to leave me. You're coming home with me today."

"Baby, don't play. I'm going home with you today? Are you sure?"

"Baby, what can I say? You had the best team of lawyers working on your case," La'Roc answered with tears rolling down her face as Shawn tried to kiss her tears away.

They celebrated by holding each other, kissing, and crying as he fed her hors d'oeuvres and sipped on champagne.

They were acting like two teenagers on their first date in the back seat of a car, making out.

La'Roc pulled her jacket off, and that was when he realized that she was almost nude. "Wow! Baby look at you. And this is all mines?"

She put the chauffeur's jacket and cap back on and turned to Shawn with her hands on her hips. She asked him, "How did you like La'Roc driving you around today as your chauffeur?"

"What happened to Mr. Sanchez?" Shawn asked. "I'm your Mr. Sanchez, baby," La'Roc responded.

Shawn said with surprise, "No shit." Laughing La'Roc ordered Mr. Sanchez to drive them to the Bronx.

Shawn looked at her. "I thought something was wrong when you didn't get into the limo with me." Mr. Sanchez glided the limo back onto the highway.

They kissed and made love all the way from Westchester County to the co-op in the Bronx. He was such a good lover; his lovemaking made her feel intoxicated.

She had waited four months for this man to rotate his penis inside her private box.

She wanted him, and he wanted her just as bad.

La'Roc knew she had to keep the moaning down, although the limo was soundproof. Shawn and La'Roc were making love like wild animals.

Their lovemaking in the limo was X-rated. However, once Shawn and La'Roc reached their destination, their lovemaking would be beautiful, sweet, and more romantic. The animal lovemaking was lust, and it was out of pure longing for each other.

Continuing their ride to the Bronx, La'Roc had been stripped of her clothing that she was wearing, which was nothing but a black bra, stockings, five-inch heels, and a black thong.

Shawn loved every inch of the way she was dressed. He put his tongue into her mouth and proceeded to kiss her down her neck. He ran his tongue around her throat and the back of her neck, which made her scream out his name with love and passion.

He took his two fingers and inserted them inside of her vagina as she moaned with pleasure.

He then placed his gigantic penis in her vagina as he rotated very slowly around in and out. As he worked his magic, he whispered into her ear, "Daddy will be gentle, I promise you. I will not hurt you. Just let me give you what I have been saving for the past four months. Sexiful, please open up your legs and let daddy slide it into you deeper."

She opened up her legs as wide as she could; she was moaning and groaning for Shawn's penis.

"Shawn, please take control of my body and give me everything you have. I want all of you inside of me."

Shawn pulled his penis out of her vagina as he began kissing her all over her body, from head to toe. "If you know what I mean?" His lovemaking was magic. He made his tongue became his penis as he poked his tongue in and out of her inner box between her legs.

La'Roc yelled out, "If I am dreaming, please don't wake me!"

Shawn and La'Roc were screaming each other's names with pure pleasure and enjoyment.

After that round of beautiful lovemaking, Shawn kissed her and held her in his arms. "Baby, I love you. Let's get married right away," Shawn said.

"Baby, we will get married as soon as we get you free, which will be very soon. Oh, by the way, we have a trial date on the calendar for next Friday. That was your other surprise. Now you know. And by the way, I love you too." They talked a few more minutes before Shawn fell asleep.

It had been four months since that terrible incident happened to Kelly Carlota Brown, and that was the last time Shawn and La'Roc slept together.

Oh, how she had missed him. She missed him holding her in his muscular, strong arms and the sweet way he kissed her entire body. The way he made love to her body was a crime. Shawn should have been arrested for making love and not for allegedly pushing Kelly down three floors in his building complex. Shawn was in prison for four months; now he was back, and La'Roc was back in his arms where she belonged. The last four months without Shawn had been hell. She was dealing with the fear of having contracting AIDS from Roger, Jordan's health crisis, and the big deal of today was to tell Shawn that Shawn Jr. was not his son.

During the investigation, the DNA test proved that Shawn Jr. was Mr. Johnston's son and not Shawn's child.

Mr. Johnston was ordered by the court to do a DNA test for both Shawn Jr. and the fetus that Ms. Kelly Brown was carrying on the day of her accident.

Both tests came back positive, which proved that Mr. Johnston was the father of Shawn Jr. and the unborn child.

If the DNA could not prove that Mr. Johnston was not the father, Mr. Johnston admitted that he was the father. La'Roc thought to herself, *my team is always on point.*

Now La'Roc had the privilege of telling Shawn the ugly truth that this boy was not his child.

Shawn is going to be devastated when he hears the horrible news about him not being a father, and if he marries me, he may not ever be a father.

She exclaimed, "Oh my God!" She could never have a child for Shawn.

She was thinking of ways to tell Shawn about his so-called son; how would she do that? Just tell him point-blank and get it over with; that is what La'Roc would do.

Being subtle was not La'Roc's style. La'Roc was very outspoken; she would tell Shawn her way: very bluntly. Sexiful was subtle; La'Roc was straightforward, and she pulled no punches when it came to business, family, her man, and her friends.

La'Roc dozed off in Shawn's arms. After that lovemaking and the champagne, she was exhausted. It had been so long since she felt so good. It was like having Courtney and passing the bar exam. They were the happiest days of her life. Lying there in Shawn's arms was like those two days all in one. La'Roc was on cloud nine. *My dear Father above, if I am asleep, please do not wake me.*

She took one more look at Shawn and then kissed him before falling to sleep. She knew that they would be arriving at the co-op soon, and she would be all alone with her man one more time. Three days in bed with Shawn. *Wow!*

She decided not to tell Shawn about Jordan until they get to Westchester on Sunday.

She needed to find a way to reward the team for a wonderful job they did during the bail hearing.

She snuggled in Shawn's arms and fell asleep.

La'Roc was awakened by Shawn kissing her. "Wake up, Sexiful. We're in the Bronx. It is time for you to wake up. Come on; let's go inside."

She heard him tell the driver that he could leave.

He wrapped her in his jacket and lifted her from her seat; he carried her into the co-op and took her into the bedroom, where they first met three years ago.

She pulled him down on the bed and kissed him hard on his beautiful lips. "Baby, is this for real?" she asked.

"I can't believe that I'm home with my Sexiful. Pinch me, baby, and make sure that I'm alive. This is unbelievable. I am home!" He yelled out, "Home!"

Ms. Cotton heard the rumble coming from La'Roc's bedroom. She knocked on the door to see if there was a problem. La'Roc assured her that it was just Shawn celebrating being home.

Shawn came to the door, wrapped his arms around La'Roc, pressed a kiss to her forehead, and reassured the housekeeper that he was fine and just extremely happy to be home. Ms. Cotton smiled and left the two lovers.

"Sexiful, you know what I missed besides you?" Shawn asked. "What is that, baby?"

"We making love to you in the Jacuzzi."

"Baby, you can make love to me all over this co-op: in the Jacuzzi, the whirlpool, and give me a bubble bath in the hot tub. We will do all of these things together for the rest of our lives," La'Roc answered with a playful grin.

"Shawn, you know what I missed most of all besides you?"

He asked, "What was that, Sexiful?"

She said, "That no one called me Sexiful." "Baby, you know why?" She answered, "No!

"Baby because you're my Sexiful, and no one else's." La'Roc smiled at Shawn's remark.

Shawn was checking out the different rooms he wanted to make love in on his first night home.

La'Roc had five bedrooms in her co-op: a great room, living room, den, entertainment room, and her gym. Shawn wanted to make love in each room. Including the whirlpool and the Jacuzzi.

"Shawn, baby, I need you and a drink in your hand. I am burning up for your steaming-hot lovemaking."

When Shawn walked into the bedroom, he was nude, and to his surprise, she was also nude and lying across the big, round, king-size bed waiting for him to make love to her.

He said, "Wow! Please don't move, Sexiful. Stay right there. Oh, baby, I want you to lie just like you are. I am going to make love to you all night in between snacks etc. I love to eat my snacks out of your platter, if you know what I mean," Shawn said jokingly.

The lovebirds took a quiet shower first before getting into their heavy lovemaking.

Sexiful, looking at her young, soon-to-be husband, said, "Shawn, I want you to make love to me like you never loved any other woman before. Make love to me like I'm a virgin and this is your first time making love to a virgin." She wanted to be his first, and she wanted him to be her first. "We'll pretend that this is our first date night. Like that idea, baby?" she asked Shawn with a sexy smile licking her bottom lip.

"Okay, baby, let me be an inexperienced virgin because right now I just want to love you like a pro … like the man that I am." Shawn looked at her, and his eyes seemed to be making love to her body that he loved so well. "Baby, I want to scream your name so loud that the whole word will be able to hear me calling, *'Sexiful!'* I want you to make love to me all night, nonstop.

"Sexiful, I'm going to love you like you have never been loved before. I have so much love built up in my body, and, baby, I'm going to give it all to you. I've been saving this juice of love in my body for four months. On the drive home, what I gave you was just a sample. Baby, you are in big trouble. Daddy is going to be gentle and patient with you because I know you have been waiting just as long as I have." He pulled her into his arms, kissed her lips, and moved down her neck, kissing her softly.

He played with her nipples as he kissed her body. He ran his tongue from her breast down to her navel. La'Roc moaned with pleasure as he continued to make love to her flesh.

She asked through her bliss, "Shawn, baby, what are you trying to do to me?" At that moment, she never felt more love. He was making love to her like he did the night before he was arrested. He made 1love that night like he was never going to see her again. And it was his last time making love to her for four months. Thanks to his team of lawyers that fought for his freedom.

He stopped kissing her stomach and looked into her eyes. "Sexiful, I love you. Marry me tomorrow; baby, I love you so much. If I lose you to someone else, I will die. Sexiful, when I was away, you were all I thought about. I would close my eyes and pray that you would be waiting for me, and not as my lawyer but as my fiancée."

"Shawn, I love you too. Yes, I'll marry you, sweetheart. However, tonight I just want you to continue making love to me and convey to me how much you missed your little sweet Sexiful."

Shawn grabbed her by her waist and carried her from the bedroom into the great room to continue their lovemaking. He placed her on a very thick blanket in front of the fireplace and massaged her inner thighs with his tongue.

He took his pointer finger and his middle finger and slowly guided them into her vagina as she squirmed and begged for his big penis. She wanted him to give her every inch of his manhood. Shawn knew what spots to touch when he was making love to her.

That night they made love all over the co-op.

At four o'clock in the morning, they decided to take a long whirlpool bath. Before going into the whirlpool, she made love to Shawn's body from his head to his navel. "Oh baby, keep doing what you are doing. Whatever you're doing, please don't stop."

"Baby, don't worry I'll never stop loving you. I'll always love you, and I'll never leave you again, I promise you.

"Sexiful, remember, I have what every man dreams of—that is you, and you are all mine. I love you so much. La'Roc, you are my life. Sexiful, when I am with you, nothing else really matters. You take care of all of my needs. I have everything right here in one big package." After making love, he carried her into the whirlpool.

After the whirlpool bath, he carried her back into the master bedroom and placed her on the bed. He dried her off and moisturized her body.

She got up from the bed and moisturized his body all over. He removed himself from the bed and went into the kitchen to bring up some snacks and champagne. He put on some soft music as they sat in the middle of the bed, enjoying each other. After they finished eating and drinking their champagne, he said, "Baby, it is good to be home. It just seems so unreal. I'm sitting here with the woman I love." Shawn looked at her. "You're beautiful when your hair is wet. With your hair wet, you look even sexier."

They kissed each other long and hard. Shawn asked Sexiful to lay her head on his chest.

Before falling asleep, he kissed her good night.

Sexiful fell asleep with her head on his chest. She had had a long day and had an even longer tomorrow.

Tomorrow she'd inform Shawn at breakfast of his so-called son, and she'd update him regarding Jordan's health crisis. In spite of what she'd tell Shawn, she'd ask Jordan to give Shawn the details himself about the virus he had contracted. It would be Jordan's call to tell Shawn whenever he was ready.

La'Roc and Shawn were awakened by her house phone ringing. Shawn removed his arms from around her waist and reached over to answer the phone. "That will be fine, Ms. Cotton. As soon as you reach the co-op with Paris and Biscuit, you can send them both up. I would love to see them," Shawn responded.

"Wake up, sleepyhead. Your babies will be on their way upstairs in a few minutes."

Before Shawn had finished his sentence, Paris and Biscuit were jumping on her bed, licking and wagging their little tails. They were excited to see their mother and father. La'Roc was just as excited to see her babies.

Ms. Cotton knocked on her bedroom door; La'Roc said to enter. Ms. Cotton entered the bedroom. "Good morning, Mr. Parker. Good morning, Ms. Rose. I am sorry, but Paris and Biscuit just jumped right out of my arms so fast, I couldn't hold them."

"That's all right, Ms. Cotton. Don't worry; I'll take them out of your hair." They both were happy to see the babies. Shawn was especially excited to see Paris and Biscuit.

"Ms. Cotton, we'd like a nice hot breakfast,"

La'Roc looked over at Shawn and smiled as he played with Paris and Biscuit. "Shawn, would you like to have something special for breakfast?" La'Roc asked.

Shawn reached for her and pulled her to his chest and whispered something in her ear. They both laughed. "You're a bad boy, Shawn. No! You can't have that for breakfast; maybe for dessert."

They looked at each other with a seductive grin.

Shawn gave the housekeeper his order for breakfast as he continued to twist a lock of La'Roc's hair through his fingers. La'Roc stated that she just wanted coffee. Ms. Cotton left the room, smiling at the lovers who were now completely oblivious to her presence.

"Get over here, Sexiful, and let Daddy hold you before we take Paris and Biscuit out for their walk." Pulling her close to his body, Shawn held La'Roc tightly in his arms. "Baby, I love you so much, and believe me, I will give my life for you,"

"I love you too," La'Roc responded.

The two of them watched in amusement as Paris and Biscuit scrambled across the bed to play with each other. While Paris and Biscuit were playing, La'Roc's mind drifted back to Shawn and his so-called son.

Ever since the boy's birth, Shawn had seen to his financial needs. La'Roc was pissed when she found out that Shawn's sister April had known all along that her brother was not the father of Kelly's baby. How could a sister do that to her brother? What a slut!

La'Roc knew that Shawn was going to take the news about his son very hard.

After breakfast, Shawn and La'Roc strolled through the garden with the two small dogs running in front of them. They walked arm in arm, silently taking in each other's company. La'Roc's thoughts kept racing through her brain as to how she was going to break the news to Shawn about Jordan's deteriorating condition. Then there was the information about Shawn's son.

La'Roc knew Shawn could handle the news; she just wanted to pick the right time to drop all of this on him.

La'Roc just could not believe a sister could be so cruel.

Shawn walked into the den. "Honey, let's go upstairs and take a shower and a nap before dinner. I feel like holding you in my arms and making sweet love to you. Baby, I craved your love each and every day when I was away. Those four months were the hardest I ever had to endure," Shawn said with a smile.

"You want to make love to little old me, sweetie?" La'Roc blushed. "I can't wait."

He picked her up into his arms and carried her into the bedroom shower. Putting her down gently, he removed her clothing very slowly as he made love to her petite body. He was holding her as tight as he possibly could while he kissed her lips and her tiny frame.

"Baby, I am burning up inside for your love, and I want to go inside of you and set you on fire so we can burn together. I want to make love to you all night," Shawn said.

He sat down on the bathroom chair and pulled her to his lap; she sat down on his penis slowly as he began to ease his penis inside of her. She rotated her body clockwise as Shawn's rotation followed. Shawn loved the movement of her body as he held her close to his chest and continued to whisper sweet words in her ear. Shawn was irresistible, and she just adored him.

"Sexiful, you're my whole world, and I can't believe that I am home with you in my arms, making love to the woman I love once again."

She kissed Shawn's lips passionately. She wanted him to go deeper. She said with excitement, "Shawn, please give me more of you. Go deeper inside of me deeper baby." She missed his rotation inside of her, his kisses, and his wet tongue all over her body.

"La'Roc, I'm going to give you all of me, and I'll be gentle, baby. Do you feel me inside of you, baby?" Shawn asked with sweat running down his face.

The shower will come later. This man is more important to me. That shower will have to wait, La'Roc thought to herself.

They made love for what seemed like hours, and she loved every moment of it.

After making love, he held her in his arms and kissed her gently.

Sometime later, Shawn was in the shower, slowly drizzling shower gel down La'Roc's back. He watched as the liquid made a slow trail down his lover's back and continued down to the crack that separated her smooth, round ass. He followed the gel with a trail of kisses. He listened with aroused pleasure as his lover slowly started to move her body in a seductive rhythm.

La'Roc turned and placed her arms around Shawn's neck and whispered, "My turn." Taking the gel she rubbed some in her hands and started soaping Shawn's neck then moved in slow circles down to his chest and gradually made her way between his legs. Shawn stilled her hand and gently raised her hand and kissed her fingers. "Enough. If you continue, we'll never get out of here, and I'm starved," he whispered.

Shawn teased La'Roc about still getting married, and she assured him that he was stuck with her for life.

After the shower, Shawn wrapped La'Roc in a towel and dried her off. She turned to look at Shawn; she felt at that moment she was falling in love all over again. What a good feeling that was.

La'Roc reached for a towel to dry Shawn's hot body. Of course, he had to sit on the shower stool so she could do a good job of drying him off.

They finished and got dressed for dinner.

Ms. Cotton was waiting downstairs in the small dining room. The table was beautiful and set for two.

La'Roc and Shawn would have the whole place alone for the next several hours, which would give her enough time to tell Shawn about Kelly's son and him not being the father.

La'Roc felt Shawn's hurt already; she hadn't even told him yet. The phone rang. "Shawn, will you please answer the phone?"

"No problem, Sexiful," Shawn responded.

"Hello, Courtney," Shawn answered.

Shawn looked over at La'Roc and motioned to the phone. "It's Courtney." Shawn handed over the phone, sat back down at the table, and started sipping on his wine.

"Hi, Courtney is everything all right?" La'Roc asked.

"Yes, Mom, we're great. I just called to tell you that we're all looking forward to seeing you guys on Sunday. I am going to pick up Grams later on today—you know how much she hates taking the long drive to Westchester by herself," Courtney said, laughing.

"Okay, baby. I'll call you back after dinner," La'Roc said goodbye and hung up the phone.

La'Roc and Shawn had a lovely meal; while sitting at the table, having lunch, staring at her husband to be … she was thinking of a way to tell him that the son he thought was his child was fathered by another man. Finishing up her meal, La'Roc informed Shawn that they needed to talk over a few things.

Shawn looked over at her and smiled. "Okay," Shawn said. "Baby, why so serious?"

Shawn removed himself from the table and walked over to La'Roc. He looked into her eyes. "What is so serious, baby?

"I can handle anything as long as you still love me and you will never leave me." Shawn was looking down at her with those beautiful brown eyes.

"Okay, baby. Come with me, and we'll talk in the great room."

"Yes, baby, let's go get this over with because I don't like the seriousness in your voice. You're scaring me, Sexiful," Shawn said.

"Believe me, baby. I am very anxious to tell you."

At that point, La'Roc's cell phone rang. "Hello sis. What's up, kid?"

"Did you tell Shawn yet about his son? How did he take it? L'Oreal asked with concern in her voice.

"L'Oreal, I am a little apprehensive in starting the conversation because I don't know where to start," La'Roc answered.

"Don't worry, sis. You will figure it out," L'Oreal said.

"Well, let me get back to my baby. I will call you later or give you full details tomorrow. We should be arriving in Westchester around 2:30 p.m.—no later than 4:00 p.m.," La'Roc responded.

"Okay, La'Roc. I am looking forward to seeing you and my future brother-in-law."

"Okay, babe, see you tomorrow," La'Roc responded as she hung up the phone.

She looked back at Shawn as he was looking out the window. She called out his name, and he responded.

"Yes, baby, I am here, looking out the window at this beautiful view that I have been missing for the past four months. Sexiful, I had no idea this view was so gorgeous until now," Shawn said as he looked at her with that beautiful smile, showing off his stunning white teeth.

La'Roc walked over to Shawn with a glass of red wine in each hand. Handing one glass to Shawn, she gracefully sat on the sofa and patted the seat beside her.

He gripped his drink and sat beside her on the sofa.

Sitting there gazing at Shawn, La'Roc realized that there wasn't going to be an easy way to tell him about Kelly's deceit. At that moment, she felt that it was just best to deliver the blow and be there for Shawn.

La'Roc placed her glass on the side table, reached for Shawn's hand, and started stroking it gently. She still couldn't bring herself to say the words that she knew would wreck Shawn's world.

Shawn watched La'Roc rubbing his hand and was becoming a little concerned by the slight tremble he could feel coupled with the fact that she wouldn't look directly at him.

"Baby, you're really scaring me. Is there something wrong with you, Courtney, Devon, your mother, or anyone in the family?" Shawn said, his concern growing. "Please tell me what wrong," he continued, concern putting a slight edge in his deep, smooth voice.

La'Roc tilted her head so that she could look into the eyes of the man she had come to love beyond reason. Speaking softly, she said the words that she knew would break her lover's heart.

"Shawn, during the investigation, we discovered that you aren't the father of Kelly's child or the baby she was carrying."

Shawn was very quiet for a moment, shaking his head. Turning his face to her, he said, "Sexiful, you're telling me Shawn Jr. is not my son."

"Yes, Shawn, that is what I said," La'Roc responded gently. Shawn sat stunned; then the tears started to flow down his cheeks. La'Roc sat and watched the play of emotions run across Shawn's handsome face. Suddenly Shawn's expression changed, and he looked as if he wanted to attack something, anything.

Both of them sat quietly, side by side, for a while. La'Roc gradually reached out a hand and gently rubbed his arm; it was then she realized he was shaking. Turning toward Shawn, she reached over and gently pulled him into her arms and held on tight.

La'Roc continued to explain to Shawn about the results of the DNA test that verified that he wasn't the father of either child. At that point, Shawn broke down and cried as if his heart were broken. Through tears, he said, "La'Roc, she lied to me for two years. I can't believe she would do that to me." Shawn removed his head from La'Roc's lap and rose from the sofa. Walking stiffly, he eased himself out to the balcony.

La'Roc watched as Shawn paced back and forth, trying to come to grips with the information he'd just received. Her heart hurt for him. He had loved that little boy. She understood that kind of love. Didn't she love Courtney and Devon in the same way? She continued to sit on the sofa and waited for Shawn's return.

La'Roc sat on the sofa with her unfinished glass of wine. She was really worried about Shawn. He really loved that little boy.

The person who was going to be hurt the most would be Shawn Jr.

Finally, Shawn rejoined La'Roc in the great room. His eyes were red and swollen from crying for a boy he thought was his child. Knowing that the child was not his beloved son hurt him deeply. He didn't say a word. He just sat down on the sofa and gathered La'Roc in his arms and held her as if she would slip away from his grasp. Silent tears rolled down her face as she joined her man in his grief.

Much later that evening, the two of them made their way to bed; it had been an exhausting day.

The next morning, Shawn apologized for his behavior the night before. La'Roc was amazed by his statement. "Baby, what are you apologizing for?" she asked.

"Baby, I should have handled the news a little better than breaking down. I am sorry I acted like a jerk," he said embarrassment written across his face. "Sweetheart, you don't have to apologize for being human. You acted as any father would if his child was taken away from him."

Shawn kissed La'Roc lovingly on the top of her head and then made his way into the bathroom. What he needed was a steaming shower to help him sort out his feelings about the events concerning Shawn Jr. First of all, why would Kelly lie to him? That might be easy to figure out ... it was just trying to figure out where he would go from here.

As the steam and the stinging water soothed his body, he knew for sure that La'Roc was in his corner no matter what. His woman was awesome.

When he entered the bedroom, Shawn found La'Roc sitting in bed, propped up by several large, decorative pillows. He was still drying his hair with a fluffy towel when she looked up and reached out her hand toward him.

Shawn climbed in beside La'Roc and pulled her toward him. He smiled when he noticed that she was nude underneath her yellow silk robe. "I am a lucky man." Sliding down from her perch, she whispered in his ear, "Let me make you feel better." Shawn had no problem with that. Arms and hands became entangled as they stroked smooth skin. Soon their breathing came in short, raspy bursts. His hands massaged her breast and rubbed the nipples into hard peaks. Her hands were busy too, stroking the velvet skin of his hard manhood. Both of them needed to reaffirm their love for each other.

In a smooth move, Shawn slid into La'Roc's hot core. With every stroke, he was met by her response. As both of them reached their climax, he could feel her inner walls closing and tightening around him. He was home. He knew that he could face all as long as he had this woman: his Sexiful Rose.

La'Roc awoke. Shawn was still asleep, and she didn't want to wake him. Now that he knew about Shawn Jr. not being his child, she knew the information about Jordan's health might be a bigger blow. She was going to have to cross that bridge soon, and she wasn't looking forward to it. Life could be so unfair.

La'Roc left the bedroom and headed to the kitchen. Ms. Cotton was preparing lunch and assured her that their seafood lunch would be spectacular and worthy of Mr. Parker's homecoming.

La'Roc left the kitchen to wake Shawn for lunch. In her hands, she was carrying Paris and Biscuit.

She ran upstairs. When she reached her bedroom, she didn't see Shawn in bed where she left him. She began to panic. *Oh my God. Where did he go?* She ran back into the bathroom. No Shawn. *Where could he be?* She asked herself. *Maybe he is in one of the guest rooms in a deep depression. I must find him,* she thought.

Oh, maybe he is out on the terrace. He was on the terrace, just starring out into space. She thought, *Shawn has slipped into a deep depression.* She was terrified.

She called out his name. "Shawn, are you all right?"

"Yes, baby. I was just thinking about Kelly using me like she did and how my sister could allow it to happen. Sexiful, did you ever think that my sister had that much hate for me?"

"Shawn, I don't know your sister like that. I'm not going to judge her on her inappropriate behavior. However, you know how I feel about April," La'Roc responded. His eyes held unshed tears.

"Baby, how could anyone be so hateful? I don't want to have anything to do with April or Kelly again. Sexiful, I've made my decision. I'm not going to put SJ in the middle of Kelly's crazy mess. I came to this decision: I'll not confuse him. I've decided not to see him again. I love him too much to continue to pretend that I'm his father. Sweetheart, it hurt something awful to not to have him in my life. I'm very lucky to have you and your family in my life. How can anyone be so wicked to play with a child's life? This is horrible."

Shawn paced around the terrace.

"Shawn this is your decision to make, sweetheart. If that's your conclusion to the situation, then that is your decision. I'll stand by you no matter what. Shawn, I love you, and I'll always be there for you. Remember, you're not fighting this war alone. We're in this together."

"Thanks, Sexiful. What would I do without you?"

Shawn looked at her. "Baby, I'll never, ever know if I could live without you because I'm not going to leave you to find out. I'll never let you go, Sexiful. So you see, baby, you're stuck with me until death do us apart—whether you like it or not." He grabbed her and kissed her aggressively. After that kiss, he said, "Let's go have some lunch."

The two of them ate and enjoyed Ms. Cotton's seafood spectacular. The candle light added to the romantic atmosphere. Watching Shawn enjoying his meal, La'Roc thought she should share her concerns about Jordan on their trip up to Westchester.

La'Roc informed Shawn that they would be leaving for Westchester after they finished lunch.

Lunch was great as usual; Shawn complimented Ms. Cotton on the beautiful and tasty lunch as he removed himself from the table. He walked over and kissed Ms. Cotton on her cheek. Ms. Cotton put her hand over her mouth and giggled.

Feeling her phone vibrate in her pocket, La'Roc reached into her purse and checked the ID: Jordan. After answering his question of how Shawn took the news about SJ, she confirmed that they would be leaving within the hour.

La'Roc then told Jordan that she planned to tell Shawn about his health crisis. Jordan confirmed that he was okay with Shawn knowing about his condition. She then shooed Jordan off the phone because she had to change her clothes. "Love you, bro," La'Roc told her dearest friend.

La'Roc stalled for time by setting up the dogs' travel crates. She was still debating when would be a good time to share the news about Jordan. Deciding that she was being a coward, she determined that she would tell Shawn as soon as she got upstairs. A coward dies a thousand deaths, a hero but one ... so the saying goes.

Entering the bedroom, La'Roc approached Shawn and wrapped her arms around his waist.

"Shawn, I need to speak to you before we leave for Westchester."

"I am all yours. I hope this is some good news, baby," he responded with a kiss on her left cheek.

"Baby, first of all, I would like to go visit Justin before we go to Westchester. Is that okay with you?"

"Yes, baby anything for you. I would like to see Justin too," Shawn answered.

La'Roc knew she was stalling. Why couldn't this be easier? *Because it isn't that small,* the voice inside her head responded. First the news about SJ, and now this. La'Roc had to remind herself that Shawn was a strong man, and despite the turn of events, he could handle this. She was the one having the difficult time.

"Shawn, remember when I told you I needed to talk to you? It's that time. Please sit here on the sofa with me," La'Roc said, pointing toward the love seat. "Sexiful, tell me anything, but you are not going to leave me for another man," Shawn said, looking and sounding serious.

"No Shawn, nothing like that. I love you, baby, and leaving you is the furthest thing from my mind," La'Roc responded.

Shawn watched as La'Roc twisted the ties to her dressing gown and had difficulty looking him in the eye. He was on high alert, figuring there must be more upsetting news she wanted to share. "Baby, you're looking so serious. Talk to me, Sexiful." Shawn sat on the sofa and looked her straight into her eyes. "Tell me, Sexiful. I'm tired of waiting, and you're going to tear that tie to shreds if you don't stop twisting it." He sounded as if he was getting frustrated with the anticipation of not knowing what she had to tell him.

"Sweetheart, Jordan has been diagnosed with HIV. He will be living with us in Westchester. He will give you full details when you meet with him today." Shawn looked at La'Roc with understanding eyes and a smile on his face.

"Oh, Sexiful, I understand, baby. He is your friend. I have no problem with Jordan being HIV positive. I met some people in prison with the virus. Baby, we'll beat this thing."

"Oh, you're the love of my life. Thank you so much for your understanding." La'Roc knew in her heart that Shawn would be sympathetic to Jordan's health issues.

La'Roc walked over to the intercom and paged Ms. Cotton. Ms. Cotton answered the page. "Yes, Ms. Rose?"

"There has been a change in our plans. Shawn and I are going to visit Justin. We will see you in Westchester. You will have to take Biscuit and Paris with you.

"Ms. Cotton, will you ask Hector to bring the car around? Tell him we are ready to leave for Manhattan."

Before leaving the bedroom, Shawn pulled her down on the bed, and she gently lay on top of him.

La'Roc loved every minute of it. She wanted his naked body to merge against hers and make love to her, and he did.

He made love to her like every woman wanted to be loved. Shawn whispered in her ear, "Baby, I asked Hector to come back within the hour. That'll give me an hour to eat you up." He winked as he smiled.

"No problem, baby. Did you instruct Ms. Cotton to leave for Westchester?"

"Yes, baby," Shawn answered.

After making love, La'Roc laid her head on his chest like he always asked her to do after making love; if it were within her power, she always gave him whatever he asked for, no matter what.

Shawn and La'Roc took a long, hot shower, dressed quickly, and greeted the driver, who was patiently waiting for them. Hector assured them that Ms. Cotton had already left for Westchester.

As Shawn was locking the doors, La'Roc's cell phone rang. "Hello, Courtney. Everything is okay?"

"Yes Mom. We're good, just checking on you guys. What did Shawn say when you told him about his son?"

"He took it pretty hard; I know he's pretending that he's not hurting, but I can see the sadness in his face."

"Wow! He must've been devastated to find out that Shawn Jr. wasn't his child," Courtney remarked.

"Courtney, we'll talk when we reach Westchester, okay, baby?" Before hanging up, Courtney gave La'Roc an update on the decoration.

She assured her mother that everything was going as planned and the house looked great.

"How is Jordan?" La'Roc asked. "Jordan is cool," Courtney replied.

La'Roc went on to explain that Shawn was very understanding about Jordan and his health.

La'Roc and Courtney said their goodbyes and hung up.

On the drive to visit Justin, La'Roc filled Shawn in on Justin's medical update.

"How is Justin doing now after the new treatment?" Shawn asked.

"The treatment he's receiving now seems to be helping. There's been one good thing: he's left the hospital and been transported back to the rehabilitation center."

As they walked down the corridor to Justin's room, Courtney and Dr. Kim were already there, talking to him; he was responsive to Dr. Kim's conversation. She called her conversation with Justin therapy.

She further explained that Justin understood when Courtney was there. He also was aware when she walked into the room. He would smile.

When Shawn walked into the room, Courtney couldn't help herself; she threw herself into his arms. She stated repeatedly how much he had been missed.

Shawn leaned over to kiss her. "Courtney, thank you. I'm happy to be home with my future wife and my extended family. Believe me, Courtney, I missed you guys too."

Dr. Kim updated La'Roc on Justin's progress.

Tears started to appear in La'Roc's eyes as she listened to Dr. Kim's positive report.

Dr. Moore entered Justin's room. "Well, well, how're you today?" Courtney walked over to Dr. Moore and introduced him to Shawn.

The two men shook hands, and Dr. Moore continued to explain, "The new treatment has done wonders for Justin. However, there has been no change in his ability to walk or to have children. He was able to hold a short conversation with his speech therapist this morning. He had just a little tremble in his voice, which will soon go away with this new treatment. Thank you, Courtney, Ms. Rose, and you, Dr. Kim, for all you have done for Justin and this hospital. If it weren't for you, Ms. Rose, I really don't know what would have happened to Justin. Thank you," Dr. Moore said with teary eyes.

"Thank you, Dr. Moore. Where is Dr. Woo?" Courtney asked. "I would like to thank him for his participation in Justin's recovery."

"I'll be meeting with him in Atlanta next week, and I'll give him your regards. I'll go a little further and ask him to give you and your mother a call," Dr. Moore responded. Dr. Moore's hazel eyes lit up every time he spoke to Courtney. Unfortunately, Courtney only saw Dr. Moore as Justin's doctor.

"That'll be great, Dr. Moore," Courtney responded.

Dr. Moore and La'Roc left the others to visit with Justin as they went to his office. While in the office, La'Roc presented the doctor with a check for $5,000 toward the new wing of the research center dedicated to spinal injuries. The new wing would carry Justin's name.

Dr. Moore thanked La'Roc as she walked back to Justin's room.

La'Roc entered Justin's room to spend some time with him and Courtney before going to Westchester.

"Mother, isn't it great news? Justin will be able to go home soon on day passes if he continues to make positive progress like he has been in the past months." Courtney walked over to her mother and hugged her with tears running down her face.

La'Roc and Shawn visited with Justin a while longer and then made their farewells in order to continue to La'Roc's other home in Westchester. As they were leaving, Courtney informed Shawn that she had received a call from Devon.

"Devon asked me to tell you to call him because he is waiting to see you. Please call my son."

"Thanks for the information. I'll call him right now and let him know that we're on our way," he responded.

Shawn left Justin's room with La'Roc on his arm.

The ride to Westchester was beautiful, long, and exhausting. La'Roc was overwhelmed from her wonderful weekend of Shawn's intense lovemaking; she laid her head on his shoulder and went to dreamland.

Once Hector arrived at the townhouse, Shawn kissed her softly on her forehead. "Baby, it's time to wake up."

Hector walked around and opened the door to the limo. Shawn stepped out and reached for La'Roc's hands to assist her out of the limo.

Chantal, Denise, L'Oreal, Casey, Alex, Devon, his girlfriend, and, of course, La'Roc's mother all ran out of the house to greet and welcome Shawn home.

Shawn's face broke into a wide grin when he saw his extended family there to greet him for his homecoming.

Smiling, Devon pulled Shawn away from La'Roc's side in order to introduce him to his girlfriend, August.

Shawn greeted her with a hello and a smile. He then walked over to La'Roc's mother. After a brief moment, he pulled her into his arms, hugging and kissing her cheek as she kissed his in return. He bumped shoulders with Alex and thanked him for the work he had done on his bail hearing.

Alex called out to Shawn, "Hey, man. Good to have you home, and remember, we have more work to do to prepare you for the trial on Friday."

Shawn was looking around for Jordan. "Baby, where is Jordan?" Shawn hugged Ms. Holiday.

"Ms. Holiday, where are Jordan and my babies?" La'Roc asked.

"Your babies are upstairs with Mr. Diaz, taking a nap. They seemed to be really tired when they arrived. Ms. Cotton gave them a bath and put them down for a nap," Ms. Holiday responded.

They all turned around to the yelling that was going on behind them, coming from the terrace.

It was Jordan and one of his lawyer friends from LA, holding up a big poster. The poster read, "Welcome home, Shawn."

Shawn eyes were watery as he looked and waved up to Jordan.

As they walked into the townhouse, there was food all over the place. Everything was beautiful. They all yelled out, "Welcome home, Shawn."

During this time, Courtney and Dr. Kim arrived and walked into the great room.

Jordan bumped shoulders with Shawn, and he had a hug for La'Roc. La'Roc kissed her mother. As she walked away from her mother, she noticed her sister walked over to her and kissed her. She looked over her right shoulder and spotted her two best friends, Chantal and Denise. She kissed them both.

"Thank you, guys, for everything."

They both said, "Please, girl, we love you!"

La'Roc turned to Devon and hugged him as tight as she could and gave him a big kiss. She said hello to August.

"Jordan, let's talk; how is it going?" La'Roc asked.

"Oh, baby girl, I'm happy as long as you are happy. You are happy, right?" Jordan asked.

"Yes, baby. I am very happy thanks to you and my team of the best lawyers in New York State. That is what got Shawn home."

While the other guests were meeting and greeting, Shawn found the time to pull Jordan aside to thank him for being one of his defense lawyers.

La'Roc joined Chantal, L'Oreal, and Denise to check on Shawn's surprise welcome home party.

Chantal said very excited. "Courtney has the party under control. She has been working day and night on that homecoming party."

Denise said with a smile, "It's going to be the bomb."

"Denise, are you bringing a date to the party?" La'Roc asked.

Chantal said, "That bitch doesn't have a boyfriend. Martin dumped her ass. Didn't you hear about the big fight they had? And Martin just walked out without saying goodbye! Then to top it all off, the MF took ten thousand dollars from Denise's bank account!" Chantal concluded angrily.

"Chantal, what the fuck are you talking about?" La'Roc asked, looking back in surprise at Denise.

Denise continued to glare at Chantal as she replied, "Chantal, please stop running your big mouth. I'll tell her. It's my business, not yours."

Denise looked at La'Roc and motioned for her to come upstairs with her. Before following Denise, La'Roc looked over her shoulder to see how Shawn was doing. She observed him smiling and hugging everyone; he was fine.

Denise and La'Roc entered one of her offices for some privacy.

As the two of them were getting settled, there was a knock on the door. La'Roc opened the door to a tearful Chantal. "Denise, I'm so sorry about what I said earlier. Please forgive me and my big mouth." Denise stared at her friend and then looked at La'Roc, who remained silent. After a moment, the two friends hugged and then invited La'Roc to join their circle.

Denise said she and Martin had been having problems for the past several months.

"I did talk to Alex about the problems I was having with Martin a while ago. He made a promise to me that he wasn't going to tell or talk to anyone about it. It was my place to tell you guys. Alex is a good man, La'Roc. He was totally straightforward and honest when giving me advice, how he wouldn't put his job on the line by keeping secrets from you because of your friendship.

"La'Roc, I knew that you and Chantal thought that Alex and I were having an affair. He was only a friend to me in my time of need. During that time, La'Roc, you were busy with Shawn's trial, and, Chantal, your job had you all over the world. Alex was the only friend I could talk to when he would drive me home from the townhouse sometimes."

La'Roc said, "We are together now. Let's talk, Denise. What happened?" "I've always met the wrong type of men. My love life has always been shady. I could never find love like you and Chantal. Remember when you first met me; I was living in the streets? I've been in the streets ever since I was nine years old. If you and Chantal hadn't taken me in, I would've been dead by now. You guys saved me from myself, and I thank you each and every day for my life," she paused.

"I'm now a successful businesswoman with my own company and three beautiful friends to thank for it."

Denise was a very private person when it came to her family background. "Maybe I am just like my mother—any man will do as long as I feel they love me. I never knew my father; my mother left me and my sister with my drunken aunt. I was five years old, and my sister was eight when my mother left us with Aunt Mary.

"My sister and I worked the streets like we were adults. At twelve, my sister and I had a pimp. He was mean as hell. He would beat the shit out of the both of us. If we didn't make money, we didn't eat. One night, he was drunk, and while he slept, my sister stabbed him to death. I really don't know where my sister is now. That is one of the reasons I don't talk about my past."

Denise changed the subject because it seemed that it was too painful for her to continue discussing her past. La'Roc and Chantal respected Denise for changing the subject and didn't push the issue any further.

"Now let me tell you about Martin: Martin and I broke up several months ago, like I told you earlier. He quit his job long before he stole my money. He moved out and started living in one of my apartments, hanging out with other women, and partying all night. Remember, Chantal, when I was missing in action?"

"Oh, that was about a month ago, right?" Chantal asked.

"Yes. Around that time, Martin had beaten me black and blue. I was too embarrassed to come out or tell anyone. I learned in the past to take care of my own problems. Well, he's gone with my ten thousand dollars. Life goes on."

La'Roc removed herself from the sofa and walked directly over to Denise and sat by her with tears in her eyes. "Denise, will you please forgive me for not being there for you when you needed me? I'm here now, baby. This can never happen again, and it'll never happen again, I promise. Denise, we're your sisters, and we'll always be here for you, no matter what," La'Roc responded as she pulled Denise into her arms.

"We'll make a pact—we'll never keep secrets from each other again." The three friends bumped their glasses of wine together to seal the pact. Chantal said, "Denise, again, I'm so sorry. I didn't know, and I'm angry with you because you didn't tell me about Martin. I can understand you not telling me about your past, but not telling me about Martin—I just don't understand that." Chantal picked up her glass of wine, looking directly at Denise. "I was the one who introduced you to that *damn rat*."

La'Roc said, "What's done is done. We have to move forward. Denise, call Martin and put him on speaker phone."

Denise dialed Martin's cell phone. He picked up on the second ring. "Hello, who is this?" Martin answered.

"This is Denise's attorney, La'Roc Rose. I think you have something that belongs to me, like ten thousand dollars. You have ten thousand dollars of my money, and I am ready to collect," stated La'Roc.

"La'Roc, I don't understand what you are talking about; what money?" Martin exclaimed.

"Martin, I don't have time to argue with you about my money. I want my money within two days. If not, I'll have your fucking ass arrested. And by the way, if you ever put your hands on Denise again, I will kill you myself. And you know I don't lie. I just got an order of protection against your monkey ass. Martin, you have been warned," La'Roc concluded in a quiet voice that promised retribution. La'Roc was lying about the order of protection. She wanted to shake him up a little. "You will stay away from Denise, her friends, and her property, and you will turn the rental car back to the dealer as well as your BlackBerry phone. You will leave with what you brought into the relationship, which was nothing. The dealer will pick up the car within an hour if you have a problem with returning the car yourself. Your BlackBerry will be shut off once this conversation has ended," La'Roc continued.

"Ms. Rose, I am sorry. It will never happen again," Martin begged.

"Martin, say bye to your BlackBerry; this conversation has ended." With that, La'Roc disconnected the call and winked at her girlfriends.

La'Roc, Chantal, and Denise were toasting when Jordan walked in with Shawn and L'Oreal.

"What is this?" Shawn asked.

"Just a little catching up that we had neglected. Everything is good now." La'Roc said, "Yes. La'Roc is back." Denise whispered her thanks as she hugged La'Roc.

Chantal and Denise kissed La'Roc and left the office.

La'Roc walked over to L'Oreal and gave her a big sisterly hug. "We have some catching up to do as well, about the organization. How is that going, by the way?"

"Oh, Shawn, I've got so much to tell you about the Jordan Foundation and so much more good stuff."

"Baby, I'll be here. I am not going anywhere. I'm here for the long haul," Shawn responded with a smile.

"Jordan, after the party, I'd like for the team to get together to discuss the plan for Friday. There's no working tonight, only a discussion," La'Roc said.

"Okay, sis you got it."

"Jordan, I want you, Alex, and Devon to excuse you and the rest of the team from the party; come to my office for a minute. Shawn and I would like to thank you guys for the wonderful work you did in court three days ago. I will also announce it at dinner."

"Sexiful, I will get Alex and Devon for you so you and Jordan can talk," "Okay sweetheart. Thank you." La'Roc gave Shawn a message for her mother. "Tell her I will be outside to join her in a little while."

Shawn left Jordan and La'Roc alone. La'Roc ran over and hugged him as close to her chest as possible. "I love you, Jordan."

"I love you too, baby girl. I missed you, but I knew you were being taken care of." Jordan was holding her just as tight as she was holding on to him.

"Jordan, did Courtney tell you that there is a possibility that Justin will be coming to Shawn's party on Friday?"

"Yes, she told me. That's great news. I couldn't be happier for the both of them,"

There was a knock on the door. "Yes," Jordan said. "You may enter." Devon, Alex, and Shawn walked into La'Roc's office. She was so proud of her team of lawyers and especially her grandson.

La'Roc stated she wanted them to know how much she loved them and how professional they all looked in court. She looked around the room, shaking her head. "Alex thanks. You did a damn good job using your expertise in leading your team to victory; you handled the DA like a champ. Good job, partner. Jordan, you also did a wonderful job conducting the introduction of the bail hearing, and your opening statement was out of this world.

"I always save the best for last. Devon, you did a great job as a participant. Thank you all for doing a beautiful job. I want all of you to go out and have a good time and prepare yourselves for next Friday. Remember, next Friday is the main trial. Anything could happen."

Shawn added his thanks to the team for their hard work. After Shawn finished his speech, the team bumped shoulders and left for the party. Shawn and La'Roc followed with love in their eyes.

La'Roc grabbed her mother by the hand and walked down the driveway, laughing and talking.

"Hi, baby," Geneva said. "I know that you're a happy person because Shawn's back home. Baby, I told you not to worry because I knew all the time that Shawn was innocent. Shawn is a good man, La'Roc. You're one lucky woman to have found a man like Shawn. Keep him happy, baby. You know what I mean." Geneva winked and smiled.

La'Roc pulled her mother into her arms with tears in her eyes; she hugged her as tight as she could. "Mother, I love you so much. I wish Dad were here."

"Baby, he is always with you in spirit."

"Thanks, Mom; in some way, I think I needed that validation from you. I guess I needed your approval." La'Roc kissed her mother as they both walked over to join the other guests, holding hands.

"Thanks, Mom, for our time together."

After dinner, the guests danced and sang to celebrate Shawn's return.

While everyone was enjoying themselves, La'Roc noticed that someone was missing. Her eyes scanned the gardens and surrounding area; however, there was no Jordan. La'Roc became worried because this kind of behavior was not like Jordan. Jordan liked to entertain and make jokes with Courtney. She said to herself, *Oh my goodness. I hope that Jordan isn't having another episode alone.*

La'Roc dialed Shawn's cell phone.

Shawn answered on the second ring. "Hi, sweetheart excuse yourself from the guests," La'Roc said in a nervous voice.

"Slow down, baby. What's up, Sexiful? First of all, are you all right?" he asked with concern.

"Shawn, please meet me in the great room. We need to find Jordan and make sure he is all right."

"Okay, baby. I'm on my way." La'Roc went into the great room to wait for Shawn to arrive.

Shawn quickly entered the great room with Courtney and Devon at his side.

"Hi, Grams we escorted Mr. Parker back into your lovely arms.

Courtney asked, "What's up, Mom? Where is Uncle Jordan?

La'Roc told them that she was also worried about Jordan. She voiced her concern since she hadn't seen him since dinner. La'Roc also revealed how Jordan sometimes reacted to his medication.

Courtney responded in a nervous tone, "Me and Devon will look in Uncle Jordan's bedroom."

"Courtney, wait. Shawn and I will look in Jordan's bedroom. You and Devon go check out the gym. After you guys check out the gym, go back out to the guests and thank them for coming by to greet Shawn. Shawn already said his goodbyes."

"Okay, Momma. We'll meet you back in to the great room,"

La'Roc couldn't get Jordan's last episode out of her mind. It was frightening and very scary; she thought her friend was going to die.

That was La'Roc's reason for not wanting her daughter and grandson to go to Jordan's room; she didn't want them to see what she saw when she witnessed Jordan having a reaction to his medication. She wanted to protect her daughter and grandson from seeing Jordan fight his demons.

La'Roc ran upstairs to Jordan's bedroom, and Shawn followed behind her. She knocked on Jordan's bedroom door. No answer.

Shawn opened the bedroom door, and there was Jordan, lying on the floor near his bed in his own vomit and excretion all over his body. Jordan always kept gloves on his nightstand and clean pads by his bed. The pads were large enough to wrap around you like a sheet. La'Roc took a pair of gloves and gave Shawn a pair of gloves to put on, and put a pad over the vomit and defecation.

"Shawn, please help me. I don't think he is breathing. Shawn, he is bleeding profusely from his mouth." La'Roc was unsure if Jordan was still alive or dead. She was paralyzed with fear that her best friend was dead.

She was screaming so loud. "Shawn, please, please help Jordan." As Shawn was holding her in his arms, she was trying to explain to Shawn about the reaction to the medication. The bleeding was coming from Jordan biting his tongue. He was shaking and bleeding from the mouth. Shawn told La'Roc to call a doctor while he tried to insert a spoon into Jordan mouth to prevent Jordan from chewing his tongue.

Shawn said, "Sexiful, stop crying. Jordan will be all right."

La'Roc continued to scream, trembling and frightened that she was losing her best friend.

Through his agony, Jordan could hear La'Roc crying. He struggled to respond to her cries. He didn't want his dearest friend to worry about him. He had to tell her he didn't need a doctor. This would pass. He had to make her understand he would be all right. This would go away. "Baby girl, why are you crying? I'm still here. I made a promise to you and Shawn. I'll be in court on Friday, fighting for his freedom. La'Roc, I'm not going to leave you—not yet, anyway."

She ran over to where Jordan was lying on the floor near his bed and gave him a playful punch on the right side of his face. Tears ran down her beautiful face as Shawn tried to comfort her. Shawn left La'Roc and went into the bath bathroom to get a washcloth for Jordan and a glass of water.

"Oh, Jordan, I'm so happy you still have jokes, but I'm not in the mood for your jokes right now," La'Roc said as she tried to control her emotions.

"I am angry with you because you didn't give your best friend a heads-up on your reaction. Jordan, dammed, you can't go through these episodes alone!" La'Roc shouted in outrage.

"Jordan, do you have the list of your medications I asked for several days ago? I want the names of all of your medications and the reactions that you get from them," demanded La'Roc.

Shawn watched the two friends from the bathroom doorway. He made a mental note to talk with Jordan about these episodes. He didn't need La'Roc to be so worried about Jordan.

They cleaned up Jordan and the room.

"Yes, baby girl, it's in my computer. I will print you another copy tomorrow. Please don't worry about me, baby girl. I will be okay as long as you have my back."

Courtney and Devon entered Jordan's bedroom, laughing with each other. "What's wrong, Momma?" Courtney asked as Devon looked on.

La'Roc responded, "Uncle Jordan doesn't feel very well." "Uncle Jordan, what's up?" Courtney asked.

"I am fine. Your mother is overreacting, as always. I am doing just great, little ones. Don't worry about me. Go enjoy yourselves."

"Courtney, did all the guests leave?" La'Roc asked.

Devon answered, "Aunt L'Oreal, Uncle Casey, Chantal, and Denise are still outside, sitting around the pool."

"Devon, what happened to August? Did you drive her home?"

"Yes Grams, I drove her home about two hours ago."

"She seems to be a nice girl, Devon. However, I would like to meet her again with her parents. Will that be possible?" La'Roc asked as she looked at her grandson with great admiration in her eyes.

"Devon responded "anything for you, Grams."

"La'Roc replied thank you, baby. I'll keep that in mind," she said with a wink.

While Jordan finished his shower, the group remained in his sitting room, discussing the upcoming trial. Everyone concluded that it was going to go well and that they would win. Courtney and Devon returned to the great room, leaving Shawn and La'Roc in the room. Jordan finished his shower and came out of the shower looking like his old self. La'Roc and Shawn walked away. Before leaving Jordan's room, La'Roc looked back and gave him a smile.

The two of them walked down the hall to La'Roc's bedroom, holding hands. Shawn put his arms around La'Roc and picked her up in his big, strong arms. "I am so happy to be here in this beautiful townhouse with a family that loves me and a woman to die for."

"First, let's go take a quick shower." They took a nice hot shower after leaving Jordan's room.

He looked into her eyes and then kissed her hard and aggressively. She knew he wanted her as bad as she wanted him.

"Baby, I've waited all afternoon to be alone with you. Now I have you and I'm not letting you go—ever." Shawn held her tight in his arms. "I'm all yours—now and forever.

"Shawn, I love you too. Stop talking and make love to me," La'Roc responded with a playful smirk on her face.

"You only have to ask me once. I've waited all day to make love to you," Shawn said, smiling.

"Shawn, sweetheart, did you lock the door? We don't need any surprises, like my mother busting into our bedroom," La'Roc said, smiling at her man.

"Baby, I'm on it. Doors are locked, and your babies are well taken care of by your top employee Ms. Holiday."

"Shawn, since you mention it, I only played with my babies twice today. Oh, well. We'll play with them after you make love to me. I need you to walk over to this bed and undress your *Sexiful Rose* like you missed her,"

La'Roc wrapped herself in her robe before going into the whirlpool with her future husband.

After taking her robe off, Shawn carried her into the whirlpool and laid her into the champagne bubble bath. He kissed her gently on her shoulders, neck, and upper body.

After Shawn quickly undressed himself, he sat behind her in the whirlpool and handed her a glass of Cristal Champagne. As she sipped on her champagne, she grabbed onto his manhood and held it tight. She wanted him to make love to her right then and there. He reached for her glass of champagne and set it down on the bathroom stand beside his empty glass. He lifted her wet body from the whirlpool and carried her into the bedroom. He laid her on the bed softly with love in his eyes.

Shawn then turned Sexiful around to face him; he put his tongue into her ear and sucked on her earlobes. She was burning up as if she were on fire. He kissed her and worked his tongue all over her body. Sexiful was wild with burning desire like she was in flames. She moaned and groaned as he made love around her vagina. She begged him to continue to give her what she had been waiting for the entire day. She wanted his penis inside of her right at that moment.

She wanted him to make love to her that night as if she were the only woman he had ever made love to.

After making love, she laid her head on his chest and listened to his heartbeat.

With Shawn around, she felt protected and loved.

"Sexiful, let's take a shower and take a ride to downtown Brooklyn. I need to go and check on my house. I know you kept it together for us. Am I right, babe?" Shawn said, smiling.

She responded, "Yes, baby. You know I did."

"That sounds like a plan, baby. We could stay there until morning."

She smiled, looking back in Shawn's direction. "Shawn, after you were incarcerated, I had no incentive or motivation to visit the brownstone again. Every time I thought about going to visit the brownstone, I would break down and cry because it was such a painful place to revisit. Shawn, you're here now, and we can overcome anything together."

After showering, they headed downstairs and out to the Hummer.

"Oh! Baby, wait I have a surprise for you. Open the door and look in the backseat." La'Roc did as Shawn asked of her; Paris and Biscuit were lying in the backseat in their doggie bed, fast asleep.

La'Roc looked up at Shawn with a gratified smile on her face. She pulled his face down to her lips and kissed him softly. "Thanks baby."

"I'll do anything for my baby," Shawn responded.

"Shawn, when did you have time to facilitate this beautiful surprise? Sweetie, how did you to pull this off?"

"Courtney and Devon put all this together. Sexiful, this surprise is because we all love you, sweetheart. Ms. Holiday also stocked the refrigerator with wine and some other goodies that you enjoy," Shawn replied.

Driving down I-95, La'Roc looked over at her handsome man with joy in her heart, and Shawn appeared content and relaxed. However, there was also some sadness lurking around in Shawn's eyes. La'Roc knew that Shawn needed to express his feeling about losing his son to another man, the son he had been taking care of for the past two years. To lose him now was devastating.

La'Roc moved her body closer to her handsome prince, raised her lips to his face, and kissed him gently on the cheek.

He held her hand and pulled her closer to him with his arm around her shoulders as he continued to drive down the highway. He whispered in her ear, "I love you, Sexiful."

"I love you too, baby. However, we need to talk about Shawn Jr. Shawn, I know it's hard for you to talk about him, but this matter cannot wait forever. He is not getting any younger," La'Roc reminded him.

"I wanted to wait until after the trial is over. It hurt a lot after two years of taking care of that little guy. And to find out he is not mine—that is disturbing. If it wasn't for you, I don't know what would have happened. Thanks, baby, for keeping me rational. Sexiful, when you told me Shawn Jr. was not my son, I thought you were just punishing me for something I had done. I could not believe that Kelly or my sister could do that to me. Sexiful, I was infuriated with myself for getting involved with a nut like Kelly," Shawn said, his voice trembling nervously as he spoke.

La'Roc touched his hand for reassurance, to let him know that she was there for him no matter what happened.

They soon arrived at Shawn's brownstone. The brownstone was well kept; his lawn was well manicured, and the backyard looked great. Everything was beautiful, including the gym that Shawn worked so hard to build for her liking.

Shawn said, "It's unbelievable that I am standing in the middle of my living room with my fiancée, the woman who I so deeply love and adore. This can't be for real. Touch me, Sexiful. I want to make sure I'm not dreaming."

In Shawn's home, La'Roc was always Sexiful.

Sexiful climbed on top of a stepstool in the living room to reach Shawn's height and pulled him into her arms and held him tight before kissing him.

"Baby, we're together now, and we'll always be together as one. Shawn, first of all, we'll have to get your freedom on Friday and then figure out what to do with Shawn Jr.," La'Roc responded. La'Roc continued to try to engage Shawn in a conversation about SJ because she wanted him to express his feelings and the pain he had to endure. La'Roc needed Shawn to keep an open mind about his so-called son. He was trying to suppress his feeling like Shawn Jr. never happened, but La'Roc wouldn't allow him to put it on the backburner. She wanted him to talk about the situation because it happened and he had to express it.

"Yes, I can't wait to be a free man again."

"Have you had time to think about what part you want to play in Shawn Jr's life?" She just couldn't allow Shawn to ignore this issue.

"I know one thing that I don't want to do, and that is to play his father. It's a good thing that Kelly's little secret came out while Shawn Jr. is still a young child. Being two is in his favor because it won't hurt as bad as it would if he were older. I just don't want to confuse him anymore; I want him to know that I am not his biological father. However, after he is older, I'd like to be there for him if he needs me to help him in terms of his education, etc. Sexiful, can we discuss this after the trial?" Shawn said, changing the subject again.

"Of course we can, handsome," she answered with concern. She noticed his voice had begun to shake.

She knew that Shawn was hurting inside; she could see it in his eyes and could hear it in his voice when he tried to cover it with his lame jokes.

That night, Shawn and La'Roc talked about everything under the sun. They talked about everything except Shawn's court case.

She didn't need to confuse him with the trial; she didn't want to say something that she hadn't discussed with Alex and the team.

La'Roc and Shawn played with her babies before retiring for bed. Going to sleep that night was so peaceful. She slept in Shawn's arms with her head on his chest, like she always did; that is what he requested every night before going to sleep, and she always provided him with whatever he wanted.

The next morning, he made breakfast and served her in bed with a chef's apron and chef's hat on his head. They both laughed so hard about the outfit Shawn was wearing until tears ran down their faces.

They were still laughing and didn't notice her babies were sitting in the middle of the floor, staring at the two of them and putting their paws over their eyes.

Shawn and La'Roc looked over at Paris and Biscuit. They laughed even harder.

After breakfast, La'Roc asked Shawn to come outside with her to do some laps around the grounds. "Don't forget to bring Paris and Biscuit with you, okay, babe?"

"Sexiful, Paris, and Biscuit were out earlier with me. We went for a long walk downtown this morning. I did some banking and had Shawn Jr. checks stopped. I also looked at another truck for business while you were sleeping." "Shawn, that's great. *I'm* proud of you baby." La'Roc was pleased with the decision he had made concerning Kelly's son.

La'Roc thought to herself, *My God, how could you treat another human being the way Kelly treated Shawn? How could she tell Shawn that Shawn Jr. was his child? It wasn't as if she kept the secret for a day or a week; she held this secret for two years.*

Shawn's sister was just a bitch to allow Kelly to engage her brother in such wicked behavior. How could April hurt her brother so badly?

La'Roc knew in her heart and soul that she would never forgive Ms. April Parker. What she would love to do is to put April and Kelly away for life.

La'Roc and Shawn walked around his property, holding hands, laughing, and enjoying the outside world.

La'Roc's cell phone rang. She answered, "Hello, my child. What is going on?"

"Mommy we're all right. Just checking in. What time are you guys coming to Westchester?"

"We'll be leaving the brownstone in an hour. We are still at Shawn's brownstone in Brooklyn."

Courtney said, "Mom I have a surprise for you and Shawn when you return home."

"All right, baby. Can't wait."

"Sexiful, who was on the phone?" Shawn asked.

"Courtney."

The two of them ran into the brownstone and headed toward the shower room. Paris and Biscuit followed and jumped into their doggie bed that were placed outside the shower room.

Shawn undressed her, and after undressing himself, he stepped into the shower with his Sexiful Rose.

He rubbed shower gel all over her body—from her head all the way down to her toes.

There was no penetration in the shower that day; he just wanted to make love to her beautiful body, and she obliged him. Standing in the shower, she opened her legs wide so he could rub some shower gel in between her legs and thighs. He provided the tools to give her a good massage.

He massaged her inner thighs with his tongue. He kissed his way back up to her breasts and massaged her breast, and she loved every minute of it. As the warm water from the shower ran down her body, she prayed in silence, *Please, Shawn, make love to me*. She asked him in silence, but he was unable to give her what she wanted because they made a promise to each other that day in the shower. The promise was not to make love for the whole day.

"It was a very stupid promise. Don't you agree?" La'Roc laughed to herself as she reevaluated her crazy promise.

Shawn making love to her body was all she needed; after the heated shower, Shawn carried her into the bedroom to dry her off.

"Shawn, please mix some drinks so we can relax," La'Roc yelled from the bedroom. "Today is Sunday; we must get to the townhouse. Ms. Holiday will have dinner ready around five o'clock, and I informed Courtney that we would be there on time," La'Roc said.

Shawn gave La'Roc her drink and sat on the bed next to her as they sipped on their white wine.

"Sexiful, sweetheart, don't worry. We'll be there on time," Shawn assured her. After they had their drinks, La'Roc and Shawn fell asleep.

Three hours later, they were on their way to Westchester.

La'Roc wore her hair in a high ponytail; she and Shawn wore matching outfits that he had purchased earlier that morning.

Biscuit and Paris were fast asleep in their car seat. They were beat after their walk with Shawn.

"Sexiful, after the trial, I'd like to be on board with the Jordan Foundation. I think that is a great idea to start an organization in Jordan's name," Shawn said with concern in his voice.

"Oh, baby, that would be wonderful. The team would just love to have a handsome guy like you on board." Sexiful smiled.

"I'll talk to L'Oreal and Casey as soon as we get to Westchester. I know they'll be overwhelmed with joy to know you want to be a part of the foundation," La'Roc responded.

Finally, Shawn pulled up in the driveway and into the garage. "Baby, we're home," Shawn announced, speaking loud enough to wake up Paris and Biscuit.

Paris and Biscuit sat up in their car seat, looking at Shawn as if to say, "Are you done with the loud noise?"

Shawn unbuckled his seatbelt, got out of the hummer, and walked around to the passenger side to open the door for her.

La'Roc reached for Shawn's extended hand and stepped out of the hummer. She and Shawn reached into the backseat to retrieve Paris and Biscuit.

Ms. Cotton, Courtney, Devon, and Jordan ran outside to greet the loving couple with hugs and kisses.

"Hello, my family. I guess we were missed, Shawn," La'Roc said jokingly. Shawn nodded his head with approval.

"Hi, baby girl. You look happy. I love to see you smile," Jordan said.

"Come over here, Jordan, and give your sister an extensive hug."

"Baby girl, you only have to say it once. Get over here and hug me," Jordan responded. La'Roc ran into Jordan's open arms.

"Mom, we have a surprise for you and Shawn inside," Courtney said, smiling from ear to ear."

"What is it, Devon?" La'Roc asked.

"Grams, it wouldn't be a surprise if I told you."

"I know what the surprise is: Denise and Chantal," La'Roc said, guessing. As they walked into the house, Shawn and La'Roc were led into the great room by Courtney and Devon. La'Roc said, "Wait a minute. I'm not walking any further until you tell me the surprise." Denise said, "Stop being a spoiled brat."

Chantal burst out laughing in amusement at the smart remark from Denise. La'Roc put her hand over her mouth as if she had seen a ghost. "Oh my God. It's Justin with Dr. Kim."

La'Roc and Shawn walked over to Justin; she hugged him, and Shawn shook his hand.

La'Roc asked, "Courtney, Devon, and Dr. Kim, how could you guys keep something like this from me?"

It was so nice to see Justin sitting up in his wheelchair, laughing and playing around with Devon and Jordan.

Justin's speech wasn't clear, and when he spoke, his voice would quiver. It was hard to understand what he was saying through the shaky voice. He wasn't able to form sentences. For example, he couldn't say Courtney's name. He called her Court.

It was a miracle that the new medication Dr. Woo gave Justin really worked. Thank God for Dr. Woo and his team.

"Justin, this is a wonderful surprise," La'Roc said as she gave him a welcome home kiss.

Shawn walked back over and gave him a high five.

"Dr. Kim, how long have you known Justin was making such positive progress, and did Courtney know about his recovery?" La'Roc asked.

"Yes, Ms. Rose. Courtney and I knew for a while. She just wanted to surprise you and Mr. Parker. She was thinking of telling you at the party Friday night. But she decided to do it today because Friday night was for Mr. Parker and only Mr. Parker," Dr. Kim answered.

La'Roc looked over at Dr. Kim. "Good answer, Debbie." She winked and walked away with a smile.

Ms. Cotton yelled out, "Dinner is being served in the south wing of the house today. Ms. Rose, Mr. Sanchez left your gifts in the entertainment room."

"Thank you, Ms. Holiday." The gifts were from the shopping spree that Courtney and she had gone on several days ago.

"Thank you, Ms. Cotton."

La'Roc saw her two best friends walking into the great room, smiling. Chantal said, "La'Roc, you should see the mansion. We did a wonderful job, if I may say so myself."

"Sis, we've been working every night to get this party together for Friday evening. I tell you, you're going to love the decorations. L'Oreal and Courtney worked their asses off on the decorations, day and night," Denise said.

They all sat down to a wonderful dinner. After dinner, Courtney, Devon, Dr. Kim, and Shawn drove Justin back to the rehabilitation center.

Before driving Justin back to Manhattan, La'Roc and Courtney decided to give everyone their gifts from their shopping spree. All the presents were accepted with tears and thank yous, and the whole team showed gratification with hugs and kisses. La'Roc looked over at Shawn. "Baby, I'll give you your present later on in the week." She smiled at her handsome man with a wink.

Devon and Courtney asked Shawn to take the ride to Manhattan because they had a plan. The plan was to get Shawn off so L'Oreal and the women could drive La'Roc to the mansion to show her the decorations for Shawn's welcome home party.

Devon asked for the keys to the Hummer to drive Justin back to Manhattan. La'Roc informed Dr. Kim that there was a van especially equipped for Justin's home visits. She further revealed that the van was to be used any time Justin came to visit.

As Devon pulled out of the driveway, La'Roc decided to get her babies ready for their little trip to the mansion.

Denise yelled over her shoulder, "L'Oreal, we'll take Chantal's SUV, and, Chantal, you ride with Jordan and La'Roc. Casey, you get in the car with me and your wife if you don't mind listening to two females yapping the whole trip."

Jordan arrived at the mansion. La'Roc said, "What the hell happened? This looks like a different place. Jordan, what did you do? Did you rebuild?" La'Roc asked jokingly.

Chantal said, "My dear sister, you haven't seen anything yet."

La'Roc was in shock. The outside of the house was gorgeous. She couldn't believe her eyes.

La'Roc had no idea what had been going on during the past several months. She was so busy with Shawn's trial; she basically forgot she owned a mansion.

Tears began to flow down her face. These tears were of happiness and thankfulness for all of her friends and her wonderful family.

L'Oreal said, "La'Roc, close your eyes before you walk into the house." "Okay sis. My eyes are closed," La'Roc said with a smile.

Jordan said, "Keep your eyes closed. We're almost there." Denise yelled out, "Open your eyes!"

Everyone said, "Surprise!"

"Oh my God this is unbelievable." La'Roc couldn't believe what they had done to her house in such a short time.

Jordan even had the contractors build more swimming pools. There were lights all around the house, parking lot, and the pools; all of these beautiful decorations were for Shawn's welcome home party. The grounds were beautiful.

He even had a big parking lot built on the side of the house. The parking lot was built on a big sheet of concrete with lights surrounding La'Roc's greenhouse.

The girls had decorated one of the rooms like a ballroom; the dining area was set up with long-stemmed candlesticks in all of Shawn's favorite colors.

Everything was exquisite.

La'Roc was so overwhelmed with joy. She cupped her hands under her chin and began to cry.

She felt in her heart that Shawn would be just as excited as she was right now.

Jordan's cell phone began to rang. He checked his caller ID before he answered.

"Hello baby. Is everything okay? Oh, baby, she loved it. She is crying as we speak. She is really happy about the outside as well as the inside," Jordan answered with a wink at La'Roc.

"Jordan, is that my baby?"

"Baby girl," he motioned for La'Roc to come over to him as he handed her his cell phone.

La'Roc reached for Jordan's cell phone. "Thanks, Jordan. Hi, baby. You guys did a wonderful job on the decorations—the place looks magnificent."

"Baby, when I walked into the ballroom, it was breathtaking. I am overjoyed with all the work you guys put into the decorating. I love it. Shawn is going to be extremely happy when he sees the decorations and knows this house is mine. He is going to be delighted when he walks in and sees the party is for him. Sweetheart, you did a fantastic job. Are you guys on your way back?"

"Yes, Mother. We're almost home," Courtney answered. "Courtney, how is Justin?"

"Oh, Mom, he's fine. He's looking forward to coming home for the party on Friday. Mom, I need to hire a nurse for Friday because Justin will be there for the whole day," Courtney said.

"Courtney, Justin has a nurse at the center, right? We have a nurse on payroll. Ask her to come with him. That is what I pay her for: to take care of Justin. Dr. Moore will attend, and we have Dr. Kim. Please don't worry, kid; we have it under control," La'Roc responded. Before they completed their conversation, Courtney informed her mother that she had invited Dr. Cummingham as well.

La'Roc smiled to herself upon hearing this piece of news. She had recently spoken with the good doctor when he gave her the results of her HIV test: negative. All was right in the world for now.

La'Roc walked back into the sitting room and joined her friends as they drank their wine and chatted about the upcoming party. She really loved this group.

La'Roc joined the clan with a glass of red wine.

"L'Oreal, how did you manage to do all of this, the foundation, and helping with all the decorations? Baby, how can I ever thank you? I love you, sis. Thanks again," La'Roc said with tears in her eyes.

"Just to see your face light up—that was thanks enough for me. That was my gratification," L'Oreal said, hugging her sister. Casey joined in on the hug.

"I want to thank all of you for being my best friends. I love each and every one of you. Thank you, guys."

As she continued to talk with her friends, La'Roc's phone chimed a familiar ring; it was Shawn.

"Hi, handsome you miss me?" La'Roc asked playfully.

"Yes, I miss you. Where are you?"

"Oh poor baby, you missed your little Sexiful?" she said, teasing him.

"I asked the girls to take a ride with me to look at another Jeep for Devon and a Hummer for Courtney," La'Roc answered. She hated lying to Shawn; as she was talking to Shawn, she kept her fingers crossed. (Like cross my fingers was going to stop the lie.)

Maybe she would be forgiven for telling that little white lie. It wasn't a real lie because she and Shawn were going to buy the car and the hummer for her daughter and grandson anyway.

"Oh, baby, that's cool. Let me buy the Jeep for Devon. I want to show my appreciation for what he did during my bail hearing."

"Okay, baby. We'll go looking for Devon's Jeep tomorrow. That's a great idea," La'Roc answered. *That's a good idea because I didn't buy the Jeep or the Hummer today.*

La'Roc was happy to see how seamlessly Shawn had fit himself into her family. She was especially happy with the relationship that had developed between Shawn and Devon.

"Chantal, what is it that you and Jordan find so funny?" La'Roc asked, smiling.

"Tell you later, nosy," Chantal responded to La'Roc. "What's going on, Denise?" La'Roc asked.

Denise answered, "I've no idea, sis."

"Come on, guys. Let's get ready to go back down to the townhouse. My baby is missing his Sexiful Rose," La'Roc said with excitement.

"I'm ready for a nightcap....after the nightcap I want to take my wife to bed so we can get a good night's sleep," Casey said, looking over at his wife and giving her a sexy smile.

After leaving the mansion, they drove back to the townhouse to meet up with the other part of the team.

La'Roc thought, *Oh, tomorrow will be a work day; the lawyers will be working on Shawn's case most of the day.*

"Baby girl, I know you'll be excited when this trial is over. Everything is going to be great. Please, don't worry about the case since we already have it in the bag," Jordan said, looking at La'Roc with concern.

When the group arrived at the townhouse, La'Roc noticed Shawn was outside, playing with Paris and Biscuit.

Shawn left the dogs as they continued to play with each other. He quickly opened the car door for La'Roc.

"Hi, baby. I missed you, Sexiful," Shawn said as he kissed her lips.

"Oh, I missed you too," La'Roc responded. "Well, sweetheart, you'll be missing me tomorrow because you're going to be busy with your lawyers, working on your trial for the next few days. I need you ready for Friday when you face the judge. I want you to be well rested, looking good, and showing confidence in yourself as well as in your lawyers." She looked at him with a serious face in her lawyer mode.

"Baby, I'm ready to face the judge. As long as you're by my side, I can face anything. Guess what, baby? I made a decision about SJ and the Brown family. Let me just run this by you.

"I was just thinking today about cutting all ties with the Brown family, including Shawn Jr. I think it's better for me to step out of his life while he is still young and doesn't understand what's going on. If I continue to lie to Shawn Jr., then I'm no better than his mother. You understand, Sexiful."

"I agree, baby. It's your decision. I'll always support you, no matter what. Shawn, I love you, and I'll always be on your side as long as you are honest with me." La'Roc and Shawn continued to walk her babies around the complex while holding hands.

La'Roc looked up into Shawn's eyes. "Shawn, take me into your arms and pretend there is no tomorrow. Shawn, you have fulfilled my life with all the good things you have given me and my family, especially Courtney and Devon. Handsome, when I see you, I just want run into your strong, muscular arms and whisper sweet nothings into your ear. Take me, baby. Make love to me, and let me do what I want do with that strong body of yours."

Shawn picked her up and kissed her softly on her lovely lips. "Baby, let's go upstairs and mix some drinks and relax in each other's arms because tomorrow I will be out of commission. Remember, I will be busy all day. Come on, baby. Let's go inside."

Shawn positioned her on his back and picked up both babies and walked up the driveway to the townhouse.

Jordan was standing on the terrace, looking down on them, laughing. Jordan yelled down from the terrace, "Man, you better not drop my only sister. Hold on, baby girl," Jordan said jokingly.

Once inside the townhouse, she noticed that Chantal and Denise had fallen asleep in the great room. Courtney and Devon were on the sofa in the living room, fast asleep.

L'Oreal and Casey were the only ones who went upstairs to bed.

Devon had driven Geneva home earlier that day. She was tired and wanted to go home so she could attend church with her friends later that evening.

Shawn and La'Roc went quietly upstairs. The terrace door was open. La'Roc noticed that Dr. Kim and Jordan were sitting on the terrace; they seemed engaged in a deep conversation.

La'Roc and Shawn continued on their journey up the stairs to the master bedroom to make some much-needed loving, which she had dreamed about all that day.

Shawn was the best lover in the world, and oh how she missed him when he was away at Upland. *Shawn means everything to me,* La'Roc thought.

La'Roc's thoughts were always on Shawn's lovemaking and how great he made her feel. Shawn had that special ability; you know when your lover makes love to you and put that hump in his back, he is a keeper. That man knows what he is doing. That type of lovemaking make you want to call him daddy. Shawn's affection was so deep that when they made love, she became his slave. He was so irresistible and devoted in his lovemaking. He made her feel that she was the only woman in his world.

She adored him and worshiped the ground he walked on.

La'Roc asked herself, *how could Kelly have treated Shawn like she did and lie to him about fathering her child? Kelly is a sick human being.* Or maybe there was something La'Roc didn't know about Shawn and Kelly. Because there's no way a person could be that bitchy.

Shawn carried Paris and Biscuit to their playroom. La'Roc waited patiently for Shawn to enter the bedroom to take out his tool and start his machine.

Shawn entered the bedroom with nothing on but a towel wrapped around his waist. He smiled, showing off his six-pack.

La'Roc looked at her handsome young man walking into her bedroom. All she wanted was for him to hurry and get in bed with her and insert his penis inside her womanhood. As he approached her, she could see his manhood rising beneath the towel he was wearing.

"Shawn, please come to Momma and give her what you promised."

Shawn leaned over to her and kissed her gently on her right earlobe. She loved the sensation and feeling of what his kisses did to her. When he kissed her she was at his command.

She whispered in his ear, "Baby, please make love to me and make me beg for more."

"Sexiful, Daddy is here, and I'm going to give you what you asked for." Shawn gave her a bath with his tongue all over her sweet chocolate body.

She moaned with pleasure as he continued to make love to her. He massaged her vagina with his long tongue.

He continued to make love to her as gently as possible, sliding his penis inside of her.

The lovemaking was good; they made love in all the soundproof rooms because she was yelling his name as loud as possible as he pumped his penis inside of her. He whispered in her ear how much he loved her.

Shawn's deep velvet voice caressed her ear. "Baby, am I giving you what you want? If this is not enough, I'll give you more. Sexiful, I don't want to hurt you. Is that too much of me inside of you?"

La'Roc barely recognized her own voice when she whispered in Shawn's ear, "Shawn, I am not glass—I will not break. Baby, just give it all to me. Push your penis all the way, and don't hold back,"

Shawn then put a hump in his back and gave her everything he had; she cried with pleasure and fulfillment. During that moment of passion, she became his slave. She wanted to keep his penis inside of her forever.

After reaching the satisfaction of her pleasure, she rolled over on top of him and made love to his entire body.

She wanted to extend their lovemaking and let Shawn enjoy the same pleasure and fulfillment that she felt.

Shawn enjoyed the pleasure that she was giving him. As the pressure built, they both felt that they couldn't take any more. Shawn yelled out, "Sexiful, what are you doing to me that feel so damn good? Please don't stop, baby. I am yours forever."

She sat on his manhood and rotated her body on his penis as he closed his eyes and rolled with the flow.

Sexiful and Shawn reached their climax ... then he pulled her into his arms playfully and kissed her hard on her lips.

He then looked at her with a smirk on his face. "Sexiful, you know you are mine, right? I'll never let you go, no matter what."

"Shawn, you're stuck with me forever," La'Roc responded.

As La'Roc leaned back on the many pillows near the padded headboard, Shawn walked across the bedroom to the small bar located near the far wall. She watched the play of his muscles in his back as he crossed the room. He smiled as he filled their glasses of wine.

After finishing their wine, they took a steamy shower, this time for cleaning. Then they fell into bed to sleep in each other's arms.

Early in the morning, Shawn slipped silently from the bed to shower. La'Roc was easing into awareness when Courtney jumped on her bed, with Paris and Biscuit in her wake.

La'Roc rolled over and tried to focus on the familiar voice. "Courtney, what's wrong? everything okay?" She searched the room to find Shawn and breathed a sigh of relief that he was still in the shower.

"Mother, we need to talk about the setup for the party. How did you like it?" Courtney asked, looking like La'Roc's little baby.

"Sweetheart, I loved the decorations. The whole house is beautiful. How did you guys accomplish so much in such a short time?"

"Mom, we had a lot of help, and Jordan hired extra help. Mom, you really liked it?" Courtney asked again to be sure.

"Come over here, little La'Roc, and give your mother a big hug." Courtney liked it when she called her "Little La'Roc." La'Roc smiled.

Courtney jumped from the bed and did a Michael Jackson moonwalk to the door.

She turned and looked back. "Thanks, Mom. If you like the house decorations, Shawn is going to love them."

Courtney opened the door. Standing there were Jordan, Devon, Alex, and, don't forget, Denise and Chantal, looking stupid.

They all decided to have breakfast in La'Roc's bedroom. L'Oreal and Casey stood in the background, saying nothing, just standing.

"Okay crazy people. What's going on? Tell me or get your asses out of my room, pronto."

L'Oreal said, "I will tell her. No, Casey, you tell her."

"Somebody better tell me what's going on," La'Roc said in a low, slow tone that warned the group that she was tired of their nonsense.

Casey said in a low, husky voice, "Shawn, just donated one of his buildings and ten thousand dollars to the foundation. That's not all;

he'll be volunteering his spare time to the foundation." Shawn stood in the doorway leading to the bedroom and listened to the excited chatter of the group. However, he mainly focused on La'Roc's face. Lord, how he loved this woman. Pushing off the doorway, he made his way into the room and sat on the bed beside his love.

The team took their seats in La'Roc's office outside of her bedroom. Shawn and La'Roc joined the team in the outer office next to her bedroom.

Jordan removed himself from his seat and walked over to where Shawn and La'Roc were sitting. He reached for Shawn's hand. Shawn responded by shaking Jordan's hand. Jordan made a speech and thanked all of his sisters and brothers for the wonderful job they were doing.

La'Roc turned to Shawn and thanked him with a kiss and tears in her eyes. She said to herself, *what a wonderful man to give that much to Jordan's foundation, and he was just released from prison. I have some good friends, and most of all, a good man.*

"Thank you, Casey, for sharing that good news with me." Jordan started to cry. As La'Roc looked around the office, there was nothing but sadness. La'Roc said, "Come on, team, let's break up the sadness in this room. Whose idea was it to bring breakfast to my room?" La'Roc asked.

"It was mine, Grams."

"So my grandson thought of this all by himself. Hmm. You're fired, grandson. Alex, you didn't tell him I am not one to accept practical jokes. Alex, you are fired as well," La'Roc winked at the team. "Alex, you and Devon can pick up your checks on your way out and leave my car in the lot at the office." Alex looked back as he was walking out of the office door. "La'Roc, does that means I won't be working on Shawn's case on Friday?"

"Alex, I think we can handle it," La'Roc responded. She looked over at Shawn and Jordan. "Do you guys think we need them for Shawn's case on Friday?"

Shawn spoke first. "I think I need Alex and Devon on my side. They're two good lawyers, and I don't want to lose them."

"Let's keep them for a little while longer," Jordan responded.

"Okay, guys. You heard the votes. You are now rehired," La'Roc announced. Devon walked over to his grandmother and gave her a hug. "I love you, woman."

"Devon, you knew that I was joking right? I would never fire you unless you did something really unprofessional. Devon, remember, you always need to be on point for little things like that. Jokes could be a symbol, a sign of something happening in the courtroom. Devon, you see, your grandmother is always in lawyer mode. Just stay on your toes, and do not ever be surprised about whatever is coming in your direction. Always be ready for any surprises you may have to face, and never say never.

"Devon, remember, the word *can't* is not an option. The word *can't* is not in your vocabulary. Come; let's eat. You guys have to get to work. Alex, I am holding you and Jordan for details. Shawn needs to explain every little detail of what happened on the day in question; and, Shawn, you have to be honest. You must tell everything as you remember it on that morning of the accident. They have your statement, and you'll be asked to go over it again and again in several different ways," La'Roc said. "I'll be around if you need me for anything. I don't think you will because I have faith in my team. Remember, team, Devon doesn't have to put in as many hours as you guys. He's a student, not a certified lawyer," La'Roc reminded Alex and Jordan.

"Now get out of my office and go rest up for the trial."

Casey and L'Oreal went downstairs with Devon.

Dr. Kim and Courtney left for Manhattan to do the paperwork for Justin's overnight pass for Friday night.

Chantal, Denise, and La'Roc went onto the terrace carrying glasses of juice in their hands.

La'Roc was giving thanks to her friends. "First of all, I would like to thank you again for helping Courtney to prepare for Shawn's welcome home party."

"We loved helping Courtney and L'Oreal. L'Oreal hooked that shit up,"

Denise said.

Chantal said, "We wouldn't have it any other way."

"Your sister, L'Oreal, she knows her business when it comes to organizing and planning a party. I want her to plan my next birthday party or maybe my wedding," Chantal said as she looked over at La'Roc with a childish smirk.

"Tell me, bitches: what's going on? It has been a while since we talked," La'Roc asked.

Chantal said, "Well my long-distance love affair is still going strong with my doctor friend from California. He'll be here on Friday for the big party."

La'Roc said, looking at Denise, "Slut, you finally made it. You're a long-distance whore. Chantal, you made it." The three girls looked at each other and bust out in a loud laugh.

They were laughing so loud, L'Oreal and her husband ran up the stairs to check out what was going on.

L'Oreal asked, "What's going on with you teenagers?"

"Sis, we're all right. We're sorry we scared you. Please forgive these girls and their stupid behavior. I apologize; we were just having some long overdue fun."

"We forgive you this time. Just don't frighten my wife again." Casey smiled and left the terrace, holding his wife's hand.

After L'Oreal and Casey left the terrace, La'Roc, Denise, and Chantal continued their conversation about their love lives.

"Denise, what's up with your love life, or do you have one?" Chantal joked.

"My love life stinks. I kicked Martin out two months ago. He has no job and has been living off me for the past year. His meal ticket ran its course. He's calling every day with his threats, what he's going to do when he sees me, etc." La'Roc turned to face Denise with a disappointed look on her face. "I thought we had this discussion some time ago when I asked him to drop off your car and give you back your keys? Chantal, do you remember that conversation and did you know about this?"

Chantal turned confused eyes toward her friend. For the life of her, she couldn't understand how and why a bright woman like Denise held on to a louse like Martin. She thought that after the conversation a few weeks ago that Denise would have kicked him to the curb—evidently not. Chantal had a feeling that this relationship was not going to end well. She loved her friend and knew she would stick by her, but this was going to be hard.

Denise held her head down as if she were being reprimanded for stealing a cookie from the cookie jar.

Denise explained her reason for thinking she still loved Martin. "I don't know what happened. I just took him back because I thought I still loved him. I know now that I don't love him. I think I hate him."

"Denise, are you ready to let Martin go this time? I will have him picked up right now. You just say the word, and he will be on his way to jail. Denise, don't get me confused with someone who gives damn about Martin because I don't. I never liked Martin. He is a fucking opportunist." La'Roc expressed.

"Denise, what are you going to do about Martin? You have to make up your mind. If you're going to take him back, it doesn't make sense to have him arrested. Don't waste La'Roc's time," Chantal said in an angry tone.

La'Roc looked over at Denise with sadness. Denise was the weakest one of the three of them. The two of them were always fighting for Denise at school. She was the shy one, and La'Roc and Chantal were the talkative ones.

Denise was a foster child. Denise said her mother left her in the hospital when she was born. She never met her mother or father. When La'Roc and Chantal met Denise, they both fell sorry for her and started taking care of her the best they could. La'Roc's family didn't have a lot, but she shared what she had with Denise. Chantal's foster parents helped Denise as well. Denise had one sister—no brothers or any other family members that she knew about. She became part of La'Roc's family. La'Roc felt that was one of the reasons why Denise couldn't let go—because she was afraid of losing more family.

We're her family, and we have to protect her from herself and people like Martin.

"Denise, what do you want to do? Do you want Martin to continue to mentally and physically abuse you, or do you want him arrested? Denise, you're the only one who can make that decision. Are you ready to close this chapter in your life?" La'Roc asked, care and concern visible in her voice.

Denise left the room to make a phone call to Martin.

Chantal's approach toward Denise may have seemed a little harsh because she felt that she had to protect Denise. "I let Denise down because I wasn't there when she needed me." La'Roc and Chantal were both aware of Denise's upbringing. They remembered her trusting them enough to disclose all the horrors she and her siblings suffered. Denise had a horrible upbringing. At a very young age, she raised herself, with a pimp whom she had to depend on just to eat and sleep. The streets and motels were Denise's home.

"Chantal, you are not responsible for Denise's action; she is a grown woman. Denise is responsible for her own decisions. She made her choice to be with Martin," La'Roc said. "We have to help her to get over her fears of being alone."

Denise entered the terrace with tears rolling down her face. Chantal jumped up from her seat. "What's wrong, Denise?"

"I am so ashamed of myself. What was I thinking by not telling you guys? You're my two best friends. I feel like a damn fool. La'Roc, I'm ready to have that nasty bastard arrested."

"Are you sure, Denise?" La'Roc asked.

La'Roc made the phone call and set up everything with the Sixty-Third Precinct. The police would arrest him, and they would meet them at the precinct to press charges. La'Roc looked over her shoulder with pride at her two best friends.

"Come on, girls. We have to get ready to meet Martin at the Sixty-Third Precinct."

Ms. Cotton was summoned to the great room for instructions on making lunch for Shawn's team of lawyers.

Ms. Cotton walked out onto the terrace where La'Roc was standing. "Hello, Ms. Rose. Is everything all right?"

"Hello, Ms. Cotton. Yes, everything is fine. I have to go out. Mr. Parker and his lawyers need their lunch set up in my office. Also, don't forget to make Jordan his special platter and mix his special juice."

La'Roc continued to give Ms. Cotton instructions for the remainder of the day.

"Did Courtney and Dr. Kim leave for Manhattan yet?" La'Roc asked Ms. Cotton.

"Yes, Ms. Rose. They left long ago. Courtney took your babies with her. She said to tell you her cleaning lady will watch Paris and Biscuit while she and Dr. Kim visit Justin," Ms. Cotton responded.

"That will be fine, Ms. Cotton. Thank you."

After getting dressed, La'Roc, Chantal, and Denise left to go downtown to the precinct to press charges against Martin, Denise's ex-boyfriend.

La'Roc looked at Chantal with sadness in her eyes for Denise.

She also felt guilty, just like Chantal, because neither one of them were there to protect her from crazy-ass Martin.

"Denise, was Martin physically abusive toward you? I'm asking you for the truth. If you lie to me, I can't help you. Denise, you know how I feel and how angry I get when it comes to my family and my job. So whatever you do, don't lie to me as your lawyer, and, most important, as your friend," La'Roc said with love and concern in her voice.

Denise had said months ago that Martin had beaten her black and blue.

But La'Roc needed to hear Denise repeat that conversation again. She was building up a case against Martin and needed the truth. Denise could have made up the physical and mental abuse because she was angry at that time. La'Roc had to be sure Denise was being serious.

Denise cleared her throat before answering La'Roc's question. "Yes, on several occasions he has beaten me so bad that I could not go to work. Remember when you and Chantal couldn't find me? I had gone to North Carolina because I was embarrassed to show my face. I was afraid to tell you because he said he would kill me. Remember when I took my car back? He came to my office and almost killed me because I told you and because I wouldn't give him anymore of my money.

"I was terrified of that man. Two months ago, I was just fed up with his bullshit, and I knew I had to tell my friends. However, I needed the right place and right time to fill you in about Martin abusing me physically and mentally. Today seems like the appropriate time to let you guys know how big a fool I've been. After I kicked him out, I changed the locks on my doors as well as my office doors. I'm not afraid anymore. I'm ready to get a new life, and that life will be without Martin." Denise was crying as she talked about her abusive relationship with Martin. "La'Roc, that's the reason why I've been so distant with you and Chantal. Please forgive me for being so secretive.

You have to understand, I was afraid of what Martin would do to me. You guys thought I was dating Alex. I wanted to, but he wouldn't give me the time of day. Alex was a way of getting away so you and Chantal wouldn't find out about me being abused by Martin. Alex is a wonderful man, La'Roc.

"One night I asked Alex to take me to one of my office suites just to make love to me. He refused. He said, "La'Roc would kill me on the spot and wouldn't give it a second though. Denise, I won't take advantage of you. I like you as a friend. Let's just be friends." He became really upset with me. 'You're an attractive woman. Why are you so unhappy?' I wanted to tell him, but I was too embarrassed. I feel better since I told my two best friends. You are still my best friends, right?" Denise questioned her friends about their relationship. Now she had no more secrets to tell about Martin. Denise needed validation about her friendship with Chantal and La'Roc.

Once they arrived at the precinct, they removed themselves from Chantal's SUV and did their college hug. Crying together seemed to help the girls to move forward. This time, the crying was to empower Denise.

The three women turned around, and there was Martin in handcuffs, escorted by two police officers.

"Denise, are you going to get me out tonight? I can't stay in lockup all night," Martin yelled out.

"Denise, don't respond to that bag of shit. Ignore that piece of shit," La'Roc said.

Chantal said, "Motherfucker, you are going to jail for a long time. We'll see you in court and hell! Oh, Martin, guess what? We're here to press charges against your black ass."

"Hello, Ms. Rose. Good to see you again," one of the officers said as they walked past La'Roc and her friends.

"La'Roc, you got to help me. Please don't let them lock me up in this place. Denise, talk to La'Roc," Martin begged.

La'Roc looked at the officers, her eyes icy. "Get him out of my sight. Martin, you better get yourself a good lawyer because Denise has a good lawyer. She has *me*."

La'Roc and her friends followed behind Martin and the officers, into the precinct.

La'Roc overheard Martin say, "Damn, that bitch got a lawyer and one of the best in New York."

Chantal looked over at La'Roc and Denise and smiled. After Denise pressed charges against Martin, he was escorted to a holding cell. "Denise, please don't leave me here. I am sorry, baby. I love you," Martin cried out.

Denise ignored Martin's pleas and continued to follow her friends out the front door of the precinct.

The three friends left the precinct and headed for their favorite restaurant, Charlie's Seafood. They hadn't gone to dinner in a while. Yes, it was about time to celebrate all the good things in their lives.

During dinner, Denise started to cry uncontrollably—nose running, shoulders shaking, and perspiring like someone poured a bucket of water on her.

Her friends looked on in shock.

La'Roc and Chantal jumped from their seats and ran over to Denise. Chantal grabbed her and held her in her arms, rocking her back and forth. La'Roc yelled to the waiter, "Please call 911."

Denise raised her hands. "Stop La'Roc please, don't call 911. I'll be all right. I just need a minute." Denise removed herself from Chantal's arms and dried her eyes.

Denise said, "I need to tell the both of you about my past. I didn't tell you before because I was afraid you wouldn't be my friends. That crying was a way to let my frustration out. I feel better now, thanks to you guys.

"Denise, calm down. Chantal, give me a glass of water please," La'Roc yelled out to Chantal.

The waiter gave La'Roc a glass of water; she gave the water to Denise. Denise calmed herself down and looked at her friends with tearful eyes. Denise called for the waiter to bring her and her friends some red wine. After the waiter served the wine, the girls toasted to each other.

Denise said with another toast, "To my friends forever." The three of them raised their glasses and sipped a drink.

Denise started out by saying, "I'm sorry about keeping secrets from you both. As long as you have known me, I've never talked about my childhood—there is a reason for that. I was a child prostitute for my foster parents. My foster father was the first man to sexual abused my sister and me; after him, it was his friends, brothers, cousins, and etc. I was everybody on the block's whore.

"I remember one day, I refused. My foster father beat me into a coma. I was never allowed to tell anyone about what was going on. After that, I stopped talking for almost a year because if I did, he would have killed me on the spot. Remember when I first met you guys; I was afraid to talk to you. I thought you were going to hurt me like my foster father's family and his friends hurt me. When Martin started to beat me, I went back into my childhood—afraid to talk about the abuse that I endured at the hands of Martin.

"I would give him a check every week, as if he had worked for it. If I didn't give him money, he would beat me severely. On some occasions, he would rape me and fuck me in every hole that was available. I used to go to work bleeding and sore as hell." La'Roc was so angry at Martin; she removed herself from the table. She turned away from Denise and Chantal with tears running down her face. The thoughts running around in her head were making sure that Martin got ten to twenty years. She put her hands in the front pockets of her skinny jean with her back still turned away from her friends.

"Sorry, guys. I had to think for a few minutes." She wiped her eyes and returned to her seat at the table with her friends.

"La'Roc, you and Chantal were the best things that ever happened to me. You accepted me as I was. You saved my life, and you guys never questioned me about my past. La'Roc, Chantal, I love you more than life itself. Don't forget our friend, Jordan. He is the best. If it wasn't for you, my friends, I wouldn't have been able to graduate from high school and would have never seen the inside of a college," Denise responded.

"I'm so angry with you for keeping all of this bottled up inside of you. Denise, where's yours foster family now?" La'Roc asked with tearful eyes.

"La'Roc, I have no idea. I ran away when I was ten years old. I told you about my sister, and I told you what happen when we worked the streets; we started working for a pimp. His name was Jimmy. Jimmy is the man my sister stabbed to death. I really miss my sister; I wish I knew where she was. I hired a detective to search for her with no luck."

La'Roc said, "We'll search again. I'll ask my agency to put out a search for her. Denise will you be able to meet with my agency tomorrow and give them a description of your sister?"

"Yes, La'Roc. I'll be free to meet with your agency at any time tomorrow," Denise answered.

"Thank you for sharing your story with me and Chantal. To answer your question, we helped each other during our college days. Remember, we were short of money, and if it weren't for Jordan and my professor, I myself wouldn't have been able to go to college," La'Roc responded.

Jordan helped Chantal and La'Roc through high school, and they did all they could do for Denise to get her through high school. They were all lacking in the financial department ... all except Jordan.

Denise had a sad and unpleasant childhood. The three of them sat at the table and continued to drink wine. There wasn't a dry eye at the table.

Chantal stared at her friend wordlessly, and that was so unusual for Chantal. La'Roc, Chantal, and Denise held hands and promised each other that they would always be there for each other, no matter what.

They talked a while longer, paid the check, and left the restaurant holding hands.

La'Roc's cell phone rang as soon as they got into Chantal's SUV. La'Roc looked at her cell phone's caller ID.

"Hello, handsome. How is it going?"

"Hi Sexiful. We're getting ready to wrap it up for today. I really didn't know April played such a part in this frame-up. I cannot believe she could be so vindictive to do this to her own brother. What kind of person does that? How could April and Kelly be so spiteful? Sexiful, I was listening to my lawyers today going over the trial documents, and it seems as though I was rehearsing for a movie. It was hard for me to believe that someone could have had that much animosity toward another human being. I had no idea that April's hostility had turned into hate. She was always trying to antagonize me. I don't understand any of this. Why would they do this to me?" Shawn questioned, still confused. "I'm so angry with my sister right now." La'Roc felt for Shawn; she could hear the anger and disappointment in his voice.

"Shawn, baby, let's talk about your feelings when you get home. I'm not allowed to talk to you about your case, sweetheart. See you in Westchester, handsome," she said as she disconnected the call.

"Was that Shawn on the phone, La'Roc? your fiancé?" Chantal asked. "Chantal, who else would it be calling Ms. Sexiful?" Denise said, laughing. "Denise, how're you?" La'Roc asked.

"I really feel better thanks to you and Chantal," Denise said, looking at her friends with a shy giggle. "I'm okay. Thank you, again. I feel so relieved since I told you about my childhood and about Martin. I have no more secrets."

Chantal looked over at her friend. "Denise, you need to go into therapy to get some insight on your state of mind." Chantal was waiting for La'Roc to agree with her.

"Good idea, Chantal. Remember, we have Dr. Kim on payroll. Give her a call and set up an appointment with her." Although she will be busy with Justin and Courtney for the next couple of days," La'Roc said in agreement with Chantal.

Denise said, "We have to tell Jordan about my childhood as a young prostitute etc."

Chantal said, "No Denise. You're going to tell Jordan about your childhood—there will be no *we*." They looked at each other and laughed.

La'Roc said, "Chantal, please take me home to my baby."

Chantal answered La'Roc with a smile. "Do you want me to drive like Chantal, or do you want me to drive like La'Roc?"

"No bitch drive like yourself. You could never drive like La'Roc. Don't get it twisted. There's only one La'Roc."

Three friends made their way up I-95 going north, with Chantal behind the wheel, laughing their asses off.

La'Roc fell asleep during the ride back to Westchester.

Chantal and Denise drove in silence. Denise had a lot on her plate; Chantal looked over at her friend with sadness in her eyes. She wanted to stop her SUV and just hold her close to her heart and tell her how much she loved her.

"Denise, I'll never let anything else happen to you. I'm sorry I wasn't there to protect you from your demons from day one. La'Roc and I are here now. Whenever you need either one of us, do not hesitate to call. We're here for you. Okay, baby?" Chantal said with sincerity.

"Yes, I know you guys are there for me. Chantal, I feel so much better since I've talked to you and La'Roc this afternoon. I feel like a different person. Thanks to you two."

La'Roc's cell phone started ringing. Denise reached over from the passenger seat into the backseat to retrieve La'Roc's cell phone.

"Hello," Denise answered.

"Hi Aunt Denise this is Courtney. Where's my mother?"

"She's sleeping. Where are you guys? We're almost in Westchester."

"Dr. Kim and I are in Manhattan. We just left Justin, so we're going to stop by the condo before heading back to the townhouse. Dr. Kim decided to make us dinner. After we eat, we will be on our way to Westchester."

"Courtney, how did it go with Justin? Will he be coming home on Friday for Shawn's party?"

"Yes, everything has been arranged for the van to pick him up at noon on Friday. That's why I'm calling my mother to tell her the good news. Aunt Denise, please let mother know that everything worked out just fine. Justin will be coming home on Friday. Oh, don't forget to tell her that her babies are doing just great, and tell Aunt Chantal I said hi. Love you guys."

"Okay, baby. I will definitely let her know. Love you, Courtney," Denise said and disconnected the call.

As Chantal pulled into the driveway, she noticed the guys were already there, sitting on the lawn, laughing and shooting the breeze.

Shawn walked over to the car. "Where is my fiancé? Or should I say my wife-to-be?" Shawn asked in a gentle voice.

"Well, hello, Shawn," Chantal responded. "She is in the backseat, sleeping."

"Oh, Chantal, I'm sorry I didn't say hello to you guys. Hi, Chantal and Denise. I missed my baby today. However, that is no excuse for not greeting you. Forgive me, young ladies."

"Okay, we forgive you, Mr. Parker. Now go and wake her," the girls said as they walked away.

Devon came running out to Chantal's SUV. "Aunt Denise, where's my grandmother?"

"She's is in the backseat, sleeping," Denise answered.

Shawn called out to Devon, "I'll wake her up and bring her inside."

Shawn got into the SUV and called La'Roc's name. "Baby, wake up. You are home. Let's go inside; come on, sleepyhead. Wake up. Time to wake up," Shawn said as he pulled her gently into his arms.

She looked into these beautiful brown eyes. "Oh, Shawn, it is you. I heard your voice, but I thought I was dreaming. Handsome, put your arms around me and hold me before we go inside the house."

"Sexiful, did something happen today?"

"No! I really missed you today. I was told that you guys would wrap the submission up by noon tomorrow. How do you feel about everything so far?" La'Roc looked at her handsome fiancé, rubbing her eyes from sleep.

"Baby, everything went well. It was fun working with my team of lawyers. Devon is going to make a top lawyer one day, mark my words. I can't wait until Friday gets here and this trial is over so we can get on with our lives and get married. Once this is over, we can start our lives together as man and wife," Shawn said while holding her in his arms.

La'Roc pulled Shawn's face to hers and kissed him gently. "Come on, baby. Let's go inside before they think we're MIA." La'Roc looked at her man, licking her lips with a provocative smile.

La'Roc's cell phone started to ring. She checked her caller ID. It was Chantal.

"Hi, Chantal what's up kid?" La'Roc answered.

"Denise asked me to call you and let you know she was going upstairs to tell Jordan about her childhood and also about Martin. She's upstairs now talking to him," Chantal said.

"That's good news," La'Roc said. "I agree she should tell him. He is part of the team as well as a good, loyal friend. I'd be very upset with her if she didn't tell Jordan."

With the conversation concluded, she slipped her phone into her pocket and turned her attention back to Shawn. She pulled him close to her lips and gave him a kiss, and he playful pushed her down on the backseat of Chantal's SUV; he held her down, kissing her with so much passion and love in his eyes. She felt so much affection from his kisses.

They decided to go inside before Devon came back looking for her and Shawn.

He removed himself from the Jeep and reached for her hand to help her from the Jeep. After she removed herself from the Jeep, he picked her up and placed her on his back for a piggyback ride. He loved giving her piggyback rides.

"Oh, Shawn, put me down before someone sees you," La'Roc yelled to him with a childish giggle.

"Too late. We got it on video, baby girl," Jordan, Denise, and Chantal yelled down from the upstairs balcony.

Devon ran to the front door. "Shawn, man, if you drop her you won't be going to court on Friday. You feel me, Shawn?" Devon said jokingly.

As they were entering the townhouse, Alex pulled up in the driveway in his BMW SUV.

Alex greeted everyone as he entered the house.

"Partner, when you get some free time, we need to collaborate on the case for Friday," Alex said, looking at his boss.

"Alex, I'll always have time for you. Talk to me, Mr. Power. Tell me what's so pressing that you need to confer with me," La'Roc asked.

"I require your expertise to go over my opening statement." Alex smiled. La'Roc motioned for Alex to head toward her office; she kissed Shawn and walked, with Alex in tow, to her office.

Alex gave La'Roc his notepad and took a seat. La'Roc sat behind her desk, and Alex took a seat across from her.

Alex asked La'Roc if it was okay if Jordan joined them in the meeting. "Good idea, Alex. Yes, by all means, call him in. He could be a good asset to your opening statement."

Alex took out his cell phone and called Jordan and asked him to come into La'Roc's office for a meeting.

Jordan entered the office. "Hi, baby girl." He walked over to shake Alex's hand. "What's going on with the case?" Jordan asked.

"Nothing man. I've the opening statement, and I asked La'Roc to proof it. I'd like for you to give me your opinion," Alex answered.

La'Roc read the statement and looked over at the two best lawyers in New York. Of course, La'Roc stopped reading Alex's statement to give him a compliment on his work.

"Alex, your opening statement is very good, I must say. I couldn't have written it any better." La'Roc looked at Alex, acknowledging his good work.

"Jordan, what are your views on Alex's opening statement?"

"Baby girl, I think it is a remarkable statement. Alex, that opening statement will blow the jury's mind away. You don't need me; you got it down pat. Love it, man," Jordan responded.

"Okay, guys, how did it go today in terms of preparing Shawn for his trial? I hope we're ready. You have everything you need; you have all of your witnesses lined up and your documents are ready," she asked. "And you have me as your consultant. What else do you need?" La'Roc said jokingly.

Alex was pacing the floor while La'Roc continued to read his opening statement. Alex had calmed down and relaxed in the chair across from La'Roc where he had been sitting before she started reading the statement.

Alex removed himself from his seat.

"Thanks, Jordan, for the support. We got this one, right?" Alex said. "I have to run, partner—I need to go back to the office to pick up some documents for one of my clients. La'Roc, you remember that young teenager we defended for shoplifting? You remember him; his name was Jeffery."

"Oh, right. I remember him. How is he?" La'Roc asked. "Yes, I remember him very well because he couldn't pay me for my services." Alex laughed.

"He is doing great. He just got a full-time summer job at Charles's Drive-In." Alex left, and Jordan sat down to talk to La'Roc. "Baby girl, did you really like what we did with the house, the grounds, etc.?"

"Brother, I loved it. How did you guys do all of that in such a short time?" La'Roc said, looking at her friend with watery eyes. "Jordan, did Denise speak with you today about her messed-up childhood and her crazy relationship with Martin?"

"La'Roc, I held her in my arms and cried with her. After all these years, we are just finding out who Denise really is. Wow! La'Roc, if I could have gotten my hands around Martin's neck at the time she was telling me all the shit he did to her, I would've killed him," Jordan stated with ice-cold anger.

"Yes, it was a sad story. Chantal feels that it's her fault because she wasn't there to protect her," La'Roc said. "How are you doing, Jordan?" La'Roc asked out of concern. Every time La'Roc saw Jordan, her eyes began to tear because of what the virus could do to his well build body.

"I'm good, baby girl. No more little episodes, if that's what you're worried about," Jordan said with a smirk.

"That's great news. Now get out and tell Shawn to meet me upstairs."
"Okay, sister. I'm going to help Ms. Holiday and Ms. Cotton with dinner. What time is Courtney coming up?"

Denise said, "She and Dr. Kim are having dinner in Manhattan. After dinner, they'll be on their way to Westchester."

"Will Devon be back for dinner? Jordan asked."

Devon has a date with August this evening. But he should be home for dinner," La'Roc responded.

As Jordan was walking toward the door, he turned around to face La'Roc. "Baby girl, I love you, and thank you for being so understanding."

"Get out." La'Roc picked up a piece of paper and tossed it at him playfully. Jordan ran out the door, laughing. La'Roc smiled to herself, thinking of how lucky she, Courtney, and Devon were to have Jordan in their lives.

Before La'Roc could leave her office, there was a tap on the door. La'Roc said jokingly, "If you're not handsome, don't enter. However, if you are handsome, please enter without hesitation."

Shawn opened the door and poked his head in with a dozen red and black roses. He also had a bottle of Cristal Champagne.

Entering her office, he locked the door behind him.

Shawn, teasing his fiancé, said, "Ms. Rose, I'm so in love with you. Please kiss me before Mr. Fiancé walks in on me kissing you."

He picked her up and carried her over to her large oak conference table, laid her gently on top, and kissed her before he poured them each a glass of champagne. After ripping their clothes off, Shawn reached for her hand and gave her a glass of champagne. He sat down in a lounging chair, pulled her into his lap, and made love long and hard with her sitting on top of his big penis. They both got naked in a split second. They both were hungry for love.

As she rotated her hips round and round, they both cried out in pure ecstasy. The excitement was exhilarating; her entire body seemed to be on fire. She confided in her sister one day that when she and Shawn stopped making love, she could still feel him inside of her for the next two to three days. That was how good his lovemaking was.

After making love in La'Roc's office, Shawn kissed her and poured another drink before taking a shower. After taking a quiet shower, they both sat on the floor; she sat in front of him so she could stay in contact, with his manhood touching her body. It's a good thing there was a shower attached to her office.

La'Roc heard a scratch at the door; they both got dressed, and Shawn removed himself and walked to the door. Paris and Biscuit were sitting there, wagging their tails, looking sad but happy.

Shawn picked them both up with a kiss. "Who left you two out here alone?" La'Roc grabbed her babies with a big kiss and a hug. (She put her puppies back on the floor.)

Biscuit and Paris ran to the door and ran down the hall into Courtney's room.

Shawn and La'Roc followed her babies down the hall. Courtney, Jordan, and Devon were watching TV, pretending they weren't aware La'Roc and Shawn were in the room.

"We want some answers—who left my babies outside my office door? And, Courtney, when did you get home? Is everything all right with Justin?"

"Oh, Momma, it is you and Shawn! About time you guys came up for air. Actually, we just got home. Dr. Kim is taking a shower, and Jordan just kidnapped me, and he let your babies out. So get on his butt." Courtney looked over at Jordan, who was laughing and making a funny face because she told on him. Courtney and Jordan were always playing games like children.

"Did you guys miss your parents?" La'Roc laughed. "Shawn, I'm going to spend some time with my daughter and my babies. I'll see you and Jordan later."

"Okay, baby. I need to talk to Jordan about the foundation anyway."

"That sounds like a plan. Casey and L'Oreal are upstairs. All four of you should get together and discuss your position within the organization."

"Good idea, baby girl," Jordan said.

Courtney, La'Roc, and her babies went for a long walk to spend some much-needed time to together. La'Roc hugged her daughter. "Baby thanks for setting up the party for Friday. Everything is wonderful: the lighting, even the colors you chose to hang around the swimming pools and the yard are unforgettable. It's going to be a great party. If not, it'll be the most decorative and expensive home ever."

"Thank you, Momma. I'm delighted you like the arrangements we did with the house. I forgot to tell you, Jordan had the lights installed all over the parking lot. It looks really nice." Courtney returned the hug.

"How's everything going with you and Justin?"

"Everything is fine at the moment. We're taking it easy for now. Remember, Mother, I still and always will care about Justin, but for now, that is as far as it goes. He's looking forward to coming to the big party Friday night. He's so excited to be hanging out with Jordan and Devon. He is so happy, he can't wait." Courtney looked over at her mother and smiled.

La'Roc and Courtney sat down on the ground and played with her babies before going in to dinner with the family.

"I'll be content when Shawn's trial is over," sighed La'Roc.

"I know, Mom. I'll be thrilled when it is over too. I have to get back to school to finish so I can get my law degree. And I need to start planning for your wedding. Aren't you happy about how everything is coming together? Even uncle is looking better," Courtney added.

"Baby, I'm happy because I have you and Devon home with me, and Shawn will soon be free. I'm a lucky woman to have so much love around me," La'Roc said, looking at her daughter. "Courtney you and Devon have made me so proud. I'm happy to be your mother and Devon's grandmother."

"Mother, Devon and I are the lucky ones. We're so lucky to have you as a mother and a grandmother."

"Speaking of Devon, where is he?" La'Roc asked.

"Oh, I forgot to tell you. He went to pick up August; they're going to a movie tonight with friends."

La'Roc called out to Paris and Biscuit, "Come, babies. Let's go in to shower before dinner." Biscuit and Paris ran to their master with wagging tails. "Courtney, I'll race you to the front door—you with Biscuit, and me running with Paris," La'Roc challenged her daughter.

"You're on, Mother. Get ready to be left in the dust, lady."

"On your mark, get set, go!" La'Roc yelled, looking over at her daughter.

Shawn yelled, "Run, Sexiful, run!" Shawn was giving her a thumbs-up as he clapped his hands together.

Jordan was rooting for Courtney. "Run, run, baby," Jordan said, laughing and clapping his hands together.

By the time La'Roc and Courtney reached the front door, they both looked up to the terrace. To their surprise, Casey, L'Oreal, Denise, and Chantal had joined Shawn and Jordan, clapping their hands.

Chantal said, "Good job. That is what you call a job well done." They all continued to clap.

La'Roc and Courtney ran up the stairs to take their showers. Courtney said, "I will see you downstairs later for dinner."

"Okay, baby," La'Roc said. "Courtney, I enjoyed our little discussion today. We must do this more often, just the two of us."

"Okay, Mom. I'd love that."

As La'Roc stepped into the Jacuzzi, Biscuit and Paris walked in and took a seat next to the Jacuzzi in their little doggie beds.

La'Roc looked down at their beds and smiled. She relaxed in her Jacuzzi with a glass of wine and thought about the last time Shawn made love to her. After drinking her wine, she closed her eyes and drifted off to sleep. She was awakened by a tap on the door. *Please, let it be Shawn.*

"Baby, it's me, Shawn."

"Come in, handsome, and lock the door behind you," La'Roc answered. Shawn undressed and slid into the Jacuzzi with his soon-to-be wife.

He poured himself a drink and refilled her glass of red wine. They sat in silence, sipping on their wine. Shawn had grabbed a bottle of wine from the freezer on his way to the Jacuzzi room.

La'Roc looked up at Shawn. "Oh, baby, I see you brought a bottle of wine up with you."

"Yes because I didn't know you had already brought up a bottle. I'll put this bottle back in the Jacuzzi locker freezer."

"Good idea, Shawn."

"Shawn, how do you feel about your upcoming trial?"

"I feel confident and certain that I'm going to walk out a free man." "Shawn, you have a magnificent team of lawyers on your side, and they are brilliant, including my grandson, even if he is a student." La'Roc looked up at her fiancé and smiled.

"Baby, I just want to focus on you and this beautiful body of yours right now." He pulled her face up to his lips and kissed her tenderly. "Sexiful, I want you right here, right now," Shawn said in a touching and sexy voice.

He carried her to the bedroom and put her on the bed gently. He continued to make love to her body. He rolled his tongue around her body as his finger was making its way down to her vagina in slow motion.

Shawn touched her vagina and stroked his hand across her body. She reached for his hand and put his fingers into her mouth; one by one, she proceeded to make love to his fingers. He was making her body feel as weak as she let go of his fingers.

Tears ran down her face as Shawn made love to her. La'Roc began to weaken as he removed his finger from her vagina and placed his penis inside of her open vagina. At that moment she fell unto his spell as she always did.

La'Roc knew that she would never let him go, under any circumstances.

She said in a very low, sexy voice, "Shawn, please don't stop, baby. Keep making love to me, and don't you ever stop."

"Baby, look at me. I'm going to love you forever, and I'll never leave you again. I promise," Shawn said as he pushed his penis deeper inside of her.

"Baby, is this what you want? Sexiful, are you okay? I won't hurt you. I promise. I just want to give you what you want. Baby, this penis is all yours. You'll never have to worry about sharing me with any other woman. I'm here, baby." Shawn stopped talking and continued making love to the woman he loved. Sexiful responded in a sexy, provocative voice.

La'Roc was overwhelmed with Shawn's lovemaking ability. He made her feel like a weak two-year-old child when he made love to her.

La'Roc loved Shawn more than life itself. She would do anything for him. Shawn and La'Roc finished their lovemaking and went downstairs to join the others for dinner.

Jordan looked down at his Rolex watch and said jokingly, "You guys are a little late for dinner, but we saved some for you two."

Shawn said, "Thank you, man. We're starving."

Ms. Holiday said, "I didn't want to wake you and Mr. Parker. Ms. Rose, did you have a good nap?"

La'Roc looked at Shawn and winked her left eye. "Yes, Ms. Holiday. We had a good nap. Thank you for asking."

After dinner, everyone retired to the great room to finish their deserts in front of the fireplace.

Dr. Kim gave La'Roc an update on Justin's condition and reported that he would be home on Friday.

Shawn overheard Dr. Kim say that Justin would be able to come home Friday. "Sexiful, didn't I hear Dr. Kim say that Justin will be coming home on Friday for another day pass?" Shawn asked out of concern.

"Yes. Dr. Kim and Courtney will pick him up on Friday and bring him here to Westchester for a day pass. He has made quite a bit of improvement since he started his new treatment," La'Roc answered.

"That's great, baby. I'm happy for him and Courtney. They deserve to be Happy … just like you and me."

Shawn had a gleam of joy in his eyes for Courtney and Justin.

Shawn reached for La'Roc's hand and led her up the stairs to their bedroom for a good night's sleep.

Shawn's trial was a day away; unfortunately, Judge Perkins would not be the judge on the Friday in question. The judge who would be presiding happened to be one of Judge Perkins's friends. Judge Jin would be presiding on the day in question.

La'Roc felt confident it was an open-and-shut case.

However, the team had to go through the formalities: presenting the witnesses, etc.

La'Roc's team was ready to go in to fight, and they would win.

La'Roc was informed of Kelly Brown going back into the hospital because of complications.

Shawn and La'Roc went to Courtney's room to say good night. "Courtney, is Devon in his room?" La'Roc asked.

"No, Momma. He said he was going to be late. He and some friends went out to a basketball game.

"After the game, they will be stopping by his condo to hang out for a while," Courtney explained.

"How nice I'm glad he is going out with his friends," La'Roc responded. "Shawn, are you ready for your court date on Friday?" Courtney asked. "Yes, I'm a little nervous, little La'Roc."

I can't wait to see Uncle Jordan, Alex, and my son in action, Courtney thought to herself. *Although Devon is a student, I just want to see him standing next to the best, knowing that one day he'll be one of the best.*

Shawn said, "Congratulations on Justin's recovery." "Thanks, Shawn."

"Well, good night, baby," La'Roc said as she and Shawn walked out of Courtney's bedroom.

The next stop was Paris and Biscuit's room. They were in their doggie bed, fast asleep. Ms. Cotton had fed them and given them their bath and put them in bed.

"How cute is that? Paris and Biscuit are sleeping in their little beds," Shawn said, laughing.

Shawn picked La'Roc up and carried her back into the master bedroom to get some much-needed rest. He said, "Tomorrow is another day."

They undressed, got in bed, and went to sleep in each other's arms.

La'Roc awakened the next morning, looking for Shawn. To her surprise, he was not in bed or in the bathroom, singing his usual out-of-tune songs. She was a little disappointed because he always told her when he was leaving and where he was going.

Oh well. Maybe he left with the team to finish their submission for his case on Friday.

La'Roc decided to relax for a little while longer; Shawn walked in with Paris and Biscuit in his arms. "Good morning, sleepyhead."

He walked over to the bed with her puppies; he laid them on the bed with her and kissed her. As he walked toward the door, he turned and said, "I love you, Sexiful."

"I love you too. Shawn, where did you go this morning?" La'Roc asked. Shawn turned and looked in her direction. "It's a surprise. I'll tell you about it later."

Shawn had gone shopping that morning for a Jeep for Devon and a Hummer for Courtney. That was the surprise.

"Okay, baby. I'll call you later."

The Hummer and the Jeep were going to take some time because Shawn was having them customized to fit Courtney and Devon's tastes.

Shawn closed the bedroom door and ran downstairs to meet with his team of lawyers.

La'Roc's cell phone rang. It was Alex. "Good morning, Mr. Power. How can I help you this morning?"

"La'Roc, we will be finished with the submission today. I will need about an hour of your time. We need to go over the submission. We, as a team, need your approval."

"No problem. What time are you talking?" "Noon will be great," Alex responded.

"That'll be fine Alex. I'll wait for your arrival."

"Thanks, partner." Alex ended his conversation and disconnected the call. Shawn ran back upstairs, pulled La'Roc into his arms, and held her real tight. "Baby, I love you so much. I don't want to leave you for a minute."

"Shawn, I love you too, so go and learn how to become a free man."

Shawn and La'Roc both laughed at her joke. Shawn walked out of the bedroom, smiling from ear to ear. "See you later, Sexiful."

La'Roc thought to herself, *Wow, Shawn will soon be a free man, and by this time next month, I will be Mrs. La'Roc Rose Parker. The sound of Mrs. Parker sounds damn good.* She jumped in the middle of her bed with excitement like a child in a candy store. Paris and Biscuit just looked at her in amazement.

In puppy talk, they said, "What the hell is she doing, Paris?"

"She is getting ready to throw another remote control; run for your life, Biscuit. I have gone through this before. *Run, bro!*"

La'Roc was a lucky woman to have all of her family and friends in her life, especially her mother. She was so delighted to have a group of people like her three best friends and a sister like L'Oreal. She had her brother-in-law, Casey; Courtney, her daughter; and her grandson, Devon. La'Roc couldn't ask for a better family and to find a wonderful man like Shawn Parker—he was all she needed, now and forever.

La'Roc heard a soft knock at the door. *Well no, sleep for me this morning.*

La'Roc said, sitting up in bed, "Come in."

Devon walked toward La'Roc's round, king-size bed.

"Hi, Grams I heard you've been asking for me. You missed me last night?" He lay on the foot of La'Roc's bed, telling her about his girlfriend and how he was excited about working on Shawn's case. They talked for what seemed like hours.

Ms. Holiday was summoned to bring up some toast, muffins, drinks, and other snacks.

La'Roc was looking for Ms. Holiday to enter through the door; however, it was Courtney who entered the bedroom with a tray in her hand, and Ms. Holiday was carrying the drinks, coffee, juice, etc.

"Mother dear, are you and Devon having a party without me?"

Devon looked over at his mother. "Mom, we're talking about law stuff— something you don't know anything about. Isn't that right, Grandmother?" Devon looked over at his mother and smiled.

"Stop teasing her, Devon. She is going to make a good lawyer, just like her mother," La'Roc said to her grandson in Courtney's defense.

"Mom knows I love her," he said, hugging and kissing his mother.

Courtney set up the food in the middle of the floor in La'Roc's bedroom.

"Momma, Uncle Casey and Aunt L'Oreal left an hour ago to go home. They'll meet you at the courthouse Friday morning for the trial," Courtney announced.

"Thank you, Courtney, for that information."

"Have you heard from your grandmother, Courtney?"

"Dr. Kim and I stopped by her house yesterday to check on her. She was on her way to play bingo with Ms. Gray. Remember, her friend next door." Courtney stated.

"Thank you for checking on my mother. I have to thank Dr. Kim as well. Where is Dr. Kim, Courtney?"

"She is upstairs, counseling one of her patients over the phone," Courtney responded. "Momma, are you guys ready for the big gala Friday night?"

Devon said, "I can't wait to see Shawn's face when he walks into that big house and hears that the house is yours, Grams. He is going to faint when he finds out that the party is for him. Man, I can't wait."

"Devon, will you be bringing August?"

"Yes, of course. Who else would I bring?" "Just checking," Courtney responded.

The three of them stayed in La'Roc's bedroom for what seemed like hours, talking about the trial, Justin, and the welcome home party.

La'Roc loved having her children around, but it was time to go take a shower and get dressed for her appointment with Alex.

Courtney and Devon kissed La'Roc and left the room, taking all the breakfast trays and the leftover food downstairs.

La'Roc took a long shower and got dressed in her yellow skirt, green blouse, and a pair of yellow sandals. She then went to her office to greet the team for the meeting that Alex had requested.

La'Roc's summoned Ms. Holiday and asked her to come into her office.

A few moments later, there was a tap on the door. "Who is there?" La'Roc asked.

"It is Ms. Holiday, Ms. Rose."

"Hello, Ms. Holiday. How is it going downstairs?

"Everything is fine, Ms. Rose."

"Ms. Holiday, are you and your staff ready for Shawn's welcome home party Friday?"

"Everything is ready. All the food has been precooked, and the flowers have been ordered. Ms. Rose, it's going to be great—the best party of the year. Courtney, L'Oreal, and your friends did a wonderful job. Don't forget, Ms. Rose, Jordan did a lot of the work himself. Don't worry, Ms. Rose. Everything is going to be fine." Ms. Holiday looked at La'Roc with eye contact and smiled.

"Ms. Holiday, could you please ask one of your staff to make a lunch for Alex and his team? He should be arriving with his team around noon; Shawn will not be meeting with the team for lunch. However, I'd like for you to make his lunch separately. Ms. Holiday, make him his special seafood dish,"

La'Roc instructed.

"All right, Ms. Rose I'll make Mr. Parker a real special lunch, I promise." Alex arrived on time, as usual. He walked in with Jordan, Shawn, and Devon. "Hi, partner ready for the case breaker on Friday?"

"Hello, guys. Hi handsome" She looked over at Shawn and winked. "Hi, baby," Shawn said with a kiss.

Ms. Holiday's staff served lunch in La'Roc's office.

La'Roc called Shawn to the side and explained to him that she needed to speak with his lawyers and it was inappropriate for him to attend the meeting. He said he understood; he kissed her, and as he walked away, he said, "I'll see you after the meeting. Okay, Sexiful?"

"See you within an hour."

The meeting lasted for almost an hour. They had their lunch as they went over their opening statement for La'Roc approval.

She approved all statements and gave Alex and the team excellent compliments on their work. "Alex, from your statements that you presented to the team, I have to say you are ready for the prosecutor on Friday. Okay, guys, the meeting is over. Get a good night's sleep and be at the courthouse on time. On time mean 9:00 a.m. Got that, Mr. Devon?" La'Roc stated.

"Grandmother, I'll be there before you because I'm really excited to work with Uncle Jordan and Uncle Alex. And don't forget my big paycheck."

Devon did a moonwalk step and danced his way out the door, giggling, pleased with himself. La'Roc just shook her head in amazement at her grandson. "Alex and Jordan, please stay. I need to talk to you a bit more about tomorrow's trial. I just want to thank you two for doing such a fantastic job on this case.

"You have worked long and hard hours to get Shawn his freedom. Jordan, you came all the way here from California to help with the case, although we didn't have a case at the time. You put your personal life and everything else on hold to come to New York to help free Shawn because you believed in his innocence.

"Jordan, I just want you to know that I appreciate what you have done for this family. Shawn and I will always be here for you. After the trial next week, we will go to California to take care of your property, etc. Brother, I love you for your faithfulness, trustworthiness, consistency, and dependability." La'Roc said, "Thank you, brother," with teary eyes.

"I love you, baby girl, and you know I'll always be here for you and your family, especially my godchildren."

"Alex, I made you a partner for many reasons. One of those reasons is that I knew you would make a damn good lawyer. Remember, I trained you.

"I have to say you have done a hell of a good job. You have been there every step of the way with Shawn and his baby momma's drama, and you were the person who put the detective on Justin's father to bring him back to New York to save Justin from his death. Although you didn't bring Justin's father back to New York, you were responsible for getting him to sign the medical documents to save his life. I'm grateful for that.

"You know, Alex, if you hadn't found Justin's father in time to sign the medical documentation, he would have died. You made Courtney very happy. Alex, thank you for your loyalty and your devotion," La'Roc said to Alex with tears in her eyes.

"La'Roc, you have been so good to me and my family. I love your family as if they were my family. I'd do anything for you. If it weren't for you, I would not be the lawyer that I am today. You made me what I am today. Thank you, La'Roc, for giving me this opportunity to become a good lawyer.

"Although I'm not really your partner, you treat me with the utmost respect. Thank you," Alex responded.

"Alex, please get out of my office and tell Shawn I will meet him upstairs. Thanks, Alex, and don't be late tomorrow morning."

La'Roc picked up her cell phone and dialed Courtney. Courtney answered on the first ring.

"Hello, Momma. What's up?"

"Hi, baby. I need you to call Chantal and Denise and remind them to meet the team at the courthouse tomorrow at 9:00 a.m., and tell them not to be late,"

"Momma, Denise and Chantal are at the Golden Circle. That is the name I gave the house until we come up with a name that we all like. They went up last night to do some last-minute decorations and to make sure that everything is ready for tomorrow night," Courtney answered.

"Okay, baby. But call them and give them the message. We'll talk," La'Roc said as she disconnected the call.

La'Roc heard Shawn walking up the stairs.

She was standing in the middle of the floor, wearing one of his shirts and nothing underneath. She had a glass of wine in each hand. Shawn walked into the bedroom, a wide grin on his handsome face. He accepted the drink that she handed him; he hugged her tight and whispered, "I love you," with his tongue in her ear. She dropped the shirt to the floor, looking at him with her sexy eyes and licking her gorgeous lips.

"Damn, baby, what are you doing to me? I have to be in court tomorrow morning with you by my side, and if you keep showing me that beautiful body, we will not be able to go anyplace but here in bed."

La'Roc wanted her handsome man to take her to bed and make love to her as he had done so many nights. She asked Shawn to pretend that she was a virgin and it was her first time making love; she wanted him to play around in her vagina with his fingers to get it moist and wet ... put his tongue inside of her womanhood and bring it in and out to really open her up so he could ease his penis inside of the open lips of her vagina. He did as she asked; after making her moist with his tongue, he put his penis inside of her, easy and slow. He moved his body in slow motion as if he were going to break her. He was so gentle, tender, and affectionate; she couldn't help but yell out his name. It was painful yet enjoyable.

His penis inside of her felt like something she never had before. It was all good. She felt something that night she had never felt before.

She felt electrified, exhilarated, and in shock from the way he rotated his penis around in her vagina.

She was thrilled to have a man like Shawn to satisfy her sexually and make her feel like a young teenager again. She hoped and prayed Shawn would never leave her again under any circumstance. Shawn held her in his arms, close to his chest as sweat poured down his body from making beautiful love to his Sexiful Rose.

Shawn left the bedroom to get two glasses of chilled wine to relaxes. "Sexiful, I've been thinking about SJ a lot this past week."

"Shawn, have you spoken to Kelly's mother about telling Shawn Jr. you're not his father?"

Pausing at the bar, he replied, "No, Sexiful. I don't think that Junior will be able to understand that I am not his father. I think he's too young to understand. I'm going to let them handle it. I'm going to keep my distance. However, I will set up a trust fund for him and ask his aunt to be power of attorney. Is that all right with you, Sexiful?"

"That is a wonderful idea. I'll support you in whatever discussion you make," she responded.

La'Roc knew that one day Shawn Jr. was going to have to learn the truth about his parentage.

"We'll deal with the Shawn Jr. issue later. Okay, handsome?" La'Roc responded.

"Baby, I am sorry. You're right, Sexiful. Like I told you earlier, I was just thinking about that little guy. Honey, I'm not going to forget him overnight because he was a part of my life for two years."

"I know, baby," she responded.

He came back into the bedroom and gave her a chilled glass of white wine. "It's just the way you like your drink—icy and cold, right, Sexiful?" Shawn said with a smile on his handsome face.

She looked up into his face and gave him her sexiest smile ever. He kissed her and sat beside her on their bed.

"Shawn, are you worried about tomorrow's trial? If you are, don't be, because there is no need to worry. You have a good team of lawyers, and everything is going to work in your favor. Trust me, handsome," she reassured Shawn of the outcome of the trial.

"Baby, I'm cool. I'm not worried because I know my team is the best. I trust my lawyers, including Devon. Sexiful, you know how I know? You stand behind your name. I've witnessed your anger firsthand when it comes to your profession. You are a tiger when it comes to your career. Nobody messes with my baby."

Shawn looked at La'Roc and winked. They both smiled. Taking each other's hands, they walked into the wet room and took a leisurely steamy shower.

"Shawn, please unlock the bedroom door before going to sleep." Okay, babe.

He pulled her against his chest, enjoying the feel of her silken skin touching him. They relaxed in each other's arms and went to sleep.

Two hours later they were awakened by Paris and Biscuit jumping on the bed, licking her and Shawn's face.

La'Roc called out and instructed Courtney and Devon to come into her bedroom. "Come in here right now!"

Devon and Courtney walked in with their heads down.

"Momma, we're sorry about sending Paris and Biscuit into your room. We wanted to talk to Shawn before court starts tomorrow morning," Courtney explained.

"Devon, I'm still waiting for your story, and it better be good." La'Roc requested an explanation from Devon for his behavior.

"Grandmother, like my mother said, we wanted to see you and Shawn before going to court tomorrow morning. I know I'll be working tomorrow, but this is a personal matter. Tomorrow in court, Grams, we're going to be his lawyers/student. I'm not a law student tonight I'm your grandson, and Shawn is going to be my grandfather.

"Please forgive me on this one, Grams. It'll never happen again," Devon pleaded to his grandmother.

"Look, guys, when you need to talk to me or Shawn, just knock on the door and asks permission to come in. Don't use my babies as your cover."

La'Roc looked over at Paris and Biscuit, who were hiding their heads behind a love seat. "Come here, Biscuit and Paris." They both eased from behind the sofa very slowly and walked over to where La'Roc was seated.

Shawn picked them both up from the floor and handed them to La'Roc. "Thanks, handsome."

She grabbed her babies into her arms and walked into the sitting area near her bedroom. She sat there and played with her babies while Shawn, Devon, and Courtney had their little powwow.

They talked while La'Roc and her babies took a nap on the sofa.

After Courtney, Devon, and Shawn finished their little chat, Shawn joined La'Roc on the loveseat, holding her gently in his arms. La'Roc looked over to her bed, and there were Devon and Courtney, lying across her bed, sleeping. Sometime later that night, La'Roc was awakened by Jordan coughing. La'Roc woke Shawn. "Wow! When did this happen?"

Shawn woke up, rubbing his eyes. "Baby, what's wrong?"

"Nothing is wrong, baby. I thought we had a party, and I didn't remember being invited. Handsome, look, they took over our bed," La'Roc said, looking up at Shawn and smiling.

"Sexiful, I've got an idea. Let's take another shower and go downstairs, and I will make you the best snack ever." Shawn pulled her up into his strong arms and kissed her gently.

"Good idea, baby. First, put me down so we can tiptoe to the shower. We don't want to wake the guests," La'Roc responded with her hand over her mouth, trying to whisper into Shawn's ear. La'Roc and Shawn made it to the shower without waking Courtney, Devon, Jordan, or her babies.

After a nice hot shower, they both went downstairs to get a snack.

Once they got downstairs, they were surprised to see Dr. Kim, Ms. Cotton, and Ms. Holiday sitting in the kitchen, having a cup of coffee.

"Oh, Ms. Rose. We're sorry. Did we wake you?" Ms. Holiday asked.

"No, Ms. Holiday. We were invaded by my family," La'Roc said, laughing. "We have three bodies in our bed, and my babies on the sofa. Shawn and I came downstairs to get a snack. Would you all like to join us?" La'Roc asked.

Shawn interjected, "I won't take no for an answer, and I'll clean the kitchen."

"All right, Mr. Parker. If you insist," Dr. Kim responded.

Shawn made one of the best grilled cheese and bacon sandwiches. After they finished eating, Ms. Holiday, Ms. Cotton, and Dr. Kim wished Shawn good luck on his trial and went upstairs to bed.

"Thank you."

Shawn and La'Roc cleaned the kitchen together. Once they finished clearing the dishes, they went upstairs to Courtney's room and then went to bed for a good night's sleep.

Shawn and La'Roc looked at each other with love in their eyes and said good night. He pulled her into his arms, and she laid her head on his chest as always and went to sleep.

This was the day they'd all been waiting for: Shawn's court date.

Ms. Holiday and Ms. Cotton made a good, healthy breakfast with a lot of blessings.

Shawn and La'Roc finished their breakfast, left the table, and went upstairs to get dressed.

La'Roc and Shawn walked downstairs dressed like they just stepped out of *Vogue* magazine.

Devon and his mother looked like they were on the runway. Devon was six feet four inches tall. He looked good in his white Calvin Klein two-piece summer suit, and Courtney was in a white one-piece jumpsuit with five-inch Louis Vuitton heels. She reached for her Louis Vuitton bag and her cell phone and walked out of the door, following her son to his SUV.

They were all dressed as if they were going to a gala; however, they were on their way to a long-awaited trial to free La'Roc's man from a crime he did not commit.

"What a year this has been!" she thought out loud to herself.

She and Shawn hugged each other before walking out the door.

La'Roc yelled to Ms. Holiday, "Ms. Holiday, did the puppies' sitter sign in yet?"

"Yes, Ms. Rose. She signed in an hour ago. I gave her all the instructions that she'll need. Ms. Cotton and I'll meet you at the courthouse. Oh, Ms. Rose, Ms. Chantal and Ms. Denise called. They'll meet you there with your mother," Ms. Holiday responded.

"Thank you, Ms. Holiday." La'Roc forgot Denise and Chantal stayed over at her mother's house the night before. "Thank you."

Shawn decided to drive his Benz. Shawn was dressed in an off-white Calvin Klein two-piece suit, light-blue shirt, thin, off-white tie, and off-white shoes to match. As Shawn drove down the driveway, La'Roc looked over at him with love in her eyes. She wanted him to stop the car and go back upstairs, rip her clothes off, and make love to her. She just wanted him to love her always.

Shawn looked at her with concern. "Baby, are you all right? You seem so distant. Are you worried about the trial? Tell me if there's something I should be worried about," Shawn asked.

"No, baby, I'm fine. Just thinking about tonight when you become a free man and the next step is our wedding," La'Roc responded.

"Sexiful, I can't wait for you to become my wife; Mrs. Parker—that does have a nice ring to it. I love that name. Mrs. Parker," Shawn said jokingly.

La'Roc and Shawn pulled into her assigned parking space at the courthouse. She noticed that Shawn's team of lawyers was already there, waiting for her and Shawn to arrive.

Alex walked over to where Shawn parked the car and headed over to the passenger side to open the door for La'Roc.

"Good morning, partner." He walked over to Shawn and high-fived and shoulder bumped him. "Shawn, are you ready for this trial, man?"

"Man, I'm as ready as I'll ever be," Shawn answered.

"Shawn, don't worry. We've got this one. This is an open-and-shut case. You have the two best lawyers in the state working on your case. La'Roc is also on your side. She's your consultant, and you know she is the best. Please don't worry about this case. Come with me, Shawn, and let me get you settled in," Alex said.

"Alex, where's Jordan?" La'Roc asked. "He's right behind you," Alex answered.

"Good morning, baby girl." Jordan kissed her on her cheek. Jordan had decided to drive La'Roc's Lexus to the courthouse.

La'Roc stood there with her mouth wide open because what she was seeing was a model from *GQ*.

La'Roc wondered if Courtney, Devon, or Jordan would ever go back to modeling. *Pull your dreams back into your head. Maybe one day.* Modeling was Jordan's happy days during college. Although he didn't need the money.

La'Roc said, "Oh my God. You look like your old self—as handsome as ever." She hugged him and gave him a kiss.

With tears in her eyes, she said, "Your client is waiting for you to free him. Go and defend my future husband." They both laughed and walked their separate ways.

La'Roc waited outside for her friends, sister, and her mother so they all could walk inside together. After they all arrived, they walked into the courtroom together and took their seats at the back of the courtroom. La'Roc was wearing a two-piece white suit with a light-blue blouse to match Shawn's outfit. Her bag and shoes were designed by Chanel. Her suit was also designed by Chanel.

La'Roc sat at the back of the courtroom. Heads turned, and all eyes were on her. She said to her family and friends that she had to give Alex some pointers on the case. What she really wanted to do was to give the nosy people a good look at Ms. Rose and all of Shawn's supporters. She walked down to Alex and whispered in his ear, "Don't worry. You'll do fine. I promise." As she walked back to her seat, all eyes were still on her.

La'Roc knew most of the females disliked her because of Roger, her ex. The females wanted Roger, and the males wanted her.

A brunch of haters, as Denise would say.

Chantal and Denise were smiling when she returned to her seat. La'Roc took her seat next to her mother and held her hand. Court began.

Judge Perkins had called La'Roc days ago and explained to her that he wasn't going to be in town on the day of Shawn's trial. Judge Jin Philips would be presiding at the trial and not to worry. He stated he turned over all the documents to Judge Philips.

Everyone sat in the courtroom in silence. As Judge Philips entered the courtroom, the bailiff announced, "All rise. The court is now in session. The Honorable Judge Philips presiding."

The judge announced, "You all may be seated."

The defendant, Shawn Parker, was asked to stand. "Counselor, how does the defendant plead?"

"The defendant pleads not guilty, Your Honor." "You may be seated, Counselor."

The prosecutor made his opening statement. He made Shawn out to be a monster. The prosecutor tried to make Shawn look like a cold-blooded murderer. He stated that Shawn had motive as well as opportunity to push Ms. Brown. "I will prove beyond a shadow of a doubt during this trial that Mr. Parker pushed Ms. Brown three landings down for his own selfish reasons. "Jury, you must bring back a guilty verdict." Throughout the trial, the prosecutor painted Shawn's character as if he wasn't a human being.

The prosecutor painted Shawn as a coldhearted woman-beater and stated that Shawn had murderous intent in his heart when he pushed Kelly C. Brown down three floors in his complex building.

"Shawn Parker is a menace to society." The prosecutor said in his statement that the police were reportedly called on several occasions to Mr. Parker's home for domestic violence by Ms. Brown. After the prosecutor finished his opening statement, he thanked the judge and the jury.

La'Roc sat in her seat quietly, watching the jury's facial expressions. "Counselor," the judge said. "Counselor, your opening statement."

Alex cleared his throat and walked over to face the jury. "Good afternoon to each and every one of you jurors.

"We intend to prove today that Mr. Parker is innocent without a shadow of a doubt. As jurors, you are not to be swayed by sympathy. Keep a clear mind and bring back a not guilty verdict. My client's character has been mischaracterized by the prosecutor, but I will prove that Mr. Parker is innocent. After you hear the witnesses' testimonies, you will find my client Mr. Parker is not guilty. Thank you, ladies and gentleman." Before walking away, Alex said, "Remember to listen for the evidence, and you will find Mr. Parker *not guilty!*

"I ask you as jurors to listen with your ears and leave all doubt outside the door. This man is innocent, without a doubt, and we will prove it here today in this courtroom."

Alex's opening statement was to the point.

The judge said, "Mr. Prosecutor, you may call your first witness."

"Thank you, Your Honor." His first witness, then the second, third, and fourth were called.

A surprise witness was called. "Ms. La'Roc Rose, will you please take the stand." The prosecutor called La'Roc to the stand. The bailiff asked La'Roc to raise her left hand. She placed her right hand on the Bible. "Do you swear to tell the truth and nothing but the truth?"

"I do, Your Honor." The prosecutor asked her, her occupation. La'Roc responded without hesitation, and she responded with pride.

Alex asked for five minutes with the witness. The judge allowed Alex the five minutes to confer with the witness. The prosecutor objected; however, the judge overruled, and Alex was able to speak with La'Roc. After he conferred with the witness, he walked back to his seat, and the judge said to the prosecutor, "You may precede, counselor."

He questioned her about her relationship with Shawn. He suggested that Shawn had been using La'Roc and planning the murder of Ms. Brown because he was dating a high-profile attorney. La'Roc laughed off the accusation in silent to herself. Alex said, "Objection, Your Honor. Hearsay. The prosecutor is misleading the witness."

The judge responded, "Objection sustained." The judge asked both lawyers to approach. The judge spoke to the prosecutor about the question that he had asked Ms. Rose. "Mr. Halls, refrain from asking your questions if you want to continue this trial. The next time you ask an inappropriate question, I will find you in contempt. You may proceed." Alex walked back to his seat where Shawn and his team were sitting.

The prosecutor continued to question La'Roc about what Shawn thought of Kelly. Alex said, "Objection, Your Honor. Ms. Rose is not a professional mind reader."

"Objection is sustained," announced the judge.

The judge looked over at the jury. "Members of the jury, you are instructed to disregard the last question that was asked by the prosecutor." The prosecutor asked if he could approach the bench. The judge motion for both lawyers to approach; whatever the question was, the judge agreed. La'Roc reluctantly revealed the strong words Shawn used when describing Kelly Carlotta Brown. The prosecutor used her testimony to show that Shawn wished Carlotta would stop bothering him.

After the prosecutor finished and before Alex started his cross-examination, he asked the judge if he and the prosecutor could approach the bench; the judge gave the lawyers permission to approach. Alex asked for a short recess.

The judge granted a thirty-minutes recess. After the thirty-minute recess was over, court resumed with Alex's cross-examination. Alex began his cross-examination. "Ms. Rose, you are still under oath." Alex was very nervous because he was questioning his boss. The first few questions were asked about how the couple met and the tension surrounding Kelly. La'Roc detailed the various ways that Kelly manipulated Shawn and how it negatively affected her and Shawn's relationship.

Alex asked if Kelly made her angry. La'Roc replied, "Yes." Alex asked if she had an alibi for the time in question.

La'Roc said, "I was home alone." She also admitted that she knew Shawn had an appointment at that particular location. All of Alex's questions lead up to a final climactic accusation: that La'Roc lured Kelly to the building and pushed her off the third-story landing. La'Roc denied the charge vehemently but was unable to offer a valid alibi. La'Roc and Alex weren't worried about Alex's questions. The case was in the bag. Shawn was a free man.

The audience and reporters murmured amongst themselves. The jury was intrigued. Alex said, "I have no more questions for this witness, Your Honor."

The judge looked over at La'Roc. "Ms. Rose, you may step down."

As La'Roc walked back to her seat, she heard Alex call another witness. As soon as La'Roc sat down in her seat, she heard someone calling her name. She turned and looked around to see who was calling her. She noticed that Ms. Holiday and Ms. Cotton were sitting two rows behind her. La'Roc wrote Ms. Holiday a note asking her if that was her who had called her.

Ms. Holiday wrote a note back to her. The note read: *No Ms. Rose. The lady sitting next to me called you.* La'Roc turned around again, and the lady calling her was April. April was a witness for Shawn. She had helped put him in prison; now she was trying to help get him out of prison. She was two weeks too late.

April raised her hand to say hi. La'Roc turned her back to her as if to say, "Go to hell, bitch."

The defense witnesses were called to testify: Mr. Johnston, Kelly's sister, her husband, Kelly's mother, her father, and Shawn's sister, April were also called as Shawn's witness.

Mr. Johnston was Shawn's last witness.

The prosecutor cross-examined the witness, but the prosecutor had no case. Closing arguments were short and to the point. Alex reminded the jury they could not find Mr. Parker guilty if there was reasonable doubt. Alex pointed to La'Roc and reminded them that other people had motive and opportunity. The tension mounted as the jury listened to the judge's ruling.

After hearing all the witnesses, the judge gave the jury the ruling and excused them for deliberation.

Mr. Johnston and April were arrested before the deliberation was finished. They were arrested for withholding evidence to destroy and harm another human being.

After three hours of deliberation, Alex came out to the waiting area where Shawn and La'Roc were sitting with family and friends. Alex said the jury was back. "They have reached the verdict."

"Alex, don't worry. You did a damn good job," La'Roc said.

The bailiff said, "All rise. The court is now in session. The Honorable Judge Philips presiding."

The judge said, "You all may be seated. Have you reached the verdict?" The bailiff answered, "Yes, Your Honor. They have."

"Mr. Parker, will you please stand?" Alex and Shawn followed the judge's directions by standing as requested.

The judge looked over at the jury. The bailiff passed the white piece of paper to the judge. The judge looked at the white piece paper and gave it back to the bailiff. The judge asked the jury if they all agreed with the verdict.

The jury answered, "Yes, we agree with the verdict, Your Honor."

"Bailiff, please read the verdict," the judge instructed.

Jordan, Alex, and Devon took a stand next to Shawn as the bailiff read the verdict.

"The verdict: Mr. Shawn Parker found not guilty of all charges."

La'Roc and her friends hugged and kissed each other with teary eyes. La'Roc ran down to be near Shawn's side when the judge gave him the news.

The judge said, "Mr. Parker, you are a free man. Go home with your family. The court is sorry for all the inconvenience that we have caused you and your loved ones."

La'Roc ran over to Shawn and kissed him. He held her tight. "Baby, I love you."

Two police officers were leading April and Mr. Johnston out of the courtroom in handcuffs.

"Sexiful, I have something to say to April. Come with me. I need you to be by my side."

"Okay, baby. Let me speak to the officers to get you permission to speak to your sister." La'Roc spoke to the officer, and he instructed her that she and Shawn had to wait in the waiting area before she was booked.

The officer explained, "After she's booked, she won't be able to meet with you until she is arraigned."

La'Roc rubbed Shawn's hand for acknowledgment. Shawn walked with La'Roc by his side to the waiting room, expecting April to appear though the door to meet with Shawn.

April walked into the waiting room in shackles, escorted by two officers. She walked with her head down, and when she looked up at Shawn, tears were running down her face. She was crying uncontrollably.

Shawn walked slowly over to his sister; still trying to imagine what would make her hate him so badly. La'Roc watched Shawn from across the room as he walked to greet his sister.

La'Roc tried to relax but couldn't stop fidgeting in her seat.

She was restless, waiting for Shawn to finish his talk with April. La'Roc walked closer to hear what April was saying to Shawn and what Shawn was saying to her.

"I am sorry, Shawn; please forgive me."

Shawn looked at his sister, shaking his head in disbelief. "April, how could you? You're my sister. April, what happened to you? I don't think I can ever forgive you for what you tried to do to me. April, you were going to send me to prison for life, and if it weren't for my lawyers, I would be heading back to prison. Then there's the matter that you helped re-enforce the idea that I was the father of Kelly's child, and you knew I wasn't. Here I am, thinking I'm the boy's father, and I'm not. How am I supposed to explain all this to a two-year-old, that I'm not his daddy?

"No, April. I will never forgive you. Have a nice life," Shawn stated in disgust.

I've never seen Shawn this angry, La'Roc thought to herself.

Shawn walked back to La'Roc and held her in his strong arms. He then kissed the inside of her hand.

April called out, "Ms. Rose, please help me."

La'Roc looked over her shoulder. "April, there's nothing I can or will do for you. I believe Karma will be your judge. Have a nice life."

With that being said, Shawn and La'Roc left April and headed out of the holding room.

Shawn and La'Roc walked out of the courtroom hand in hand.

Outside, Alex, Jordan, Devon, and friends were waiting for the couple to arrive.

Ms. Holiday and Ms. Cotton left the courthouse as soon as they congratulated Shawn on his freedom.

La'Roc called out to Courtney, "Yes, Momma."

"Ms. Holiday and Ms. Cotton are leaving. Tell them to make sure that everything is ready for tonight. Ask Ms. Holiday to make all the calls she needs to make for the temp staff and the caterer," La'Roc informed Courtney.

"Oh, Momma, it's going to be great," Courtney said, laughing. "Dr. Kim went to pick up Justin. That is why she wasn't in court today."

"Courtney, are you kidding me? That was a wonderful thing for her to do," La'Roc said with pride.

"Denise, where is Chantal?"

"She left for the airport to pick up her friend Mitchell. Where is Shawn? Girl, what happened with April when Shawn confronted her?"

La'Roc laughed before giving Denise the answer to her question. "April said, 'Oh, Shawn, please forgive me. I'm sorry.' I wanted to kick the shit out of her with my four-inch heels.

"Alex worked his ass off today. Actually, they all did a good job digging for information on Mr. Johnston and Kelly's family. If I ever get in trouble, I want your whole team on my shit. La'Roc, you and your team are the best, girlfriend," Denise said, laughing.

Shawn sneaked up behind La'Roc and whispered in her ear, "Baby, let's go home. I need and want to make love to you right now."

"Okay, baby. Go get the car and bring it around to the front of the courthouse," La'Roc said, looking up at her man and smiling.

Baby, you're a free man! La'Roc shouted in her mind as she watched Shawn head for the parking lot.

La'Roc said to her team and friends, "We are going to Westchester to the townhouse, and later, I'm taking the whole crew out to dinner. All the invitees knew where to go for the welcome home party.

Everyone laughed and clapped their hands in excitement for Shawn's release from a crime he did not commit.

"Okay, you all know the drill. Be on time," La'Roc said.

"Hi, baby girl," Jordan said with a hug and a kiss.

"Oh, baby, you guys did a damn good job today with disclosing information that the consultant didn't even know. Jordan, how can I ever thank you for your expertise? I'll think of something," La'Roc said with tears of happiness running down her cheek.

"You've already thanked me. La'Roc, you have given me a home, a loving family, and great friends—what more can I ask for?"

"Jordan, I see Shawn's back with the car. He is waiting for me. I'll see you tonight in your tux, looking your best," she said as she walked away.

Jordan called out, "La'Roc, wait up for a moment."

La'Roc stopped in her tracks. "Yes, baby. I'm all yours. What's up?"

"I forgot to inform you that I won't be able to meet you at the townhouse. I have to see one more contractor to finish putting the doors on Devon and Courtney's garage. It'll take about an hour. I'll meet you at the gala." Jordan smiled as he and La'Roc walked in separate directions.

La'Roc said thanks and continued to walk toward Shawn, who was patiently waiting for her in his new car.

Shawn got out of the car and walked to the passenger side to open the door for his future wife. She got into the car. He shut the door and walked back to the driver side to get into the car.

After getting inside, he pulled her to him and kissed her on her lips. "Let's go home, Sexiful," he said with a smirk on his face.

Once on the highway, La'Roc pulled herself closer to Shawn, held his hand, and laid her head on his shoulder. She felt so safe when she was with him.

La'Roc closed her eyes and let her mind drift back to the trial. She recalled the part where Mr. Johnston testified that he and Kelly lured Shawn to a particular subdivision. They planned to have him attacked and beaten; this was in response to the way he allegedly treated Kelly.

Mr. Johnston also testified that he had hired two men to come to the apartment after Ms. Brown left the building.

Once Ms. Brown came into the apartment, she was asked to leave by Mr. Parker; however, Ms. Brown refused to leave. She followed Mr. Parker up the stairs. "Kelly, please leave. I have an active restraining order against you. I'm going to call the police." Mr. Parker pulled out his cell phone. Kelly knocked the phone from his hand; she turned to walk away, lost her footing on the landing, and fell three floors to the bottom landing. Mr. Johnston further stated that the guys that he hired never showed up at the complex.

Mr. Johnston also testified that he and Ms. Brown had been together, off and on, for eight years.

"After she started dating Mr. Parker, we were still dating each other." Mr. Johnston further stated that if they looked at Shawn Jr.'s birth certificate, they would see that he was the father of the child. Shawn Parker was not the father. Mr. Johnston shocked the jury when he stated, "Ms. Kelly C. Brown stated that I was the father of her unborn child that she was carrying when she had the fall. Mr. Parker is not the father of Ms. Brown's son or the father of the unborn child.

"Shawn, Jr. real name on his birth certificate is Tray Johnston Jr., just as my name is Tray Johnston Sr." Mr. Johnston turned to look at Shawn. "I'm sorry, Mr. Parker, to have put you and your family through all of this turmoil."

Throughout Mr. Johnston's testimony, La'Roc noticed that Jordan handed Shawn a box of tissues as he wiped the tears from his eyes.

Mr. Johnston informed Alex that April had nothing to do with hurting her brother.

"She didn't know what the plan was. The plan was to hurt Shawn. April knew nothing about it. However, she did know that we were trying to scam money from him. She also knew about me fathering Kelly's children."

La'Roc refocused and looked over at her future husband and held his hand as tight as she could, and he acknowledged it by holding her hand even tighter. She knew that sooner or later, she and Shawn would have to deal with whatever lay ahead with his so-called son; with the two of them together, they could defeat the world.

"Sexiful, we're almost home, baby. I can't wait to get you into my arms and thank you properly." Shawn placed his hand gently on La'Roc's thigh and massaged it softy, showing off his beautiful sexy smile.

La'Roc said, "Baby, you're my life, my friend, my soul mate, my lover, and soon to be my husband."

She popped a CD into the CD player: "Can You Feel Me" by Anthony Hamilton.

"You did wash your hands when you went to the bathroom, right? I asked you because I have a plan ..." They both laughed.

La'Roc placed Shawn's hand on her mouth and kissed his hand. "Baby, I'm so happy when I'm with you. Sweetheart, you make me feel so full of life and so alive. Everything about you makes me feel like a newborn woman. Shawn, you are an extraordinary man, and I love every bit of your capability to keep me happy."

Shawn stopped the car and looked at her with his sexy brown eyes. "Come over here, Sexiful, and let me hold you in my arms. My arms, lips, and tongue are lonely for you."

He pulled her into the driver's seat and kissed her aggressively.

La'Roc said with a return kiss, "Baby, let's go home so I can give you what you want."

"I know what it is you want, and I want to give it *all* to you." Shawn started the car. La'Roc put in a CD by Whitney Houston. *I want to run to you.* She laid her head upon Shawn's shoulder and closed her eyes. She opened her eyes for a moment, looking at her fiancé, and whispered in his ear, "Baby, I want to run into your arms and just stay there forever.

"Shawn hurry. Make me your wife before I run away with someone else," she said jokingly.

Shawn playfully grabbed her hand and held it tight and as firmly as possible. "I'll never let you go, Sexiful. And I can't wait for you to become Mrs. Shawn Parker." Shawn was smiling from ear to ear. "Oh, baby, I'm so happy right now."

Shawn and La'Roc were interrupted by the ringing of her cell phone. She checked her caller ID. It was Courtney. "Hello, my only daughter. How can I help you?" La'Roc answered.

"Momma, I just wanted to update you on what's going on for the gala tonight. Everything is all in order. Justin and Dr. Kim are with Jordan at Golden Circle. Once Jordan finishes his business there, he'll be coming to the townhouse to get dressed for the gala. Before he comes down, he'll get Justin dressed.

"Dr. Kim will dress there at Golden Circle. Everything is ready to start on time. You and Shawn are going to love the house," Courtney said with excitement.

Before La'Roc hung up with Courtney, she said, "Why don't you guys get dressed at Golden Circle? I think personally that will be better because there are more room for you guys to get dressed without running into each other."

"Okay, Mom; good idea," Courtney responded.

"We are about ten minutes from the townhouse, and, Courtney, we'll finish this conversation once we arrive," La'Roc responded.

Shawn glanced over at La'Roc. "Baby, I'm going to invite my guys out to dinner and thank them each personally."

"That sounds like a very good idea, baby; let's not do it tonight. You should wait until one day next week," La'Roc answered.

"Okay, if you say so. I wanted to take them out tonight to celebrate our victory. Okay, baby. Next week it is," Shawn said, looking disappointed. Shawn yelled out "Home sweet home. Baby, I'm so damn excited. I don't have to worry about going back to

Upland Prison. I'm home to stay, baby. I didn't ever think that I'd ever be home again. But here I am, back in my Sexiful arms again.

"Sexiful, let's go in and get Paris and Biscuit and take them for a long walk and tell them that Daddy is home to stay. I know that we have guests in the house; however, I want to stay outside and walk around the grounds, holding your hand and being thankful and blessed that I have a woman who loves me."

"Shawn, that sounds like a good idea. Come, let's get the babies and disappear through the basement so we won't be noticed." They both giggled like two teenagers stealing a kiss.

Shawn and La'Roc ran downstairs to the basement and out the door with Paris and Biscuit. La'Roc knew that the walk would be a short one because they had to get dressed for Shawn's party.

La'Roc's cell phone began to ring. La'Roc checked her caller ID. It was Courtney.

"Hello, beautiful. What's up, kid?" "Mom, where are you and Shawn?"

"Courtney, look out the second-floor terrace and it's a possibility you may see me and Shawn taking a walk with the puppies," La'Roc replied.

"Oh, you are here. I see you, Shawn, and your puppies."

Shawn walked away from La'Roc with Paris and Biscuit after La'Roc started her conversation with Courtney.

"Yes, baby; we're here," La'Roc responded.

"Momma, we'll be leaving in about an hour. We decided to take your advice and get dressed at the big house."

"Courtney, who is riding with you?" La'Roc asked.

"Grams and her friend, Ms. Thomas, will be riding with me to the party as well. Ms. Thomas lives next door to Grams. You and Shawn will have the townhouse to yourself. You guys can get dressed at the townhouse. We all will get dressed at Golden Circle."

"Everything that you and Shawn will need for tonight is in the master bedroom, hanging in the closet," Courtney said.

"I don't understand why you didn't call a driver. That is what I pay the drivers for: to drive you to wherever you want to go."

"Okay sweetheart, no more talk about the driver. We'll see you soon," La'Roc said. "I'll have Shawn call you when we're on our way, so make it good when you talk to him. Don't let him know what's going on."

La'Roc wanted Shawn to take the message so he wouldn't get suspicious about his welcome home party.

"Courtney, when you talk to him, just say, 'Shawn, tell Momma everyone is here.'"

La'Roc reminded Courtney to have the car pick her and Shawn up around eight o'clock … no later. The guests should be there at seven thirty … no later than seven forty-five.

"Momma, I have everything under control. Trust me." "Courtney, tonight is in your hands, and, baby, I do trust you."

La'Roc called out to Shawn as she ran to catch up with him and her babies. She yelled out for him to wait for her.

They walked for a few minutes more before returning to the house.

Before entering the house, Shawn picked her up into his arms and kissed her. He was about to carry her upstairs when La'Roc's phone started to ring. "Hello, Mother dear. We're leaving and going to Golden Circle; see you there. Love you," Courtney said and hung up her cell.

"Later, baby," La'Roc responded.

La'Roc placed a call to Hector to pick up Paris and Biscuit. He was also instructed to come back for her and Shawn at the appropriate time.

Good thing Shawn had gone upstairs and didn't hear the conversation. "Ms. Rose I am on my way."

A few minutes later, Hector rang the doorbell; La'Roc met him at the door with Paris and Biscuit in hand.

"Sexiful, are you coming upstairs?"

"No, baby, we don't need to go upstairs. Let's make love here in the great room. We're all alone. Make wild love to me right here on the sofa bed," she said. "I want you to fuck me like there is no tomorrow." She was breathing hard as she looked into his beautiful, sexy eyes. "Shawn, make love to me now!"

Shawn ripped his clothes off without hesitation, and he undressed her slowly and gently. Piece by piece, her clothing fell to the floor.

He threw her on the sofa bed and gently massaged her vagina with his long, hard tongue.

She cried out his name in pure ecstasy. Oh, how she liked it when the two of them made love to each other. He was the best lover on the planet.

Yes, he is a keeper, and soon I'll be Mrs. Shawn Parker, La'Roc thought, smiling.

"Sexiful, after I've made love to you, I don't ever want to sleep with another woman. I'm yours forever."

After Shawn and La'Roc finished making love, they laid in each other's arms and took a quiet nap before getting dressed for the welcome home party.

After what seemed like hours of sleeping, Shawn's cell phone rang. "Hello, Devon. What's up, man?" Shawn responded.

"What time are we meeting tonight for our celebration?" Devon asked. "Thanks, man, for waking me and your grandmother. We'll get up now, take a shower, and get dressed," Shawn responded.

"Sexiful, wake up. We need to start getting dressed before Courtney, Jordan, and Devon sends an emergency car to escort us to the celebration dinner tonight."

Shawn and Sexiful took a shower and got dressed. Shawn headed downstairs ahead of La'Roc to call Hector to bring the car around to the front of the townhouse.

Hector pulled the limo around to the front of the house and waited by the back door for the couple to arrive.

La'Roc headed downstairs to greet Shawn. She took one look at Shawn and fell in love all over again; La'Roc stopped in her tracks.

She said, "Oh my God, Shawn, you look stunning in your tux. You're the handsomest man alive." La'Roc complimented Shawn on his neat body.

Shawn looked up the stairs with his mouth open. "Baby, don't move. You are so beautiful. Oh my God, I need this picture. Baby, please don't move. Sexiful, you are the most gorgeous woman I have ever known, and I am delighted we will be sharing our lives together forever." Shawn kissed her lightly.

They were wearing matching colors. Shawn was wearing an off-white tux with a peach shirt, and she was wearing a peach fitted gown to match Shawn's shirt.

They were dressed to impress, and for her, she wanted to show off her man. They looked drop-dead gorgeous.

Shawn set up the camera to take their picture together before leaving for the welcome home party.

As La'Roc and Shawn walked out to the awaiting car, Hector was there with the back door open. Shawn helped La'Roc into the limo, and he followed behind her.

Hector closed the door and returned to the driver's seat.

As Hector started to drive off, Shawn decided to mix some drinks. Shawn sat across from La'Roc, holding her hand.

"Sexiful, you look good enough to eat. However, since we are on our way to a dinner, I'll have you for dessert after the celebration." He looked at her and smiled.

La'Roc looked at Shawn. "Baby, I've got to keep my eyes on you tonight since you'll be the most handsome man at the dinner and the most important man there tonight. I'm going to make you my man of honor tonight."

Having arrived at the Golden Circle, Shawn looked surprised as the driver opened the door. Shawn stepped out and reached for La'Roc's hand and helped her to exit the car. Shawn looked up at the house. "Wow! What a beautiful place." Shawn couldn't see all the cars parked because the parking lot wasn't visible. The parking lot was built on the far side of the house.

"Oh my God. Whose beautiful home is this?"

La'Roc said, "In time you'll find out who owns this beautiful paradise."

She looked up at Shawn and smiled. "Baby, you like the celebration so far? We're having dinner here at the Golden Circle. Courtney invited a lot of people for this celebration." La'Roc smiled.

Before going into the house, La'Roc took Shawn's hand and pulled his face down to her lips and kissed him. "Baby, I love you so much. Just enjoy tonight."

"Sexiful, I love you too." He kissed her gently. Shawn rang the doorbell. One of the waiters opened the door.

Shawn and La'Roc walked into the house; everything was quiet. Out walked Jordan, Alex, Devon, and Courtney, yelling out, "Welcome home, Shawn!" Then all the guests ran out. "Surprise, Shawn!" Shawn clutched La'Roc's hand and pulled her close to him; surprise was written all over his face. It was a pleasure to see the excitement in his face. Courtney had pulled it off; the place looked amazing. All of their friends were there, cheering for Shawn and his lady.

La'Roc was ecstatic. She looked around in the big room at all the people that night and felt nothing but love.

Shawn teared up when he saw Dr. Kim pushing Justin in a wheelchair.

"Oh, Sexiful, why didn't you tell me that you were going to give me a party? Seeing Justin here is just too much." Shawn walked toward the wheelchair to greet Dr. Kim and Justin. He hugged Justin and kissed Dr. Kim on her cheek.

La'Roc looked up into Shawn's face with a smile. "Baby, if I told you about the party then it wouldn't have been a surprise, right?"

La'Roc looked around for her best friends, sister, her sister's husband, and her mother.

She saw her mother in a corner, talking to one of her friends and Ms. Cotton. Jordan had a bandstand built inside the ballroom; a live band and a DJ were on hand for the evening.

Chantal strolled over to La'Roc and Shawn with her doctor friend and reintroduced the couple. Dr. Mitchell shook Shawn's hand and kissed La'Roc on her cheek. "Shawn, are you enjoying yourself? This beautiful party is for you. Courtney did a fantastic job," Chantal said.

"Hello, Dr. Mitchell. Good to see you again and thanks for coming to Shawn's welcome home party. I'd also like to thank you for your assistance in getting Justin into that great rehabilitation center. If it weren't for your help, Justin wouldn't be with us today." Dr. Mitchell looked to his left to where Justin was sitting and smiled.

Dr. Mitchell shook Shawn's hand and congratulated him on his victory.

Then, taking Chantal's hand, he walked away to talk with Justin.

"Shawn, I am going to find Denise. I am a little worried about her," La'Roc said.

"Okay, Sexiful," Shawn responded.

La'Roc spoke with L'Oreal and Casey for a moment and then maneuvered her way over to her mother and gave her a loving kiss. "Mom, I love you." She walked away from her mother, greeting other guests as she continued her search for Denise. After Martin had been arrested, she and Denise hadn't had much time to chat.

"La'Roc," Denise called out.

"Denise, where are you? I need to talk to you," La'Roc responded.

"I am right behind you, sis," Denise said, tapping La'Roc on her shoulder. "How is it going tonight, baby sister?" La'Roc asked her friend.

"Oh, La'Roc, I feel like I am a reborn woman since we had Martin arrested," Denise said, smiling. "Thanks friend."

"Denise, we didn't have Martin arrested. You did. Remember that," La'Roc said, empowering Denise to be strong.

Devon tapped La'Roc on her shoulder.

"Grams, I've been looking for you. Remember August? Shawn is looking for you; I think he has a surprise for you. Come, ladies. Follow and trust me." Devon turned his head toward August and smiled.

"August, are you taking care of my little lawyer?" La'Roc said jokingly.

"Yes, I am, Ms. Rose. I'd like to thank you personally for inviting me to share in this wonderful evening with you and your family. I'm really enjoying myself," August said.

"I'm glad you are enjoying the party," La'Roc responded.

La'Roc maneuvered her way over to Shawn, where he was busy talking to Jordan.

"Hi, handsome. Miss me?" La'Roc asked, looking up at Shawn and winking at Jordan.

"Baby, I've got a surprise for you. However, I don't think I can top this gift that Jordan gave you. This house is breathtaking. I've only seen the downstairs. I asked myself what it is like upstairs."

"Sweetheart, I'll give you a private tour when we're alone tonight," La'Roc said as she walked toward Jordan.

"Jordan, you okay?" La'Roc asked.

"Yes, baby girl. I'm doing great. I feel so much love in this house tonight. Just look around you, baby girl. Look at Courtney's face when she looks at Justin. She's so happy. Oh! I almost forgot," Jordan said, smiling. "Shawn has something to ask you. Go to your man, baby girl," Jordan said as he walked away, dancing and popping his fingers. He looked so good, spinning around on the dance floor.

"Shawn, I am all yours, baby."

Shawn was standing up on the bandstand when the DJ made the announcement. "Ms. La'Roc Rose, will you please come up and join Mr. Parker on the stage?"

As La'Roc was making her way to stand by her man, she kissed her mother, who was standing in front of the stage. Shawn walked to the edge of the stage and reached for La'Roc's hand to help her onstage. He held her hand gently as he walked her to the middle of the stage. Shawn thanked the DJ for doing a wonderful job.

Courtney came to the stage to congratulate Shawn on being a free man. She asked the team to come up on stage.

Once on stage, they all thanked the guests for making Shawn's party a big success.

All the guests raised their glasses toward La'Roc and Shawn. Shawn asked the guests for their attention.

"I'd like to take this time to thank everyone for coming out to help me celebrate my homecoming," Shawn humbly stated.

The DJ had soft music playing in the background; Shawn asked for La'Roc's right hand.

"Sexiful, I want you to know I love you more than I love myself. Before I go to sleep at night, you're on my mind. When I wake up every morning, the first thing I want to see is your face. I want your head always lying on my chest. Sexiful, you are the air I breathe. Every time my heart beats, one beat is for you. I love you, Sexiful."

La'Roc looked up into Shawn's eyes with tears running down her face.

"I love you too, handsome," she said with tears continuously running down her face.

Shawn picked her up and kissed her tears as if he could kiss them away. "Sexiful, are you all right?"

"Yes, handsome. I am great as long as you are here beside me," La'Roc said, wiping the tears from her eyes.

Shawn got down on one knee, and Devon gave him a black box.

"La'Roc 'Sexiful' Rose, I know I proposed to you long ago, but this time I'm going to propose to you properly." Shawn felt that this party was the appropriate time to propose to La'Roc in front of her family and friends.

"La'Roc 'Sexiful' Rose, will you marry me? I am asking you to marry me in front of your friends, family, and, most of all, your daughter and your grandson."

Shawn opened the black box Devon had given him. From the black box, Shawn removed a three-carat oval blue sapphire and diamond ring. Denise, Courtney, Devon, Chantal, and Jordan left the stage.

La'Roc yelled out, "*Yes*, Shawn. I will marry you!"

Shawn kissed her long and hard. "She said *yes,* she will marry me," Shawn yelled out as loud as he could.

Shawn called Courtney and Devon back to the stage. He presented Courtney with a diamond bracelet and Devon with a Rolex watch. He then announced that they were all engaged. He called La'Roc's mother up and gave her a gift-wrapped box.

"Thank you for accepting me into your family, Mother Rose,"

Shawn grabbed La'Roc's hand and led her to the dance floor. He had requested the DJ to play "Send for Me" and "Can You Feel Me," two of La'Roc's and Shawn's favorite songs.

The two of them clung to each other and smiled at each other, tears staining both of their faces.

"The party was a success, Sexiful. The decorations are out of this world. This house—I can't believe Jordan gave you a house like this."

"Oh, handsome, we have to give you a tour as soon as the guests leave," La'Roc said with pride.

Shawn and La'Roc joined their guests for dinner in the large dining room. The room was filled with conversation and laughter. After dinner, drinks were served and the music continued for several hours before the guests started to say their goodbyes for the evening.

Shawn and La'Roc walked hand in hand to bid their friends goodnight. Every one of her guests walked down the hallway to the front door, bidding the couple goodnight and taking a good look at Sexiful engagement ring, especially the women.

After the last guest and the DJ left, Shawn and La'Roc thanked all the staff with a big fat check. Shawn noticed Courtney walking into the entertainment room; Shawn called out to her. "Courtney, I heard you set this party in motion. Ms. Little La'Roc, this party was off the hook. I never had a party before; this is the first. Thank you, my adopted daughter."

"Shawn, putting this party together was fun. The team and I enjoyed hooking it up just for you and my mother," Courtney responded.

Shawn smiled. "Great job Courtney."

Shawn took his lawyers into the office (while La'Roc chatted with her family and friends) to thank them with a bonus check, which Jordan refused.

Jordan said, "No hard feelings, man. I just can't accept your money. It would be like taking money from me. Thanks, but no thanks. What I did, I did from my heart and the love I have for La'Roc and her family. And, Shawn, you are a part of that package. Tonight, Shawn, you became a big part of my family. I love you, man," Jordan said as he and Shawn high-fived.

"Another thing ... my job is to free innocent people, like you. You are innocent, right?"

Jordan hugged Shawn and smiled as he walked away. "Thanks for the lesson, Jordan," Shawn responded.

Jordan left the room, and Alex walked over to Shawn and high-fived him.

"You did a damn good job this afternoon. I had no idea that Sexiful was going to be called to testify. When did you guys come up with that one?"

"That was La'Roc's brilliant idea. She knew it would work, and she is never wrong," Alex said, smiling.

"Thanks, man. I am a free man because of you guys," Shawn responded. He handed Alex a check.

"Shawn, I can't take this check. I appreciate it, but I've already been paid," Alex said.

Shawn said, "I know, man. Buy your girl something nice." "Man, I'm sorry. I can't accept the check," Alex insisted.

"Okay, we'll all go out to dinner, just us guys," Shawn said with a disappointed smile.

Alex said, "That sounds great. Dinner it is."

"You and Jordan decide the time and the place. Get back to me, okay." "Sounds like a plan," Alex said.

Shawn and Alex left the office, laughing. Shawn walked over to join La'Roc and her family. Chantal left with her doctor friend. Devon left to drive his girlfriend home, and Denise was upstairs with Jordan. Dr. Kim was upstairs with Justin and his nurse. Justin needed his rest; he was getting tired, so the nurse and Dr. Kim decided to take him upstairs to medicate him and get him ready for bed.

Courtney ran over to give her mother a big hug; she congratulated her and Shawn on their engagement. "Shawn thanks for making my mother the happiest woman in the word. Thank you."

L'Oreal and Geneva were just as excited as La'Roc was about the engagement.

"Casey is going shopping tomorrow to get me another diamond ring. Girl, that ring is to die for," L'Oreal said.

La'Roc's cell rang. She checked her caller ID: it was Chantal. "Hi, girlfriend. I can't wait to get a good look at that big diamond you have on your finger, but I got a quick glance at it at the party. Denise called. She said it was a rock and a half. Sis, I'll see you tomorrow morning,"

"Chantal, come for breakfast and invite Dr. Mitchell. You all need to get together and start planning the wedding. I want to be Mrs. Shawn Parker within three months." La'Roc said goodnight and disconnected the call.

Shawn and La'Roc said their goodnights and went upstairs to bed.

Before going to bed, they decided to get into the Jacuzzi. Shawn picked up a bottle of champagne and two champagne glasses from the bar; he set the tray on the Jacuzzi stand. That's when La'Roc presented Shawn with the diamond ring she had purchased some weeks prior to his homecoming party.

He thanked her with a gentle kiss, a beautiful toast, a glass of champagne, and a whole lot of loving. "Shawn, this ring is a token of my love." She had his name engraved inside and "ILU."

"Thank you baby. I'm going to show you my appreciation. By the way, whoever helped Courtney hook up my welcome home party; they did a damn good job. I'm going to thank each and every one of them personally. Or did Courtney do all of this all by herself?"

La'Roc responded it was her idea but she had lot of help from the team. "L'Oreal, Denise, Jordan, Chantal … just thank the whole team."

He pulled her close and unzipped her gown. The gown fell to the floor. He eased his hand into her thong and inserted his finger into her vagina. She moaned with pleasure. He placed her into the Jacuzzi gently and then undressed himself. Once in the water, he kissed her body and placed her on top of his manhood.

La'Roc though she was dreaming as her body shivered with pleasure. As she reached her climax, she became emotional, with tears rolling down her cheeks. She yelled out his name with great satisfaction and felt exhilarated because this man knew the art of making love.

Shawn knew how to make her feel excitement and always leave her anticipating more of his untamed lovemaking.

After making love, they sipped on champagne and went to bed with her head on his chest, as always.

She admired her big diamond before going to sleep. "Shawn, I love my ring and will never take it off my finger. When did you have time to shop for it?"

"Remember when we were in Brooklyn and I left you in bed? I told you I took the babies downtown to take care of some business. That was the day; I purchased the ring because I knew you would love it. Did Daddy do well?"

"Yes, baby you did a wonderful job. Go to sleep."

Shawn said, "Good night, Ms. Rose, and soon I'll be saying, 'Good night, Mrs. Parker.'"

"Good night, Mr. Parker. I can't wait to become Mrs. Parker."

There was a knock at their bedroom door. Shawn said, "Enter." Devon entered through the door with Paris and Biscuit in each hand.

La'Roc said, "What a big surprise! Devon, how did you know that I missed my babies?" La'Roc was smiling with joy.

"Well, my future grandfather asked me to bring them up to surprise you. So I guess it worked, Shawn. She is surprised and happy to. Four out of four. Not bad, Grams. You have all you wished for tonight: your big diamond ring, your man is home, the party was a big success, and you have your babies here with you. What more can you ask for? You have everything right here in the palm of your hand," Devon said.

"Well, one thing I don't have is you standing near me so I can give you a big hug and thank you for a wonderful job you performed today in court." La'Roc thanked her grandson with a big fat kiss.

Devon walked over to his grandmother and gave her a hug and a kiss. He then walked over to Shawn and gave him a high five, and they made shoulder contact.

"Good night, Grams. Good night, Shawn," Devon said and walked out of the bedroom.

La'Roc asked Shawn to hold her. "I promise I'll never let you go, handsome. You're stuck with me." La'Roc playfully kissed Shawn on his lips.

"Sexiful, I love you, and I'm here at your beck and call," he spoke in a serious tone.

"Oh, baby! Let's go on a tour of the house, or did Jordan show you Golden Circle already? Courtney came up with the name Golden Circle. As soon as we take the tour, we can get back to bed," she said, smiling at her man.

La'Roc showed Shawn all the rooms that were available at the time. Most of the guests had gone to bed.

Jordan had the team, family, and friends' names engraved on the bedroom doors: Casey, L'Oreal, Courtney, Devon, Chantal, Denise, Geneva, and—he saved the best for last—Shawn and La'Roc on the second master bedroom. All rooms had their own bathrooms with a shower and hot tub.

She then showed Shawn the staff quarters. As they walked toward the elevator, he held her hand oh so tightly as if she were going to run away.

La'Roc and Shawn took the elevator to the third landing of the house. Once they reached the third floor, she glanced at Shawn, admiring his name on one of the office doors. "This is great, Sexiful." She looked up into his eyes, and she knew he had fallen in love with Golden Circle and all it had to offer.

"Sexiful, this is unbelievable. I can't thank Jordan enough for taking care of you while I was away. I can't get over him buying this house."

"Baby, I'm glad you like it, but as I told you before, I have great friends." La'Roc smiled.

"Shawn, who told you this, was my house? Who gave the secret away?" "Sexiful, if I told you, I would have to kill you. Okay, I will tell you. It was your mother, by mistake. She thought you had told me. Geneva said, 'Shawn, what do you think about my baby's new house that Jordan gave her.' I said, 'Wow! This is Sexiful's house? Mom I love it.' She said, 'Oh my God, you didn't know?' Geneva put her hand over her mouth with shame. I told her, 'This would be our little secret, Mommy Rose.'"

"Okay, so Mom told you.

"You can check out the gym, tennis court, pools, and the garages tomorrow on your time," La'Roc's said jokingly.

"Oh, I forgot the big parking lot. It is on the side of the house." Shawn and La'Roc returned to the main house, arm in arm, and traveled upstairs to retire for the night.

A month later, Courtney, Chantal, Denise, L'Oreal, and Geneva started planning La'Roc's wedding.

La'Roc wanted the wedding to be held at the Golden Circle Drive.

Shawn asked Devon to be his best man; La'Roc asked Jordan and Devon to give her away. Devon said, "I can do both; nowadays, we youngsters multitask, and I can be Shawn's best man and still give you to Shawn with no delay in the wedding. That is what you call *multitasking*." Devon did his fancy footstep and laughed his way out the door. "Everything will go as scheduled. I promise you, Grams," Devon said.

The groomsmen were Casey, Alex, Chantal's date, and Shawn's friends from his old neighborhood ... the same friends that he grew up with. One of the friends was the person that he lived with when he ran away from home as a child.

The bridesmaids were close friends from La'Roc's office and her coworkers. There were eight groomsmen and bridesmaids. The matrons of honor were L'Oreal, Courtney, Chantal, and Denise; La'Roc couldn't ask one to participate as matron of honor and not the other ones because she loved them all.

Biscuit would walk down the aisle as Shawn's ring bearer, and Paris would walk down the aisle as La'Roc's ring bearer.

La'Roc met with the girls and the wedding planner. The planner Courtney had hired was well known for working with celebrities, so she was prepared to handle the large affair.

La'Roc felt as though she was in seventh heaven; she would soon be Mrs. Shawn Parker. She laughed out loud. *Huh, Mrs. Parker has a great sound to it.* She smiled to herself in excitement.

Shawn was upstairs with the boys; Shawn, Jordan, and Devon were on the fourth floor, trying on their tuxes for the big day. Shawn liked to go out and shop for things; he wasn't use to being pampered; on the other hand La'Roc sometimes liked to be pampered. She asked Courtney to have her wedding gowns and all of her accessories sent to the townhouse for her fitting.

Ms. Holiday and Ms. Cotton were having a meeting with the staff to instruct them on their duties on the day of the wedding and make sure all the drivers were in place.

"Ms. Rose wants everything perfect for her wedding day. Get it together!" Ms. Holiday yelled out to her staff.

Shawn walked into the gym where La'Roc was doing her exercises; he decided to join her in her workout.

"Hi, handsome. Are you ready to marry the woman you *said* you love?" La'Roc asked.

"Yes, I was ready three years ago. Baby, I just want to be your husband and love you forever." He sat down next to her on her mat and held her real tight; he whispered in her ear, "Sexiful, I can't wait to see you walk down the aisle to greet me as your husband. When I see you walking down the aisle toward me, I know that you'll be mine," he said in his sexy voice.

"Shawn, sweetheart, it is three weeks before the wedding." She looked at him, speaking with a very serious tone. "This is your last opportunity to back out of this wedding—get out while you can because once you get married to me, as I said, I'll never let you go. Am I the one you really want in your life? Remember, we have an age difference, and we have to think about children because I can't give you children."

"Yes, Sexiful, I've thought about all of the above. I'm ready to be all yours, and like I said before, age is just a number. I love you, Sexiful, and I want to spend the rest of my life with you. I thought about Shawn Jr., and I decided to give him a trust fund and stay out of his life. He is only two years old; thank God for that. Kelly had already turned him against me anyway. The last time I saw him, he started to cry when I picked him up. He seemed to be afraid of me. I knew then that I needed to stay away from him. Junior will get his trust fund at age twenty-five for college only. If he drops out of college, the money stops. So, yes, I'm ready to become your husband. Are you ready to become my wife?" Shawn asked.

"Yes, Shawn. I'll marry you anywhere, any place. Just say the word, and I will be there to say *I do*." She laughed.

Shawn laughed.

"Sexiful, let's go out tonight, just you and me. I want to take you to the same place we had our first date. Remember that night I told you about Shawn Jr., and you talked about your daughter, grandson, and the feelings that you have for your babies? Once I met your family, I could understand why your feelings for your family and friends were so deep. I'm delighted that I've become a part of your family. Come on, Sexiful. Go out on a date with me tonight."

"Shawn, that sounds wonderful. I would love to go on a date with you. Handsome, let's make it a real date. You get dressed upstairs on the second floor, and I'll get dressed downstairs in the master bedroom. Oh, Shawn, since the wedding is going to be here at Golden Circle, we'll have to go to the townhouse tomorrow evening or we can go after our date tonight," La'Roc responded.

"Okay babe. We can go tonight after our date. The townhouse it is," Shawn said with a little giggle.

The date was fantastic—Shawn rented the whole restaurant as he did on their first date; Shawn gave the DJ a list of the music that was played on their first date. *How did he remember those songs? I have no idea.* Shawn also ordered the same meal they had on their first date. That night, she was the happiest girl in the world. She was with the man she loved and would be marrying in three weeks. She forgot a long time ago about the fifteen-year age difference.

After their date, Shawn and La'Roc returned to the townhouse. Shawn drove the car into the garage. After parking the car, he walked around to the passenger side to open the door and help her out of the car. He picked her up and carried her into the house, straight upstairs to the bedroom. He placed her on the bed very gently and started making love to her. He pulled her dress up to her waist and pulled her thong to the side. Breathing hard, his heart was pounding as his manhood became harder. La'Roc liked feeling his penis rise as he sucked on her nipples. He was so steamed he didn't take the time to take off her clothes; he was so turned on, he made love to her as if he were going away and would never return. She felt as though she was actually having an out-of-body experience that night; she had no control over her body.

She loved it when he took control of their lovemaking. With her dress pulled up around her waist and her thong pulled to the side, it made her feel like a teenager. Remember when you were sneaking around, making out with your boyfriend (you girls know the feeling), and you were afraid of getting caught by your parents? That was a damn good feeling.

As Shawn reached his climax, he was moaning and crying out her name. "Shit, Sexiful, what are you doing to me?"

"Oh, baby, keep doing what you are doing just don't stop making love to me." Shawn started to rotate his lower body into her as she felt his penis go deep inside of her. She moaned in pain but liked every inch of it. It was painful yet so good. She asked for more of his penis, and he gave her more of what she requested. He started to rotate the head of his penis slowly and gave her more as he entered more of himself inside of her.

"Oh damn." She cried out his name, "Shawn, *baby*."

As they both reached their climax, they yelled out with enjoyment and pleasure.

After they made love, he pulled her clothes off and carried her to the Jacuzzi. He put her in the Jacuzzi and left to get a glass of champagne for each of them. He walked back into the room with two glasses of champagne and a towel wrapped around his strong body.

He set the glasses on the nightstand and reached over into the Jacuzzi to kiss her; she snatched the towel off his body and pulled him into the Jacuzzi. After playing around in the Jacuzzi for a while, they talked about the wedding and then went to bed with her in his arms and her head on his chest, as usual.

The bridal shower was X-rated. It was a wonderful night, hanging out with the girls and about twelve muscular, handsome male strippers who could have put Magic Mike to shame.

All of La'Roc's friends and family were there to celebrate her bridal shower. La'Roc had a wonderful time, laughing and joking with her mother and her friends. Although, La'Roc missed not being in Shawn's arms.

Three weeks later:

La'Roc leaned against the open French door to her bedroom, looking out at the new day. She cherished this time of day when the house was quiet and she could pull her thoughts together with no interruptions. She thought about the fact that she and her man were finally going to be together forever. What a journey it had been. She ran her hand over the beautiful invitation that was lying on the side table. She knew that the three hundred or so guests would be impressed. The invitation read:

You are cordially invited to attend the wedding of the century. Mr. Shawn Parker and Ms. La'Roc "Sexiful" Rose are to become husband and wife on July 14, 2012 at 2:00 p.m. at 1545 Golden Circle Drive Westchester County 00099.

La'Roc's gown had been flown in from Paris. She was so happy and excited that the dressmaker she had met on a previous trip had been able to design and create her special dress. Who would have guessed that a crazy shopping spree would one day pay off like this?

Shawn and La'Roc decided to stay apart the week before the wedding. Oh, how she missed him. She wanted to be held in his strong arms and to be able to sleep on his chest, as always. He called every night to say, "I love you, Sexiful."

She would respond with, "I love you too, handsome. Good night."

It was hard for the both of them, being separated from each other.

That week of the wedding without Shawn was the hardest thing she had done since Shawn was released from Upland Prison; she thought about the time when he was in prison and how lonely she was.

Due to all the preparations that were taking place at Golden Circle, nobody was going to be living there.

The day before the wedding:

La'Roc got up that morning, ran three blocks, did some exercises, played with her babies, and took a long, hot bubble bath. She missed Shawn's hands around her body as they would take a bath or shower together; after tomorrow, they would be able to take a shower every night as Mr. and Ms. Parker.

La'Roc asked Ms. Cotton to call Hector and ask him to drive the car around to the front of the building within the hour.

"Ms. Cotton, we'll be staying at Golden Circle tonight," informed La'Roc. She reasoned that it would be more convenient to have all the female members of the bridal party there on site. Truth be told, she knew that tomorrow was going to be a whirlwind, but she wouldn't have it any other way. Her Parisian dressmaker had flown in last night and would meet her at the mansion. The makeup team would be there right after breakfast. Let the wonderful madness begin.

"Yes, Ms. Rose. Don't worry; you and Mr. Shawn will have a beautiful wedding. I can't wait to see you in your wedding gown." Ms. Cotton responded by singing "Here Comes the Bride" as she danced around the room with a broom. They both looked at each other and laughed. La'Roc glanced over at Paris and Biscuit. They had their paws over their eyes as if they were ashamed of Ms. Cotton.

La'Roc and Ms. Cotton laughed so hard, tears were running down their faces. La'Roc said, "Come on, guys. Let's go get married."

La'Roc was thinking to herself, *this wedding should be perfect; everyone should know their steps as well as their turns.*

La'Roc had hired an animal trainer to train Biscuit and Paris to carry their rings down the aisle. The rings would be placed around their little necks until the best man removed them during the ceremony. She yelled out, "Oh my God, my wedding is the most important day of my life. My beautiful wedding will be the talk of Westchester County and even New York State!"

The day of the wedding, everyone had their own space to get dressed. Shawn and his groom party were downstairs; La'Roc and her party were upstairs.

La'Roc would be walking down the spiral staircase that Jordan had built just for the wedding. Her matrons of honor would be walking down the spiral staircase first, and La'Roc would follow. As La'Roc walked down the spiral staircase to meet her long-awaited future husband, the music would be playing: "Run to You" by Whitney Huston.

One hour before the wedding, La'Roc was so excited. She never thought she would ever find a man like Shawn: someone to love her for her and not for her money or to explore her as a showcase, as Roger did.

"Ms. Rose, your grandson is at the door," one of the workers announced. "Show him in; thank you," La'Roc responded.

Devon entered the bridal suite, smiling. "Wow! Grandmother, you look great. You look just like a picture from one of those magazines. I think it is the one with all the pretty models. *Vogue* ... that's it. Grandmother. I'll be so happy when you get married because Shawn is driving me *mad*," Devon said jokingly.

"Oh, baby. It'll be over soon. Devon are you happy for me, sweetheart?" La'Roc asked as she hugged and kissed her grandson.

"Yes Grams. I'm really happy for you. I know that Shawn is the right man for you. When someone can make you smile, he is my man. I like him a lot. I told him if he ever makes you cry, I'll have to check him out. And we both know what that means, right, Grams?" Devon said, looking very serious.

"Oh, my little attorney." Don't worry about your old grandmother. She will be just fine with Shawn. Shawn loves me, and I love him," La'Roc responded with a hug from her grandson. "Now go back to your groom party." She smiled.

Devon left the room, smiling, looking just like his father. He looked so damn handsome in his tux and dark shades. As he walked out the door, she thought to herself, *Wow! I am so proud of him.*

The photographer's assistant informed all the female members of the bridal party to gather in La'Roc's room.

The bridal party gathered in La'Roc's bridal suite. The suite was filled with white roses and dusty purple calla lilies that had been handpicked from her garden. The photographer took photos of the bride and the bridal party. La'Roc's designer gown was off-white with a high-low hemline; the U shape above her knees showed off her beautiful long legs. Her waist was very small, and the gown fit her perfectly. The back of the gown had a very low U cut to show off her beautiful toned back. Sparkling stones lined the hemline of the gown; they also circled the waistline.

The gown was one of a kind. On the day of the wedding, La'Roc decided to wear a tiara to show off her beautiful hair, which she wore in an up-sweep with a bun at the crown of her head.

Shawn's tux was off-white with a light-blue cummerbund. The groomsmen wore light blue tuxes and off-white cummerbunds.

The bridesmaids were dressed the same as the groomsman. The matrons of honor dressed in light-blue one-shoulder gowns, showing off their toned arms. They had off-white roses on the sides of their heads.

Courtney gave her mother something blue, Chantal and Denise gave something old, and L'Oreal gave La'Roc something borrowed. The bridal party and La'Roc did a group hug for the last time as Ms. La'Roc Rose. Soon she would be Mrs. Shawn Parker.

The wedding:

The bridesmaids and groomsmen lined up on each side of the spiral staircase. The staircase was designed like a U. The groomsmen walked down the spiral staircase on the left, and the bridesmaids walked down the spiral staircase on the right. At the bottom of the staircase, the groomsmen and the bridesmaids joined together and walked to the center of the ballroom where the wedding was to take place. The four matrons of honor walked down the spiral staircase, two on each side. At the end of the staircase, the four of them joined together and continued to walk to the center of the ballroom. La'Roc's music started to play as she walked down the stairs "I want to run to you."

As La'Roc walked down the stairs, everyone sighed. "Wow, she's a beautiful bride. La'Roc is a beautiful woman." La'Roc looked out to the front-row seats and saw her mother crying with Ms. Holiday standing nearby. The inside of the Golden Circle ballroom was packed with loved ones ... beautiful people dressed in their tuxes and long designer gowns.

She scanned the floor to find Shawn. As La'Roc walked slowly down the spiral staircase, she glanced to the center of the big hall where the wedding was being held. Shawn was standing in the middle of the floor with his two best men standing by his side.

La'Roc was thinking to herself, *Damn, will I ever get to my man? This walk seems to have no end. Is there an end to this shit?* It seemed like she was walking the green mile. She smiled to herself. Her bridesmaids and matrons of honor were standing in a perfect line to accommodate the bride as she entered the ballroom.

Paris and Biscuit reached the bottom of the staircase without a problem and took their places next to Shawn.

La'Roc reached the end of her long walk down the spiral staircase to greet her grandson and her best friend, Jordan. Jordan and Devon each reached for La'Roc's arms to escort her to the man she loved.

She continued her long journey down the red carpet to marry the man she adored. As she got closer to Shawn, her eyes were filled with tears; she could not believe that she was walking down this red carpet to marry the man of her dreams.

After the rings were removed from Biscuit and Paris's necks, they were given to Geneva.

Geneva played an important part in the wedding; she gave the rings to the appropriate person, Rev. Ward. Rev. Ward passed one ring to Shawn and the other ring to La'Roc. After their vows, they placed the rings on each other's fingers.

La'Roc and Shawn had written their vows; after they read their vows to each other, the reverend said, "With the power vested in me, I now pronounce you husband and wife. Mr. Parker, you may kiss the bride."

Shawn said, "I have been waiting for this kiss all week." He pulled her into his arms and kissed her gently. "Baby, you are the most beautiful woman in the world. Thank you, Sexiful, for giving me a family and, most of all, for giving yourself to me as my wife."

"Handsome, you are stuck with me. You are my life, Shawn. Tell me, baby, just look around you. I have everything I need. I have my family, friends, and now I have a husband—the man I love."

The wedding was a beautiful success. The flowers were gorgeous; everything about the wedding was exquisite.

All the guests received a small Waterford crystal bowl with a rose engraved inside. And all the staff received a bonus in their little yellow envelopes.

Paris and Biscuit looked wonderful in their little tuxedo jackets with bowties around their tiny little necks. The trainer did a wonderful job training Paris and Biscuit for the wedding; they were so well behaved, she couldn't believe her eyes.

After the wedding ceremony, the puppy sitter escorted them back to their room to eat and rest. They had a long and exhausting day.

La'Roc and Shawn maneuvered their way over to Geneva; La'Roc hugged and kissed her mother. "Mom, are you enjoying yourself?"

"Yes, baby. This was the most beautiful wedding I have ever attended. La'Roc, there were so many people. I've never been to such a gigantic wedding before. I'm really enjoying myself. I just wish your father could have been here to witness this event of his daughter getting married to the man she loves. Shawn, you better take care of my baby." Geneva walked away with her friend, laughing and talking about the wedding. The wedding was performed in the west wing ballroom, and the reception was held in the east wing of the house. The room was decorated in white and blue, two of La'Roc and Shawn's favorite colors. It was beautiful!

When the guests walked into the reception, there was a lot of, "Oh Wow! What a gorgeous room."

After their first dance as a married couple, Shawn and La'Roc maneuvered their way to greet the guests to thank them for joining their nuptials and for participating in the festivities throughout the entire evening. Shawn decided to make his thank-you speech at the top of the stairs, with his wife by his side.

Shawn and La'Roc changed from a wedding gown and tux to something more comfortable. La'Roc changed into a designer yellow gown with a split down to her navel and very low cut in the back. Shawn changed into a Michael Kors two-piece beige suit and yellow shirt to match La'Roc's yellow gown.

They walked up the spiral staircase as husband and wife, hand in hand. At the top of the staircase, Shawn made a speech, looking down into the ballroom, in the east wing where the reception took place. He thanked all the guests again for coming to the wedding of the year. They also thanked the wedding party for putting such a beautiful wedding together.

"Special thanks to La'Roc's mother, Courtney, Chantal, L'Oreal, Denise, Devon, Alex, Jordan, and Casey. Thanks, to Ms. Holiday, Ms. Cotton, and all the staff for this wonderful layout."

It seemed like a million pictures were taken during the day. La'Roc said to Shawn that she was tired of smiling for the camera—she just wanted to go upstairs and relaxes.

Shawn and La'Roc came back to their table in the reception area and joined the wedding party. Devon and August came over and congratulated the couple again. Alex, Denise, Chantal, Dr. Kim, and Courtney came over to La'Roc and Shawn's table to congratulate the loving couple. Courtney had a special table set up just for Shawn and La'Roc Parker.

"Where's Jordan?" La'Roc asked.

"I'm here, baby girl. Congratulations," Jordan responded, kissing his best friend. He high-fived with Shawn.

La'Roc asked her friends to sit down at her table. "We'll have the food served at this table. Chantal, invite your doctor friend over and bring my mother and her friends back to our table. Debbie, where's Justin?"

"Justin is taking a nap," Debbie answered.

Casey and L'Oreal came over to congratulate the happy couple.

Shawn invited L'Oreal and Casey to come and join the wedding party at their table. "Let's eat and drink some champagne." The wedding party joined the newlyweds' private table.

Shawn looked around the table and didn't see Alex. "Where's Alex?"

"On the dance floor," Devon responded. Shawn asked Devon to invite Alex and his guest to join them at their private table. Alex and his female friend accepted the invitation. Devon and Alex returned to the private table together with his guest. Alex introduces his date to the bride and groom. "This is Ashley."

"Congratulations on your beautiful wedding. It's a pleasure meeting all of you."

"Pleased to meet you Ashley; have a seat."

"Thank you, Ms. Parker."

"A toast to La'Roc and Shawn—this was the most beautiful wedding that I have ever attended," L'Oreal said with teary eyes. Courtney presented a long speech with her blessing to the couple.

While Courtney was making her speech, Dr. Cunningham was holding her hand, smiling from ear to ear. After she finished her speech, she introduced Dr. Kevin Cunningham to Shawn. Shawn extended his hand to Kevin, and they shook.

They did the shoulder-bumping thing, and she knew than Shawn had approved Kevin and Courtney's relationship. La'Roc thought to herself, OMG. *My baby is in love with Dr. K. Cunningham.*

Devon, Alex, Jordan, Chantal, and Denise made their speeches, and the wedding party was over. After the guests left for the evening, Shawn and La'Roc left the family downstairs.

"You all have your own rooms, so please do not bother me and my husband for the next three weeks. Just to let you all know, in one month, we'll be going away to Africa on our honeymoon. Good night, my family," La'Roc said.

She and Shawn decided to use the elevator to their hideaway for the next three weeks. During this time, La'Roc told Shawn about the scare she had about the AIDS virus. She told him the whole story about Roger and his sexual activities. Shawn understood, as she knew he would.

"Ms. Holiday will just work for the happy couple during the next three weeks. We have everything we need upstairs. We'll take only emergency calls." Three weeks later, the lovebirds left for Africa on their honeymoon.

Five months after the wedding, Alex received a call from one of his colleagues that Kelly Carlotta Brown had passed away from complication. After suffering, a massive heart attack and too strokes.

Ms. Brown passed away quietly in her sleep.

La'Roc and Shawn returned from their honeymoon, still hugging and kissing as if they just had just gotten married.

Chantal always said, "La'Roc, why don't you and Shawn go buy a room at Bates Motel?" She smiled. "You are always kissing and hugging. I pray that when I get married, I'll find a husband like Shawn. Welcome home, guys." She kissed La'Roc on the cheek and went upstairs to find Jordan.

"Shawn, sweetheart, what are your feelings about Kelly's death? Have you thought any more about Shawn Jr.'s well-being?"

"Sexiful, I really feel sorry for Kelly's family and Shawn Jr., but my feelings for Kelly are zero. Remember, I spoke to you about the trust fund that I was going to set up for Junior. His aunt will be power attorney of the trust fund until he is twenty-five. He'll only get the trust fund for his education, nothing more. When he graduates or drops out of school, the trust fund stops. Even after he graduates, money stops. Either way, age twenty-five, money stops! I really want him to forget about me since he has a father who will be released from prison in another year. I don't want Shawn Jr. to be more confused than he already is. I'll love him from afar. Sexiful, did you forget—I have a daughter and a grandson, so I am good," Shawn answered his wife.

"Okay, handsome, as long as you're happy, I'm good," La'Roc responded. Three years later, Chantal married Dr. Mitchell and moved to California. Although Chantal still had keys and a room at Golden Circle.

Denise and the team would always have keys and a room at Golden Circle. Denise was shot by her ex-boyfriend, Martin. Martin had been released from prison three months before he shot Denise. Martin was returned to prison for attempted murder. La'Roc made sure that he got the time he deserved. Martin got twenty years to life for attempted murder. Denise recovered from the gunshot wound and started a new life with Alex.

Denise started dating Alex, and they became a couple. Alex and Denise are married now and have two children: a boy and a girl. She asked Courtney to be her daughter's godmother. Courtney accepted.

Denise and Alex named their daughter Courtney La'Roc. Alex continued to work in the firm as La'Roc, Devon, and Courtney's partner.

Devon graduated and passed the bar with the highest score in his class. He is now a full-time attorney working with Alex at La'Roc's firm. Courtney will graduate in another month from Preston University at the top of her class. La'Roc is very proud of her daughter and grandson following her in her footsteps.

Courtney continued her practice as a doctor. She is now engaged to Dr. Cunningham. They have been dating ever since he tested La'Roc for HIV. La'Roc had no more worries about HIV; all tests came back negative. She was HIV free. La'Roc never told Courtney about that little ordeal. La'Roc thought to herself, *if Courtney is happy, I am happy.* No wedding date has been set. Devon and August are still dating; she will be graduating from law school in the next three months.

La'Roc is so proud of her daughter, her grandson, and the accomplishments they have made with the help of family and friends.

Casey and L'Oreal renewed their vows, and L'Oreal had her first child. They are both ecstatic about the new addition to their family. Casey and L'Oreal had a six-pound baby boy.

Jordan is keeping busy working with L'Oreal and Casey at the Jordan Foundation. The organization has been a big success. The organization has helped millions of people so far, and they are working on three million more. The organization has two locations: California and Atlanta. They are all fully staffed. Jordan's health has begun to show signs of deterioration. He has more bad days than good days.

Ms. Cotton passed away from colon cancer two years ago. La'Roc, her family, and friends were devastated over her death. La'Roc was really angry with Ms. Cotton; she felt that Ms. Cotton keeping her illness to herself was selfish. Maybe she could have gotten help to save her; maybe not saved her from cancer, but she would have gotten her the best treatment in the world.

La'Roc was very sad over Ms. Cotton's death. After the death of Ms. Cotton, Shawn was worried about La'Roc's health. At the time of her death, he was always by La'Roc's side.

Ms. Holiday has the run of the houses and is in charge of the housekeeping department.

Biscuit passed away not long after Ms. Cotton. La'Roc was devastated over the loss of her baby. She didn't eat for days. She stopped working out for months. Shawn knew it was a problem when La'Roc stopped working out. He was really concerned about her well-being. Her primary doctor was called to the home as well as Dr. Kim. Dr. Kim flew from California the same day of the call.

Her primary doctor diagnosed her with depression. That is the reason Dr. Kim was called in: to treat the depression.

Biscuit died of old age. La'Roc was in bed with Shawn's arms wrapped around her body for days. She became overprotective of Paris because of Biscuit's death.

She refused to allow the staff to take Paris out for her walk or give her a bath. She only allowed her family and Ms. Holiday to take care of Paris.

"Baby, you need to eat something. Please eat something for me, Sexiful," Shawn said out of love and concern.

Courtney, Devon, family, and friends were worried about La'Roc's health. After the burial for Ms. Cotton and Biscuit, things seemed to fall into place.

There will always be an empty place in her heart for Ms. Cotton and Biscuit. "Okay, handsome. I'll eat some soup. Life must go on. Shawn, let's go to the gym and work out," La'Roc said.

"Okay, Sexiful. I'll do anything for you," Shawn responded. La'Roc appointed Ms. Sanchez to be Ms. Holiday's assistant.

Courtney and Justin were still friends; however, Justin was dating someone from his rehabilitation center, and he continued to make positive progress. Jordan sold his properly in California. Roger's murderer was found guilty and is locked away for life. Thanks to La'Roc.

Dr. Kim visits the Parker/Rose family whenever she's in New York or just to get away from California.

A year ago, Mr. and Mrs. Parker bought a luxurious Gulf Stream jet. Devon wanted to become a pilot. The four of them took pilot lessons: Courtney, Devon Shawn, and La'Roc.

"Grams, I can fly you and Shawn around the world." He gave a laugh and left the room.

Shawn said, "Sexiful, we can fly all over the world whenever you like." He looked over his shoulder and winked his left eye at his lovely wife.

"I love you, Shawn. Yes, I'll fly around the world with you," Mrs. Parker said and winked back at her husband.

Devon returned to join the family conversation, drinking a glass of juice. Devon said, "Shawn, I heard you. I said I'll fly you guys around the world. Did I not say that, Grams?" Shawn smiled and gave Devon a set of keys to a new Jeep Shawn had purchased to thank him for the work that he did on the Kelly Brown case. As Devon accepted the keys, he gave Shawn a hug.

"Thank you, man. Shawn, are you trying to tell me that's my Jeep parked over there next to my mother's new Hummer? Oh man, I'd kiss you, but I don't love you like that." Everyone laughed at Devon's joke. Devon's Jeep and Courtney's Hummer were customized.

The Jeep and the Hummer were delivered earlier that day. Courtney was just as surprised as Devon was. "Oh, Shawn that's my hummer? Thank you, Momma and Shawn. Just give me my keys. Man, I can't believe you guys. How did Devon know that was my Hummer?"

Shawn told him that the car dealer was going to deliver the Hummer that morning. Shawn had the dealer to cover both vehicles.

"Devon always keeps you laughing. He is a very funny guy." They all got into their cars and drove off to the landing field.

Shawn and La'Roc boarded the plane; Shawn was in the pilot's seat, and La'Roc was the copilot. Shawn looked over at La'Roc. "Sexiful, I was told this was a man's world; but, baby, this world wouldn't be nothing without you. Sexiful, do you feel and understand me, baby?" Shawn said as he winked at his beautiful wife.

"Yes, baby, I understand you," La'Roc answered with a smile.

La'Roc looked at her handsome husband. "Let's fly this dam jet before I divorce you." She winked back and smiled at her handsome husband.

As they took off, La'Roc looked out her side window to wave at her family and friends. She could see Courtney, Devon, her mother, Jordan, Chantal, L'Oreal, Casey, Denise, Alex, and Ms. Holiday.

She remembered it had been a tearful departure. She had kissed all of them goodbye and then informed them that she and Shawn would return in two months.

"Sexiful, you still love me?"

"Yes, handsome. I still love you; take me to our destination. Shawn, I still Miss Ms. Cotton and Biscuit."

"Sexiful, I miss them too." Shawn thought it would be a good idea to change the subject away from Ms. Cotton and Biscuit; he didn't want his wife to feel sad on her second honeymoon. He wanted her to focus on their trip and start a new life.

"Baby, I love flying this plane; it is so easy to handle," declared Shawn as he looked at her with those beautiful brown eyes.

During the almost eight-hour flight, Shawn and La'Roc talked about their future and what they hoped it would bring.

"Handsome, we'll be landing in Paris in about a half hour," La'Roc announced after checking her instrument panel.

"Good job, baby; you know where we are. Sweetheart, I am so proud of you," Shawn teased her.

As they descended out of the clouds, Shawn's face showed some concern. "Oh, damn, baby. It's raining pretty hard out there."

Shawn descended through the thick gray clouds. The air currents were buffering the private jet back and forth.

Shawn looked at his wife and whispered, "I will always love you, Sexiful." La'Roc reached over with her left hand and placed it over Shawn's and whispered, "I love you too." She could see the fear etched on his face.

The plane continued to buck in the wind, and they could hear the concern in the voices coming from the tower. Shawn's greatest fear was that they were going to crash.

For La'Roc, the world seemed to shrink into a small circle. She could hear Shawn's voice telling her he loved her. Somewhere in the background, she could hear music playing, and then the world faded to black.

Early in the morning, Courtney received a phone call from Paris. "Hello, this is Officer Colon. May I please speak to Courtney?"

"This is Courtney. May I help you?"

"Ms. Rose, I found your phone number in a note pad in a plane cabin. There has been an acc ..."

Courtney didn't hear the rest before she slid to the floor.

Jordan took the phone from Courtney's limp hand. "Who is this? *Hello, hello hello?* The line is dead." Jordan tracked down the call. The call was from an airport in Pairs. He founded out that Shawn and La'Roc were in a Paris hospital. Courtney started making a reservation to fly to Paris. The team and the family left for the airport.

Three days after their plane crash, La'Roc woke up at a hospital in Paris with a broken leg and two broken ribs. She looked around the room and realized she was in a hospital with an IV line securely injected into her wrist. All she could think was, *where's Shawn?* Then she cried out, "Hello, hello … could someone please come in and tell me *where my husband is?*" She reached for her buzzer and pressed for the nurse while continuing to cry out, "Hello, hello … someone, anyone, please tell me *where is my husband?*"

Finally, the doctor came into La'Roc's room. "Mrs. Parker, please calm down. You are going to be just fine. I will make sure you get some information on your husband as soon as possible," the doctor said as he gave her an injection to calm her down; seconds later, La'Roc was fast asleep.

The next day when La'Roc awoke, she felt better and happy to see family and friends surrounding her bed, except for Courtney, Devon, and Shawn.

"I really appreciate you guys for being here with me … but where are Courtney and Devon? And where is my husband?"

Jordan came closer to La'Roc. "Courtney and Devon are in the corridor, and I promise you, we'll find Shawn." The thought of not knowing whether Shawn was alive and the pain she was suffering made her cry uncontrollably.

Devon and Courtney entered La'Roc's room with tears rolling down their faces. Courtney ran to her mother's bedside and held her close. "Oh my God, Mother, I'm so happy you're awake and okay," Courtney said excitedly. Devon was anxious for Courtney to release his grandmother so he could get his chance to hold her close to his heart because she was just that to him … his heart.

After waiting patiently, Devon held his grandmother and then cried. "Grams, I promise you, we'll find grandpa."

Paris and Shawn were nowhere to be found. Three days later, after making phone calls, Jordan and Devon were able to locate the hospital where Shawn had been admitted. They spoke to Dr. Gucci. He said, "Paris was a little shaken up but no broken bones. Paris had been examined by a vet, and the report was given to me. Shawn had a mild concision and a cut above his left eye."

Devon left his grandmother's room with tears running down his face. The doctor said, "Come with me, young man. I am the doctor you spoke to over the phone." The doctor was holding Paris in his arms.

"Oh sweet Paris, my grandmother is going to be so happy to see you." Paris was licking Devon's tears and whining as Devon cried. The doctor, Jordan, and Devon drove across the hospital grounds to the other wing of the hospital where Shawn had been admitted. As they walked into Shawn's room, Devon was holding Paris in his arms. They all were crying happy tears. Paris was so happy to see Devon and Jordan; his little tail was going around and around. The doc discharged Shawn with a great report.

Shawn's first question was, "How's my wife? Please tell me she's all right."

Devon assured Shawn that they were going to see her right away. "She has been asking for you. Now you can see her, and she can see you. Thank you for flying here to take care of my wife and me. I love you guys."

"Mr. Parker, you are going to be just fine. I will take you to see your wife now."

When they reached La'Roc's room, Shawn started to cry, begging for La'Roc to forgive him. "Baby, please wake up. I told you I will never leave you again, and I always keep my promises. Please talk to me, Sexiful." She was half-awake and heavily sedated, but still, tears were rolling down her swollen face.

"Shawn, please tell me that I'm not dreaming. Please hold me and tell me that we're both all right."

"Sexiful, I'm here, baby. I love you."

"Shawn, where is Paris?"

"She's right here." After looking at Paris she dozed off to sleep again. Shawn cried uncontrollably. Devon and Courtney tried to console him; however, it was useless. The doctor came and gave him a mild sedative to calm him down. He loved La'Roc so much, and he vowed if she stopped loving him, he wouldn't know what he'd do. Shawn dozed off to sleep, calling Sexiful's name.

The doctor explained to the family that La'Roc should make a full recovery; however, when they arrived in the emergency room, they both had blood work and X-rays completed. "We're just waiting for the results. Mr. Parker is just fine, just a bit sleepy from the sedative. He should be awake soon. They are very lucky to come out of that plane alive. Mr. Parker did a beautiful job landing their plane." As Dr. Gucci was leaving La'Roc's room, he looked back at Jordan. "Mr. Diaz, it was a pleasure meeting you and your family; hopefully one day we will meet again under different circumstances."

Devon spoke on behalf of the family when he said, "Thank you, doctor, for all you have done for my grandmother and grandfather." The doctor turned, looked at Devon, smiled, and left the room. Courtney, Devon, and the rest of the family were sitting by La'Roc's bed, holding her. They noticed a change in her breathing patterns and became worried. They pressed the buzzer for the nurse to come. Chantal and Denise started yelling calling La'Roc's name.

"Please don't leave us. We need you." Alex tried to calm Courtney, and Devon was holding onto Jordan. Shawn was still fast asleep.

The doctor and his assistants entered the room and began working on La'Roc right away. "She's slipping into a coma. We're losing her … we're losing her. Everyone must clear the room," said the nurse as she closed the curtain to separate Shawn and their attempts to save La'Roc. "We are doing all we can, but we need room to work. Please leave the room. Everyone left the room." After twenty minutes, the doctor came out of the room and spoke to them. "The next several hours are going to be very critical. I've already requested a rush on her blood panel, and we will know within the next half hour whether Mrs. Parker is suffering from a staph infection or some other type of infection."

L'Oreal said, "Okay, guys, let's all go to the chapel and pray."

Denise wrapped her arms around Courtney and began to assure her that her mom was going to be all right. "I promise you and Devon, your grandmother will be just fine." Although Denise hoped for the best, she wasn't really sure if La'Roc was going to make it or not; she could only pray and pray some more. Finally, the dog sitter arrived to pick up Paris and take her to doggy care. Jordan made a mental note; *I must remember to thank the doctor for referring us to Wendell's Doggy Care.*

After several hours, La'Roc began to respond to Courtney and Devon's voices. The whole team whispered in La'Roc's ear in the hopes she would respond to hearing their voices. Shawn was now alert and scared to death. He aroused from his seated position and walked over to La'Roc's bed and began singing to her; she started to shake her head and then said in a weak voice, "Please stop it." Everyone started to laugh. The nurse ran out of the room to get the doctor, who returned into the room with a smile on his face.

"Ms. Parker, you had all of us a little worried there for a minute." Shawn asked the doctor what had happed. Dr. Gucci explained to Shawn about the coma that La'Roc had slipped into. "But I assure you, she is fine. Her blood work shows she has a little staph infection."

"MRSA?" asked Chantal.

"No, thank God. Not MRSA." Denise, along with everyone else, breathed a sigh of relief. The doctor continued, "We will need to keep Mrs. Parker here for a few more days, though, and as long as all continues to go well, she will be released with antibiotics to take for seven to ten days. Now that we know for sure it's not MRSA, you guys will not have to wear the masks. However, for precautionary measures, you may continue to do so. Mrs. Parker may have some hallucinations over the next few hours, but this is to be expected. If it becomes severe, please make us aware as soon as possible."

Shawn was holding La'Roc's hand and smiling from ear to ear. "My baby, my baby, came back to me ... thank you, God, thank you." Devon and Courtney were consoling each other. Courtney was so happy that she began to cry so hard that her body was shaking as if she was having a seizure. Devon asked the doctor to give her something to calm her down. Courtney laid her head on Devon's shoulder and fell asleep.

"Doctor, will my wife survive this infection?"

"Mr. Parker, may I have a word with you in my office, please?" All eyes turn to Shawn as he looked at his wife lying there helpless in her weakened state.

"Doctor, she's my mother. I am coming with you," Courtney said, her voice very weak from the medication the doctor gave her to calm her down.

Courtney and Shawn followed the doctor into his office. Shawn and Courtney each took a seat across from Dr. Gucci, anticipating the worse. "There is nothing to worry about. Ms. Rose will be just fine. I just needed to get you out of her room for a while because, in your emotional state, you are not helping her. Ms. Rose, I need for you and Mr. Parker to maintain your emotions, if that's possible. She can hear every word you speak; she is not in a deep coma; she is in a semi-coma. That means she is aware of her surroundings. I know that is your mother and your wife, and I know it is hard to see her in that physical state, with tubes inserted in her body and monitors constantly beeping." Dr. Gucci paused, his accent getting thicker as he tried to assure La'Roc's loved ones. "Mrs. Parker needs lots of rest, and I am counting on you to help me to keep the family calm. We want her to get better so you can take her home, back to America, where she will make a full recovery. Remember, she is a strong woman, Mr. Parker and Ms. Rose. Don't worry so much; you are a wonderful daughter, and your son is a great young man." As the doctor let Shawn and Courtney out of his office, he quietly remarked, "What a family!"

La'Roc made a full recovery. She and Shawn are back in New York, living happily with their families. The loving couple has been on several honeymoons since the plane crashed. They are still very much in love.

ACKNOWLEDGMENTS

I would like to thank God first, for giving me the willpower, strength, and patience to make my second book possible.

I would like to thank my mother and my family for their support—for believing in me and *Sexiful Rose 1 and 2.*

I would like to give thanks to my team at Xlibris for making *Sexiful Rose* become a reality for me as a writer.

I would like to thank my daughter, Tia, for being so helpful when I was busy writing my second book; she would always go to the hospital to visit her grandmother (my mother) when I was too tired from writing to visit her myself.

Tia, how could I ever thank you for my Mother's Day present? On Mother's Day, when you presented your gift to me, I was in shock. I had no words to say to you at that moment but "I love you." When you gave me the plaque, I was speechless. Tia that was the best gift anyone has ever given me. To open that box and see *Sexiful Rose* embedded on a plaque, I almost fainted. Thank you, Tia, for giving me your support and the best gift ever. Tia, your input means more to me than you know. Love you!

Thank you, Rodney (Shakiel), for reminding me each and every day about my writing and how many pages I had written that day or that week. Your reminders kept me focused and it made me work even harder to finish this book. Love you, little man.

I would like to thank Al for his patience and understanding in giving me my space to complete my project. Thank you for being there when I needed you. You are always there to pick up the pieces.

I would like to thank my sister, Sylvia—although she moved to North Carolina, that didn't stop her from checking on my writing each and every night. Sylvia, you have been a great influence on my writing; you have continued to encourage me to stay focused and on point. When I needed help, you were there for me. Thank you for being my sister. What would I do without you, kid? May God continue to bless you?

I would like to thank my brother-in-law, Jahi, for his support and listening to me vent when I was overwhelmed with work. Thank you, Jahi, for giving me your reassurance and for believing in me.

I would like to take this time to give my brother, Wallace, special thanks for promoting my book to all of his friends in South Carolina. I love you, Wallace. I would also like to give my sister-in-law, Judy, thanks for listening to me vent late at night about my book and family issues.

I would like to thank Dianna and Tameka C. for their support. I would like to thank Frank and Branda for their support.

I would like to thank my family from Boston: Mattie, Ruth, Robert, and friends. Thanks, each and every one of you who purchased a copy of *Sexiful Rose*. Thank you for your support. Love you.

I would like to thank Zadie, for your support and kind words of endearment. Love you, girl.

I would like to thank Brittany for always being there to give me positive compliments on my work and encouragement to keep writing.

I would like to thank Tyler and Avery for their support.

I would like to give thanks to Lillian and all of my coworkers from B.C.P.C for purchasing *Sexiful Rose*.

I would like to thank Ginny for giving me positive and kind words of encouragement throughout the years.

Thank you, Ginny. I thank you all for your support. God bless. I would like to take this time to thank my brothers, Ricky and Jesse, for their support.

To my dearest friend Geraldine (Gerri) Howell, I would like to thank you for all of your kind words of encouragement. Ms. South Caroline lady, you have always had my back. Love you, girl.

I would like to thank Na'im Ali for all of his support and believing in me.

Thank you, Dr. C. D. Cohen, for all of your positive advice and for keeping me focused.

To my loyal readers, this one's for you!

I would like to add some sad news …

My brother-in-law Jahi passed away August 31, 2013, during my corrections on my second book.

Before he passed away, he and my sister presented me with a beautiful gift—a plaque. Embedded in the plaque was their expressed admiration and love for me for the completion of my second book. Pulling the plaque out of the box, I sat on my bed and cried. The words were so exquisite. It read, "Sexiful Rose II: Back with a Vengeance."

What a beautiful sight to see my second book on a *plaque.*

My brother-in-law always believed in me and my writing.

Love you, Jahi.

"Understated Greatness"

Thank you, guys.

www.ingramcontent.com/pod-product-compliance
Lightning Source LLC
Chambersburg PA
CBHW022136060526
44654CB00043B/565

9781648265488